Laura,
"Let

you roar
for us."

Signed With Love

Duet

J R Dust

JRDust ♡

Authors Note & Important Information / Trigger Warnings

The contents are occasionally very dark with triggering situations and scenarios, such as one explicit sexual assault scene, graphic violence, and explicit sexual situations. Please take these trigger warnings seriously. Your mental health is of the utmost importance.

The following Trigger Warnings and the 'Further Warning' does have spoilers included. If you do not have any triggers and would prefer to read on without spoilers, please feel free to avoid the following page.

Trigger Warnings

Sexual Abuse
Sexual Coercion
Rape
Gore
Torture
Stockholm syndrome
Kidnap
Graphic violence
Psychological abuse
Child Abuse (past tense)
Physical abuse
Dub-Con
Non-Con
Degradation
Suicidal Thoughts
Necrophilia
Murder
Miscarriage
Self-Harm
Mental Health (depression and anxiety specifically)
Character death

**This story does have an unconventional/realistic
HEA (Happily Ever After)**

Further Warning/Potential Spoiler

Not all characters will make it through this story. If you feel that this puts this book in a space that isn't suited to you for any reason, please do not read on.

Similarly to real life, I feel that everyone deserves the truth - even the ugly truth as well as happiness after trauma and loss. This is something that is explored in this story.

Recommended for readers 18 years and older.

Language Differences

I'm a UK based author that writes using British English. For anyone based and reading outside of the UK, this may mean that some phrases, words, shop names or locations seem strange or as though a mistake has been made but this isn't the case (unless it really is a mistake 👀😅). If you do find a mistake, feel free to send a message my way!

If you ever need to contact me, please feel free to do so at j.rdust_author@yahoo.com

Part 1

Signed for You

Chapter 1

I need to find out what is going on. He is acting so sketchy and secretive – even more so than usual, but I can't ask Crow about it at home. There will be no chance of him telling me anything if Dad is around.

The rain is a relief. I am a winter lover - rainfall and all. I have only just walked out of my house, and yet I am thoroughly drenched. My favourite hoodie has droplets of rain being thrown its way. Even as a child I loved the rain. Dancing in the rain, making mud pies, and going on hikes, much to my dad's displeasure. Gray always used to play with me when Dad wouldn't, even though his friends always told him what a loser he was for hanging out with his little sister instead of them. It is one of the countless things I love about him.

I place my earphones in their rightful place, squeezing and moving them slightly to get them to fit just right. Looking down at my phone, I wipe away the droplets of rain that have already started appearing on its surface, click on the Spotify app, and put my running playlist on.

I look ahead at the houses beside my own, knowing that everyone that lives inside of them are no longer there apart from a few of the Cobras' wives. Not as though many of the men have wives around. Those that do are probably cooking their men dinner or cleaning the house in a hurry, running around after their children, or

1

worrying about if their partners will come back tonight or not. It is never simple, never a certainty, always a worry. My father always promises me that he will return, and he hasn't disappointed me yet, even if he has returned home beaten black and blue on occasion. My dad is passionate about very few things, but keeping a promise is one of them. The others being me and the Cobras.

The Dark Cobras. His little, or not so little, part in the circle of men that surround us. He's in charge of them and the Clubhouse that so many of them call home. His best friend is the owner, the true Pres, so while he's in prison my dad is in charge. He nearly beat someone, or possibly multiple someones, to death. I was so young when it happened, no one ever really told me why he was gone, but I do remember hearing snippets of conversations. He asked my dad to take over his role, which as his best friend my dad gladly did.

I turn on my heel to look behind me as I hear Crow pounding down the steps after me. He's new to the Cobras, and he's been tasked with keeping watch on me – acting as my bodyguard.

My dad worries about me and thinks it will be best to have someone around, which I initially hated the idea of. I know it comes from a good place though, and sadly it often comes with good reason. I know that the dangers often lurk nearer than we would like, especially as a family member to a Dark Cobra.

2

My dad did his best by me though. He taught me to fight young, how to wield a knife and aim a gun. Now, just because he taught me, that does not mean that I am any good. I have admittedly never put my skills, or potentially lack of skills to the test, but I like to think that if I freeze and forget everything else, I could just kick whoever in the crown jewels and run. In my head that would totally work. I'm hoping I don't have to put it to the test anytime soon though.

"You couldn't have waited for me, Char? I've just searched the whole damn house for you!" Crow pants.

He's at the bottom of the steps that lead to our three-bedroom house, leant over catching his breath. He looks as if he's just run a marathon, not run around a small town house.

My eyebrows raise as I smirk at Crow. He's young, though he doesn't particularly look it. He's four years older than me. Just. He had his twenty-second birthday a few weeks ago, and he just loves to remind me how mature that makes him and childish it makes me. Even though I know he's only joking, it still drives me crazy.

He's been on my watch for about six months, and we've gotten to the point where we're inseparable, not just because he's there to guard me but because we get on a lot better than I think either of us expected.

He's still leant over catching his breath.

Good thing I hadn't turned my music up too loud or I wouldn't have had the luxury of hearing him huffing and puffing. I roll my eyes and start a slow jog away from my house, past the front of the other homes that belong to my dad's fellow men. I'm not sure how it started, if it was done on purpose or not, but so many of my dad's friends that work with him live on the same street as us, or in the Clubhouse full-time.

"We're running, Crow, get your arse into gear or you won't catch me at all." I turn around, jogging backwards, silently hoping that I don't trip over anything or anyone, keeping my pace as I yell at a still hunched over and out of breath Crow.

He brings his eyebrows together and looks at me with the same fiery look they all have when they're angry, and I can't help but smile.

Crow is about six foot in height, possibly even a little taller, so he overpowers my five-six appearance. He has shaved, short, jet-black hair. Where my appearance is plain, with freckles covering my face and a healthy body to match, with no bones on show but not enough fat to actually call me chubby, he is anything but plain. He has the most annoyingly perfect body, so much so that you can see through however many layers of clothes the man is wearing that his body is ripped. He has muscle everywhere and looks like he should be in some fighting ring, instead of following an eighteen-year-old girl around town.

We're opposites, Crow and I. He likes to act grumpy around practically everyone and yet I am happy. Well, most of the time. Most women, hell

4

not even just women, most people in general would cower at the look of annoyance, anger, or frustration that the men around me seem to collect when they become part of Club life. It's got to be some sort of initiation. If you can't pull some crazy deadly face, then you can't join. I mean probably not, although that would be a funny rule to implement.

"Fuckin' hell, I hate you sometimes, woman." Crow sighs as he begins a light jog behind me.

I turn back around and face the road ahead once again as I speed up and turn the volume of the music that I'm listening to up so that it drowns everything else out, and then I run.

The rain is slowly stopping. It is now a slow intermediate shower of soft liquid falling from the grey clouds above.

Between the rain and the droplets of sweat running down my brow from the run, I don't notice that I'm at the place I need to be until I practically run into the large oak tree in front of me.

I transform my high-speed run into a gentle jog as I aim for the top of the hill above the park. The park is silent, not a person in sight. It's always overcrowded and filled with people throughout the summer, but at the peak of winter, around mid-January, there's no one around and there probably won't be anyone around for a few months to come yet. The hill I'm running up is one of the most popular hiking spots in Yorkshire, surrounded by forestry, biking paths, and little benches that are now rusty and breaking, desperately in need of some serious maintenance that it appears they haven't seen any of in years.

The trees protect me from the last of the rain. I sprint to the top of the hill, seeing my spot isn't far away. In the winter, no one bothers with this place, so until the summer arrives, with it being just four miles from my home, it's my favourite place to use for the peace I crave away from anyone else.

I grab my phone out of the pocket of my grey hoodie, panting from the run as I turn the music off and take the earphones out, folding the lead around my phone until it's neat enough to put back in its previous home.

Just as I reach the top and find the space between the trees where Crow and I made our makeshift shelter a few weeks ago to take a seat that allows me to see the park below, I turn back on myself, looking for Crow, and notice that he's still a little way behind me.

I sit down on the leaves, bark, and dirt on the floor, crossing my legs and take out my book, and my flask of tea as well as two cups from the backpack that I carried up here, pouring the still scalding water carefully into the camping cups and then placing one in front of me and one next to me, ready for Crow.

Reading is one of my greatest pleasures. I get through a different book every day or two. I love to read anyway, but I'll be starting university next year to study Publishing and English Literature, so part of my love for books comes from my desire to be a publisher. I tend to read and worship romance novels, albeit dark romance novels, but romance all the same.

I see love every day in my dad's fiery eyes, and that of the men and women around me, but it's not the kind of love that I yearn for.

Crow finally reaches the top and collapses beside me, picking up the camping cup filled with tea ready for him.

We sit in comfortable silence for a while, with me reading my book and Crow sat peacefully, between checking his phone and simply using the silence to breathe for more than a minute, between the Club's angst and drama.

The Clubhouse and The Dark Cobras seem to have this stigma attached to it. The stigma that allows everyone to think those inside of it are violent, angry, aggressive killers. They are the rumours and taunts I grew up with as a child, and although that's not completely inaccurate in some aspects, it's also a big fabrication in other areas. My dad does his best to keep me sheltered from the life he leads, though when he shows up wounded, there's only so much he can hide. I've read stories about motorcycle clubs, gangsters, the mafia, and so much more, and I'm sure that's what the little town around me perceives the Club and the Cobras to be, but it's not. It doesn't hurt to have them think that though, because it means people won't mess with you which is what my dad always reminds me. Let people think what they want as long as you know the truth.

"Did you put any sugar in the tea, Char? You know I need sugar in my tea." Crow and his obsession with having half a pot of damn sugar in his tea is madness. Six spoonfuls are his minimum – yes, minimum.

"There is sugar, Crow, just not enough to give you a heart attack and shut you up, sadly." I don't look at him as I speak, my attention still on the book in one of my shivering hands.

I turn back to my book, until I notice Crow moving in my peripheral. He's pushing himself up from the floor with one hand whilst still smoking with the other. As I look up at him, he takes off his leather jacket, embroidered with the Cobras emblem on the back, and puts it over my shoulders.

Immediately, I feel the weight of it. It's real leather and to be big enough to fit the giant next to me, it's bound to be too big for me which only adds to the weight around me, but I love it. I don't particularly like my body being on show. It's not as though I don't like it, although there are parts I'd change, the same as anyone I suppose, it's just for comfort that I love to wear things that overwhelm my body. That and my belief that I shouldn't need to show my body to receive the looks from men that my dad and Crow are certain I get constantly – I don't ever notice it but I don't argue with them either. I glance up at Crow as he reaches his hand out for me to take it. I do. His hands feel rough on mine, and for the millionth time since he came around, I wonder if there could ever be more. I've been feeling closer to him for some time, idly wondering if the possibility of more than what we have could ever be real.

"It's getting dark, let's take a stroll home before your dad gets back." His voice sounds rough, though not anywhere near as affected by the cold as what I'm sure mine would be if I said anything right now. So instead I give him a small nod and let him lift me from the floor.

"What's going on with my dad and the Cobras, Crow?" I ask. It's why I wanted to venture out today, to see if he knew anything.

"What do you mean?" He begins shifting uncomfortably at my question.

"He's been acting weird. I dunno, he's always out more and he won't tell me where he's going lately, which is unlike him. I know something is happening, everyone's always at the Club having meetings and no one will tell me anything. Is it about Gray? Have they found out who it was?" I know I could be wrong, but no one could find any solid proof around Gray's disappearance and although they suspected it was The Devils Henchmen, a rival motorcycle club, no one could do anything without some sort of proof without causing uproar and chaos.

"You know I can't tell you anything, Char. You know I would if I could, but I just can't risk it." So there is something going on. There must be or he would just tell me there was nothing.

"Can you at least tell me if it's about Gray? He's my brother, I deserve to know." Crow knows how much Gray's disappearance has affected me.

He rubs at the back of his neck, sighing before turning back to me.

"They don't know where he is, but they have someone who might. That's all I can say, alright? I shouldn't even be telling you that. You know your dad would skin me alive for telling you anything, Char." I know he's right, that no matter how much my dad adores Crow, he doesn't want me involved or knowing anything more than the essentials, the bare minimum.

"I know. I know you telling me anything is a risk and I'm sorry to ask but thank you, thank you for telling me." I appreciate it more than he could possibly know.

I pick up my tin, the flask, and empty cups before placing them in my backpack and closing the zip. I put the backpack straps over my shoulders, on top of Crow's jacket, and began the walk back home with him.

"I can't tell you what but there is something your dad is planning on approaching you about though, Char. Not Gray, but something I need you to think very carefully about before you commit. Do you understand?"

"Not even a little bit, no. What is it?" I wonder.

Crow doesn't say a word, just sighs and shakes his head as he puts his hand on my lower back and tells me we should go.

"Well? What do I need to think very carefully about?" I ask lightly as I echo his serious tone.

"You have to swear to me you won't say anything, Char, and I mean it. I'm only telling you because I think it's a shit idea and I think you have the right to have the heads up about it."

I nod my head, apprehensive suddenly, nervous. Crow is very rarely this sceptical or serious.

"They're talking about merging with The Laidens," he says as we continue to walk. He takes my hand in his, rubbing my palm with his fingers.

The Laidens are a motorcycle club not far from us. There are often tense ties between clubs and although there are very loose connections between the Laidens and The Dark Cobras, from what I can gather it seems they have been trying to join bands for a while.

"OK, but that has nothing to do with me."

"It could have everything to do with you if you marry their president's son." Crows voice comes out quiet, yet cold as ice, similarly to how the pit within my stomach drops as every ounce of blood within me freezes.

"Marriage? What are you talking about?" I rush out as I stop mid-step and turn to Crow, grabbing hold of his arm as he halts and sighs before finally turning to look at me.

"You can't tell him I've told you, Char, but that's the offer. You marry the son and the clubs

11

merge." His words hit me like a tonne of bricks, knocking the oxygen out of my constricting lungs.

"There's no chance of a merge without that?" I question.

"No. Your dad tried every possible angle he could think of but they're insistent that the only way to truly merge and stand as one against The Devil's Henchmen and The Enforcers is to truly tie us all as one."

The Devil's Henchmen and The Enforcers. I remember thinking what stupid names they were for motorcycle clubs when I heard them as a child; and yet, now all I feel when hearing the names is dread.

We have two rival clubs determined to see us drown in our own blood, and we have no way of beating them without help. We need the help but I desperately want out of this life and love so much more.

Chapter 2

"Crow, will you turn the heating up for me?" I call behind me as I walk into the kitchen.

Our home is my reserve space, modest in its size and littered with old furniture that has been around for as long as I can remember. We're not really the type of people to update things or buy new unless it's really needed, and our home is perfectly rustic because of it.

I'm still reeling from Crow's revelation about the marriage pact that The Laidens have offered my dad. A large part of me is unsure if he would even approach me and ask such a thing of me, but then I know how much the Club and The Cobras mean to him. I know he would do anything for them, but does that include sacrificing his child's happiness?

I'm not even sure I want to get married, let alone anytime soon. I mean, I probably will get married one day, but to someone I love, someone that I have spent time getting to know, not a stranger that will tie me to Club life forever.

"Do you think your dad will mind if I stay again? I hate going to the Club to sleep." I wipe the thoughts of marriage from my mind and turn to Crow. Crow is always moaning about the Club house.

It's a nightclub, with rooms upstairs used as a hotel for our crew whenever they need it, a bar downstairs, a cafe in the day, a meeting ground, a place that manages to transform into whatever is needed really.

Crow doesn't like the girls that hang out there. The girls are usually after anyone with status. A lot of them are lovely, but there are a few that are only there because of the rumours they have heard and their incessant obsession over being with a 'bad boy'. It doesn't really work that way, not only because the Club is nothing like what the outside world perceives it to be, but also because most of the men there either have wonderful wives they would never waver from or simply aren't interested in girls, nor women that want them for anything other than them - but that's something many of the girls don't understand.

Crow doesn't want the women there and he can't stand the men fighting for their masculinity every time someone looks at them the wrong way. They aren't all like that, it's more often than not the younger members and prospects that feel they need to earn their way in through fighting.

"You know he won't mind, you're here all the time, you're like a son to him, Crow. Don't stress," I tell him as I collect the mince from the fridge and the potatoes ready to start peeling and cooking.

Crow sits down on one of the chairs at the table in the middle of the kitchen. He gets his phone out and scrolls aimlessly through Facebook, Twitter, Snapchat, or whatever other app he can find to amuse himself with.

The one thing I've wondered about since he came around is how he ever finds time to do anything, have friends, girlfriends, or let loose if he's always with me.

The idea of him having a girlfriend makes me cringe. Though he's not been with a girl that I know of since we've been around one another, I know the day will inevitably come if I never make a move or confess to the brewing feelings I have for him. Hell, even then it may still happen if he doesn't feel the same way.

I guess he must be okay with the lack of time away though. Even if he wouldn't say anything to Dad, he would have said something to me by now if it was something that bothered him.

"Are you coming with us to collect Liam next week?" Crow asks me. He hasn't met Liam before since he's not long joined and found his way up the ranks when he had the job of looking after me assigned to him.

"What do you want to know about him?" I ask with a chuckle.

He's not interested in if I'll be there. He's only interested in finding out what Liam's going to be like as the president. He's never seen anyone apart from my dad as President and a new one can change things drastically, although I know that won't happen. Well, I hope it won't.

Liam and Dad have been friends since my dad was ten years old. Liam and my dad were still young when he got sent down, and I was only eight myself. I remember him being there all the time, living with me and Dad because he didn't have any family, or a partner to go home to, and since my mum left when I was only four, my dad raised me, and Liam sat on the sidelines as the uncle that was never really my uncle.

"What's he like? Do you think he'll get rid of us lot?" Crow wonders.

He's hesitant, as are most of the new members that have never met him. They've all been told the stories about him. He's ruthless, filled with anger, willing to kill if you breathe wrong and fiercely closed in on himself. From what I remember, most of them are just stories though, or at the very least exaggerated stories based on small sections of truth.

The stories about him are endless. One of the newer prospects told me one last week that he had heard. Apparently, Liam had beaten ten men by himself, all because they walked into his club and didn't leave a tip for the bartender who had put up with their egotistical bullshit all night. Every time someone tells it, they add a little bit more to the story, meaning that at this stage I'm pretty certain it's a complete lie.

Having grown up with him for eight years of my life, and through the phone calls that took place when he first got locked up until I was thirteen and no longer had any interest in talking to my dad's friends, and would much rather see or speak to my own instead, I know more about him than a lot of the men and women that will soon be under his control. So, I give in and I tell Crow what I know. Which isn't really much of anything considering I only know of Liam what I witnessed through a child's mind.

"He always used to be pretty hard faced, but fair." I take a breath, thinking of the times he would reprimand me as a child but was never cruel. "Strict, but understanding..." I pause again. "Undeniably and fiercely protective of those he's loyal to and those that are loyal to him," I tell Crow. "But then I don't have a clue what he's like now. Other than shouting hello when Dad's been on the phone to him, I've not spoken to or seen him in years."

I think back to all of the summers throughout my childhood when Liam would take me to the park if Dad was busy with club business and watch over me as if the world stopped and started with my ability to be happy and carefree. Dad always says that Liam had a terrible life before he joined the club and that's why he always made sure that I was happy, because watching a child be born into the same dynamic that he was made him want a different life for me than the one he had growing up.

"Your dad wouldn't let him get rid of us all, would he?" Crow wonders as he sits fidgeting with his hands and the ends of the sleeve jacket. He's nervous.

"You know my dad speaks to him on the phone every week, he tells him everything he's done, and Liam's happy with it. He believes in my dad and has had just as much of a say as Dad has in bringing new people into the club, Crow. Don't worry, I promise, you'll be fine," I tell him.

I turn back around and continue on with the cooking that I had started. I can understand why he's concerned. I'm anxious to see him and to find out what changes he plans to make, if any at all. No matter how much he trusts my dad and his judgement, things are bound to alter. I just hope it doesn't negatively affect Crow. Or me, for that matter.

Crow didn't have a home or a family that loved him when he joined us. He wouldn't have anywhere to go if he got kicked out.

"Not as though you will be, but you know that even if you were kicked out that I'd come with you, Crow. You can come with me to uni, or we could find somewhere of our own," I tell him with a smile as I turn around and notice him giving me what is one of his most genuine smiles. It's warm, honest, and everything that this world isn't. Crow's a pure man, no matter what he's done under orders of the club. Crow's good.

"I wish it were that simple, Char. There are things at play that no one even knows about."

"What do you mean? What hands are at play?" Is he talking about The Devil's Henchmen? Does he know something? Or is it the marriage, or even Gray? With the way things are going lately, it could be just about anything that he's referring to.

I put the food in the oven and take a seat next to Crow.

"I wish I could tell you, but just know that there's more happening around us than I think

18

anyone here realises." He knows something about the Club that he's not telling me. If he can't tell me, I need to make sure that Dad does. And if he won't then I'll just have to find out for myself.

I hear the door open and close as the scent of diesel comes into the house. My dad. He's a mechanic by trade and although there are other mechanics within the ranks of the Cobras, my dad likes to work on his bike himself.

"You two alright?" my dad shouts through to us as he takes off his boots in the hall.

"Yeah, just making tea," I yell back at him.

"Can I have a word with you before tea, Charlie darlin'?" He says it so casually, with no hint of worry or uncertainty.

I know what it is. Thanks to Crow.

Crow and I exchange a look before I nod at my dad, telling Crow to keep an eye on the food as I follow my dad through to his study.

My dad's study is rather bare, consisting of his desk with a plush chair behind it and one in front of the desk. The only other items in the room are filing cabinets and a few pictures scattered around the place.

I take a seat at the chair on the opposite side of the desk to my dad and wait while he gets a glass and fills it with whiskey. I can't stand the stuff.

He takes a sip before turning to face me.

"You know we want to join with The Laidens, don't you?" He hasn't told me that himself but he knows I'm privy to Cobra gossip and talk when in

19

the Clubhouse. He's aware that I know a lot through others even if he doesn't like it.

I nod, not saying a word, knowing exactly where this conversation is heading.

He nods at me and takes another sip before putting his glass down on the desk in front of him and clasping his hands together.

"They've offered us a merge."

"Well, that's good, isn't it?" I ask, knowing it's very well not a good thing considering the stipulation they've added to the merge taking place.

"Yeah, yeah it is but they'll only merge if we do something for them."

Here it comes.

"They want you to marry the president's son, darlin." The words are said steadily, with little to no emotion behind them. He's attempting to gauge my reaction, as I am his.

I make sure to widen my eyes and sit forwards in my seat, at least attempting to feign shock even though I already know what he's telling me.

"And you told them no, I assume." It's not a question, though it should be and it's one I want answered anyway.

My dad shifts in his seat uncomfortably before facing me again.

"Well, here's the thing, Charlie darlin', you're a grown woman now. You'll be getting married at some time anyway, I have no doubt, and if it can benefit the family then I, I'd like you to think about

20

it." He looks sheepish and so he should.

I truly thought he wouldn't dare ask me. That he wouldn't even question it and yet he did. He is. He wants me to do it.

"Benefit the family? Dad, you've never wanted me involved in Club life and now you want me to marry into it and to a stranger?" I practically yell.

I can feel myself getting worked up, angry, frustrated at the lack of care he's showing. He doesn't seem phased at all by any of this, and yet it was only a few weeks ago that he was ranting at me for wanting to be involved.

"I can't and won't force you, but you know what's at stake here, I don't have to tell you. They may even be able to help us find Gray." That's what this is. He's trading me in for the hope of finding Gray.

I want to find Gray more than anything in the world and he knows that. Everyone knows that, but surely there is another way. There has to be another way.

"That's a low blow and you know it," I hiss at him as I get up and leave.

"I've set up a meeting with the son, so you can get to know each other. Day after tomorrow." His face is unforgiving, completely void of emotion. So, unlike the man that he's been up until this very moment.

"You didn't even wait for me to say yes?"

He doesn't respond and with my hand on the doorknob, I find an idea entering my mind.

21

"I'm not a virgin, you know. That's what he'll want, isn't it? He won't want damaged goods." I lie. I am a virgin, but if pretending I'm not will cancel this ridiculous set up then I'm all for spending the rest of my life covered in the web of lies I can create.

He winces at my words, the first show of any feeling since this conversation started.

"He doesn't care about that. And I really don't want to know about that, Charlie, but since when have you been around anyone without me or Crow or Gray long enough for that to happen? Jesus, darlin'." I roll my eyes at his berating tone.

As if right now is the time for that conversation. Not as though there's even a conversation to be had about my fake loss of virginity.

"Oh, for fuck's sake, Dad, I didn't tell you that so that we can have the bloody bees and the birds talk again," I tell him with a sigh.

"Fine, but just meet him. Please. He'll be at the Club, somewhere comfortable for you. His idea." He says it as if I should be grateful to the man that is trying to steal my right to choose.

Fucking men.

Chapter 3

Crow and I fell asleep together watching some documentary on Netflix last night. As I wake up to the sun shining through my cream curtains, I look to my right and see that Crow is still sleeping soundly. I fell asleep in my fluffy teddy bear pyjamas, long pyjama bottoms and a flannel fluffy top. Crow's in his boxer shorts as usual. He fell asleep on top of my duvet. Dad must have come in to check on us at some point, because Crow's now got a light blanket on top of him.

Dad is normally adamant that I don't even speak to men, which is ironic really considering he's currently trying to marry me off, but when it comes to this heavy sleeper next to me, I think he has a soft spot for him. Even though I'm Crow's assignment to protect, Dad knows that he means more to me than just that.

I watch Crow for a few minutes, taking in the abs any guy would kill for, his tanned skin that never seems to pale, even in the adverse weather we seem to be having this winter. He always looks like he's just been on holiday somewhere warm. He has skin that's so blemish free it's easy to imagine him on a magazine cover.

I put my bare feet to the ground and as they rest on the warmth of the carpet below my bed, I look to my left, towards one of the two double windows in my room, and spot the clock on my bedside table: 6.09am. It's no wonder the house is still so eerily silent.

I groggily wipe my face and clamber from the bed gently, careful not to wake the now sleeping and snoring man next to me, and find myself in front of my dresser, picking out some dark denim skinny jeans and one of Gray's black hoodies out of my drawer that makes me look tiny. It's ridiculously baggy, but I like the fact that it overwhelms my body and I love that it's my brother's.

I used to like wearing Gray's dressing gowns, jumpers, and jackets when I was little just to wind him up. I loved that he never objected even though they were practically dresses on me. Now they serve as a reminder of Gray.

I made a list of the ways I could attempt to find him. I just need to make sure that no one knows what I am attempting. Despite his recent very abrupt change of mind about me being involved in Club life, I know my dad will still object to me doing anything that will endanger myself in order to find Gray.

I shake my head in an attempt to wash away the thoughts of Gray for now and wander into the en-suite attached to my bedroom and quickly strip out of my pyjamas before jumping into the warmth of the shower. I ease my head back as I let the water trickle over my face and down my chest and into the abyss of the plughole at the bottom of the bathtub that my shower head hangs above.

Signed with Love duet
J R Dust

It doesn't take me long to shower, wash my hair, clean myself, brush my teeth, and get dressed again before opening the door and leaving the steaming room behind.

I towel dry my hair before untangling it with my trusted Game of Thrones brush that Crow got me for Christmas, throw the towel into the laundry basket, and pad quietly out of my bedroom door and down the stairs, careful not to wake anyone. I unlock and open the front door and sit on the steps in front of my house.

As I sit and look out at the houses around ours, their occupants beginning to wake up and start their day, I think about what my plans are.

I need to go shopping in town with Crow and decorate Liam's old room so that it's ready for him to come home to. He'll be moving back in with us. You would have thought he would want a place of his own, so that he could bring women back, or have meetings in, or do whatever it is that he wants once he's free, but when Dad asked him, he had apparently said he couldn't live away from us. God knows why, he hadn't lived with us for years and we're not very exciting, but that's his mistake, I guess. Maybe that's what he wants though, away from the chaos of club life, maybe he just wants some normality, much like Crow I suppose.

I remember suddenly that I'll also need to wake Crow soon, so that we can get into town and back before we're expected at the clubhouse for two pm. Dad has got some work for us. Well, for Crow but Crow and I are inseparable so I tend to go with him to the Club whenever he's needed there.

It seems so absurd to be spending the morning and potentially the rest of the weekend decorating a room for someone I haven't seen in years when I have a brother that's missing and a potential forced marriage to contend with.

I wonder how Gray would handle this. What he would do or say. I knew he wouldn't stand for it and although part of me wants to completely ignore the meeting my dad has set up, I know that for the sake of Gray and hopefully gaining information, I have to at least meet the man that my father seems intent on pawning me off to.

As much as I want to find him myself, since no one will let me help, I have very little to go on.

It is so out of character for Dad that I am curious how the Laidens had even got him to come round to the idea. He was hesitant about putting Crow with me at the beginning, simply because Crow was a man; and now here he is, willing and even encouraging the idea of me marrying someone I have never even met.

Dad has always done his best to keep me out of the areas of the Cobra life that he deems too much for me. He doesn't involve me in it too much and I don't ask. Any time I ever dare to question it, he tells me I'm being silly, that nothing illegal goes on, but I highly suspect that's a lie.

I've become more and more inquisitive since Gray's disappearance. I know he was involved with the Cobras and although he didn't tell me much, he told me enough for me to know that there is a lot more going on than what Dad would have me know.

I notice Tin and Dove walking towards the house.

"What are you two old fuckers doing up this early?" I shout down at them as they begin to climb the stairs to our front door.

They both chuckle at me, and Tin, one of the Club's counsellors and a close friend of my dad's, lands next to me in a sitting position, with his legs outstretched onto the steps before him. Dove scoots round him, putting a hand on my hair and ruffling it up as he always does when he sees me.

"We're here for breakfast, you little sod." Dove laughs as he talks to me, shaking his head as he opens the front door of the house to go and start breakfast. They come around most mornings. Neither of them have partners or kids so they spend a lot of their time here.

When I look next to me and see Tin sitting there, I notice that he's now smoking alongside me.

"Couldn't sleep or just missed this beautiful face?" I ask as he blows out the smoke inhibiting its space in his lungs.

Tin smirks and knocks my shoulder with his.

"Well, hell, little lady, you can't be beating on me this early in the morning." Tins voice is gruff, though his words are anything but.

27

Signed with Love duet
J R Dust

As well as Liam, both Tin and Dove have been around since before I was born. Tin, Liam, and Dove aren't the longest standing men in the club by any means, but they are the ones that are closest to my dad and I.

———————

"Where are we going then? Or am I just driving aimlessly for a while?" Crow asks me.

He's driving, as always. I have my driving license but I can daydream when someone else is driving and the last time I started daydreaming when I drove, I nearly crashed, not as though I told anyone that. I don't even seem to notice when my mind takes off to a different dimension. Trying to pay attention and drive alongside it does not go well.

"Okay, we need to go to B&M first, we'll see what we can find in there," I declare as I close the book in my lap before tucking it neatly into my backpack.

"I think we're going to go with neutral colours for him, you think that'll be ok?" I ask eagerly, not wanting to mess up, but needing a man's view, because no matter how much I know about men, which isn't much at all really, I'm not sure I'm quite on par with what a nearly forty-year-old bloke is going to want in his bedroom.

"You do remember that I haven't met him, right? I haven't got a clue what he'd want, Char," he tells me as his eyes scan every mirror the car

28

has for signs of danger behind us.

I notice that Crow does this constantly. The reason I notice is because I do it too. We've both been taught, although through very different means admittedly, to constantly keep an eye out for danger and being the daughter of the man in charge of a motorcycle club invites danger, meaning that both Crow and I are constantly on the lookout.

There have been so many times I've been followed, it's only natural to be paranoid. Paranoia's horrible but it keeps you safe most of the time, so I don't mind it.

"Grey's a safe colour though. Can't go wrong with grey." Crow interrupts my thoughts, and as I look at him, I find that he's got his coffee in his left hand whilst he uses his right to steer.

Grey's safe.

"We gonna get some lunch after this shit show of a shopping trip, Char? I'm hungry already," Crow whines. He's like some crazed dog, he doesn't stop eating and acts like it's both the first time he's ever seen the food and the last time he ever will each time he has a meal.

"You're such a pig. You ate an hour ago, for God's sake, and what do you mean shit show of a shopping trip? We haven't even got inside yet!" I tell him as he parks up in a bay space and opens his door.

I follow his lead and head out of his white Golf, slamming the door shut behind me. I walk round the front of the car towards Crow and start

29

off towards the front doors of B&M.

"I might have eaten an hour ago, but if you fed me bigger meals, then I wouldn't be hungry all the time and no, but I hate shopping, so it's bound to be bad." I can't help but scoff at this, he had the biggest breakfast out of everyone and made a mess of the table in my kitchen in the process. I do admittedly know that he hates shopping though so I give him credit for not giving me too much of a hard time about dragging him along.

"Oh, stop moaning and follow me, you big baby."

I collect a trolley from outside of the shop and head in, going straight for the home aisle.

I pick up a grey and white patterned double duvet cover and throw it in the trolley straight away, paying little attention to the phone-obsessed Crow behind me. He's staring down at the little screen as if it holds his whole life that he just can't help but look at.

There are two dark grey lamps, a floor lamp that's as tall as me and a small one you touch to activate. I stare at them both, figuring out which would go best before deciding to pick them both up and moving along. I collect matching bathroom accessories, pillows for atop of the bed, some floating shelves, a couple of photo frames, and a rug before turning down the next aisle in search of the perfect shade of paint.

Egg green? Stained ivory? Ion blue? Translucent Grey? Crayon yellow? Holy hell, can't they just have simplistic terms for colours and shades rather than about fifty different shades for each colour? I decide on a magnolia, duck grey, and vase grey (basically light and dark grey, whoever decides the names of these things just has a problem that can't be solved).

Now to see how good my decorating skills are when I put it all together in Liam's room.

"You took forever," Crow tells me as we head back towards the car.

"I was less than half an hour in there! You should be grateful, I could always decide I want to go clothes shopping too," I declare.

"You wouldn't dare."

"Oh, you know I would but luckily for you, I'm not feeling it today," I tell him with a smirk. I hate clothes shopping, but he doesn't need to know that.

"Get in the car." Crows voice is as cold as ice as he opens the door and shoves me in.

"Excuse me bu—" My words are cut off as I realise what or rather who he's eyeing up. I open the door, my hand on the back of his leather jacket.

Edgar is heading our way with a group of the Devil's Dealers not far behind him. He's the President's son, formidable in his appearance with dark, soulless eyes and a very nearly bald head that shows off the scar running across his forehead and the burns covering his head, cheek and upper chest, as well as the countless tattoos plastered along his bare forearms.

31

I watch on as Crow is facing the gruesome bunch of men that head our way.

My dad had always taught me that although fear can often be useful, it's letting fear overwhelm you that puts you in danger. Right now, it feels like I'm being overwhelmed by fear.

They haven't done anything threatening, but I know them. I know they went after Gray, whether there's any proof or not. I'm certain of it. They are the only rival Club that would have enough gall to go directly after a member, let alone the President's son.

I know what they're capable of from the stories I've heard and unlike the ones I've heard about Liam that I have no doubt are mostly false, the stories about these men come from the men within the Cobras that have seen the torture they inflict first-hand.

"What do you want, Edgar?" Crow often acts grumpy or illusive around others but this isn't him acting. He isn't just grumpy, he's uptight, angry, and ready to attack. You can see it in the stance he's holding, legs wide, hands clenched.

"Princess not coming out to say hello?" Edgar asks with a laugh as those with him follow along and laugh at his seriously unfunny joke.

Crow takes a few steps away from me, closer to them.

I hate Crow being so close to them alone. I know he can handle himself but there are six of them and only one of him. Despite how well trained he may be, those aren't great odds.

"I just wanted to come and say hello to the princess. The last time I saw her in person, she was a small wee thing. She's practically prime for fucking now. I can imagine now just how sweet she'd be to break." His words come out with a smile so hollow it's hard to imagine any woman willingly going near him.

His words make me cringe in disgust, knowing all of the awful things he's done to women in his time. So many of the women he's hurt are now protected by the Dark Cobras.

Crow inches closer to Edgar, his face taking on a look of pure fury.

"You even think about her again, and I will crush you and every one of these pussy ass sheep that follow you. Do you understand me?" His words are low, quiet yet no less threatening.

Edgar looks from me to Crow, looking him up and down before returning his eyes to me.

"I'm only playing with you. No one wants a marked girl. Not worth the hassle," he says with a dry laugh.

"What the fuck do you mean marked?" Crow growls at him.

"You haven't heard? She's for sale. Marked. Bet dear Daddy is the one that's got her up there. Always did think he was a bit dark for the Cobras with his taste for pain. Do say hello to the dear ol' Pres for me, won't you, princess?" He speaks without taking his eyes off me. I feel disgusting. My mind goes blank when I register what he's said. Marked? Questions are racing around my mind as Edgar walks off with his trail of men eagerly following behind him.

Crow gets in the car and starts driving without saying a word.

"What did he mean, Crow? How am I marked? For sale. I can't be, can I?" I ask him.

I know what it means and so does Crow. So many of the other MC clubs not only in the country but around the world sell, trade, and deal with human trafficking – women, men, children. To be marked means that you have a price on your head, that you've been marked and put on the black market for sale.

"I don't know." His words are short, abrupt, the edge to his voice like steel.

"What do you mean you don't know? You must know something, Crow! What was he talking about? He must be wrong." Even if it is about me, I know Dad won't tell me anything. Someone must know.

I couldn't be for sale. That's impossible. Who would put me up for sale? You need pictures, a trafficking passport, and who knows what else to even mark someone. I immediately dismiss his suggestion about my dad. No matter who my dad is when I'm not around, I know that he loves me. No matter what, I know he will never do anything to put me in danger.

The marriage pops into my mind, and although I've spent the time since he told me questioning his moral compass, I know for certain that he wouldn't do that unless he felt it would keep me safe. Maybe that's what it is, he does know about me being marked and that's why he wants the Laidens and The Cobras to merge. It means more protection and finding Gray.

"I need to make a phone call. Do not say a word. Not a single word, do you understand me?" I nod numbly at Crow's words.

Crow pressed some buttons on the screen in front of us and within two rings, a voice I don't recognise answers.

"Down Viper Swing." What the hell?

"Viper Whiskey Spring," Crow replies cryptically.

What on earth is going on? Are we reciting in rhyme? I can rhyme plenty, I'm just not sure this is the time somehow.

"Take her off the register. Now."

"I can't, man. I wish I could, but it's out of my hands. The Lopezs have put her on there," the strange voice says.

"Down Viper Spring." Crow hangs up.

Who were the Lopezs? I haven't heard that name before. If it isn't The Devil's Dealers that have done this as some kind of way to antagonise my dad into starting a war between the Clubs as I had first assumed, and it was instead these Lopezs, then I need to find out who they are and why they are after me.

"Who was that?" I ask Crow.

"Some computer whizz the Cobras have contact with. I was hoping he'd be able to get onto the market and get you off it."

"Who are the Lopezs? Are they worse than the Dealers?"

"FUCK!" The roar that comes from Crow as he punches the steering wheel scares me. It's guttural and filled with fury unlike anything I've seen him express before.

You would think that having lived the life I have that not much would scare me anymore, but the unhinged anger coming from Crow is unlike anything I've ever seen him showing. I've seen him mad, angry, frustrated--but never like this. His hands are shaking and his jaw is clenched as he stares at the road ahead.

I put my hand on his, gently so as not to startle him. His jawline ticks but he doesn't take his eyes off the road or acknowledge that I've touched him.

Eventually, he takes his left hand off the wheel and intertwines his fingers with mine, using his thumb to rub the topside of my hand.

"I just need you to be ok, Char."

Chapter 4

I am sitting at the bar in the clubhouse. It is always busy at this time of day, filled with workers and the public alike. In the day, it's a cafe, with sofa chairs and tables accompanying them. The atmosphere is more laid back, with club members milling around, either chowing down on lunch or goofing off, waiting for something to happen.

I am sitting, chatting to one of the barmaids, Alice, when Crow walks in searching for me.

Alice brushes her hair down and starts twisting a strand with her hand. She's had a thing for Crow for far too long without either him noticing or her telling him. It is never ending with them two - Crow is clueless, and Alice is shy. She has never outright told me that she likes him, but it is clear that she does.

Crow takes the seat next to me and immediately starts on the food I ordered for him. I got him a double cheeseburger and chips. He told me to order food whilst he was on the phone outside and without telling me what he wanted, burger and chips is the safest option. He doesn't seem to mind, wolfing it down as though he's not eaten in days.

"Do you know what's going on around here today? Everyone is acting super skittish," Alice tells us as she eyes the men around us.

There do seem to be more Cobras around

than usual and unlike normal, they're not sitting drinking or relaxing. They're on guard - alert. I wonder silently if it has anything to do with my marking and Edgar's appearance earlier but realise that Crow didn't call anyone and inform them apart from the nameless computer whizz. Maybe whoever that was had contacted everyone else.

"I have no idea. You know more than I do around here. Has anyone said anything?" I ask her.

It's the truth about her knowing more than me. Alice has been around for a few years. She doesn't dance like a lot of the girls, she instead prefers to bartend or waitress, meaning that she often overhears a lot more than what the Cobras realise. It is through Alice that I get information that no one else wants to freely give me. She's about the same height as me, though a few years older. Alice is bigger in build than I am; curvy and constantly hyper and smiley. She is beautiful.

"No, nothing," she squeaks out, looking right at Crow, who is paying little to no attention to our conversation.

"Keep your eyes open and your ears peeled. I have a feeling you'll be hearing your fair share soon enough," I tell her, and notice Crow's look of annoyance at me as I do.

Crow knows I get most of the information I know about the Club from her, but he doesn't say anything to either one of us as he rolls his eyes and continues on with his food.

Signed with Love duet
J R Dust

"Hey, Crow, have you spoken to Dad?" I ask, and as slowly as he does anything that he has little interest in, he raises his head to look Alice over quickly before looking at me again and nodding, all the while still munching on his burger.

"Yeah, I called him before. He's on his way," he gets out, barely understandable with the food in his mouth.

Before I get a chance to say anymore, my dad is behind me; I can feel his presence before he says a thing.

I turn around instinctually and my eyes fall on my father. He's a tall man, a little taller than Crow, although only by an inch or so, but the way he carries himself makes him look seven feet tall. He has pitch black hair, his is as straight as rods, whereas mine waves in annoying curls. He needs a haircut; I note as he smiles at me.

"You coming with us, my darling Charlie?" he asks.

So, we're pretending as if he isn't pawning me off now? I can do that.

"If Crow's there then so am I, gotta protect the poor fellow, haven't I?" I joke as Crow glances at me in frustration.

I don't mention Edgar or what he said. He wouldn't answer me anyway, so I certainly don't plan on asking in front of anyone and embarrassing myself by letting everyone hear him treat me like a child and refuse to tell me anything.

39

Signed with Love duet
J R Dust

Crow hates when I talk about protecting him. Even though that's exactly what I hope I'd be able to do if it ever came to it. Even though I know how capable he is, I know I would do anything for him, including attempt and fail to stick up for him.

"Alright, come on then, kids. The men are waiting," my dad tells us before rubbing my back and turning on his heel as he heads towards the stairs. We're going to the basement, I'm sure of it. The stairs lead upstairs to the bedrooms, or down stairs to the basement, and I have no reason to believe the men are waiting for us in the hotel rooms, so basement it is. Shit.

I turn to look at Crow as he soon realises the same thing that I have. They want Crow to do something bad.

It's sort of like an initiation. One that Crow has failed three times already. He never tells me exactly what he has to do, but he does tell me that he hasn't done what he was supposed to. And considering he's supposed to protect me, that's a problem, or at least for Dad it is. Fuck. They aren't going to give him many more chances if he can't do it today. If he goes, I go too, I decide. I meant what I told him about leaving together.

"You can come back for your burger later, boy, let's go!" my dad shouts back at us as he nears the stairs at the complete opposite end of the room to us.

Crow and I get up together and start after my dad.

Signed with Love duet
J R Dust

"It's fine, you'll be fine, Crow," I tell him, even though as much as I hate not believing in him, I'm not convinced my words are true.

"Don't bullshit me, Char. I can't fucking do it and you know it," he tells me.

I take hold of his hand and give it a little squeeze. I don't know how else to support him.

As we eventually enter the basement, it makes sense why it needs to be soundproof. I can hear shouting from the cells and grunts coming from the one room now in use.

Dad's holding the door open for us as we walk in. He doesn't usually let me get this far, but I refuse to speak up and remind him of that fact. Any morsels of information he's allowing me to have, I'm taking.

I recognise the man sitting in the chair. He's from one of the other clubs, I'm sure of it. I close my eyes briefly in frustration, knowing that whatever comes can't be good.

I note that I'm still holding onto Crow's hand so let go gently, not wanting to startle him or allow for anyone else to notice. I don't care if they see, but they'll see my comforting him as a weakness for Crow.

Dad stands next to the man who's bloody and bruised, and looks straight ahead at Crow and I.

"This man helped orchestrate the attack on us. He has given us the information we need, though there's one more thing we'd like to know." My dad looks at me as he says this. He wants me to know, to understand.

Signed with Love duet
J R Dust

"I'd like you to leave now, Charlie darlin. You can wait outside," my dad tells me.

I can see Crow shaking, though I bet no one else notices that part. They're too hungry for this man's blood.

Fuck, fuck, fuck.

My dad comes towards us, pushing me gently towards the door.

It's only then as I turn to whisper words of comfort to Crow that I notice the man doesn't have anything covering his mouth and yet he's not said a word. Surely, he should be angry and screaming, upset and frustrated and crying, pleading or begging or trying to get out of the chains in a last attempt to get free. Doing something. Anything.

This man is sitting perfectly still, watching and I'm sure assessing those around him. Mainly Crow as the new one in the room.

My dad nudges me to leave once more and the last thing I see before I do is the man in the chair, all bloodied and dirty watching me intently before smirking briefly at me as I walk out and mouthing three words when the others are too busy ushering me out to notice.

He'll get you.

The heavy metal door slams shut behind me. So, I wait. Thinking over the man's words. He'll get you. The man is a member of a band of men that attacked the Club not so long ago. They call themselves The Enforcers. Even the name sounds ridiculous. The enforcers of what exactly? No one's going to get me. I continue to wait. And wait. What if he knows something about the marking? I anxiously wait a while more, unable to hear a thing going on inside the room behind me because of these stupid soundproof walls.

And then, as if nothing has happened and no time has passed, they're back and closing the door behind them.

"Son, I'm proud of what-"

I interrupted my dad, "Of what?"

"He's a part of us, now more than ever, Charlie, but we may need to swap him round with one of the other guys to watch you for a while." My dad eyes me dubiously, knowing just as well as I do what's about to come out of my mouth.

"I'm not having anyone follow me around, Dad – well, not unless it's Crow. Considering I'm currently marked, up for sale, Gray's gone, and we have The Enforcers and The Devil's Dealers around trying to constantly find a reason for a war, the safest thing is for me to be with someone I trust, Dad, and that person is Crow. Please, please don't have someone else do it," I beg him.

"Char, it's only one day a week. That's all and I promise you, no one will get to you. Not the Enforcers or the Dealers," Dad tells me.

Crow says nothing, but he nods, slightly, only slightly at my dad who eyes him cautiously.

"What's going on? What don't I know now?" I ask in frustration.

I don't move beside Crow. I watch as he once

43

again eyes my father, waiting for him to speak.

"Charlie darlin', there's no way you're able to go to the city next weekend to see Nina. It's too dangerous at the moment," my dad tells me.

In all the chaos and unrest that's been happening the last few days, I had completely forgotten about going to see Nina.

Nina has been my best friend throughout high school and when she went off to University in Cardiff, I had promised to go and stay with her once a month for the weekend which up until now I have done, but I understand that my dad is right. Between Gray's disappearance, the mark on me, and the rival gangs gaining on us, it is too much of a risk. Not just to me, but to Nina as well if anyone catches me with her and uses her as leverage.

"OK. I get it, I'll have the new guard one day a week, I won't go to Nina's, but I need you to tell me what's going on. I feel like my head is going to explode, Dad," I tell him, feeling exhausted from the constant mismatch of thoughts going on in my head.

"Charlie, I'm sorry, but the less you know the better. You know this."

"No, I don't, Dad. This is about me! And Gray, and no matter how much you don't want me involved, I already am just by being your daughter." He winces at my words, knowing that no matter how hard it is to hear that it's the truth.

"It's not as simple as you think it is, darlin'. Look, I've got to go. There's a meeting here tomorrow, one that you should be here for, as you well know, and I need to make sure everything is ready. I'll see you at home," he tells me just as Tin walks up to us.

"Me and Crow are going to finish our food now," I declare as I take Crow's hand to leave.

"Is it bad? I mean, really that bad?" I ask quietly as we walk away from my dad and Tin.

"I'll protect you. I swear I will." Crows' words affect me more than I'd like to admit. Not only because him saying that means that it really is that bad but because if it is that bad then I'm just as worried about him as I am about myself.

And then I have an idea.

"What did you have to do earlier? That you couldn't do before, what is it you had to do?" I ask him.

"You know I can't tell you that, Char. I wish you'd stop asking me to tell you things you know I can't. I don't want to hide things from you but I can't not," he tells me, looking as defeated as I felt only moments ago.

"But what if you could tell me? What if I was a Dark Cobra? You could then, right?" I ask eagerly.

Crow stops me, looks both ways to be sure there's no one around and then looks me dead in the eyes. He doesn't move for a moment, looking at me so intently I'm sure he's either in shock or thinks I'm delusional. Or maybe both.

"Do not ever let your dad hear you say that. In fact, just don't ever say that again. You are not

45

now, nor ever will you become, a Cobra."

"Why? It makes sense. I've been around the Dark Cobras my whole life, my dad is a Cobra, my brother was a recruit. Why can't I be one?"

"Women aren't Cobras, Char," he says as he drops his head.

"Why?! We're not in the twentieth century anymore, Crow, women can do just a-"

"It's nothing to do with what women can and can't -do, Char. If women were Cobras then the men would automatically try and protect them, more so than they would the men around them. It's just automatic and if it's one of the men's wives or daughters then it's even more distracting because he will be spending every minute trying to protect her rather than doing his job. That leads to lives lost, problems caused and just – no. No, Char." He releases a breath, lets me go, and continues walking towards the cafe.

"What if you just train me up then so that I can look after myself? I won't mention the Cobras again, but at least if you help me train then I'll have a chance at protecting myself if I ever need to," I tell him with certainty.

"I thought your dad trained you and Gray," he says as we walk towards the bar and the seats we were previously sitting at. Crow's food was still there. Untouched.

"Well, he did, but I've never put it to practise. I don't have a clue if I'd actually ever be able to use what he taught us. Learning in a room with people you know won't hurt you is very different

46

to actually fighting off people that want to kill you. I mean, I imagine it is. I used to tell my dad to stop if I got tired, I don't think The Dealers or Enforcers will listen to me if I tell them to stop somehow," I tell him with raised eyebrows, knowing that he can't argue with that logic.

I think of all of the times Gray and I would spar as Dad watched on and encouraged us, telling us which way to dodge the other. He always used to tell me to use my size as an advantage over Gray, to be fast, nimble, and small was a good thing just like for Gray to be large, intimidating, and strong was a good thing.

"Fine. Tomorrow morning we'll start." I try and fail to hide the smile that's brewing as Crow rolls his eyes at my antics.

Chapter 5

"You need to dodge me, Char. If you can't block then you at least need to dodge." We've been at it for an hour, and nothing I do seems to make me any better. I know having the skill to fight or defend yourself isn't something that can appear within an hour of training, but I think a small part of me hoped that my dad's training from when Gray and I were younger would kick in and I would at least be able to show Crow that I was capable of something. But no.

"I'm trying!" I yell at him as he comes for me again.

He keeps repeating the same actions over and over again. Backing away, coming at me again in different directions while I try to either block or dodge him. He seems to get me in a position I can't get out of every time though, no matter which way I go.

"Stop. Just stop. God, you're worse than I thought," he says with a laugh.

"Excuse me!" I exclaim, pissed off at his blunt nature. I mean, I know I'm bad, but no need to beat me while I'm down. Jeez.

"You've got to show me something here. What can you do?"

"I can punch. Dad always used to say I could throw a good punch."

Crow eyes me curiously.

"Fine. Maybe I've been going at this all wrong

just trying to get you to defend. Maybe you'd be better off attacking," he says, walking towards me.

"Hit me."

"What, n-" He interrupts me with a hard look.

"I can't just hit you, Crow," I tell him.

"Afraid you'll hurt me?" He laughs.

"Well yeah!" I tell him, watching as he walks around me. He's circling me.

I can't keep my eyes away from him. He's just in his shorts and even though I've seen him in his shorts and boxers a million times, all I can think about is how his muscles ripple and move every time he moves. He has the body of a god and although there are plenty of things I would love to do to him, hitting him is not one of them.

"Hit me or I won't train you anymore," he tells me seriously, straight faced, as he pulls to a stop in front of me.

I need him to train me. Dad won't teach me anything anymore insisting that I don't need it and although I hope like hell that he's right, if he's not and I ever do end up in a situation where I need to fight my way out, I would currently be completely and utterly screwed.

I have power behind my punches, I know that much.

"Fine, but I can't just hit you standing there like that. You need to hit me or come at me or something. I just can't otherwise."

Crow smirks deliciously at me as he walks away and then spins and is running towards me too quickly for me to think about what I do before I do it.

I launch my body towards him, my right arm extending straight towards his face, landing below his chin as I push my weight up with my fist. Crow's eyes looked as shocked as I feel as he staggers backwards and his head lolls to the side.

"Fuck, Char!" he yells as he rubs his chin and shakes his head at me.

"You said to hit you!" I scream, unable to stop the way my voice raises at both his outburst and the shock from actually hitting him. I can't believe I just hit him straight in the face. Oh god, I knew I shouldn't have bloody hit him. Why didn't I just go for his shoulder or something?

"That was hard! I said hit me not try and fucking knock me out! Jesus fucking Christ, woman!"

"Oh, fucking hell, let me look at it," I tell him as I walk towards him, realising in hindsight that I probably should have avoided his face because now my dad will be extra curious as to what the hell is going on If I've managed to bruise him.

"Why didn't you tell me earlier that you could punch? We've wasted an hour on self-defence. If I knew you could hit like that, I'd have started there from the off," he tells me.

"I don't know, I didn't think. Let me see your face."

"Why is your lip bleeding? I didn't hit your lip!" I'm shouting again. I am so bad in these situations. This is why I couldn't be a Cobra. Not because I'm a woman but because in stressful situations, I turn into a panicked, high pitched teenage girl that doesn't know what to do.

"I bit my lip when you decided to try and whack me like Tyson fucking Fury, you lunatic!" Crow laughs as he comes closer again, letting me see the damage I'd done.

"It's already starting to bruise. Oh, bloody hell, I'm sorry." I wince as I brush my fingers gently over the already purplish skin, knowing that not only must it hurt but that I've caused it.

"It's fine, I've had worse. I just wasn't expecting a decent punch to come from you," he tells me lightly with a smirk.

"Oh, shut up and let me get some ice." I rush back into the house and get a bag of ice from the freezer before resting it on Crow's chin as he tilts his head back.

The garden is surrounded by high fencing and bushes meaning that no one can see in and with Dad at the Club getting ready for the meeting later, no one is around to witness what we're doing.

Crow's eyes are dark as I edge closer to him, our faces only inches apart. The blood on his lips has vanished, and as he looks at me, I feel the heat I've wondered about time and time again. His eyebrows crease together in wonder and as I find myself instinctually leaning closer to him, he puts his arm around my waist softly.

"How does it feel now?" I whisper quietly.

51

"It feels good." His voice is low, gentle. I can feel his breath on my face as he speaks.

"Close your eyes." I don't know where this bravery is coming from but he does as I demand. His eyelids bat shut.

I bring myself closer to his lips and place mine delicately on the already bruised mark on his face.

His skin was soft and warm, almost feather-like against my lips. The hand that rests around my waist pulls me in closer to him.

"Char." He breathes my name, igniting a fever within me. We have never spoken about how I feel, I have never questioned if he feels the same way. I am instantly warmed by the thought of Crow wanting this, us, as much as I do.

The bravery leaves me just as quickly as it had come, and it leaves me in a state of timid embarrassment for having kissed Crow. Even if it was just a peck on the side of his lip.

"Char, look at me." His voice is demanding, yet soft.

"Yeah, I don't think so. I'm sorry." I laugh awkwardly.

His hand reaches for my chin and lifts my face to look at his. I do so, sheepishly.

"What was that?" he asks, his face flat and patient.

"A kiss to make it all better?" I squeak out in question with a small laugh.

He doesn't say anything, but his brows crease as if he's never heard of anything so absurd before.

"Why?"

"Why do you think? I'm just gonna go inside," I tell him as I pull my face away from his hand and turn towards the house.

He grasps my wrist and yanks me back to him so that our bodies are flush up against one another.

I can feel the muscles of his chest on my breasts and feel the fire ignite within me once more.

"Do it again, but don't be sorry this time." His words hit me like a freight train, making my brows rise in shock. He wants me to do it again?

I look into his eyes, waiting for him to shake his head, to change his mind or laugh at me but he does none of that. Instead, his eyes bore into mine hungrily, waiting.

I look ahead and find that my eyes are the same height as his chest.

I spare one more glance at him to be sure he's not going to backtrack before placing numerous light kisses along the delicately soft skin on his chest, reaching my tiptoes as I ascend to patter kisses along his shoulders and neck before finally reaching his lips again.

All the while he stands there unmoving, staring at me in what I can only describe as awe and as he does, I feel more elated than I ever imagined possible.

Our lips touch. It's not soft or gentle, but rough and demanding. His hands nestle themselves within the waves of my hair as he pulls my head closer to his, destroying and maiming my lips with his own. His tongue darts out, eagerly swirling against mine as he uses his other hand to hold my body flush against his.

I can feel the heat of his body, his skin, the fire of the kiss we're sharing. It doesn't last long enough though. Within what feels like only a few moments, it's over and he's staring down at me once again. Only this time, I find myself unable to look away from his gaze.

Chapter 6

The Club is packed, same as yesterday. Same as every day. Crow and I are sitting in a booth towards the back with very few people within hearing distance.

The drive here took all of two minutes, meaning that no awkward silence really had a chance to happen. He's hardly said a word since the kiss aside from telling me that we needed to go to the club. He needed to be here for Dad's meeting and so did I.

I am supposed to be meeting the Laidens' President's son here this afternoon. I have already been dreading it, but adding the kiss between Crow and I into the complicated mess that is my life now intensifies the anxiety I feel about meeting a possible fiancé.

My dad has explained that there was a Cobras Only meeting first to discuss current affairs.

I would wait here, in the cafe as always when a meeting occurs; the only difference with today is that I have already planned to hopefully get close enough to listen in on the meeting. If no one will tell me what is going on then I will find out for myself.

Crow had rung ahead and ordered food. Alice had carried it over, been tipped well, and has left us alone again. Even though I know Alice has a thing for Crow and I hate the very thought of it, I am no less than petrified to be left alone with him for the fear of having some awkward 'that shouldn't have happened' conversation which changes everything.

"Pass me the ketchup will you, Char." Crow interrupts my thoughts with the most mundane demand.

I hand him the ketchup and then go back to eating my chips.

"Why are you staring at me like that?" he asks.

"I wasn't staring at you!" I insist as I look away, realising that in order to look away, I must have indeed been staring at him without even realising it.

"Look at me," he demands.

"I really wish you'd stop telling me to look at you," I tell him as I dubiously look his way.

"And I really wish you'd get out of your head and look at me instead of overthinking," he tells me with a laugh. I can't help but smile at him; he's right and he knows it. He knows me well enough to know how my mind works.

He shifts closer to me in the booth so that we're only inches away from one another.

"I don't know what's going on with us right now but I don't want it to stop, but I also don't want you thinking things have to be weird because you can't keep your hands off me," he tells me with a wink.

"Oh, shut up and eat your stupid burger." I shove him and watch as he laughs before digging into his food again with a smile.

"What times the meeting?" I ask, watching the room as most of the high-ranking Cobras begin filing out into the hall. Crow seems to notice this just as I do. He checks the time on his phone before wiping his lips with the napkin at his side.

"Now apparently," he grunts out. "Right, you stay here. Do not go anywhere unless it's inside this club, alright?" I nod at him, which is apparently enough to appease him.

"I won't be long, alright?" He gets up, grabs his phone, and heads out towards the hallway, chatting to a few of the men as he does.

I purposefully wait twenty minutes before leaving the booth, knowing that there are always stragglers that are late to the meeting.

There are still men around everywhere though. It's not hard to figure out that my dad has most likely upped the guards around the club or more specifically around wherever I am. Which is fine. I'm not leaving the Club.

I walk up to the bar and find Alice on her phone.

"Hey, Alice, can you do me a favour?" I ask quietly.

She eyes me suspiciously with a small smile.

"What's your plan this time?" She giggles.

"I'm just going to go for a walk, I'm not leaving the Club but if anyone asks, I went to the toilet, OK?"

"Sure, just don't be too long. They'll notice," she tells me as she eyes the men around the outskirts of the building.

I nod in her direction before heading off into the hallway towards the meeting rooms. The hallway is empty, so I take the opportunity and walk quickly to the room I know sits adjacent to the meeting room. There's a kitchen just off the meeting room that has access through one of the bathrooms, so I follow through until I'm at the door to the kitchen.

It must be my lucky day. The kitchen door is ajar slightly, meaning that I can see and hear straight into the meeting room.

My dad is sitting at the head of the table with Tin and Dove to his right, Crow to his left, and John beside Crow. The rest of the men are sat sporadically alongside the rectangular table.

"It's a million pounds, Matt. We've already stopped two men from getting in the Club and one at your place. It won't be long before they stop coming in ones and twos and bring a whole fucking gang of the fuckers," Dove tells my dad.

"So, what are you thinking? How do we get the mark down?" he asks him, though I have no doubt he's asking anyone that has an answer.

They're talking about me. My mark. A million pounds. Is that to get me? Who would be paying that much money to get their hands on me? When and who did the Cobras stop? I hadn't seen or heard of anyone coming anywhere near me that weren't supposed to, though I suppose that was with thanks to my dad and the men he had around me. I suspected that he had more people following me than he told me, but this practically confirmed it.

"I don't know, that's the problem. We have too many enemies to know who's behind it, though I suspect The Dealers have something to do with it," Dove tells my dad as some of the other men nod their head at his words.

"I've asked the O'Banians to help us. I've been trying to merge with them for years and they've finally got back to me. I just need them to help us sooner rather than later." My dad sighs, rubbing his forehead before taking a sip of the whiskey in front of him.

I recognised the name that they were talking about. The O'Banians, but I had no idea why or where I had heard the name before.

"They'll be able to take the mark down, won't they? Nothing's happening to that little lady under my watch, I'll tell you that much. Shit, they might even know a way for us to get some evidence of Gray's disappearance too." It's Tin that's speaking now, hopeful in the mysterious O'Banians reach.

"I really hope so. I don't know where to start with even half of the shit we have going on, if I'm honest with you men." I don't think I have ever seen my dad looking so defeated and worried. So vulnerable.

He has already lost one child, the disappearance of another would be the end of him.

"Liam's back tomorrow, he might have a

better idea of how we can face this, yeah? That little lady is the best protected little shit there is, I promise you that much, Matt. And with the Laidens joining us, no one will get near." I smile up at Tins words, knowing that he's as close to family as what my real family are, that he would do anything he could to help both me and my dad, even if it means handing me over to the Laidens in order to keep me safe.

"There's one more thing. Elio's got something on Gray, but I wanted him to wait until we were all together. What is it?" my dad asks, his eyes on Elio at the opposite end of the table to my dad.

Shit.

As I look up to see what else is happening, it's at that exact moment that Tin looks towards the kitchen door that I'm perched behind. His eyes catch mine before I get a chance to leave. My eyes shoot wide with panic as he whispers something to my dad who nods in his direction, not looking towards me. Tin stands and heads straight towards the kitchen and as he does, I look to Crow, who I find is looking straight at me as well.

Fuck, fuck, fuck

I mentally curse myself for being the world's worst spy and begin to scamper off before Tin gets to me, but he's too fast and I'm apparently way too slow. I reach the hallway through the bathroom at the exact moment he enters the hallway from the meeting room's entrance.

He looks from me to the doorway I've just

come out of.

"What are you doing?" he asks sternly.

"Going to the toilet?" I tell him hesitantly, more a question than a fact, knowing that there's no way out of this unless a miracle comes to save me.

"What did you hear?" Oh shit.

"Nothing, I swear! I just heard voices and was curious but I didn't hear anything!" I tell him in a rushed whisper-shout so as not to gain any attention from anyone else. If Tin tells Dad I'm going to be in so much trouble.

Tin grins at me and shakes his head as he breaks out a rough guffaw of laughter.

"You're such a liar, you little sod." He laughs.

I smile up at him, knowing that if anything, I'm lucky it was him that caught me rather than any of the others. Although Crow saw me, too, that's not so great.

"Don't say a damn word and stop spying on us. For your own sake, stop spying, you're bloody awful at it," he says with a laugh before walking off back into the meeting.

Now there's just Crow to contend with. One down, one to go.

"What the hell was that, Char?" Crow asks as soon as he gets back to our booth.

"I'm sorry! I'm sorry, I just need to know what's going on and I know you can't tell me or won't tell me or whatever but I need to know, especially because no matter how much Dad doesn't want me to be involved, I already am." I spew out the words, unable to stop myself before I take inventory of what I've said.

"I know you can't tell me; I know it's not that you won't, I'm just frustrated always being kept in the dark when it's my life just as much as anyone else's that's being messed with," I tell him with a sigh.

Until Gray disappeared, I had always let my dad keep me away. He didn't have to try particularly hard because I just wasn't interested. I was young, naive, and more interested in my friends and my future career than the Club, but between Gray being gone and now, I'm as involved in the Club business as anyone else in the Dark Cobras is, whether they like it or not.

I don't want to be. I know there's danger because of it but I had that choice taken away from me the moment people started to dig and found out that my dad has kids. Not as though they had to do much digging and because he has a weakness – two, that meant that despite his best efforts, Gray and I had no choice but to be involved.

And now I've got a hit on my head and I have no idea how to save myself, let alone get to the bottom of saving Gray.

"I'm scared, Crow," I tell him quietly.

"I'll protect you, I swear to you, Charlie. I will keep you safe. No one is going to touch you. I'd do more than kill and murder, I'd fucking slaughter and torture - burn the world to ashes to be sure you're safe." His words whisper to my inner worry and paranoia, knowing that he truly will do anything to protect me, but that I don't want him in danger any more than I want myself to be.

"What happened to that guy, the one in the cell the other day. What did my dad ask you to do that you could do this time but couldn't do before?" I ask curiously.

I haven't thought about it since it happened with everything else that was going on but there didn't seem to be any anxiety surrounding him afterwards, unlike the last time my dad had taken him down there to do his mysterious task.

Crow turns to look at me, his face stern, eyes cast low as he says, "Protect you."

Chapter 7

My dad had insisted that I meet Victor, the Laidens' President's son, in one of the meeting rooms. The very same one Tin had just caught me in as it happened.

He felt that I wouldn't want a show for this particular meeting, which I couldn't disagree with. I'm not sure if everyone knows of the potential deal up for the offering, but either way I don't need it to be public knowledge if it isn't already.

"Are you sure you don't want me to come in?" Crow asks as we walk towards the room.

"It's fine, I promise. Go back and finish your food, I won't be long," I tell him with a smile that has far more confidence in it than what I currently do.

He laughs abruptly, shaking his head.

"I ain't going fucking anywhere, Char. I'm waiting outside the damn door," he tells me sternly.

I roll my eyes but am silently grateful knowing that he won't be far away. It can't be the most comfortable of situations for him to be in – standing outside the door while the girl you kissed only hours ago is inside talking about marriage with a stranger. This isn't a fun scenario for either of us.

I smile up at him timidly before pushing open the door and walking inside.

Victor is the only one in here. I was expecting

my dad, or maybe Tin or Dove to be here. I didn't expect it to only be us two.

He's a big guy, with no skin on show, but large enough of a stance even when seated to clearly see that he's filled out and most likely extremely capable of causing some damage.

He has light mousy brown hair and a relatively soft face. I was expecting a hard faced, intimidating presence and although his presence could certainly scare, I don't feel that's something he is purposefully trying to do.

"Charlie, I presume?" His voice is low and the smile accompanying his words much gentler than I assumed it would be.

I can definitely see that this man oozes charm and is the complete opposite of most biker men I know. He doesn't have the same air about him. He seems more like a well-spoken lawyer than an MC President's son.

"That's me." I smile awkwardly as I take a seat opposite him.

He watches me for a moment before speaking, taking me in or so it seems.

"I know this is a little unusual but I assure you, I will not be forcing your hand if it isn't something you don't want as well. I just want to make that clear right away," he tells me earnestly.

"So, you don't mind what happens either way?" I wonder aloud.

He shifts uncomfortably in his seat before loosening the collar around his neck.

"It's not that I don't mind. If I had my way, I'd

very happily marry you. This is something both my father and I have wanted for a long time. For him, it's the merge he wants, for me, it's you I want." His brazen nature and words shock me. He doesn't even know me, how on earth could he know that he wants me?

"I'm not trying to be rude, but why exactly do you want me?"

"You're a stronger woman than what the men around you seem to realise. I've noticed that they don't allow you to do much or have a huge amount of say. I have watched you for long enough, allowing me to know enough to make the statement clear and true that I want you." I'm not particularly surprised at his admission of watching me. Given my current situation, one more person that doesn't want me either dead or sold watching me isn't necessarily a bad thing.

"OK. So, aside from me – what's in it for you? Or your dad?" I ask.

"That's simple. We have a lot of power in favourable areas and with particularly favourable people that are able to help us in our line of work and we simply wish to branch out, but we're not willing to do so without some form of guarantee that we won't be betrayed. The Cobras and the men within the Dark Cobras will not betray us if you are with us. Family first is all of our motto," he tells me with a nod of his head towards the door.

"Your family is waiting outside this very door for you as further proof that even if they disagree, they will not stand against us if you are with us."

I nod my head at him, knowing that he's right. No matter who agreed or otherwise, no one in the club would go against the Laidens while I was a part of them.

"This wouldn't be like a conventional marriage though, I want you to know that. I'm eighteen, I have plans for myself and my future, and I can't promise you that we will ever be as a normal married couple would be." My words make it sound like I'm accepting of it, of the idea of marrying this man that in all fairness to him has been nothing but honest and open with me since the moment I stepped in the room. If I'm being completely honest with myself, I don't hate the idea. I don't particularly like it, but if the safety of those around me is a certainty then I could see myself getting on board.

He has been more forthcoming about the information he has than most of the Cobras ever have been with me.

"I like someone, one of the Cobras. I'm not sure how this would work around that," I tell him quietly, feeling shy having admitted it but knowing that I couldn't rightfully go any further with this conversation without saying it.

He watches me intently, his eyes boring into my own as he slowly nods his head at my admission.

"I would like to think that one day, even if that day isn't for a long time, that we would be a normal married couple, but I understand if that doesn't happen and as I said before, I will never force it upon you."

"But how would this work? I mean, I just told you that I have feelings for someone else. I won't lie to you. I don't know what I want with them, but I know I can't be with them if I'm married." This is a me problem. It isn't his fault, nor his responsibility, to give me an answer or to find a solution to my question, but I ask anyway.

He looks towards the door thoughtfully, contemplating my words.

"Would you date me? Until a wedding is confirmed, date me and then see how you feel at the end of it? I'm not asking for a commitment to myself alone, I understand you'll be pursuing this other man as well, but it gives you an opportunity to know me while also being sure you want this."

"I can do that."

That's when another thought hits me.

"What about Gray and the other Clubs that want the Cobras gone? How can you help us there? You want to expand, that's fine, but what do we get?" This feels strangely like a business transaction as I request something for us in exchange for me.

I am disappointed in how easily I seem to be convinced that this is the right thing to do by his words. I like to think that I'm not usually the type of girl to believe and fall for everything I'm told, and yet the way Victor seems to hypnotise me each time he talks speaks volumes.

He's a good-looking guy. Probably an inch
68

taller than Crow, built a little smaller, but no less muscle seems to be covering his body.

"I'm glad you asked. I'm willing to deal with the Devils Dealers and The Enforcers before a wedding takes place and Gray afterwards. I feel he'll be the more difficult task but as a sign of goodwill and to show you our willingness to work together, we will solve the problem of the club wars before any further commitments are made." It is a good offer. A particularly generous one considering they are currently getting nothing in return and may still not if they prove incapable of doing what Victor is insisting that they can.

"OK. Deal with them and when it's done, I'll marry you so long as you promise to find Gray next," I tell him sternly as he nods at me.

"One more thing before we allow the others back in to explain the arrangement. Until either we are married or until the day upon which this agreement is deemed null and void, you are now under my protection. I have heard of your marking and I assure you that no hair on your head will be touched by you unwillingly." His words both terrify and thrill me. His voice is demanding, his presence overpowering, and as much as I don't want his protection over that of what I already have, I say nothing as he gets up and opens the door for the others to enter.

My dad and Crow file in first, eyeing up both myself and Victor as if to make sure that I was still in one piece.

"You're OK?" my dad asks quietly as Victor's

father and VP walk in.

I nod at him and pull Crow towards me to take a seat beside me.

"I'll explain everything later, I promise," I whisper to him quickly, wishing that I had the chance to explain now without everyone else around.

"So, what's the consensus then?" Victor's father, Demetri, asks.

"We've come to the decision that the marriage will take place but in exchange for that, we will deal with the problems they have with the Devil's Dealers and The Enforcers before the marriage. We will deal with the brother, Gray, afterwards," he tells his father, who nods solemnly at us all.

I have met his father before. He is so unlike his son in his demeanour – much harsher and more rugged. The complete opposite of his son who is sat in a suit with the Laidens' signage on the back and chest. His father sits, similarly to most bikers I know, with his legs spread apart and the leather jacket with the club cut surrounding it.

"I think that's fair. Don't you?" he asks my dad, who nods his head at him.

I can feel Crow watching me, his eyes boring into the side of my head as if in hope of a telepathic explanation. I wish I could give him one.

Chapter 8

Come Sunday morning, the weekend has been spent decorating Liam's room with Crow, ready for his return tomorrow and arguing with Dad when Crow's not around about Dad's unwillingness to tell me the things that I need to know. There have been hushed conversations all weekend between my dad and the Cobras that have been visiting more frequently than normal. Something is going on but I have no clue what. As usual.

Dad pulled me aside to "talk shopping", telling Crow that he just needed to add something to the shopping list—which was a terrible excuse might I add. As if Crow wouldn't know what the hell we were talking about. As if my dad really didn't think I wouldn't just go and tell him. I think my dad assumed that if Crow wasn't around when we had these snippets of conversation that I would be more willing to do as I was told - to be obedient. He was wrong.

"You are not supposed to know. There is a reason for that, darlin', you understand that, don't you? We're here to protect you, you don't need to know so you can protect yourself. That's what we're here for." Now normally when my dad gives me this macho man shit, I just let him go for it because it's easier, to put it simply, but on Sunday morning, before my run, before my morning cuppa and quite frankly, before I had the patience for shit, I wasn't having it.

"No, you know what, Dad? I might be your little girl, but you were the one that taught me to protect myself, you were the one that told me I could do it just as well as any man, so no. Now that I want to know what I'm up against so that I can protect myself, which again, you taught me to do, you won't tell me a damn thing." I take a breath and glare at my father. Not as though I can stay angry at him for long, but he didn't need to know that right then.

He sighed, rubbing his hands over his face, and looked up at me.

"It's expected, Charlie, it's what's right. You shouldn't know or be involved in all of this. It's not me being difficult, we have to protect you, you know that. It's what I'm here for," he told me quietly.

"I will find out what's going on one way or another. I get that you want to protect me and that's great because I'd quite like protecting from some lunatic that thinks he can put me up for sale like some second-hand walkie talkie, but I need to know what's going on so that I can protect myself too." I walked on upstairs and carried on painting with Crow as if my dad hadn't just been a giant ass.

And that was how my weekend went, filled with hushed conversations with my dad, and painting and decorating with Crow.

I had been honest with Crow about the conversation I had with Victor. I didn't want to hold back from him or keep anything from him, so I hadn't. I wasn't sure how we would fit into that scenario but I felt better on both ends, making Victor aware that I had something going on with Crow and Crow being aware of the potential marriage to Victor for the sake of the club and Gray.

So now comes Sunday evening, and as I look into the room that we've spent the last forty-eight hours decorating, I debate shouting my dad up to have a look.

I haven't purposefully hidden it from him, but since we've been at loggerheads all weekend, he's not been up here to see his best friend's new room.

"Dad! Come here!" I shout down the stairs, deciding against being childish and letting him see. Mainly because I am proud of how well it has turned out and no matter how frustrated I am with my dad, I know he is only doing what he thinks is best. I don't agree by any means but I also know that if I was a parent, I would probably do the same.

The grey theme works, but I've been careful not to pick out shades that are too dark or too similar so that the room still has some light even with the less than optimistic colour decorating it.

I hear my dad before I see him, heavily stomping up the stairs, hanging on to the rail attached to the wall making him look far older than he really is. At thirty-six, he is still seriously young. A lot of people start families at his age, and yet my dad has had a full life with a family, even if the members of said family have dwindled significantly in the last fourteen years.

Crow seems to shy away from my dad as he gets closer to us, dodging him as he walks our way.

"Since Liam's coming home tomorrow, we've redecorated as you know. Crow's pretty much done all the hard work and I've just told him what to do." I earn a chuckle from both my dad and Crow at this, and it dissipates some of the tension between everyone.

Crow won't say a word against my father, especially not in front of him but with him being my bodyguard and my best friend as well as a member of the Cobras and my dad as his President, I unintentionally and selfishly put him in the middle of it all.

"Why am I not surprised to hear you've been using your bodyguard for manual labour, my darlin' Charlie?" my dad questions as he shakes his head in mock disapproval.

"Oh, shush up, and listen to me old m-"

"Old? I'll have you know I'm still in my prime, young lady!" my dad growls at me as I sigh and try to continue on.

"Do you want to see his new room or not, Dad?" I ask.

I open the oak door in front of me but keep the main light off since it's only just starting to get dark. That and the fact that I left the bedside lamp on as well as the floor standing lamp.

Signed with Love duet
J R Dust

I enter first and look around again. The bed is on the left as you enter the room, with the bedside cabinet on the left of that, and a lamp and a picture frame with an old photo I found of Liam and Dad on top of it. There's a dresser straight ahead in front of the double window and more picture frames along the walls, next to the floating shelves I'd attached, just below the fifty-three-inch television. The grey rug matches everything else in the room, with the contrast of the white desk, grey and white bedding, and mismatched sized picture frames around the room.

Dad walks in and takes a stroll around before standing in front of the artwork that took me most of the day today.

He reaches his hand out to touch it, before I snap it away.

"It's still wet, Dad, don't touch it!" I tell him hastily.

"It's perfect." He looks at me then before turning again to look at the feature wall I had created.

I got my love of mountains, hiking, hills, and the outdoors from Liam, so I did my best to incorporate it into his room.

I painted grey mountains, with darker ones behind it onto the wall. Instead of the sun, I drew the moon, and filled it with light grey, almost translucent pictures of us all from my childhood. Pictures of Dad, Liam, and some with me and Gray in too. The stars in the night sky were made from glow in the dark paint, and jewels that I had found in the pound store.

"This is incredible, he's going to love it, Char." My dad turns around to look at me again and grabs me in a monstrous hug before I have time to think about it any further. Before you know it, I've got my dad's strong arms wrapped around me "Thank you, Char," he whispers gruffly. You can hear the emotion in his voice, and I forget all about his scalding of me about the questions. I'm not sure if he's saying thank you for the room or for letting him hug me but either way, I take it.

I pull back suddenly, "Oh wait, you haven't seen the best bit!" I squeal with excitement, and grab Crow's arm and pull him towards the mountains painted on the wall.

"It just looks like a nice painting, right, Dad? Nothing peculiar about it?" I question with a raise of my brow.

My dad's eyebrows knit together as he shakes his head, "Just a normal wall," he says carefully, and I can't help the smile that spreads across my face.

"Crow, if you'd do the honours," I say, bowing slightly and elongating my arms to show my dad the very normal wall once again.

Crow steps forwards and puts his hand up against the highest peak on the tallest mountain and then looking back at me and sighing in exasperation. He knew nothing would happen and yet I made him join the show anyway.

"Why are you smiling, Char?" my dad asks

76

me as another laugh escapes my lips and I skip merrily over to my dad, hold his hand and lead him towards the spot that Crow was just standing in.

"Put your hand on the top of the tallest mountain, Dad," I instruct him.

He looks at me in confusion, but doesn't hesitate other than that and does as I say before opening and closing his mouth a few times.

Crow and I made a small square hole in between the timbers of the wall. Only small, but large enough to conceal a few things within. Crow did the electric aspect of it all, I just came up with the idea but at the top of the mountain, where a small fake star lies, is a button behind the star that leads to the cubby hole opening.

After a few minutes of silence and my dad looking around the new space in awe, he comes back out to stare at me with what I can only describe as complete shock.

"Well, now I need one! What makes him so special?" my dad asks with a face of complete seriousness, making me laugh once again.

"Oh, you'll get one, Dad, you will." I sigh, taking his arm as we walk out of the room. I take Crow on my other arm, dragging him along with me.

Having two of my favourite men on my arms makes me happier than I'd like to admit. It's so simple and yet it makes me feel more complete than I have in such a long time.

I'm laying across the sofa in the lounge next to Crow, with Dad in his corner chair nearest to the television. I have my head on Crow's lap, watching Hide.

We're waiting for our food delivery to arrive, and Hide is my favourite thing to watch right now.

It's about fifteen people that go on the run, with FBI agents, law enforcement, and many others searching for them. The people on the run have three hundred pounds, the clothes on their back, and a backpack with the basics to camp and then they run. The person or people that last the full amount of time without being caught win. The winner gets a significant sum of money.

I spend the whole time either telling Dad and Crow how cool they are for coming up with the best ideas to stay hidden or shouting at the television when the Hunters are close by. Then you have my dad and Crow who think they're experts giving a running commentary on the show – why would they purposefully go home when that's the one place everyone would look for them? Why would you stay in one place for more than a day or two unless you know it's an underground, undetected area? It is constant with them two.

There's an abrupt knock on the door, and as I look up, I realise that Dad is already up and heading towards the door.

Within minutes, our food is plated and in our

laps as we continue to watch the programme that had been paused while we got comfy again.

These are the types of nights that I love. Relaxed, without trouble, peaceful and content.

We do this at least once a week, which alongside the amount of crap I eat day in and day out probably explains why I never seem to lose weight. I'm not fat by any means, but I do have more meat on me than most of the girls at the club that I look at and find myself wondering what it would be like to have a body so perfectly sculpted and beautiful.

They are all slim. No more than a size eight at their biggest, aside from Alice who might be closer to a sixteen, but she's certainly not big. She has the most gorgeous curves.

I find myself curling into Crow a little more as I get lost in my thoughts but halt when I look down at how we're now sat.

I ponder for a moment at how my connection to Crow looks. We're both eating. Me sat on his lap with both of our plates of food on my lap as we continue watching television. No one ever says anything to us or about us in that way, but I realise that us holding hands when we're shopping or me sitting in his lap eating food, sharing a bed, and so much more of our friendship looks like that of a couple. I wonder if Crow recognises that as well? Even before our kiss, we have always been pretty physically connected.

As I watch him, I take in how breath-taking his

eyes are, how soft the shape of his face is despite the harsh jawline he holds. No matter how serious or stern he looks, he has a softness to him that I suddenly notice I'm drawn to without ever recognising it before. I've thought about Crow and my attraction to him many times but it's only recently that I've begun to think about him as more because rather than just admiring his body, it's his caring and protective nature that draws me in.

We spend every day and nearly every night together.

I could definitely understand why people would assume we are together.

Crow must have noticed because he's now looking at me with eyebrows creased together, "What's the matter, Char?" he whispers, as not to disturb Dad.

I look at him a little more before answering. "Nothing. I'm just thinking," I tell him.

He doesn't say anymore and turns his head back to watch the show I've now lost all interest in, but with the one arm he has wrapped around me, he starts stroking my arm. The contact makes me shiver. He's always trying to reassure and comfort me.

Crow reaches for the blanket behind us and places it awkwardly with his one free arm around my shoulders and over my lap, careful not to get it in our food. He noticed that I'm cold and warmed me, he noticed when something was wrong and questioned then comforted me. Now that I think about it, he does it all the time.

Crow and I share a bed pretty much every night. Sometimes he sleeps on top of the duvet and sometimes under, and I've never thought any more of it. I'm surprised Dad doesn't, but I think he recognises our relationship and sees the truth in it or at least the truth in Crow, knowing that he would never harm me.

━━━━━━━━━━

"What do you want me to put on Netflix?" Crow shouts towards the bathroom door. He's probably sat lounging on my bed in his boxers as usual, scrolling with the remote through our options for tonight.

I look at the clock on my phone. 11.23pm.

"I don't think I want to watch anything tonight. I think I'll just go to sleep," I tell him in a voice so small and meek I'm surprised he heard me.

"Oh," he says. "Alright then." I hear the television's roar spinning down as he turns it off.

Crow immediately looks up in my direction as I leave the bathroom and I see him subtly look me up and down.

"Fluffies again tonight?" He laughs. He's referring to my obsession with fluffy pyjamas.

"Fluffies keep me warm, you big baboon," I tell him with a roll of my eyes.

I lie back in my bed, lay my head on the pillow, turn so that I'm facing Crow like I always am in bed, and pull the duvet up over my

81

shivering body. Crow looks at me as he lays down on top of the duvet beside me and faces me.

"What's going on in that little head of yours?" Crow asks in a whisper. His voice is rough, as if he's got a cough, although I know he doesn't.

"Nothing," I say. "You can get under the duvet if you want." I can feel the warmth that his body gives off as he climbs under the covers to join me.

"Are you going to tell me what's wrong now?" he asks. He's staring right at me, but being careful, being quiet, as if he's uncertain whether or not I'll bolt any second.

"Crow, will you cuddle me to sleep?" I answer his question with a question of my own. A brave question.

He turns onto his back and lays his arm across the top of my pillow. I slide over to him and lay my head on his chest, place my one hand between us and the other on his stomach.

He flinches. "Shit you're cold." He pulls me closer and starts rubbing my arm and my back. He feels so warm, so safe, so secure in his hold.

"There's a reason I needed your body heat under the blanket." I chuckle.

"Does it never bother you that you never get time for girls, Crow?" I wonder. I'm talking into his chest where my head is.

"I've got time for you, haven't I? And with all the mayhem you make, and all the chasing I do to keep up with you, I don't think I'd be able to stay interested in anyone else." He laughs. His stroking on my arm and my back slows now.

"Do you want time for other girls though?"

"No, you're my girl in every way. Char, I don't need another girl in my life." I'm still unsure if I believe him but I tell him "OK" and close my eyes whilst listening to his heartbeat under my head. It's fast, faster than mine and so is his breathing. Do all men breathe faster than women? Do I just breathe slowly? Without realising, I match my breathing to his as I sleepily trickle my fingers along his chest.

Chapter 9

Breakfast is served.

I am sat with Crow on my left and Tin on my right, with Dad and Dove sitting opposite me. This is how breakfast happens most mornings.

This morning was my dad's last breakfast in charge of the Club and the Cobras, but also the day that he gets to pick up his lifelong best friend from prison after serving time for a crime very few around me seemed to know anything about. Or maybe they do know and they just won't tell me – not as though I have asked in years but them knowing and refusing to tell makes much more sense than them not knowing at all. I mentally shake myself for ever believing that they didn't know. How would they not? There would have been court dates, police interviews, and newspaper articles. Hell, I could probably find out myself if I really wanted to.

There is an aura of excitement at the table this morning as everyone picks from the buffet in front of them and places their food on the plates in front of them.

I had picked up a sausage, a slash of bacon, an egg, and a few hash browns. Crow has about triple if not quadruple what I have on my plate and will probably go back for seconds and possibly even thirds. The man eats like he's starved.

Dad, Dove, Tin, and Crow are chatting

animatedly. The faces of the men around me are scattered with smiles and laughs. I join in when needed. I am nervous. For far too many reasons to count. I am nervous about seeing Liam.

I watch my dad as he chats with the others with ease. He seems more relaxed than normal.

I think maybe he is finally ready to hand over the reigns. He has enjoyed his time as President of the Cobras but I think he is happy enough to let Liam lead now. Even though he will still be Liam's second in command and be at all the meetings, the workload and pressure won't land on him as directly as it will on Liam.

I pick my book up with one hand and open it to begin reading whilst eating breakfast with the others. The chatter around me doesn't bother me as I delve deeper into the world of dark romance that captivates me in a way very few things in the real world do.

I had been obsessed with creating lists and reviews of everything I had read for the past few years, but since Gray's disappearance, the stress of the rival gangs, and now my for sale tag, I haven't given much thought to my future, apart from knowing that I want to get out as soon as I can. I just don't know how to make that happen yet. I can't leave until Gray is back or we have answers about him one way or another. That's why I have put university off until next year. It doesn't feel right moving on with my life while Gray's potentially hangs in the balance.

There's suddenly a high-pitched intermittent

ringing in the background that interrupts my thoughts and my reading. My head lifts, and I realise with a start that it's the house phone. It's Liam. He was going to ring with a time to be picked up, Dad had told me last night.

My dad smiles at the others and practically sprints to the phone to pick it up. He's impatient as he listens to the drone of the robot voice telling him that there's a call for him from Wrexham High Security Prison, from "Liam" and asks if my father wants to take the call. Press one if you'd like to take the call. Press two if this is a wrong number. Press three if you feel scared, afraid or threatened in any way. I could still recite the recording they sent out to everyone before you spoke to your family member or friend. I've heard it so many times from the times that I did speak to Liam on the phone that it is reserved in my memory now as another piece of pointless information.

My father, of course, doesn't let it get any further than that. He accepts the call.

"Liam, my man!" my dad shouts excitedly, moving his free hand around animatedly as if he's speaking to Liam for the first time in ten years rather than the thousandth. Well, I'm not sure how accurate that number is, but it's certainly not far off.

My dad's brows shoot up, his eyes widening in surprise at whatever it is Liam's telling him.

"Alright, I can do that, man. I'll see you in an hour, bud!" my dad tells him and promptly hangs up the phone. That's got to have been the quickest conversation I've ever seen them have. They are normally talking and gossiping like a couple of middle-aged meddling women for over an hour. An hour for which I'm rolling my eyes usually just listening to Dad's side of the conversation.

My dad spins round so quickly, I'm surprised he's not got whiplash, and tells us, "He wants me to pick him up alone so we can talk, and then we'll meet the four of you and the others at the Club. No club girls, just Alice and Ben. We'll be there at eleven. Got it?" We all nod. No questions asked.

"Fucking hell, let's get goin!" Tin says as he jumps from his chair and practically drags Dove, Crow, and I along with him.

I stop to turn back to Dad and watch as he nods at me and begins getting his things together.

"Tin, I need to get dressed," I pant out, tired from trying to resist the pressure he's using to pull me along like an excited puppy. He turns back to me with confusion written all over his face.

"He's seen you in PJs your whole life girl, come on." The "on" in that drags like he's an excited child, dragging their parents out of bed on Christmas morning.

"I'll meet you there soon guys, okay? I promise," I reassure him and begin heading up the stairs before anyone can stop me. Crow, of course, follows me in my haste, whereas Dove's already out the door before he gets the chance to mess my hair up anymore, and Tin sighs up at me before running from the front door with nothing but glee on his normally sullen and paling face.

And now I must decide what on earth I wear to spend the day with these mad men.

———

I'm at the Clubhouse chatting with Crow at one of the tables set out for the cafe.

The men around me are loud, excited and somewhat annoying in their boisterous nature, although I can't blame them. They haven't seen Liam in years and Crow, Alice, her younger sister Kira, and Ben, one of the newer recruits, haven't ever met him.

Crow's anxious energy is obvious. His hands fidgeting with one another, clasped together in front of him on the table, his eyes darting around the room as if waiting for a bomb to go off any second, and his lack of conversation is more than anything a sure sign that Crow is as nervous as I am, although for vastly different reasons.

"Stop stressing, Crow," I tell him as I reach for his hands to pull apart the fidgeting hands in front of us.

He looks up at me and with those soft brown eyes that usually hold the hardest of looks and I can feel myself softening under his gaze.

"Easy for you to say, you've known the man

your whole life, Char. What if he doesn't want to keep us on?" He's asked me this so many times in the last few weeks. I get it. I do. New leadership is frightening and with so many of the new guys having nowhere else to go, it's a scary prospect that someone might tell them to leave.

"I won't let you leave alone, you know that. Come on, come out the back with me. These lot and their fidgeting are even making me nervous." I don't tell him that I'm nervous regardless of the drinking and hollering happening around me.

Crow slowly rises from his chair with a sigh, the squeak of the chair moving is barely noticeable in the atmosphere that surrounds us.

I don't want to be the first to see Liam, and I don't want him to see me before everyone else so I start walking to the back door of the club, knowing that Dad will bring him in through the front ready for everyone to hone in on him like he is prey, although the very thought of Liam being the prey in a roomful of animals is almost laughable.

"You know your arse is about as round as a couple of beach balls in those leggings right now, Char?" Crow asks me with a chuckle.

I'm suddenly mortified and turn around to look at him in astonishment.

Did he seriously just say that my arse looks like beach balls?! Beach balls!

"It's not a bad thing. Jeez, if looks could kill and all that," he says with a smirk on his face that I can't help but want to smile at.

I turn on my heel abruptly, shaking my head in mock disapproval. I begin to head outside but before I get a chance, I find myself knocked over by what feels like a brick wall.

I flail and look around, grabbing onto thin air to catch myself from falling, but within a millisecond there are tree trunk arms wrapped around me, supporting me and stopping my collapse to the floor.

I look up and I swear to whoever's up there, my time of breathing in this world is done for.

It's Liam.

Of course it's Liam. Why wouldn't it be? Attempting to give myself a mental facepalm hard enough that it'll knock me out doesn't seem to be helping the situation somehow.

My mind seems to be blank and what makes it so much worse is that it isn't just my mind. It's silent. No one is saying a word. My body feels like it's on fire and I realise with a start that it's because I'm still in Liam's arms. Well, shit!

I pull myself away from Liam, only to be pulled back in by him for the type of hug he's never given me before. The last time he hugged me, I was eight years old, about a quarter of the height of his six-feet-five builder's frame and also didn't feel awkward as a shit stood in his arms.

I allow myself to relax a little though and I realise that I'm not really doing any hugging, I am being hugged. His arms are locked around me, and I am just cocooned inside of his arms that seem to be unrelenting and unmoving.

Signed with Love duet
J R Dust

I can hear him breathing next to my ear, but before I have a chance to think any more of it, I hear his voice for the first time in years.

"You're so grown up, baby girl." It's only a whisper and yet his voice is deafening. Not loud, or obnoxious, just so overwhelmingly manly and deep that every fibre inside of my now grown-up body shivers at every syllable he says.

He always called me his baby girl. I used to love it and now I can't decide if I hate it for reminding me that he still thinks of me as that child he left ten years ago or love it because it's so comforting.

I pull myself away, and as Liam reluctantly lets go, I get a good look at him.

He's the same but so much more. As a child I never looked at him as anything but family but having not seen him in years, I realise through a woman's eyes he's incredibly good looking.

His head's shaved, but it's growing back. You can see the dark hair growing in every direction. His eyes are sky blue, which is the most insane contrast to the rest of him, because he looks as bulky and bad now as he did all those years ago, if not more so.

I guess there's only so much to do in prison and working out is a pastime. Clearly a pastime he took up going by the sight of Liam.

He's watching me expectantly and it's then that I know I've said nothing to him yet.

What do I say? My god, it's like it's the first time I've ever met him.

I'm frozen. My body isn't moving, my mind seems incapable of thought, and both Crow and Liam are waiting for something. Something from me.

Liam's eyes soften.

"I'm sorry, it seems crazy seeing you," I manage out, my voice and words feeling so small.

Liam frowns, his eyebrows coming together but the confusion I see on his face is gone in an instant. He brings his arms back around me in a heartbeat and I breathe, letting my body droop into his. This time, my arms wrap around him too.

I open my eyes to find that my dad has walked in behind Liam. His eyes are gentle, his face etched with concern.

———

I'm in my room, sitting on my bed reading, using the light of my fairy lights above me when I hear Dad and Liam come through the door. Probably drunk or merry at the very least.

Within minutes, I can hear my dad snoring downstairs. He's probably fallen asleep on the sofa. Dad can drink and drink and drink, but the moment he finds somewhere comfortable, his eyes close and he's dead to the world.

I hear footsteps plodding steadily up the stairs. Liam. The house is large enough to have privacy but not so large that you can't hear everything going on within it. Such as the steps that have stopped outside of my bedroom door.

Two soft knocks on my door stop my thoughts.

"Come in," I say.

I pull the covers over me, covering the vest top I have on. It's just typical that someone wants to come into my room the one night I don't have my fluffies on to cover me up.

My lights aren't on, only the fairy lights above me, which allows me to see Liam as he enters. It's still dark, but the small light that is in the room illuminates him.

He's changed in so many ways and yet also not changed at all.

It could just be my adult perception of him that's changed, maybe it's not him at all, just the way I see him now in comparison to the way I saw him ten years ago.

He stops in the doorway. Uncertain. Probably just drunk and unable to see in the dark.

"Are you alright?" I wonder, shifting in the bed so that my legs are crossed beneath me, in case he decides to sit on the end of the bed.

He notices that I've made space for him and does just that. The bed shifts under his weight, though not so much that it makes any noise, although it does jolt me slightly.

"I'm a little drunk, my girl," he tells me. "But I wanted to talk to you."

"Is something wrong?" I wonder aloud.

"No, no," he rushes out, "nothing's wrong, we just didn't get to talk earlier." His accent seems stronger, certain letters being accentuated more. I suppose that's the drink too.

"I know, I don't know what came over me." I laugh nervously, finding myself shifting again, unsure of what to say.

Things never used to be awkward between us. I wonder if he feels awkward too. If maybe I'm so different from the child that he used to know that he doesn't know how to form a new relationship with me now that I'm not sitting on his lap with him reading me a book.

"I read," I say, looking up at him now, holding up the book in my hands to show him "I think that's on you," I tell him. "Reading to me constantly as a kid has me now obsessed with reading.".

I notice a smile form on his lips, only a small one, but I notice it all the same.

"Your dad says you're a bookworm through and through."

I wait.

"Do you know why people read?" he asks me.

"To escape for a little while, to relax, to see a new world, a new perspective, a new life to live in for those few minutes that the words are in your head creating the perfect story," I tell him with a smile.

"What are you escaping?" he asks me.

I feel my brows furrowing. I wonder if Dad has told him about everything that has been going on here recently. I know he keeps him updated on most things but he probably didn't want to bog him down with everything else immediately so I decide to do the same.

"I'm not escaping anything," I lie. "Books just give me time to breathe."

He's looking directly at me. He looks unsure. Unbelieving. What does he think I need to run away from? What has Dad told him?

"Yeah, yeah you're right," he says, shaking his head as if doing so will help with clearing his thoughts.

"Are you sure you're okay?" I ask again. He seems so lost. I'm not sure that's the right word but it's the first one that comes to mind when I look at him. Lost.

"I'm fine, better than fine." He takes a deep breath, "I'm home again," he says, with more conviction and certainty in his voice this time round.

"You should get to sleep," he tells me as he lifts himself from the bed and walks back the way he came.

I don't say anything.

"Breakfast on me in the morning," he tells me with a smile on his face this time.

I smile back.

"Hash browns t-" We both stop, and I find myself grinning, similarly to the one he holds on his face, as we catch ourselves both saying so at the same time.

He remembers.

"Goodnight, baby girl," is all I hear as I see the back of him leave as he closes the door behind himself.

Maybe I'm just too tired to think properly but I'm sure there was something wrong. Maybe he's just not adjusting well, or he's overwhelmed with the day he's had. It would be understandable.

Chapter 10

Liam is true to his word, or at least I assume it is him.

I wake to the smell of bacon, and more importantly, hash browns.

I shower quickly, and throw on a plain black, long-sleeved dress, black tights, and a hoodie overtop after brushing the knots out of my semi-dried hair.

I sniff the air around me again, reminding myself of a bloodhound on a mission. The food still smells fresh, so before I have the chance to get distracted and take much longer, I launch out of my room and down the stairs.

There is a spread on the table of cereals, fruit, and fresh juices. I am watching the back of Liam as he is moving something in a pan on the hob, apparently still cooking up whatever he had planned. I can't have taken too long after all.

I realise that he hasn't noticed I'm here yet and find a smile spreading across my face.

I tiptoe over to Liam, suddenly grateful that I didn't put any shoes on after all and just as the music on the radio begins again, I jump and poke his sides.

I'm laughing at his surprised startle when he turns and glares at me in mock anger.

Still heaving from laughter, I look down at him still smiling. "Better than I used to be, hey?" I question as I jump away from him and move to

97

turn the bacon on the stove so it doesn't burn.

The laughter's still bubbling within me as he sets up the table.

"I could have hurt you, Charlie," he says sternly.

I'm not looking at him, I'm flipping the eggs now, facing the window instead of the far too serious man behind me.

I spin, ready to apologise, and find him just inches from my face and feel my breath halt.

No. This feels weird.

I'm not a lover of people being in my space at the best of times, let alone after just waking up.

"I'm sorry. I didn't think," I tell him as I stare for far too long into the silence alongside his blue eyes. "I used to try and jump scare you all the time, I just thought- I don't know, I'm sorry."

"Your dad told me about your boyfriend." I know immediately who he's talking about. I mean, who else if not Crow? There is certainly no other guy in my life coming close to anyone being labelled my boyfriend, although I highly doubt that was the word Dad used to describe him. I also note a series of emotions that cross far too quickly across Liam's face when he calls Crow my boyfriend. I don't think I'll correct him even though it's not true. Not yet at least.

Does that mean he doesn't know about the potential marriage in the works? I suppose he could be on about Victor, though I can't imagine Liam calling him my boyfriend. If Dad had in fact told him about it, the last thing he would assume was that.

"What about him?" I ask as I spin back around, tending to the food, sticking with the assumption that he's talking about Crow.

"You shouldn't be getting involved with him or the club." He huffs, takes a deep breath that I can hear far too loudly, and continues calmly, "It's not the right way, baby."

His use of the word baby freezes me for a moment too long before I flip back round, glaring at the man in front of me.

"I have just as much of a right to know what is going on. Why can't anyone get that into their heads?" I hiss out the last few words, cross at him for coming at me the first sober moment he can about my involvement with Club business.

If Crow was right with his suspicions and Liam starts changing things around here, especially with the new recruits, I'll be leaving right along with them.

"You aren't right for the club. You couldn't do what's needed to be involved. Are you a natural murderer?" he asks me lightly, softly, gently. So much so that it sounds like little more than a whisper.

What is wrong with him? First, he asks about my boyfriend and then changes the subject to lecture me on the club, calls me baby in a way I'm not too sure sounded as innocent as it should, and then asks me if I'm a murderer.

I feel my blood boiling, my hands beginning to shake. Why on earth is he asking me about being a murderer? I know he's been locked up for years, I get that he's changed, I understand that things have altered and it's going to be hard for him to adjust but if he's insinuating that because I'm not some violent bully that can pass the Clubs tests that I don't have the right to know what's happening then he's more deluded than I ever imagined.

"Murderer? No. However my specialty is in finding out what I'm not supposed to." I stare him down, craning my head slightly to see into his eyes, but refusing to give up if he insists on being such an asshole.

His face is blank, impassive, unmoving; and no matter how much it boils my blood, I'd be blind to have to say it isn't attractive too. Not to me personally but I can understand why so many women fell for him when he and my dad were younger. My dad and Tin often reminisce over the days when they were younger and had women falling at their feet – Liam included.

He laughs, and then he laughs again, moving back to give himself space from me, laughing so much, so hysterically now that he's bent over slapping his hand on his knee.

"And what exactly is so funny Liam?" If he's laughing at me, I'll be half tempted to use the punch I practised on Crow on him.

Not before breakfast though. Or not at all, let's face it, I'm not that brave or that violent.

He looks up at me, wiping the tears of laughter from his face.

Signed with Love duet
J R Dust

"My god, girl, you'd make most men piss their damn pants with that look," he tells me with laughter and lightness in his voice.

I stare at him absurdly.

He doesn't say a word.

I roll my eyes at his silence and swiftly spin and plate up my breakfast, walk towards the kitchen door, leaving his on the stove, and turning it up to the maximum so that I can smell it burn.

Is that some joke to him? My involvement with the club, or rather lack of is not a joke to me.

Honestly, is there a reason we need men around? Can I find some deserted Island where men are forbidden? That would be great right about now.

I take my plate up to my room.

The wafts of burnt food are hitting me already.

I feel myself smiling smugly.

My breakfast tastes wonderful.

———

I have been desperately trying to avoid Liam since the terrible failure that breakfast was, but no matter where in the house I go, his booming laughter and far too loud phone calls seem to follow me everywhere I go.

I am currently sitting out in the garden, reading once again. Well, mainly glaring at the asshole through the kitchen window, but reading too.

I'm sitting on a swinging bench my dad made a few years ago, and I have Crow sitting beside me on his phone making a new playlist.

We do this a lot.

Just sit in silence. We're comfortable around each other and I like that.

"Why are you glaring at him?" Crow asks me, pulling me from my thoughts.

"I just don't like him right now," I tell him, not in the mood to talk about Liam.

"You seemed to like him plenty yesterday," he says, obvious confusion threading through his words.

I find myself huffing, turning to Crow and glaring once again.

"He just annoys me," I tell him. "He's arrogant, a complete shitstick, and a frustration I do not need," I say with certainty.

Crow is watching me, his brows knitting together, the one side of his lips lifting up into a small smirk.

"I see," he says before returning to his phone.

"Where would you want to go?" I ask him. "If not here, where?" I've turned back to look at the book I'm doing a terrible job of reading, but I know he's listening.

"I don't know." He takes a moment.

"Probably somewhere kind of like this. Some place in the middle of nowhere." I find myself looking at him again, noting how similar we are.

Signed with Love duet
J R Dust

"I think I'd find myself some land, far away from everyone else," I say. "I'll have a spare room for you when you're annoying me and I kick you out of bed though," I tell him with a smile.

I can't imagine anything worse than living in a city. The hustle and bustle, endless people, lights, chaos, and sirens.

Peace, serenity, and silence on land that I can call my own, with animals, would be my release. One day it will be. I'm going to find Gray, figure out how to calm the chaos around me, and then go to university, find myself a home and live peacefully. That's the plan.

"The spare room can be for when you annoy me," Crow tells me, putting his arm around my shoulder and pulling me closer.

"I am not annoying," I tell him with a laugh. "I'm just so perfect that no one else can stand it," I say, moving back into his embrace.

"So perfect indeed, Char," he says with a chuckle.

I find myself smiling at his words but am soon rudely interrupted by the very devil I've been trying to avoid.

"How long have you two been together then?" I hear Liam ask as he wanders towards us.

"Did Dad tell you we're together?" I ask as I watch Liam saunter towards us.

It was only a matter of days ago that Crow and I kissed for the first time, and here Liam is asking us how long we have been together. We haven't even talked about if this is a thing yet, and now I have to find an answer to him that doesn't make me seem too keen to Crow in case he doesn't want anything more than this but also an answer that doesn't make me sound like too much of an idiot.

"No, but I can tell. You don't stay here though, do you, boy?" he questions.

"Yes, he does," I tell him with a roll of my eyes and a sigh. What is this? An interrogation?

His jaw sets as he looks at me. He doesn't even acknowledge Crow. I stare right back. Again. This seems to be happening too regularly, and he's only been around for twenty-four hours. These staring competitions are going to end up with me having my face stuck permanently in a scowl at this rate.

"I don't think he should," he tells me, still not looking in Crow's direction.

I feel Crow shifting uncomfortably, unsure of what to do with himself.

"Dad's fine with it," I tell him, ice lining my words. This man. He thinks he can just say whatever he wants, to whoever he wants, and get his damned way. Well, not here, not now, and certainly not with me.

What happened to him? I feel horrible even thinking it. Prison happened. I know he changed, but the shade he has been throwing my way since this morning is becoming too much when he seemed so happy to see me yesterday.

He doesn't respond. He comes to sit in the wooden chair opposite us. He's trying to

104

intimidate. His arms crossed, legs ajar slightly, his glare alternating between me and Crow every second his eyes can roll around to it.

"I'll come back later," Crow says, pulling his arm from around me slowly.

I latch onto his arm with speed, agility, and a crack that makes it sound like I just slapped him.

"No," I say. I look at Crow. "Stay," I tell him.

"Look, I'll come back later, Char," he says. "I need to get some stuff done anyway." He's pulling his arm from my grasp. This time I let him go.

I know it's hard for him. He would stand up to anyone for me, I know that much, but I also know that he hardly knows Liam, has him as a new Pres, and can't put himself in a vulnerable position with him.

Crow's gone and yet Liam and I are still left staring at each other. More like glaring actually. The only passion shown is anger, frustration, and on his part happiness that he's intimidated my "boyfriend" away.

"Not sure he should be able to scare that easy if he's here," Liam says, "with you."

I do not respond.

I stare and stare some more.

Liam smirks, and it's the most frustrating thing I've seen since breakfast.

Chapter 11

Victor must have gotten my number from my dad. Or from his stalking ways, who knows, but either way he had text me Tuesday afternoon asking if I was free that evening to go for a walk with him.

I was initially shocked that he hadn't asked to go for food to some fancy restaurant or to a film. That seems to be the normal type of first date that people go on, but then I remembered two very important things. The first being that he was a MC President's son so his idea of a first date would be very different to most teenage boys I had known in school; and secondly that he had himself admitted to having me watched which meant that he probably knew I liked to be outside – hiking, walking, running – just about anything so long as I had fresh air around me.

I had asked Crow how he felt about it, not wanting to go without speaking to him about it first, even though I didn't have a huge amount of choice in the matter.

I didn't doubt that Victor would take no as a solid answer without question if I suddenly changed my mind but with Gray's life on the line and that of my father's men; my family, I couldn't very well turn him down and change the rules of the deal now. I mean, I could, but I wouldn't. It wouldn't be fair to Victor or to those around me that are relying on this deal going well.

I know that I could have just said screw it all

and either marry him without getting to know him or just say no to it all, but both felt too hasty. I have to give him a chance. I hardly know him but from what I do know, although I don't see myself falling for him when I have Crow that is slowly but surely stealing my heart, I feel that Victor deserves a chance and so do I. If I do end up marrying him, I want to know him, really know him – even if the marriage never ends up being a conventional one.

Crow had been surprisingly easy going about it all so long as I promised to be honest with him throughout, which of course I had and intend to be, but now that he is walking me to the club to meet Victor, he seems more tense. Understandably so. Just before we enter the Club grounds, I halt and grab hold of his upper arm, feeling his bicep tense as I do.

"Crow, will you stop for a second?" I ask him, ready to beg. I can't lose him, not over this or over anything for that matter. I need him more than he could possibly know.

His jaw is set, his eyes dark and his face a mask, showing no emotion. This isn't Crow, and I can't even blame him.

"I'm sorry. I wish it didn't have to be like this," I tell him as I fasten my body to his in a hug I have no doubt we both need.

His arms wrap around me tightly as he sighs into my hair.

"You don't need to be sorry, Char. I get why you're doing it, I just wish you didn't have to," he tells me as he lifts my face and places a gentle kiss on my forehead.

I look up towards him and find his soft gaze burning into me. It's more than just physically being able to feel him, it's all of him. His presence, his safety, his constant reassurance that overwhelms and completes me. Being in Crow's arms makes me feel like the world could stop, the people could disappear, and it wouldn't even matter because he would somehow find a way to make it OK. The warmth of his breath, his arms, and his love surround me in ways I spent my childhood dreaming of and it's in that moment, the moment I can feel myself falling for the man that I know I shouldn't, that I hear an abrupt clearing of one's throat. An intentional cough that breaks up our faces veering for one another.

I startle and pull away, worried that it could be my dad catching us in a compromising situation. No matter how much he likes Crow, I don't doubt that he would be unhappy finding us seconds away from kissing. But when I turn to see the face the noise came from it seems even worse than my dad catching us.

Victor.

His face is blank, much like Crow's was only moments ago.

Crow tugs me closer to him, kissing the side of my head possessively, his eyes not straying from Victor's.

"You go on, Char, your dad will be picking you

up here afterwards and I'll see you at home later," he tells me as he releases his hold on me.

My body shivers instantly, not only from the cold around me but from the immediate disappearance of his warmth around me.

I nod at him and walk to Victor, ready to apologise.

I open my mouth to speak, but he starts before I have the chance to fumble and say I'm sorry.

"No need. You did warn me. Let's get going." He nods to Crow before putting his hand on my lower back and guiding me away.

"I am sorry, I know I told you but it's not fair for me to parade it around in front of you."

He lifts the helmet off his bike and hands it to me, helping me fasten it below my chin before putting his on.

I realise now that he's still dressed impeccably. He's in a suit again. Does he not get it ruffled and dirty on his bike, I wonder.

"I haven't had a woman on the back of my bike before so yank on my shirt if I'm going too fast," he tells me before lifting his leg over his bike and encouraging me to do the same.

I circle my arms around his large chest, feeling the muscles beneath his shirt rippling and moving under my touch.

I can feel his heart pounding against his ribcage, the rhythmic beats keeping up with my own.

Maybe he is as anxious as I was about this.

109

Even if he does feel he wants me, if what he had said was true about not having had a woman on the back of his bike before he probably hasn't had any woman that he has been particularly close to either. I don't fool myself by assuming that he is a man that doesn't have one night stands and hook ups, I have no doubt he does, but perhaps he hasn't ever been serious with anyone and the idea of truly getting to know someone and dating someone is as foreign to him as it is to me. Or maybe I am completely wrong and over thinking as usual.

The bike engine roars to life, vibrating beneath us.

As Victor takes off and the landscape surrounding us begins to blur, I notice that his body starts to relax. His tense posture eases and my body seems to follow along. My rapidly beating heart slows and I let the wind blow away the worries that plague me for a while.

It isn't often I ride on the back of someone's bike. Dad didn't like or allow it, but I understand now why so many of the Cobras wives say they loved it. I feel more free than I have in a long time.

The time it takes to get to the lake beneath my favourite spot is only minutes, but those few minutes feel like mere seconds. I am not surprised in the slightest that Victor has brought me here. He had admitted the first time we met that he had been keeping tabs on me, so his knowing my whereabouts and my favourite places to go isn't a shock; however, seeing him

110

dismounting his bike, putting the helmets to one side, and walking towards the path I used regularly in a suit is not something I had anticipated.

"Did you really think walking up here in a suit was a good idea?" I ask, watching as he tries to hide a smile.

"You'll find that suits are my go to attire. Biker jackets, leathers, and slacks are not something you'll find me in often. Even when hiking," he tells me with a smile.

"Do you not wear The Laidens cut?" I wonder, knowing no other club members that don't show off their clubs symbols and signage at every chance they get.

"I may be one of them but I like to think that I'm my own man, capable of my own decisions. I don't need a cut to prove who I am and who I am loyal to." His clean shoes are getting muddy. I watch his face as it shrivels up in disgust as he notices the same moment that I do.

"We can go somewhere else If you want. So long as I'm outside, I don't mind where I am. You don't need to get muddy to get to know me," I tell him with a laugh as his face falls.

"I thought this was your favourite place?"

"It is," I admit, "but that doesn't mean we have to be here. Come on, we'll walk around the lake. On the pavement, save your shoes," I tell him with a wink as I turn on my heel and head back down the dirt track.

"I only came here because I thought you

would like it," he tells me.

"I do like it. I love it here, but that doesn't mean that you have to pretend that you do too."

"I hate hiking, or even just walking out like this. I don't see the point in it."

I laugh at his abrupt nature, appreciating his honesty.

"So, what do you like to do?" I ask as we follow the curving path around the silent lake.

He ponders my question for a moment, looking thoughtful as he gazes off into the distance.

"I don't have hobbies, or a huge amount of spare time, to be honest with you. I read before I sleep every night though, so I suppose that would be something I enjoy."

"What do you read?" I can't imagine him reading romance and fantasy novels somehow, so I find myself surprised when he admits the types of books he enjoys.

"It's a little silly," he tells me as he watches me for a reaction. I make sure I keep my face straight, not wanting to make fun of him for whatever it is he finds so silly.

"I enjoy reading dystopian and apocalyptic books. I don't read any non-fiction, which my father has always found ridiculous. He didn't like me reading fantasy and fiction books growing up so I always hid them."

"I don't think that's silly at all. I mainly read romance and fantasy, but I like a few dystopian novels too."

"I'll make you a library when we have our own home. We can read all the fantasy books we like." The smile accompanying his words is like a child's that has just been told Christmas is coming early, and it breaks my heart because I'm not sure I can commit to living together, to building a life and having what he so obviously wants.

"Your face just fell. I'm sorry, I just…" The ease from his voice disappears.

"You don't need to be sorry, I just don't know how things are going to be just yet."

"Of course. My apologies." And I've ruined it.

"Under normal circumstances, I'm such a hopeless romantic, so in love with the idea of love that I would be planning a wedding and searching up kids names already and sighing at your charm, I just feel so tense at the moment with everything going on and with Crow that I just can't seem to let loose, you know?"

"I understand," he says solemnly.

"So, you're in love with the idea of love? What does that mean exactly?" He chuckles.

His laugh is contagious, his smile so open and honest that I can't help but smile back. It's true what I said. I am a hopeless romantic and with the honesty he's given me, I have no doubt that if Crow weren't a factor, I would be able to easily forget the arrangement and very genuinely try.

"It means that I have spent years reading romance novels and have always been desperate to have someone love me the way the characters in my favourite stories love each other. I've always wanted that overwhelming, empowering, all consuming love that takes you by surprise." It makes me feel vulnerable admitting that, and I'm not completely sure why. Maybe because love isn't something that I talk about often with anyone aside from family, or maybe it's because Victor is practically a stranger, and yet I feel more comfortable than I imagined telling him whatever comes to mind.

"Is that how you and Crow feel about one another?"

"I don't really know. We haven't spoke about how we feel. I know how I feel and I know that I do love him, but up until not so long ago that was just as a friend. I know that the feelings I have snuck up on me slowly over time, which isn't really the love I always dreamed of, but he makes me feel cherished, safe and treasured, which is something I love in itself," I tell him honestly.

"I like the idea of having that. Is it wrong of me to crave that with you when you already have it?"

"It's not wrong of you to want it." I feel like I'm being so unfair to both him and Crow. Both know the situation but that doesn't change the fact that I feel like a fraud for intentionally getting to know Victor with the idea of marriage in our near future while also falling for Crow.

We've almost completed one lap around the lake and are nearing his bike again. There's no one around, the sky is beginning to darken around us. It feels much like my life at the moment. There's so much brightness to be seen, and yet every day something else seems to darken the atmosphere around me.

"Would you like to read with me tomorrow?"

"Read with you?" I ask, a little confused at his meaning.

"I feel that me coming to a place you like isn't really first date material, but perhaps you can come to mine and we can read together. It's not what I suppose most would consider a date and maybe it doesn't have to be, but I feel it's something we would both enjoy."

"Yeah, sure, that sounds nice," I tell him tentatively. It does. I don't think I've ever sat side by side with someone reading, but it sounds like the most peaceful thing in the world right now.

"Why don't we go now? It's still early." Both his gaze and his question is hopeful. He seems so vulnerable, so sweet that I can't do anything but nod and accept his offer.

Chapter 12

His home isn't what I imagined. At all. I'm not sure exactly what I had in mind but it certainly wasn't this.

As Victor encourages me to follow his lead inside of the block of flats at the edge of town, I am surprised to see he doesn't live at The Laidens' Clubhouse or at least onsite or nearby, but that isn't what surprises me the most.

What truly shocks me is the inside of his home, in part because it is significantly more homely than I expected it to be.

It is small, quaint even, and yet it seems to ooze personality. There are drawings, paintings, and quotes on every wall I can see, with more bookshelves on the walls than I see in most libraries. His lounge is compact, with only one two-seater sofa, a coffee table, and a television, but the main reason it is so compact is because of the books everywhere. Scattered all over the floor, on shelves, in bookcases, and his desk that sat at the edge of the room. The kitchen is open plan and behind the lounge, just a single line of cabinets and the necessities. There are even a few books in the kitchen on top of his microwave.

"Sorry, it's a bit of a mess. I don't usually have people round," Victor says as he shuffles around the room, picking up clothes that hang over the sofa and chairs before throwing them in what I assume is the bathroom. It isn't messy though.

Cluttered perhaps, but not messy. The books that take up the majority of the space within the small room look unusually organised.

"This is literally my dream. You've got your whole flat as your own personal library." I laugh as I scoot around the room and find a few books I recognise and have read and others on my to be read list. Maybe we have more in common than I thought.

"Well, you can come here anytime you want to dream." He chuckles as he puts the kettle on and holds a tea bag up to offer me a cuppa. His whole body seemed to relax the moment we walked in through his front door. Maybe the posh, well-spoken Victor is a whole other persona separate to that of the one he truly is when comfortable in his own space.

"One sugar, please." I nod as I take a seat and continue gazing around at the mass amount of books surrounding me.

"I bet your dad has a heart attack every time he walks through the door of this place if he doesn't like you reading fiction," I joke, remembering what he had said earlier on about his dad and hiding his books when he was younger.

"He doesn't come here. No one does really. I've got one good friend that visits but apart from that, this is mine and mine alone," he tells me as he hands me the warm mug full of steaming tea.

"Thank you." I smile as I wrap my hands around the mug to warm my hands up.

117

"So, what do you want to read?" He places his cup on the table before peering through his collection and picking out a few books and bringing them over to me.

He sits next to me on the sofa, though not too close. I'm not sure if it's because he's purposefully trying not to invade my space or because that's naturally what he would do with a visitor anyway. I find myself surprised at the butterflies that fill my fluttering stomach as he takes a seat so close to me.

"You'll have to tell me if you've already read them but this one is one I haven't read. I've been meaning to for a while but haven't got round to it yet. I have two of every book, so we can read together."

"Why do you have two of every book?" I ask as I pick up the one he's offering me and begin reading the blurb at the back.

"You'll think it's strange."

I look up to find him watching me intently, his gaze not faltering from my own. It feels as though he's inspecting me, unsure if he wants to reveal his truth or not.

"I sign my books. Every single one. I want to be a publisher, but I also want to write and every book I own, I sign, like a practice for when I eventually get to print and sign my own books," I tell him with the hope that he'll be willing to tell me his own book secret now that I've shared mine.

"That's strange."

"Hey! No making fun!" I exclaim with a laugh as I shove him playfully and feel my heart faltering at the breathtaking smile he gifts me with in return.

"Fine, fine, no judgement here," he says as he holds his hands up innocently.

"So, what's your strange secret then? Why do you have two of every book?" I wonder.

"I lied before, when I said that I don't have any hobbies. I do. I beta and ARC read for new and upcoming authors. I do it on the page. I got into the habit of annotating all of the books I read which means that there are scribbles, notes, and highlighted sections in all of my books but I like to have the original copy too so I get two of each. One I can annotate and one that's clear of any annotation."

"Loads of people do that, that's not that strange. I mean, it's got to cost you a bomb with the amount of books you have, but my secret is definitely more embarrassing than yours." I laugh.

I'm not sure if it's a conscious move or not, but he seems to shift closer to me. So close that our outer thighs are touching. Only slightly, but I can feel the impending heat from the contact. Victor doesn't seem to notice though as he picks his book up and leans back comfortably.

We sit in serene silence as we read side by side, catching each other's eyes with little laughs or smirks as we get to similar pages and find funny sections in the same book we are reading.

It feels like we are reading for no time at all but before I know it, an incessant buzzing starts.

"What's that?" I ask curiously as I flip across the next page.

"That, my dear girl, means it's time for me to take you back. Your dad wanted to pick you up from your clubhouse at ten and it's nine thirty now, so we'd best get going," he tells me as he collects the book from my hand, takes a bookmark, and places it in the pages I had got to.

As we make our way down to his bike outside of the building, I realise I was right earlier when I noticed his body relaxing when we got inside of his flat. The moment we reach the outside air, he seems to be on edge again. His posture is more upright, his body tighter almost.

Being on the back of his bike with my hands around his waist as he speeds through the night seems even more of a comfort now than it did before. The vulnerability I often feel when on the back of a motorbike doesn't seem to peak once. I feel like I am flying, rushing through as the world passes us by on a machine that feels as alive as I do. I had experienced the thrill before, but I unexpectedly feel more joy and freedom than I have in a long time. As I grip onto Victor's shirt and feel him bringing his hand to squeeze mine, I can't stop my immediate smile from the contact he is initiating, no matter how small. His hands are warm compared to mine being ice cold from the weather and the rushing wind.

Signed with Love duet
J R Dust

The clubhouse gates came into view only moments later, leaving the adrenaline and euphoria to drain from my body almost instantly.

I notice almost immediately that the jeep my dad ordered Liam is outside in the parking lot, meaning that either Dad has borrowed it or Liam is nearby which, after the peace I've had with Victor, is the worst thing to think about. I used to adore Liam as a child but as an adult he seems to wind me up and think he can control me which does not bode well.

"Are you OK there?" Victor asks as I dismount from the bike, place the helmet back, and brush down my windswept locks with my fingers.

"Yeah. Yeah, that felt amazing." I laugh as I continue to brush myself down.

Victor chuckles at my admission before taking a step closer to me, leaving us only a foot or so apart.

As I look up into his eyes, I feel somewhat hypnotised by the attention that he gives me.

"I had a really lovely evening. If you're available, I would love to do it again in a few days." The statement isn't posed as a question, though I know it is one. I suspect he is more uncertain and more self-conscious than I perhaps realised to begin with. He doesn't seem as confident as I anticipated that he would be. I had assumed that a man in his late twenties that practically ran a motorcycle club would be filled with cocky charm but Victor seems the complete opposite of anything I had ever envisioned.

121

"I'd really like that," I tell him with a small smile, feeling shy under his intense gaze.

"Let me walk you into the club. I know we're inside the gates, but I still don't like to leave you alone at night," he tells me as he places his hand on my lower back and leads me into the front doors of the club.

The heat and instant desire I feel from his touch startles me.

As we walk in, the eyes of the men and women around us seem to land on us, both watchful and wary.

To all of these people, both Club members and the women that escort and join them, Victor is a powerful and intimidating source of violence. To see the previous President's daughter with him is either a shock or a sign of probable things to come if they know anything about the arrangement that has been made.

While spending time with him, though it had only been a few hours, I note that I seem to have grown used to his size and his demeanour, so much so that the initial intimidation I felt from him has diminished completely.

"Thank you for walking me in," I smile shyly. "Do you want a drink before you go?" I ask him as I walk towards the bar, seeing an excited and smiley Alice most likely waiting for every piece of information I could give her.

"As much as I appreciate the offer, I should probably get back. We have a big day tomorrow. A meeting with the Devil's Dealers." His eyes seem to darken at the mere mention of the Dealers, a newfound look I haven't seen from him before. If he hadn't been so soft and sweet with me from the moment we first met, I could definitely understand why everyone was so awestruck and intimidated by him. He is a devastatingly handsome man that holds power and dominance in his every stride and word he speaks.

"OK, well thank you again for tonight, and thank you for what you're doing with the other clubs. I really do appreciate it, and I know everyone else does too."

"I'm more than happy to. I'll text you later if that's OK?" he asks as he lifts my hand and places a kiss on it before smirking at me slyly, most likely at my wide eyes showing both the shock and blush that seems to overwhelm my cheeks at his bashful and charming nature.

"OK," I squeak out as he smiles affectionately at me before turning to leave.

"Tell me everything!" Alice squeals in my ear as I watch Victor leave.

I turn to face her and laugh as she shakes my shoulders, squeaking with excitement awaiting any small piece of information she can get out of me.

"I feel so bloody bad, Alice, he's amazing," I gush, gladly taking the drink she hands to me.

"Why do you feel bad?" She laughs.

"Me and Crow have been getting closer," I tell her hesitantly, having suspected for a while that

123

she likes him. "I'm sorry, I know you like him, Alice."

"What? No I don't!" She laughs, "Why on earth would you think that?" she wonders as her head rolls back with laughter.

"You're always blushing and giggly around him, I just thought.,." I drift off, now unsure about my internal assumption.

"Have you ever watched me around any man under thirty? I'm awful around men, Char. If they're handsome or cute, I turn into a shy and blushing mess. That doesn't mean I like them," she tells me, still giggling.

"Oh, OK, well that definitely makes this less awkward than I thought it would be." I laugh.

"Where's your boyfriend?" I recognise the voice and roll my eyes instantly at the question being posed in my direction.

Liam.

I turn to face him, finding him right beside me.

"My not-yet-my-boyfriend is probably at home or working," I tell him sourly, wishing this conversation could end there but knowing without a doubt that he'll carry it on.

"So how was your fiancé?" I freeze at his words, the insensitivity behind them.

He's technically not necessarily wrong, but if he's been told about the arrangement then he should also surely be aware of the fact that the situation between myself and the two men that seem to be overtaking my life is a rather difficult and sensitive one.

"I'm not answering that."

"Oh, come on, between your boyfriend and your fiancé, you've got to have some gossip to give me." His eyes seem hollow and empty, devoid of emotion, and I feel so bitter at his lack of care that I decide to leave.

"I'll text you later, Alice, I'm heading out," I tell her with a stiff smile as I take a step off the barstool I had taken place on and begin walking away. He may be the Pres but he is acting an awful lot like a cocky, nosy teenager instead and unlike everyone else, I am not a Cobra and will not give him the same bloody respect they do if he can't at least be decent to me.

"I'm giving you a lift home, baby, your dad's busy!" he shouts in my direction as he speeds up to catch up to me.

I hate when he calls me that.

Of course, my dad left it up to him to give me a lift home.

"So back to your boyfriend then."

"He's not my boyfriend," I tell him as I steer my steps towards his jeep.

Chapter 13

I'm sitting in Liam's truck waiting for him and when he finally gets in, he doesn't go to start the engine. He sits there and stares at me strangely.

"What?" I ask. Knowing exactly what is bothering him.

"That kid's your boyfriend," he tells me. Not so sure of his words now as what he was only minutes ago.

I turn to look at him now, noting and reeling in his confusion.

"First of all, he's not a kid," I say before taking a breath that's loud enough to make me sound like a frustrated school teacher. "And secondly," I edge on, "he's not my boyfriend."

I watch as his face knits together, as if it possibly could anymore.

"You said he's your boyfriend."

"No, you said he was my boyfriend," I tell him with a smirk. "I didn't say anything of the sort. Crow's my best friend and maybe he will be more but right now we're just – in between," I explain, using my hands to express the said in between space.

"So, you don't have a boyfriend?" he questions. "At all?"

"Well, I mean, I wouldn't say not at all, but no I don't have an official boyfriend." I'm not sure if I would call it relief I can see on his face, but there's definitely something there that wasn't there before, but it flashes by so quickly, it's hard to place. I remind myself that it's just because he looks at me like a daughter, or a sister, like family, that he's relieved. Though with the way he's been treating me since he's been home, it's been the complete opposite of care that he's shown.

"Huh," he grumbles, finally starting the engine. "Your dad's out tonight, won't be back until morning." He puts his left indicator on to take us onto the village. "Just you and me." Of course it is.

"And Crow," I tell him.

"Afraid not, he's going with your dad." I imagine that would be Liam's doing. Why did he even ask where he was before if he knew? Does he genuinely just enjoy winding me up?

"Where are they going?" I ask instead of asking what I really want to know.

"He says he has to go and meet some friends," he tells me. Not that my dad doesn't have friends because he does, but that is a lie. Dad doesn't go and meet some friends, all of his friends are Cobras and they either meet at the Club or come to our house. More lies. Why am I not surprised?

———

"Shit, that smells good!" I turn to find Liam walking into the kitchen, taking a seat opposite me. I place a plate in front of him, and head to the freezer in search of some ice cubes for my juice. My dad bought us a juice machine a few years ago, and I've used it daily since. It's the most incredible tasting thing ever. Even better with ice, though I normally forget to fill the trays up every night so it's not often I actually have the ice parts of that equation.

"Do you want a drink?" I ask.

"Juice will do, please," he says as he investigates the cottage pie.

"No beer?" I ask. It's not very often any of the Dark Cobras go long without a drink of alcohol in hand.

"You trying to say I'm some alcoholic?" he asks as I roll my eyes at his argumentative tone.

I pass him the juice and sit down to start. It does smell good.

"It's not often you used to go without a drink. I just assumed you'd want one now, too, especially after going so long without," I tell him honestly.

I dig in, and he soon follows suit.

"I'm changing, Charlie, is that so hard to believe?"

"What type of change exactly?" I wonder aloud. The only change I've noticed is that he seems to have it in for me since coming home.

"I'm making some changes to the Club and the Cobras to start with," he says, and with that I find myself frozen. This is exactly what Crow has been worried about.

"I'm cleaning my act up, taking charge like I

128

should have back in the day," he tells me. "I want a family one day, a wife, a child or two, and I want the Cobras to be a safe place for them." What a contradiction. Dad always told me that Liam had a rough home life as a child and that's why he insisted on helping my dad raise me well and give me good experiences as well as keeping me away from the Club and the Cobras. Surely if he wanted a safe life for his future wife and child, he would want out. That's the safest way. Anyone related or attached to any Club member is in danger, no matter what.

We eat in silence for a little while.

Before I get too caught up in my own thoughts, I take my plate and his, expecting him to go back to wherever he came in from before he smelt the food, but I turn towards the fridge to find him sitting in the same position, no move to be made.

"I take it you're after dessert?" I ask. He used to take me nearly every day to a cafe that specialises in desserts after tea as a child. It closed down a couple of years ago when the owners moved away.

"Well, if it's on offer, I'm certainly not turning it down." He sniffs the air like some dog before turning back to me.

"You get the chocolate, it's on the counter, and I'll get the fruit," I tell him, shaking my head at him.

We're soon sat back around the table with a bowl of melted chocolate in the middle and

129

skewers filled with fruit and marshmallows by the side of it.

The melted chocolate and fruit seems to be the only thing we've spoken and not argued about so far since his return.

I take one before he has a chance and dip it into the chocolate heaven.

It. Tastes. Amazing.

"Your eyes are rolling, baby girl."

"Try it and you'll understand why," I tell him, ignoring his baby girl comment.

I'm too busy enjoying the treats on the skewer I'm holding to pay him much attention.

"I haven't had melted chocolate in years."

"Maybe if you didn't go get yourself caught with whatever you were doing, you'd have been enjoying it for ten years longer and telling me you're sick of it by now." My mouth starts to feel sticky from all the gooey sweetness, so I pick up the napkin next to my drink and wipe at my lips before taking a sip of juice to wash it down.

"You don't know why I was there?" he asks hesitantly, looking at me inquisitively now.

"Am I supposed to know?" I ask him.

He doesn't say a word.

"No one really tells me anything," I explain before getting my next skewer and dunking it into the chocolate again.

His hand is on my arm, stopping me from putting anything into my mouth. He pushes my arm to put the sweet stick onto my plate.

I find myself gazing curiously at him.

130

"Did your dad not tell you?" he asks.

"No." We're watching each other rather intently considering there's far nicer things we could be doing right now. Like eating chocolate covered strawberries and marshmallows.

"Are you going to tell me?" I ask him.

He comes out of his daze, shakes his head as if to get rid of the thoughts inside of his head.

"There were two men in our family, our club, not literal, biological family," he explains, "that I'd had my eye on for a while. They'd been planning something and I needed to know what." I wait patiently, wondering where this is going. "So I go into their rooms when they're not around, look around and I find some notes." He stops, looks down.

"Plans to kidnap a child." He takes a deep breath, a breath so large it's as if it takes a physical toll on him to tell me.

"They'd planned it perfectly, and no one would have found them if they'd gone through with it," he says. "They were supposed to go through with it that night. So, I found one of the men, tied him up, and went through his phone. They were going to kidnap the child for a ransom from her family. They had a list of kids they were going to take. It wasn't just the one. They were undercover, dealing with The Enforcers." He stops for a moment. His face is breaking, his arrogance gone. This is obviously difficult for him.

"There were messages between them on

131

their phones about who would get to rape the child first, the things they'd do to her." I unintentionally gasp, covering my mouth with my spare hand to try and derail the shock spiralling through me. I'm not stupid, I know awful things happen in the world but to hear that it had nearly happened so close to home is terrible.

"The things they had planned for her I can't even repeat, I don't want to and I can't. They had a man on the inside, in prison at the time that was in on it too."

I watch him as he brings his face up to find mine.

"I killed the one man there and then. I was beyond angry, I was furious. I slaughtered him, ripped him limb from limb, Charlie. I couldn't stop myself even if I had wanted to. I had never, and to this day have still never, lost control like that before." Jesus. I can't even imagine what I'd do if I found information like that.

"I found the next man, but before I got there, I realised that I had to do it in public because I needed to go down to get this man on the inside. We have ties, connections, and many of them, but none of our men are behind bars," he says as he takes a deep breath again. "I found the second man in the square in town. I went up to him, paralysed him, ripped his cock off, and shot him in the head, and got sent down to do the same to the other one that was involved."

"I was supposed to be in there for eight years, even though I'd given the police all the evidence

132

to prove why I'd done it. The judge commended me for my service to the child." He chuckles at that. "As if he was grateful. The extra years were for killing whilst inside."

"I'm so sorry." I don't know if he needs to say more, if there is more to his story, but I need him to know. I had judged him so harshly for so long, I can't help but feel awful.

I stand up, walk towards him, and crouch at his side.

"I always hated you for leaving," I say. "I mean I don't think I could ever actually hate you but it felt that way. I hated that you'd left me, that someone I loved so much had put the Club before me." I'm so ashamed of myself. Even if I didn't know, I should have known that he wouldn't get himself locked up for a reason that wasn't good. Wasn't needed.

He looks down at me, and I see something different now. I'm not sure if it's in his eyes, or in the reflection through his of my own, but the hate, the anger, the frustration. It's all gone.

"I sure hope you don't hate me, baby girl." He stops for a moment, though I know there's more.

"There was more than one child and even though I would have done it for any child, it was you that fuelled the killing spree. You were on the list of names."

I freeze. I'm still on the floor next to Liam, staring up at him. Me. Whoever these men were, they were going to take me. Do horrible things to me. Possibly even kill me. I picture myself ten

133

years ago, the innocence, the child that I was, and I want to cry in both anger and frustration but also in gratitude for Liam. Knowing that he did that for me. He spent ten years in prison to protect me. I'm sure he would have done it no matter who the child was, but to know that it was me both breaks and wrenches apart my heart completely.

"I'm so sorry." My voice is soft, barely there. I feel both ashamed and so grateful that I'm not sure which way my mind is taking me.

Before I have chance to stop him, he's on the floor with me, pulling me into a hug. Caring for me even after I've taken ten years of his life away from him. Guilt is overriding my senses even though I know rationally that it shouldn't be.

I feel his hand under my chin, lifting it up to look at him again, and it's only because of the guilt and shame I feel that I'm doing it, otherwise I'm not sure I'd be able to bear looking at the man in front of me. Not the asshole. This poor man that threw away so much of his life to protect me. I was hating him this morning and now I can't even comprehend what I feel. Something between adoration and overwhelming guilt.

"I'm so sorry you lost your life because of me," I tell him with a shaky breath, my words cracking.

"I haven't lost anything. You're safe, and I'd happily do it again," he says, "I needed it." He sounds so strong, so sure.

I'm not convinced by his words, but after so long suffering because of me, or what could have been, I remind myself that he doesn't need tears. He doesn't need some girl crying and slobbering all over him. He's the one that's suffered, not me. So why am I crying?

I wipe my face, my hands wet from the tears that managed to leak, no matter how much I hate crying.

"I need some fresh air," I declare, lifting myself from his embrace. "Wanna come?" I ask weakly.

"I'm pretty sure coming would get rid of a lot of tension right about now," he jokes, and besides myself I literally burst out into the stupidest, most abrupt laugh in a long time.

Did he just? He just made a sex joke. He actually did. My God.

"Where are you going?" he shouts as I walk outside.

"To hell most likely," I yell back towards him. "But for now, I'm going to go sit on the swing," I say with a grin, watching as he chuckles to himself.

"It looks nice out here at this time of night." We had been sitting in silence for a while, both in our own heads. The stars have joined us, and it is at times like this that I'm more grateful than ever for the lack of street lights, so that we can truly see the stars.

"It's my favourite place to be," I tell him. "Second favourite next to my bed, and the lake," I explain with a smile. "Have you seen your room?" I ask, having completely forgotten about

135

the transformation I'd completed in there for him through the haze of anger and frustration.

"Yeah, it's insane in there, baby girl! Have you seen it?" Have I seen it? I bloody did it!

I turn to him now, wondering why Dad wouldn't have told him.

"I designed and decorated it, Liam." I laugh. "Of course I've seen it".

"Are you being serious?" I laugh again at his lack of belief in my skills.

I nod at him, taking a breath in and blowing it back out, watching as the cold air turns it to what looks like smoke.

"Do you know what it means when you blow smoke at someone?" he wonders, obviously thinking the same as me about how it looks like smoke.

"That you're a rude bastard?" I ask.

He chuckles at me. "No, that you want to kiss them." He smirks at me, but this one, unlike the smile from earlier, is filled with his usual arrogance.

"No, it does not!" I hiss-whisper at him, remembering I can't shout since we're outside with neighbours that probably don't want to hear us at this hour, shoving him in my annoyance. I'm not really annoyed, though I won't tell him that if he can't already tell. He laughs again, regaining himself from my probably far too forceful push of him.

"What is it with you and your terrible jokes today?"

136

Signed with Love duet
J R Dust

He chuckles heartily at my words, shaking his head from side to side lightly. "Ten years away from women, and I think I've forgotten how to act like a gentleman."

"I'm not so sure that's true. Apart from the terrible jokes, you're not doing so bad," I tell him.

I look towards him in question when he goes silent, wondering if I had started another argument. I hope not after we have finally cleared the air between us.

I'm not sure what I expected to find when I face him, but it isn't the hunger in his eyes as he looks at me. The strange sensation I've experienced a few times since his return resurfaces.

He is handsome, I can't deny it, but the type of handsome you would think of an older man to be. He isn't old by any means, but too old and too close to family for me to find him attractive; and yet the way he looks at me—not just now but in a few separate moments before this—makes me think that perhaps he doesn't think of me as family in the same way that I do him.

It both surprises and creeps me out to think that he is looking at me with desire. He feels like an uncle, and yet the look he is surveying my way makes me question what I am truly seeing. Surely it isn't what I think.

Ringing.

It turns out that it's my phone chiming with a text that puts the odd moment to an end.

I grab my phone and stand, wanting distance

from Liam and his uncomfortable gaze.

"Things got a little confusing for you there, didn't they?" Confusing for me? Right. Of course this is being blamed on me.

I'm not confused. I'm creeped out.

I look at him, my eyebrows shot up, attitude I'm sure covering my face.

"Confusing for me?" I repeat. "And why would that be? What am I confused about?" The damn cheek on this man!

"I'm more of a man than that boyfriend of yours for su-"

"Don't even bother, that's bloody disgusting!" I exclaim, cutting him off before he has a chance to say any more. I stand and walk away, heading back towards the house.

Just as I'm about to reach the kitchen door, he shouts over to me.

"Charlie!"

I begin to turn, though if he thinks I'm going back over there then he's as crazy as every man around me makes out he is.

"It got confusing for me too." He's quiet now, but it confirms what I had already known or at the very least, suspected. The desire I sensed oozing from him wasn't in my imagination; he really has changed and not for the better.

My mind can't fathom that both the man that saved and the man now looking at me with eyes filled with hunger are the same. How could he save me from that torture and abuse and yet look at me with the eyes of a man wanting more than he should?

I can't tell Dad how uncomfortable he makes me, but I also don't want to be around him. I feel uneasy and vulnerable and I hate that.

I check my phone. Midnight. I seriously need some sleep.

Just as I go to drift off, my phone vibrates with a call from Alice.

"Hey, everything OK?" I ask as I wrap myself up and get comfortable.

"Yeah, I was just wondering if you wanted to come over soon. Kira's missing movie nights with you," she says with a small laugh. I hear Kira, her sister, mumbling something in the background.

"I will soon. I feel like we've hardly seen each other lately," I tell her glumly, realising how terrible of a friend I've been.

We used to see each other daily but lately I feel like my mind has been overrun with problems, Gray's disappearance, and the unrelenting tension between Crow and I—and now, of course, the proposed marriage.

"Did you find anything out when you were doing your sneaking?"

"Nope, I got caught. If you ever need a spy, do not ask for my help. It will not end well." I laugh, listening as Alice and Kira begin bickering about something before she comes back to the phone.

"I don't think I'm ever having kids. I feel like Kira is enough to deal with for one lifetime." She sighs.

Alice and I talk for a while, her telling me the incessant gossip that she overhears at the Club and me informing her of the constant chaos that sits around me before we finally hang up and I very nearly pass out from exhaustion.

Chapter 14

Liam and I have been avoiding each other for two days now. Well, I've been avoiding him so much that I don't actually know if he's avoiding me or not.

I've thought it over, wondering what would have happened if the phone hadn't gone off. I can't decide if he would have tried something, leading to me having to push him away and cause a whole new drama in my life or if he would have kept the desire to himself, though with his crude jokes, inappropriate glances, and possessive questions about my not-my-boyfriend boyfriend and potential fiancé, I can't help but suspect that he will at some point at least try something that I know I will be uncomfortable with.

He's best friends with my dad. I have never thought about Liam in that way.

I'm so screwed.

I need to be concentrating on Gray and yet between Liam being too much, Crow that I want to see more than ever while he's constantly busy, and a deepening connection forming with Victor, as well as my name having a bounty attached to it, our club being at war and everything else, I cannot think clearly.

Crow's been here daily, as usual, though he seems to be busy and disappearing for hours on end, meaning that I've not had any chance to talk to him privately about anything. I've spent the days in my room, doing very little. Reading, eating, watching Netflix, and wondering when Crow will come back. Anytime it's just Liam and I in the house, I've made sure to stay in my room with the door shut, not wanting to be near him for the fear of him making me feel so awkward and uncomfortable again while simultaneously blaming me for it.

At the start of this year, I was determined to figure out so many things. My five-year plan. My way out of this town. Finding Gray. And one day finding my peace.

I want to break away from the life I'm living and move towards the life that I have always wanted.

I don't want a complicated, dramatic, chaotic life. I want peace, tranquillity, and a home that you walk into and instantly feel relaxed in.

My mind instantly moves to images of Victor's apartment and how cosy, wholesome, and homely I felt while in there.

All my mind seemed to be able to comprehend right now is boys. Men. The useless half of the human species. OK, maybe not useless. They aren't useless, really. I just don't have the mental capacity to cope with anything other than the immediate troubles right now – finding Gray and getting myself out of trouble.

Crow had suggested a party next week and I had refused, but maybe letting my hair down and enjoying myself without overthinking every minute of every day was exactly what I need.

I've drank before but I'm not a huge fan. This party is at the clubhouse, which in one sense is great because it means I will be in a place that I am comfortable and I feel at home at. But it also means that everyone will be there, which I normally wouldn't mind, but the idea of being around both Liam and Crow doesn't appeal to me.

I suppose I could just have a few drinks and stay with Crow, and if I want to go home then I can. I can even stay at the club, if need be, and I know I will be safe there.

Maybe I will go after all. I can dress up, make myself feel nice, and if I don't like it, I never have to go again. Right?

Crow has gone out to run some errands for Dad, so I have been left bored in the house alone.

I decide to venture downstairs and look for Dad since I have very little else to do and I know he is home. I still need to get answers out of him about the meeting and what the plan is about getting me off the market. I hate that I sound like a piece of meat being put up at the local market for sale. The thought makes me shiver.

Liam was supposed to be at the Club with meetings today. It is early, so I'm sure he will still be there.

Just as I turn around the corner into the kitchen, I hit something hard. I expect a wall that I've misjudged, but as I look up I realise that it's the very same creep I've been trying so hard to avoid.

I move to the left immediately in a hasty attempt to get out of his way before anything other than the very literal bump in occurs, but he of course goes to the left along with me, and then the right.

I stop. That's what you're meant to do when you're lost, isn't it? Stop exactly where you are and wait. Well, here I am, lost and waiting.

If any heros want to come and collect me now, that would be great please and thank you. Or not.

Liam doesn't go past me when given the chance though. No. He's looking me up and down, so slowly it burns.

I'm in my baggy shirt. Well, it's one of Crow's. He left it here a while ago, and I wear it all the time.

Liam still seems to be examining me. Actually, no, that's a complete lie. He's not examining me, it's my body he's looking up and down. The disgust that forms in my mind and convulses through my body brings up an involuntary shiver.

I slap the underneath of his chin up so that he's looking directly at me.

"My face is here." I walk past him before giving him a chance to respond, knowing Dad won't be too far away, and since it's him I came out here looking for, I ignore the man behind me and carry on with my mission. Dad.

144

Signed with Love duet
J R Dust

He's sat outside on the deck chairs. God knows why since it's January and cold. Great. Now I'm going to freeze.

I halt at the back door; my dad has got his back to me so is completely unaware of my presence.

I contemplate going back upstairs to change, but realise rather quickly that I am far too lazy to go upstairs, to get changed to come back to a spot that I'm already stood in.

I groan internally and spin, prepared to pick up Dad's coat from the coat-rack to at least keep the top half of me warm, but am once again met by what I now know isn't a wall, but a muscle filled man with no sense of direction.

I don't walk into him completely this time, I just come close. I internally roll my eyes at the frustration this man causes me any time I'm near him. Too close for comfort.

He brings his body closer.

No, no, no.

This is becoming very weird, and I am not liking it. I really need to talk to Crow. Even if I have to stay at the Clubhouse with him, it's better than being here and feeling disgustingly uncomfortable anytime Liam is near.

Such a large part of me feels guilty for thinking so poorly of him after his revelation yesterday and what he's given up to protect me but I also don't want to owe him something, that something being me, because he did that.

"Do you not think you should put some

Signed with Love duet
J R Dust

clothes on?" He's the Pres, technically in charge of my dad and just about everyone I care about, and yet he's acting like a menacing and ghoulish teenage boy.

"No one in this house should be attracted to me, so there should be no problem with what I'm wearing." It's true. He practically raised me next to my dad for eight years of my life, there really shouldn't be any attraction there and yet with his incessant sex jokes, the 'confusion', and the constant bumping into one another, I'm sure there's something going on in his head that there shouldn't be.

Dad couldn't care less what I wear whilst in the house. Liam is supposed to look at me like a child, like the baby girl that he keeps referring to me as, the little girl that he used to play Barbies with, but, going by the tension between us now and the frustration on his face, I'm not entirely sure that's true.

"Are you bothered by me wearing so little, Liam?" I ask.

"Just put more clothes on." He spins abruptly and leaves.

I grab hold of a coat of my dad's, and head outside to join him. It's chilly, the winter air blowing a bit, and I shiver slightly even with the coat. I sit beside him, then snuggle deeper into the seat, pulling my knees up to my chest and covering them with both the hanging material of Crow's shirt and the coat.

"I need the results back before then." My
146

father is on the phone, talking to god knows who about god knows what. He's not facing me and obviously hasn't realised that I'm behind him yet.

I don't interfere, even as my insides shake a bit with fear.

I clear my throat beside him, and he acknowledges me for the first time, giving me a tight smile.

"I'm going. Two weeks, you hear me?" He doesn't wait for a response before hanging up.

Dad has only just figured out how to use phones that are anything less than twenty years old and now that he has, he seems to be on his twenty-four/seven.

He's only thirty-six, but that doesn't stop him from being incapable of understanding just about anything that is associated with modern technology.

"You alright, darlin'?" he asks, putting his phone down on the table next to him and swapping its place in his hand with his mug of coffee.

He loves coffee, and won't speak a single word to anyone before he's had a mug of coffee in the morning.

I can't stand the taste of coffee, but I love the smell of it. I think it's because I associate the smell with my dad, and it makes me feel safe and warm and secure.

"Yeah, I'm okay. I had something to ask you, actually, Dad," I tell him as I lift my knees up to my chest and pull the coat around myself even more. I should have gotten dressed. Well, more dressed. It's freezing out here. It looks beautiful with the way the leaves have fallen, and the sun that's sat in the sky, but it is misleading. It. Is. So. Cold.

His eyebrows lift, urging me on.

"You know the parties that Crow and all the other kids go to? There's one next week."

"That's not a question, Charlie," he says with a chuckle. I roll my eyes but laugh along with him.

"Well, I was wondering if you'd be ok with me going?"

"Course you can, darlin', you know you don't need to ask me. You are an adult now," he tells me, picking up his phone again. Probably playing some game on there. He's obsessed with Dig It, a game where you have to create tunnels to get a ball into a hole. So simple and yet he seems to find it so satisfying. The simple things, hey?

I know he's right. I don't need to ask him, but I always feel that I should. Whilst I'm living with him, it's only respectful to ask, no matter how old I am. It still astounds me that I really am an adult. That I'm in control of my life. A life I'm so lost and clueless in. I know what I want, and where I want to be, but getting there? That's where I seem to struggle. I have no idea how to get to the place I want to be.

"Ah, Charlie. We've all got check-ups with Doc that morning. The morning of the party. It's the Friday night, right?" The Doctor. That's who he was talking to. What results is he so desperately after?

"You're not ill, are you?" I jump up, putting my palm to his forehead to see if he has a temperature.

I don't know how I will cope if Dad is ill. Seriously ill. It's my worst nightmare – losing him. I have no one else. No real other family. My mum's gone, Gray is nowhere to be found, meaning that my dad and Crow are all I have left.

I know that I will probably have a family of my own one day, and as much as I can't wait for that day, I don't want to lose my dad before it happens.

I'm not willing to lose my dad until I'm enough of an adult that I don't need him, and I somehow doubt it will ever happen.

I'll always need my dad.

"No, Mother, I am not," he says with a chuckle as he knocks my hand away.

He always tells me that I mother him. Cooking him food, doing the washing, keeping the house clean.

I enjoy doing it. I hate mess. It stresses me out more than most people could imagine. A clean home means that I'm happy and Dad is less likely to trip over something and hurt himself. He still manages it mind; he's got two left feet like no one else I've ever met. It's not even that he's clumsy, he's just never paying enough attention to his surroundings when at home.

"Can I ask you about something else?" I question. He seems to be in a relatively good mood and is much more likely to not argue with me about my questioning without others around.

"Is it going to be a real question this time, darlin'?" He smiles.

"Yep, a real question this time." I laugh.

"Have you figured anything out about Gray or who or why someone put a mark on me? I know you don't want me to know but I need to know this," I tell him honestly.

He sighs, shaking his head before looking at me sadly.

"We haven't come much closer to anything with your brother. I wish we had but there's nothing, no matter which way we search. I'm not keeping that from you on purpose, we simply don't know anything," he says grimly.

"And as for you – Elio traced the Mark back to The Enforcers. The man you saw us with that day at The Club was the one that put you online, and if it was just them it would be fine but we suspect they're working with someone with more connections since no matter which angle we try and go through, we can't seem to take it down. They don't have that kind of grasp so we've asked another organisation to help us." The O'Banians. It must be them he's talking about.

"That guy, he said something to me before I left that day. With everything else going on, I forgot to mention it but he said 'He'll get you.' Who do you think he is?" I ask.

I haven't thought about the man's words since the day it happened, what with everything going on around me at the moment, but Dad's words remind me. He's not usually this open with me so while he is, I may as well at least try to get some answers out of him.

My dad's face ignites with fury the moment he takes in what I've told him.

"He said that? Why didn't you tell me before you left?" he questions. His voice has gone from quiet and soft to icy cold and nearing shouting.

"I didn't think, I'm sorry. I was panicking about Crow and I just wasn't sure if it was just his last ditch attempt to get free or if there was more to it." Lying to my dad never gets me anywhere so the truth it is.

"Let me make a call." And with that, he storms off, leaving me once again to myself.

Chapter 15

I am happily watching Crow as he works out in the gym at The Club. There is no one else in the gym at this time of night, which means that Crow enjoys the time to release any and all of his pent up energy even more. He gets on with mostly everyone, even through the natural grit and grumpy attitude he shows to most people, but he also likes to have the gym to himself and although I would usually leave him to it, Dad has insisted that he doesn't want me home alone with the bounty on me and since both he and Liam are busy tonight, I am with Crow at the club.

I spend most nights with him anyway, though it isn't usually here. I am more a middle-aged mother than a teenager, often tucked up in bed reading or watching Netflix by nine pm.

I can hear the music pounding from the main room. The night is in full swing. There is music and mayhem most nights but with tonight being Friday, the first night of the weekend, it seems to give everyone even more reason to party. I had come in through the back entrance to avoid the crowds of people. I don't know how Alice sticks it, though I know part of it is just out of necessity to provide for herself and her sister. They don't have any parents around and with Alice being the eldest, she feels that it is her responsibility to do what she can to keep them both in as good of a position as she can.

I place my book down, watching Crow as he lifts weight after weight and finding myself startlingly turned on by the sweat and grunts he is omitting. He only has a pair of jogging bottoms on, leaving his chest bare. The mirror in front of him allows me to see his face as it scrunches up, filling with tension each time he pushes his body further by lifting the weight in his hands once more. The muscles in his back constrict and release each time he moves. The sight of his strength and his powerful body leave my stomach in pieces.

"Like what you see?" I didn't realise he had been watching me as I watched him but as his eyes flit to my own, I shake my head at the smirk he has.

"I'd like it even more if you weren't working out and were over here instead," I flirt, though with my lack of experience, I'm not sure exactly what I plan to do if he does follow through with my plea and come to me.

"Well, if that's the case, I think I'm done for the night." He laughs as he places the weight down and saunters over in my direction.

"You wanna go back to yours?" he asks as he lifts my backpack from the floor and sifts his arms through the straps.

"Can we stay here actually?" I ask weakly, knowing he will question why I want to stay in his room instead of my own. He knows I don't like staying here but the choice between being near Liam or hearing rowdy men all night had me willingly listening to said rowdy men.

"Why do you wanna stay here? I'm assuming it's not just to get a piece of this?" He asks, his voice filled with sarcasm and laughter as he bangs his chest like an ape.

"Nothing to do with any of... that!" I laugh out, playfully jabbing his side as we walk towards his room.

"So, what is it?"

"If I tell you, you have to promise not to tell anyone, especially not my dad," I warn him quietly to be sure no one overhears.

"What is it, Charlie?" he whispers as he opens the door to his room and leads me inside.

I love Crow's room. It's so him. Predictable almost. Usually, predictable can be bad but honestly, in all the chaos at the moment, predictability is perfect. I know I can rely on Crow, no matter what.

"Liam has been weird, it's hard to explain," I tell him.

"What type of weird?" His eyes darken at this as he takes a step menacingly closer, his hands wrapping around the tops of my arms.

"He's making sex jokes and looking me up and down, hinting that he wants, I don't know, something more. I feel like I'm probably just being dramatic, but he just makes me feel so uncomfortable. I hate it but I can't say anything to Dad. It would destroy him to know that the two people he cares about most don't like each other, and he's just got Liam back. I don't want to be the

154

reason he begrudgingly sends him away." It feels good, better than I thought it would to let it all out.

"I knew he was fucking creepy from the minute he hugged you," Crow grinds out, shaking his head in disgust.

"He hasn't done anything, I just get this weird feeling, I don't like it. So can we stay here?"

"You can stay here whenever you want, Char, you know that," he says as he pulls me into his embrace, stroking my hair as he does. "But I do have a job tonight. A private job that I need to do. You can come if you want?" he asks with a playful smile as he pulls away from me.

"A private job? I thought you weren't allowed to do that."

I'm not one to be a stickler for the rules considering I break just about every rule I'm given – mostly unintentionally in a search for answers, but it's very unlike Crow to go against anything my father has said.

"It's about Gray. The garage that took his car from the scene of the crash gave a report to the police and your dad, but when I encouraged them to be a little more honest, they said they'd call me back. They called me earlier to let me know that the mechanic that worked on it had some extra information for me. I'm going to see him tonight," he informs me as he begins suiting up.

I watch on in astonishment, my mind whirling with the possibility of a clue, the idea of getting one step closer to finding Gray. Crow is gearing up, filling his jacket with a pocket knife and gun, though I can't imagine he would need that to go and see some mechanic but with the things going on lately, I don't question it.

"When?" I ask eagerly, watching as he rummages around his room looking for things and filling up my backpack as he does.

"Now, if you're ready."

Crow takes my hand as I nod avidly in his direction. This could be monumental in finding out not only where Gray is but what happened to him. I've spent too long wondering, crying, and wishing that someone would find him and now here I am, with the predictable Crow who has done the most unpredictable thing – being the person that is bringing me closer to Gray.

As we leave the Club, everyone is too busy dancing, drinking, and cheering at God knows what to notice us, which in this instance isn't a bad thing. The music is loud, and the way people are carrying on, they wouldn't be aware of the Second Coming if it began right now. Perfect. We open the door on a wild burst of laughter, and as we step into the cold night air, the silence is an almost instantaneous thing. The noise from inside is muffled, and I breathe a sigh of relief that we slipped out undetected.

We clamber into Crow's truck silently and drive away from the Club without anyone asking any questions.

"The garage is a good twenty minutes away.

Signed with Love duet
J R Dust

I wanted to talk to you about something else though now that we have the chance," Crow tells me as he swings the wheel around, reversing out of the Club driveway.

"What is it?" I wonder, hoping he's not preparing to tell me bad news after bringing me so much hope from the mere mention of finding out more about Gray.

"What happened with Victor?" Oh. I should have seen this coming. I knew it would come and I knew that I would have to keep being as honest as I could be with Crow, but that doesn't change the fact that I feel full of shame for enjoying the time I spent with him.

"We went to his place and read, and I had fun," I tell him, not sure how much to divulge; it's not as though a huge amount more than that happened.

"How do you feel about him?" he asks, his tone clipped.

"He's actually really nice," I tell him honestly. "He loves to read like me so we literally just sat reading for hours. I do want to get to know him though. He does seem really sweet."

"I'm not sure sweet is the word anyone I know would use to describe him." Crow chuckles. "You just have a way of getting the untouchably formidable people to be soft teddy bears around you." He laughs as he shakes his head with amusement.

"You're not mad?" I ask timidly.

Even though I like to think I'm a relatively level

headed person, I have no doubt in my mind that I would be jealous and somewhat possessive if I knew the person I was becoming closer with was getting to know someone else too.

Crow sighs and runs a hand through his hair before turning to look at me briefly.

"Nah, I'm not mad, Char. Obviously I'd much prefer if you were all mine, but I get it. Whatever is meant to be will be."

"I didn't take you as a believer in fate," I tease.

"Sometimes you gotta believe in something, girl, not much else to believe in round here." He smiles sadly.

We ride in silence the rest of the way. I spend the time contemplating how we can use whatever information we're given from the man we are going to see to help us find Gray. I really hope he knows something.

I had texted my dad earlier to say that I would be staying at the club with Crow and though he didn't usually mind and his response was a simple 'ok. Love you.', it was the text off Liam asking why I wouldn't be home that unsettled me.

"I don't think this guy's a danger, but you have got people on your tail so don't wander off, alright?" I nod to Crow, letting him know that I acknowledge and agree with his sentiment.

There was absolutely no chance I would be off adventuring the darkness without him. I like to think I was brave and strong like the characters I read about, but honestly, I would one hundred

158

percent be the girl to run away and survive in a horror film rather than run towards the danger. No creepy basement hunting for me, thank you very much.

The man is stood in front of the bright lights of the garage sign above the entrance, waiting anxiously for us. He seems to be shaking, which could usually be blamed on the cold, but given it's currently warmer than normal through the winter in the UK, I suspect in this instance that the shaking is more nerves than the weather. His eyes are shifting and checking in every direction and his hands fidgeting together. His eyes light up when he sees Crow, who he quickly ushers inside the building. I follow quickly behind.

"Do you want a drink? I think I need a drink for this." The man is older than both Crow and I, probably in his mid to late forties, with a balding spot on the top of his head and a grey beard protruding from his chin. He looks innocent enough though, beside the alcohol and shaking.

I realise that I've spoken to him before. With my dad being a mechanic before joining the Cobras, he works on most of the bikes and cars the men within the Cobras have, but on the odd occasion that he doesn't have the time or the tools, he brings them here. I remember coming a few times with him and note that must be why I recognise the man.

"I'm fine. I just need you to tell me what you know," Crow tells him.

The man shakes his head as he tips back a

single shot of what looks to be whiskey.

"You swear to me you can protect my family?" he demands, obviously scared about the safety of those he cares for.

"I already have people at your house now. They will be safe, I promise you that much," Crow assures him.

How has he got people looking out for this man's family? He said no one else knew about this and if that is the case, who can he ask to protect them? Surely, he wouldn't lie and put this man's family at risk for information. I would do anything to find Gray, but leaving people vulnerable is not something Gray would want.

I need to ask him when we are out of here.

"Right, right, well, I had this guy come up to me the day the crash happened. Before it happened telling me that a car would be coming in later that day and that I needed to cover up and sign it off as an accidental crash – dangerous driving, speeding, you know the stuff I mean." He nods towards Crow before taking another shot.

"I said no, initially. I've been working in the industry for years, I didn't want to tarnish my reputation, but he had my daughters on his phone. They were walking home from school and he had someone following them. If I didn't do it.. he didn't tell me what he'd do but I dread to think." The man practically sobs as he holds his hand to his heart.

"I didn't have a choice, I couldn't let them take my girls. So, when the car came in, I insisted that

160

I work on it, checked it all over – it was the steering rods. They were left loose," he whispers to us in a rush.

"Who was it that asked you to put the clear reports in?" Crow asks.

"I don't know, that's the thing. He had a ski mask on, all I could see were his eyes. He was big but apart from that, there's nothing else I can tell you about him."

"I appreciate this, man. Thank you. You'll all be kept safe, I promise you," Crow tells him before taking my hand in his and walking back to the truck.

"Wait, there's something else." He's talking to me this time, looking directly at me.

"I think he knew. Gray. He knew something at least. I've worked on his car before, on his bikes when Matt couldn't, and we'd spoken about certain areas within the car that I wasn't to look in. I know who you all are, what you do. I don't care but I know. I found this in one of the hidden spaces in the car." He hands me a small white, crisp envelope with my name on it.

It takes every ounce of strength and patience I have not to rip the envelope open there and then but I know that whatever is inside of it needs to be read another time. Not now.

Once we're safely inside the vehicle, knowing that we can no longer be overheard, Crow unleashes his thoughts.

"Your dad was working on his car the day before he went. He wouldn't have thought he did

161

anything wrong, but maybe he left them loose and didn't realise. Maybe it was one of the Cobras covering it up for the sake of your dad's pride, his guilt if he knew it was his fault."

"He didn't. He wouldn't, not even by accident. Trust me when I tell you that someone did it but it wasn't my dad and it wasn't someone protecting my dad either. That doesn't explain where Gray would have gone either," I tell him sternly.

My dad and I have had our differences and disagreements but logically I know that he is good at what he does. He is a good mechanic. He has never made any major mistakes before. He double, triple checks everything he does, everything he works on and fixes. He wouldn't have made a mistake like that.

"Why would someone force that man to cover it up if they hadn't done it themselves or been behind it in some way?" I ask him, knowing that my logic in this area had to at least ease my dad's burden and responsibility. It wasn't his mistake or nothing would need to be covered up.

"That's true. Whoever it is knows where Gray is," he concludes.

"Who's looking after that man's family, Crow? You can't just leave them with these people around," I tell him, the guilt gnawing away at me.

"They're protected. I wasn't lying, Char."

"By who?" I question.

"I don't agree with your dad on many things but I do in this – some things you don't need to know."

Chapter 16

I've been sitting on Crow's bed with the envelope in my hands, staring at it for what feels like a lifetime. I feel both numb and tingly—one with dread, one from anticipation. I want to know, and yet I don't.

I was so desperate to tear it open when the man had handed it to me but now that I know that whatever is inside is potentially the last thing Gray intended for me to see, I'm petrified. What if it's a suicide note and we've got it all wrong about someone sabotaging his car? I know that he had been stressed over the last few months, but I had no idea if he had suffered from depression. Maybe he had. Perhaps I didn't pay as much attention to him as I thought. Would I have noticed the signs? Were there any?

What if it was a note to say that he was running away? Or maybe it was just a list of what he wanted to get me for Christmas.

I won't know until I open it.

As my fingers dance along the seal with trepidation, Crow comes barging out of the ensuite attached to his bedroom.

He has a towel around his waist, leaving the rest of his body bare and dripping with water from his shower. His hair is ruffled and messy, his face a soft mask of concern as he looks my way, and his body as tense and godly as every other time I see him.

"Do you want to open it on your own?" he asks tensely as he dries himself off and throws a t-shirt over his head, covering the sight of his bare chest and pulling me back to the moment. Gray's letter.

"No, I don't mind you being here, I'm just nervous. I don't know if I want to know what's inside," I tell him weakly.

He quickly goes back into the ensuite to pull some jogging bottoms on and then comes to sit next to me on the bed.

"I'm here for you, whatever you want to do."

His fingers lace through mine, filling me with the warmth and protection that Crow's mere presence brings.

"Whatever it says will help us in some way. That can't be a bad thing," he tells me quietly, and I know that he's right. Even if it's a mundane note that holds no real importance or relevance to the situation Gray found himself in, we'll know that we're not missing out on information, whereas if I don't open, we won't know if it does or does not hold information that could help us find him.

"You're right." I nod solemnly as I take my hand from his and open the envelope to find Gray's messy handwriting scrawled all over the page.

I'm hoping it's gonna be you reading this, Chars, and if someone else has opened it then fuck you, like seriously. Respect a girl's privacy, will you?

Anyway, if you're reading this then I want you to know I'm going to look for mum. There's some shit going on in the world that is so much more than you could even begin to realise and I need to start working it out. Check my room, you'll find some stuff in there on where I am.

Either I've said goodbye and gone willingly in which case you'll never see this and I'm writing for no reason, or they've got hold of me because they know I know.

Either way, I'll figure it out and come back and explain it all. Promise.

Love you, Chars!

Oh and for fuck sake—stay away from Liam when he gets out. Tell Crow I was right and have proof but don't do anything about it until I'm home. I'll come back, I swear.

As I finish reading the letter out loud, my mind whirls. He was going to find our mum? What did

166

she have to do with any of this and who was he referring to having got hold of him? What did that even mean? Does that mean someone took him? I rationalise that he probably felt he couldn't delve into too much information in case the letter got into the wrong hands but a little more of an explanation would have been great.

And then there's Crow.

"What was he right about?" I demand, angry that he had kept something, anything about my brother away from me in this mess we're in.

But Crow already has his phone to his ear, saying that stupid code thing again.

"Down Viper Spring."

I can't hear what's being said on the other side of the phone call, but I'm certain it's the same set of words that were said to him in the car when I was with him, and I'm doubting more and more the accuracy and truth behind Crow's alleged connection to some tech guy that he claims this person to be.

"He was right about Liam. He left a note saying he had evidence but not to act yet."

Who is it he was talking to exactly and what on earth had Liam done to warrant both Crow and Gray knowing enough about him to want me to back away? I know and feel that he has been acting unusually with me, but I didn't assume there was something more than him being a bloody oddball.

"I trust him. Yep, I'm about to tell her now. Both. Down Viper Spring."

Signed with Love duet
J R Dust

I wait anxiously as he hangs up and turns to face me, his eyes filled with hesitance and concern.

"Right, so there's a few things I need you to know and a few things you can't know. You're going to be mad at me, but I need you to trust me. You got it?" It sounds rehearsed, his words, as if he'd practised this very speech a thousand times.

Do I trust Crow? Yes. Even if he is keeping things from me? Yes. I don't like it but that doesn't change the fact that I do trust him entirely.

"OK. I want as much of the truth as you're able to give me, though, Crow. I'm so fed up with all of this," I tell him, feeling my heart clammer and my stomach give way. I feel defeated, as if I've lost a war I didn't even know I was fighting.

His eyes soften and his face falls, my words bringing out the pain in him. He knows how much I hate being lied to and kept away from things. He knows how much it hurts me to have the person I'm closest to in the world do that, and yet I can also see the determination in his steadfast nod as he takes a breath and begins unravelling the lies that have been told to me.

"Do you know why Liam went to prison?" Crow starts.

That much I do know.

"Yeah, he told me about me and the other kids that were going to be taken by the men he killed," I tell him confidently.

Crow lets out a dark and sarcastic huff as he shakes his head at me.

"Officially, yes. But truthfully - not quite. Gray had suspected for a long time that there was more to that story than Liam had told everyone so he told me and we did some digging. We had spoken to one person who had told us a story that we weren't sure was true. He caught a lead and went solo to find out more but disappeared before I ever got hold of him to ask what he found, to find out if the story we had been told was true. That letter is confirmation that it was," he tells me with a sigh as he runs his hand through his hair before pinning his eyes on me again.

"Liam killed those men, that is true, but the reasoning behind it isn't. He didn't kill them because they were going to take you or anyone else. He killed them to cover up the fact that he was working with them and was going to take you too."

I can practically hear my mind whizzing and spinning, trying to make sense of the words leaving Crow's mouth. I almost wish that I doubted him but I don't. Not one part of me questions what I am being told. I wholeheartedly believe it to be the truth and that guts me completely.

"What's the rest?" I ask as I continue to absorb the information I've been given, feeling so vulnerable and dirty at the mere thought of the man I shared so many hours and days with as a child being not only willing and capable but actively part of a scheme to take children from their homes and do God knows what with.

"The guy I just called. He's not who I told you he was." I roll my eyes as he says this, having guessed that only moments ago.

"If you ever need someone and I'm not around, you call Kenny on your phone and say Down Viper Swing and tell them who you are. They'll protect you," he tells me seriously as I bring my phone out and check the contacts, realising that Crow must have added the number at some point without me realising.

"Char, look at me." I bring my eyes up to his, my own the shapes of orbs in the reflection of his deepening gaze.

"Do you understand what I just said, Char?"

"Yes, yeah, I understand, but who is it? Who's the person you ring every time something happens?" I inquire, looking at Crow in a whole new light knowing for certain now that he's a part of something I have no idea about.

"That's the part I can't tell you. For your own safety. I don't ever plan on letting someone get a hold of you but if anyone ever did, the less you know, the better." He stands from his bed and lifts me to encourage me to do the same.

"We need to go to Gray's room now. I'll explain more later but for now, we need to see what we can find there." I nod my head at him and watch as his gaze turns from serious and business-like to soft and nurturing.

Signed with Love duet
J R Dust

He brings his arms around me and tucks me beneath him, sighing and rubbing his hand against my hair gently.

"What's happening, Crow? I feel like everything is falling apart." I nearly sob into his chest.

"All I want you to concentrate on right now is you and me, you understand that?" he says, his voice a husky whisper in my ear. He lifts my chin gently with his finger and places a gentle kiss on my forehead, followed by one on my cheek and another next to my lips.

Before I have time to overthink and change my mind, I reach my hands around the back of his neck and bring his head down to my own, smashing our lips together in an undeniably and earth-shattering kiss.

This kiss feels like the sun is rising, the earth is melting, the floor beneath my feet is shaking. It feels like the very molecules that make up every atom of my insides are roaring to life in both the anguish and passion that is consuming me.

I let my mind forget the chaos, the pain, the despair and the worry as I worship him and everything he's willing to let me take.

I want all of it. All of him. All of everything we could be when we unite. His lips feel like a fire against my own, his tongue darting between our lips in a war to take control.

For the single soluble moment that the kiss takes, I allow him and the thoughts of him to take over my mind, my body, my whole entity. My hands ripple through his hair as he clings to my waist lifting me so that my legs wrap around his.

I can feel him against my core. His want, his need, his desire, all matching my own in the heated tendril of war that consumes me as our lips collide and my mind clears of anything but him.

The roaring in my mind is interrupted by the very literal roaring in the hallway.

Crow puts me down in a rush, pushing me towards the bathroom as the crashing and screams appear closer.

Those screams aren't drunken fights or brawls. The bellows, howls and yells sound as terrified as I feel. The sounds ricochet around me, causing me to tremble. I want to clamp my hands over my ears, but I also want to know what is going on. It sounds like we're being attacked. And if we are, then why? Who? A volley of gunshots ring out, and I cower behind Crow even as he reaches for his weapon.

The door crashes open as Victor runs in, a gun in each hand, his face filled with fury and relief when he sees me behind Crow.

"Get her out. Take her to mine. I'll hold them off," he yells at Crow as he runs back out the door and down the hall.

"What's happening?" I squeal out as Crow grabs my hand and begins running for the door and dragging me down the opposite side of the hallway in the direction Victor just ran.

"I don't know and I don't care to find out right

now. We need to go. Come on." He rushes out as we run along the corridor to the empty staircase. As we run down, the screams and deafening roars of gunshots grow.

"Fuck, stop." Crow drags me back, pushing me up against a wall as I hear more shots ring out at the side of the hallway that lead to the bottom of the stairs we are currently occupying.

Crow edges his head around to check the way is clear before he pulls me along to the back entrance door and runs for his truck, all the while holding my hand with a gun in his other hand.

Within minutes we are on the road.

"What about Alice and my dad? We need to do something, Crow, we can't just leave them all there to fend for themselves," I rush out, worry and anxiety for them building to the surface now that we are no longer in danger ourselves.

"We aren't going back. The chances are high that whoever it is wants you, not anyone else. I am not taking you back to a place where you are the one that's wanted. Between The Cobras and The Laidens, they'll be fine, I promise." His words do nothing to ease the dread that fills me; if anything, they just amplify the worry knowing that those ruthless enough to go after a woman for a bounty paycheck will also be ruthless enough to hurt anyone they need to.

I pull my phone from my pocket and dial Alice's number, knowing that she above anyone else I care for is the most vulnerable in that situation.

"Charlie! Where are you?" Alice's voice fills the midnight air around me, and I breathe a sigh of relief hearing her voice.

"I'm fine, where are you?" There is no noise in the background, no shouting or screaming, no shots, so I assume she is either hidden or has been taken somewhere safe.

"I'm at home. Edgar got me and drove me back the moment it all started. I was so scared, Charlie."

"Edgar? As in Edgar, The Devil's Dealers Edgar?" My tone shoots sky high, inquisitive and worried once more, knowing that she's in or was in the enemies' hands.

"Victor made a deal with them. I don't think everyone's exactly on friendly terms but they are willing to help. He's gone now, but he was decent enough when he was here," she tells me, her tone filled with positivity. Alice is such a preppy and happy person that you would never be able to guess at the troubles she holds within.

"OK, as long as he was fine with you and he's gone now, I don't care. Is Kira safe at home with you?" I ask.

"Yeah, she's in bed sleeping, thank god. Edgar said he's posting guards for the next few days while everyone's still on high alert in case of another attack. Do you know who it was?"

"I have no idea. Victor rushed in and told me and Crow to leave so we're on our way to his, but I haven't heard anything else. I'm gonna go, Alice, I need to try and get hold of my dad, but

you stay safe and call me if you need me, OK?"
She tells me to stay safe too and hangs up, once
again leaving my mind reeling and curious about
the Dealers' involvement with it all.

"Did you know that Victor managed to get The
Dealers on board?" I ask Crow as I dial my dad's
number and hold the phone to my ear.

"Yeah, he told me earlier."

"Victor told you earlier?" I ask, paranoia
making me wonder when they started having
contact with one another.

"Yep. You're our priority, Char, we figured
that keeping in contact would help with that," he
tells me as his jaw sets and his eyes scan the
road and the mirrors of the car to check for
anyone following us.

"And you know where he lives?"

"Like I said, we've been in contact."

I don't even have a right to be mad. I'm not
with either one of them, not really, and even if I
was, I don't have the right to know every person
they speak to. It just makes me feel like every
ounce of privacy I once had has been stripped
from me. In my mind, whether it be true or not,
they could be comparing notes for all I knew.

I internally shake myself for even thinking that
way about either one of them. I don't know Victor
as well as I know Crow, but I do feel that I know
them both well enough to know that they won't
do that. Neither of them seem maliciously
inclined to hurt someone.

"I need to get hold of my dad," I tell Crow. I'm

just venting, releasing something, anything out of my mind in an attempt to relieve myself of one more factor that's worrying me. Three times I've rang his number and he's not picked up.

I try Victor's number instead, remembering that if things were over, he would be there with my dad or would likely know where he was.

The agonising wait while listening to the frustratingly repetitive ringing on my phone drove me close to insanity, leaving my mind to contemplate every bad scenario it could come up with.

"Are you at mine?"

"Oh, thank god, you're okay." I breathe a sigh of relief at the knowledge that one more person is uninjured or at least not harmed enough that he could answer the phone to worry about me when it is him that was running towards the line of fire the last time I saw him.

"Of course I am," he says, sounding confused, as if the idea of him being anything other than fine was ridiculous. I can't help but laugh at the abrupt tone of his voice.

"Good, I'm glad," I tell him truthfully. "Is my dad there? Is he OK too?" I can hear noise in the background, men talking, both in hushed whispers and menacing degrees of anger. I can't hear what they are saying, but the anger is what presents itself.

"Your dad is fine, he's walking through with some of the others to make sure no one is hiding and that everyone got out safely. Are you going

176

to answer me?"

The relief at hearing that my dad is safe is felt throughout my body. The speeding rhythm of my heart beating decreases steadily, my breathing relaxes and my hands begin to smooth from the constant shaking.

Alice is OK.

Victor is OK.

Dad is OK.

"Answer what?" I ask, distracted, having forgotten that he had asked me anything to begin with.

"Are you at mine? It's not safe yet, there is likely to be another attack, it's how they do things," he tells me in a very matter of fact way, as if this whole thing is nothing but an inconvenience rather than a near fatal attack.

"We're nearly there. Who was it that attacked?"

"I'll explain when I'm with you. Do not leave mine." And with that, his voice is gone and the phone call is cut short.

Chapter 17

Crow and I have very awkwardly sat in Victor's flat for nearly an hour now.

I've only been here once before and I'm not sure if Crow had been here at all, though given the fact he knew where it was suggests that perhaps he has. Even so, he seems as awkward and agitated as I am. It is one thing being in someone's home when they are there to tell you to make yourself comfortable, but to be without them makes me feel like an intruder.

"Have you thought anymore about the letter?" Crow asks me as he puts his phone down on the coffee table in front of us.

I sigh, defeated, uneasy with the conclusion I had come up with but glad for the distraction, even if it is a dire one.

"Whoever Gray was talking about having taken him is with Mum in some way. I don't know if they're a gang, a MC, the bloody mafia, I don't know but the letter made it sound like mum was a part of them somehow."

"What happened to her? You've never talked about it. Neither did Gray," he admits.

I hate talking about her or giving her time in my mind because she just isn't worth it but maybe explaining why will either help relieve the burden of holding her a secret or possibly help him connect some imaginary dots to give us another clue in the mystery of Gray.

178

Signed with Love duet
J R Dust

"I hardly remember her. I think I remember her face, but I was so young when she left that I don't even know if what I remember is real or if it's just imaginary from seeing her face in pictures." I recall looking at pictures of the four of us – me, Gray, Mum, and Dad in pictures when I was little and wishing she would come back. I look just like her. The same dark, wavy and wildly messy hair. The same eyes, even the same facial structure. Looking back now I realise that I look nothing like my dad and everything like her.

"She left when I was four. She told Dad that she didn't want this anymore. The family life, the kids, the husband, and that she didn't want to be contacted again. Dad said she left in the middle of the night after putting us to bed. She didn't want to say goodbye, so she just left. Dad tried to find her a few times but didn't come up with anything. He said I cried for weeks, but I don't remember that either. I just know that whoever she is, or was, is someone that I don't want to know if she could just leave her family behind like that." I take a deep breath in an attempt to collect myself and my fraying thoughts. She isn't worth the energy I used even thinking about her.

"I'm sorry, it must have been shit, Char," Crow says as he rubs his thumb over the top of my hand in an attempt to comfort me in the only way he knew how.

I look up at him and find his eyes filled with the same deep sadness I have no doubt are in mine.

179

"What about your family? You never talk about them either."

"My family is complicated, let's just put it that way," Crow says as he chuckles.

"Oh come on, you have to tell me more than that! I don't even know if you have any brothers or sisters! Tell me something. Anything," I insist.

"Alright, fine." His eyes look around the room as if trying to find something to encourage a memory to pop into his mind.

"OK, so I do have brothers. Two. One younger brother and one older. My little brother Zak is hilarious, I mean so smart that it's hilarious. Like he'll come out with all these random facts constantly. He knows everything about everything." He laughs as he seems to be imagining him. "My older brother, Coran, reminds me a lot of Victor actually. He's the business man of the family, very straight faced. He can be harsh but he gives a shit, like really gives a shit. If he cares about you, you're set for life kind of thing, you know? They drive me nuts but I'm lucky to have them," he concludes just as the door opens.

I jump up to my feet, filled with both anxiety and dread, unsure of who to expect.

"Answer your phone, your dad's worried sick." The words come out of Victor's mouth before he's even fully entered the flat, leaving me feeling guilty for having left my phone unattended in the midst of such a chaotic situation. I pull my phone from the pocket of my coat hanging on the chair behind me and notice the numerous missed calls. All off Dad and Victor.

The phone rings again, this time allowing me to answer immediately.

"Is Victor there?" my dad's gruff voice asks. There's mayhem and shouting in the background, though it sounds more like the voices around him are filled with anger and frustration this time rather than fear and danger.

"Yeah, he just got back, Dad. Is everyone OK?"

"I need you to stay there for a few days while I sort everything out. Crow and Victor are staying with you. The house is too dangerous for you to be at and so is the club. Until I get this fucking crap sorted, you need to stay put, you understand me?" It's not a request but a demand, one I dislike but know not to argue with.

"Of course, I'll stay, but you have to keep me updated and make sure that Alice and Kira stay safe too."

"They're in good hands, Charlie. I'll call you tomorrow and let you know what's happening. I love you." And with those parting words, he hangs up and leaves me stranded with the two men that I can already tell don't want to be stuck in the same country together, let alone the same flat.

"You can have the bed, we'll sleep in here," Victor tells me as he takes off his suit jacket, leaving only the white crisp shirt underneath.

I look uncomfortably around the room,

181

wondering where they plan to sleep exactly. It's not the largest of spaces.

"I'll sleep in bed with Char, we usually sleep together anyway." My eyes immediately bore into Crow's, taking in his words and the heated glare I feel radiating through the back of my head towards Crow from Victor. I can see the smallest hint of a smirk on Crow's face, confirming what I suspected - that he said that on purpose.

It isn't a lie, we do often sleep together, but not at all in the way that Crow is insinuating, and he damn well knows it.

"Virgin Mary over here is declaring that I'll sleep in the bed by myself, thank you both very much," I say in a huff, knowing that if this is how tense it feels after only a matter of minutes in the room together that this is not going to bode well for any of us.

"You're a virgin?" The shock is palpable on Victor's face as his brows crease together and the out of place confusion fills his tone.

"Yes, I'm a virgin, job done. Thanks for coming to my Ted talk. Can we get back to a conversation that doesn't revolve around my intact hymen now, please and thank you."

"Right," Victor says as he shifts uncomfortably while Crow sits with the same smirk still plastered on his face. "Food?" he asks as he lifts what looks to be a takeaway menu in our direction.

Chapter 18

"Your dad just texted me, I have to go," Crow says, filling the awkward silence as he hastily gets up to leave.

"I thought we all had to stay here?" I ask, outraged at the fact that he can so easily leave and yet I've been guilt tripped into staying here.

"You have to stay, but your dad wants me, which means I need to go. I'll be back in a bit, princess," he says as he drops a kiss on my head before leaving.

Victor releases a sigh of what seems to be relief as Crow leaves, which makes me feel even more awful for taking over his space.

"I can ask my dad to let me stay somewhere else if you want, I don't want to be overstepping by being here."

Victor looks up at me, confusion covering his face.

"Why would you be overstepping?" he asks, seemingly genuinely unsure.

"You hardly know me and I've taken over your home and had Crow thrown in, too, who you know and like even less than me. That's kind of overstepping in my mind." I laugh awkwardly.

"I like having you here, and it's not that I don't like Crow. I just find it difficult. We're very similar even though we may not outwardly seem it, and it's just a conflict of interest with us both wanting you," he tells me earnestly.

We met through a proposed marriage deal and since I had been so honest with him about my feelings for Crow, I wasn't expecting him to feel much of anything for me other than friendship at most. Hearing him say he's interested in me, wanting me, makes my stomach do flips and my heart race and pound so loud I'm practically certain he can hear it.

"You don't need to say anything, I know that was me overstepping." He chuckles as he rubs his hand along the back of his neck.

"It's not overstepping, I just don't know what I want, and I don't want to pretend otherwise and make this worse," I tell him honestly.

"I get that. Crow text me about the letter from Gray," he says, changing the subject. "I've got some men looking for him, hopefully it won't be long until he's back home with you."

"Thank you, I appreciate you trying to help." I do. He doesn't have to help me and yet he is, so willingly, expecting nothing in return.

"OK, this is too tense, I can't deal with this. Do you want to bake a cake?"

"A cake? You want to bake?" I blurt out with a laugh as I watch him walk into the kitchen and begin getting ingredients out of the cupboards.

"Yes. I hate tension, it drives me nuts, so we're going to bake a cake," he tells me firmly, a small smile highlighting his beautiful features.

"Sure, why not." I giggle as I stand beside him and watch as he weighs out just the right amount of butter and mixes it with the eggs.

"How about you bake and I watch? You seem to be a pro," I joke, watching on at the face of concentration he's making as he weighs out the perfect amounts of each ingredient.

He stops what he's doing before looking at me in mock disapproval.

"Only if you tell me something interesting while I'm waiting. Something no one else knows." A bribe. I see. I can do that.

"A secret for a secret, I'm not trading any of mine without getting one back." I smile, watching as he contemplates my offer before nodding his head, encouraging me to continue.

"OK, change of plan, how about truth or dare?" he asks before I have a chance to say anything, looking mischievously suspicious as he smiles at me knowingly.

"Fine, but I get to go first," I insist.

The cake mixture is ready to be placed in the tray, which he does just as delicately as everything else he's done thus far.

"OK, go for it. Ladies first, I can handle that," he tells me as he offers me the spoon with some cake mixture on. I take it eagerly while I ask him truth or dare.

"Dare," he says confidently as he takes the spoon back and places some more of the cake mixture onto it before handing it back to me.

"I dare you to strip and run outside in your boxers," I tell him seriously. I expect a fight. What I don't expect is for him to hand me the spoon back with more of the cake mixture on it and begin stripping in front of me immediately. No hesitation, though if I had a body like the one in front of me I'm not sure I'd be hesitating to show it off either.

And, boy, oh boy, do I thank myself for daring him to strip. He is as delicious as the cake mixture I'm currently devouring. He's toned - everywhere. Like, literally everywhere. His neck and his shoulders are bulky, leading to more muscle beneath his crisp shirt. I should totally play truth or dare more often.

"Just a light jog, is it?" he asks as he walks towards the front door. I nod, distracted by the rippling muscles moving and contouring under his skin.

Within seconds, he's out the door. I rush to the window, intrigued to see if he'll actually go outside and find myself surprised that he does. Not only is he practically naked, letting his manhood swing free (or very nearly free), and what a sight that is might I add but it's also January. In the UK. I get cold with three layers, let alone none, but he seems completely unphased as he looks right up to the window with a confident glance in my direction before leisurely walking back inside.

"Truth or dare?" I hear shouted from the stairs before he saunters inside. He grabs his trousers and puts them back on before walking over to sit next to me on the sofa topless. I'm not complaining.

"Truth." There's no way I'm giving him a

chance to pay me back for that.

"Are you attracted to me?"

"Is that a joke?" I ask, eyeing him up.

"No, I'm being serious."

"Yes, I'm attracted to you. You're bloody gorgeous, I'm pretty sure it would be impossible not to be," I tell him honestly with a laugh.

"My turn. Truth or dare." I offer him the choice once more before he has a chance to comment on my appraisal of him.

"Truth."

I eye him curiously, his eyes glinting with mischief as he inches closer to me. I can feel the heat rising within my body having him so close and yet not one part of me wants to move.

"Don't you have club business you need to be doing?" I ask, knowing it's not the typical Truth or Dare question, but genuinely curious since everyone else I know within the MC life tends to be constantly busy with one thing or another.

"Honestly, not really. I'm called if I'm needed, and the rest of the time I'm here or with one of the few friends I have."

"Who's that?" I ask, suddenly unsure of if I've ever seen him with anyone other than the Inner circle of The Laidens or Cobras.

"Ah, ah, my turn," he tells me with a wagging finger mockingly.

I roll my eyes before choosing dare.

"I dare you to kiss me."

I wait a moment, wondering if he's joking and about to change his mind, but his face doesn't

187

move, his expression unfaltering. It feels like he's testing me.

I only have to twist slightly to be nose to nose with him. I can feel and hear his steady breathing on me as I place my hand lightly on his cheek. His eyes don't leave mine, his breathing halting, seemingly afraid to move in case I change my mind.

I bring my lips to his and feel his lips graze mine, his hand coming to the back of my head. Not forcefully but encouraging me to continue. And I do. The space between us explodes in a new found passion as I find myself lost in the mesmerising sensation of kissing him. His tongue darts across my lip, testing the waters, though it's hardly needed. My body seems to react before I even think about what I'm doing. I open up to him, my body instinctively moving closer, wanting to be so much closer. He pulls me onto his lap, his hands on my behind, massaging every part of my body that he feels like grazing.

The kiss feels hungry, like it's been forever in the making. My hands find their way to the back of his neck and head, pulling him into me further as my body grinds upon the large, hard manhood beneath my core.

"Stop, stop, stop," he insists as he sneers and pulls back, leaving me breathlessly steering away, unable to keep my eyes off his lips. That was not what I expected, and yet all I can think about is wanting more. He hardly touched me and yet I can feel how wet I am from just kissing him.

"If you don't stop, I'm going to take you to bed and fuck you." That gathers my attention as I look into his eyes and see no humour within them. He's deadly serious, and not one part of me would say no at this moment.

"I'm sorry. I got carried away," I tell him, feeling stupid for being so wound up and willing when I already have too many complications and uncertainties in my life. I don't need to add more.

He laughs before etching his head lower so he can look into my eyes.

"Don't be sorry, I fucking loved it. I just don't have much control when it comes to you grinding on my dick apparently." He chuckles as my face lights up with what must be the most furious shade of red embarrassment.

"Come on, the cakes gotta be done by now. You can help me decorate it. Just stay a foot or two away from me or I'm likely to relinquish the self-control I'm stringing onto right now and fuck you anyway." He smirks before lifting me gently from his lap, taking my hand, and leading me back into the kitchen.

Fuck. Things just got more complicated.

Chapter 19

I slept on the bed alone last night. It was surprisingly comfortable and I didn't wake once - unsurprisingly. I love my sleep. I'm now sitting in bed with Crow who carried a tray of breakfast in for me. Well, burnt toast and a glass of orange juice, but who am I to complain?

"It feels like you and Victor are purposefully ignoring each other," I tell him. He didn't come back until we were both in bed last night. Well, until I was in bed and Victor was sleeping on the sofa.

"We've spoken plenty. Besides, I can't help it. He said he got called in. That's not on me," Crow says with his hands raised in mock surrender.

"I know, it's just shit that you don't get on. I care about you both," I tell him.

"You do?" he asks hesitantly.

"I kissed Victor yesterday," I rush out, feeling the full weight of the guilt and shame hit me all at once. I had stayed up late last night, thinking and over thinking about what I had done so freely without even considering Crow until it was too late.

Crow doesn't say anything for a moment, his face doing the job of words and giving away his frustration as his brows crease and his lips purse together.

"I'm sorry. I don't want to lie to you but before you say anything, I want you to know that it doesn't mean that I don't care about you too. That's the problem, I really, really do."

"He's exactly the right type of guy for you, and I hate that, but I also know that you're the right girl for me so stay honest with me and I can deal with it. You're my girl and you always will be, no matter what happens," he says as he pulls me under his arm and into an embrace. My face to his chest leaves me hearing the erratic beating of his heart as I hear him breathe steadily above me.

"How about we make today our day? At least until Mr Kiss My Girl gets back?" Crow asks with a low chuckle. It doesn't shock me one bit to hear him be so casual in his jealousy. I know he's a possessive person and yet when it comes to me, it seems that no matter what I do or say, his care for me is never swayed. Something I hate myself for. I wish I could give him all of me.

It feels like in the moments I'm with him, he's all I want; and yet the same applies when I'm around Victor. If this is the part that a mum is supposed to help you with, I seriously need to find a replacement mother to give me answers to these teenage girls' problems.

"Yeah, that sounds nice," I answer him with a small smile.

"We've got to stay in the flat, your dad's being pretty strict about keeping you in here until he's deemed it safe everywhere else for you, but we could have a pamper day? I got some of your face and make-up stuff from your dad's when I was out. I know how much you love pamper days," he says as he nudges me lightly with a teasing grin.

"Only if you'll let me put a face mask on you too."

"Fine, sure," he says as he rolls his eyes in defeat, which is quickly followed by my smile of triumph.

I rummage through the bag he hands me and find two matching face masks before opening it and applying it to Crow's face.

"Don't pretend you don't love this as much as I do," I tell him gleefully.

He rolls his eyes once more before shifting so that he's closer to me.

"I definitely do not love it, but I can deal with it if it brings that smile out of you."

I don't think I've ever realised just how lucky I am to have that. This. Him. Since the first day I met him, he's always been so willing to do any and every thing it takes to make me smile which is when I note that I'm not sure I do the same for him. Or at least never actively. I need to set a day aside just for him. A day when I do whatever he wants, to keep him happy and make him smile. The thought brings another smile out of me. The idea of him being happy makes me happy.

"Have you heard anymore from mystery man about the mark or Gray yet?" I ask, having put the problems to the back of my mind until now.

"Mystery man isn't that mysterious, I promise." He chuckles.

"Are you going to tell me who it is?"

"No, you know I can't," he says regretfully.

As much as I wish he would tell me the things I long to know, I know him well enough to know that whatever he's keeping from me, he's keeping from me for good reason. I hope. I wonder if Victor knows. They seem to have spoken more about things than I had originally assumed.

"Well, until you do, he's mystery man," I insist.

"I'll make sure to tell him that. But no, he's made it clear how much danger you're in which is why I'm easily siding with your dad but apart from that, he hasn't got much yet. For you or Gray."

"I don't feel scared. I did when we were attacked, but I don't know. I feel like maybe I should be but I'm not," I tell him honestly.

"That's probably a mix between the adrenaline constantly coursing through you and you having two hefty bodyguards," he jokes as he pulls at his hair that I accidentally tangled in the gooey face mask.

"Maybe."

"You know I won't let anything happen to you. I don't need to tell you that. You know I'd burn the fucking world down before letting anyone touch you, so you don't have any good reason to be scared. I don't want you to be," he tells me.

I smile slyly at him, appreciating his words but not being able to take him too seriously when his face is covered in green goo.

"It's this mask, isn't it? Fucking women." He shakes his head in distaste with a small smile playing at his lips.

"What do you think your dad would say if you told him we were together?"

I freeze at the question. Unexpected and completely off topic. Partly because it's not something I really considered but also because it shows how serious he is about wanting us to be. He's usually the joker and I know he wouldn't ask if it wasn't something he wanted.

"If it ends up being that way," he quickly adds on.

"I don't think it would be a shock." I laugh. "I mean, he knows we share the same bed, we're with each other practically every minute of the day when you're not busy, and we've always been pretty handsy," I say, for lack of a better word. "So, I don't think he'd mind or be surprised."

Crow nods his head in what I assume is agreement but says nothing else as I finish plastering his face.

My phone beeps as I begin opening the second face mask.

"Can you check that for me a sec?" I ask Crow as I attempt to tear the stubborn packet open with my teeth.

"It's Alice. She says she needs you to call her."

"Oh shit, I haven't spoken to her for days!" I

exclaim, feeling like a love sick idiot for having forgotten about one of my only friends. The last time I spoke to her, she had Edgar the Enemy in her flat. I smile at my mind's own nickname for him before pressing the call button and handing Crow the packet in disdain, unable to open it myself.

"I need your thoughts." No greeting, no questions. Straight to the point. Well, okay then.

"Sure, what's up?" I laugh as Crow begins applying the same green goo on his face to mine.

"I think I like someone," she rushes out with no more of an explanation behind her words.

"OK, tell me who, why and how it happened right now please and thank you." I smile as I tell her.

"That's the part I don't want to tell you," she says hesitantly.

My face scrunches up in confusion. "Why?" I ask slowly, unsure where this is heading.

"It's Eggy. Edgar. I think I like him. A lot."

My mind doesn't seem to register half of what she's said. "Eggy? You nicknamed him Eggy? Of all the possible things in the world that you can call him, you call him Eggy?" I laugh as Crow attempts to cover up his laughter opposite me.

"Well, Kira did and it kind of stuck." She giggles.

"Wait, Kira called him Eggy to his face and he did what exactly?" I ask, unable to imagine the intensely criminal man Edgar being called Eggy by Alice's teenage little sister.

"He looked at her a bit confused and then just kind of nodded and went with it. It was pretty funny actually," she whispers.

"Why are you whispering?" I wonder.

"They're in the other room. She's doing his makeup."

"This just gets better and better. Wait, hold on, what happened to him being the bad dude? He's a baddy, like a bad baddy, Alice, not tiktok baddy but actual baddy," I inform her before realising that if he was letting a teenage girl do his makeup that he maybe wasn't that bad.

"Most of the stories about him are bullshit, he's actually really sweet," she tells me.

"I feel like I maybe need to re-meet him at this stage, Alice because I feel like we're talking about completely different people here." I laugh, holding my negative thoughts back. If she trusts in his apparent sweetness, then who am I to deter her?

Maybe I'll just ask Crow to get Mystery Man to do some checks, just to be sure. Alice is unbelievably pure in a world that doesn't deserve her kindness. I can imagine her forgiving anyone for anything but this is taking it to the extremes. Even for her.

"He's hardly left our sides since he dropped us off the other night. He's honestly been so lovely, Char. Would it be terrible of me to pursue it?" she asks, her voice filled with worry and anxiousness.

Signed with Love duet
J R Dust

I contemplate her question for only a moment. "If he makes you happy then you do you, girl. What has Kira said?" I wonder.

"I asked her about it and she said and I quote 'Slay, Queen, Slay.' Which I'm taking as good." She laughs quietly.

Kira is the most typical teenage girl you will ever meet. The most tiktok and horse obsessed, new slang that no one understands teenager. If she's been around him and is OK with it then maybe he isn't such a bad guy after all.

"You know what, if you and Kira are happy and he's not as bad as everyone thinks then screw him sideways for all I care. You deserve some bloody happiness, girl," I encourage her.

"Oh, he's opening the door! Bye!" she squeals, and then she's gone.

Crow finally lets go of his pent up laughter before bending over, holding his stomach and wheezing.

"She calls him Eggy?!" His whole body practically vibrates with laughter, which ignites my own. It's contagious. I definitely need to re-meet Eggy.

Chapter 20

"I guess I'm starting?" I ask as we sit around the coffee table together.

"We can't keep going like this, at each other's throats, and the only one that can stop that is you, so yes, please." Victor's formality seems to have reached a new high and though I can't blame him given the recent days antics, that doesn't change the fact that I wish he didn't feel he had to be anything but himself with me.

"You're right," I say with a deep breath, knowing what needs to come next. "I'm not trying to lead you both on. I've been honest, so honest with both of you because I do care, more than I'd like to admit, but I can't choose one of you and lose the other. I know how selfish that sounds, but it's true. I feel like I've lost so many people and I can't stand the thought of not having either of you in my life," I tell them both, my eyes focused on the fidgeting hands on my lap, unable to look at either of them, knowing how awful my words sound.

"I don't know about you, mate, but Char knows how I feel. She knows I love her and I fucking want her. Every fucking part of her and if that's not what you want, if this is just some fling, some fucking joke, then you need to tell her because I want a life with her." Crow's words tear at the strings that tether themselves to my heart, pulling on every wish I'd ever had of wanting someone to want and love me that way.

I smile weakly at Crow, both in gratitude and awe, before turning to a tight-lipped Victor. He doesn't say anything for a moment, nearly a moment too long as I begin trying to decipher what he's thinking through his facial expressions. A mission that is practically impossible with the blank expression on his face.

"I'm not sure why you would assume my feelings for her are a joke. I know I don't know her as well as you might but that doesn't change the fact that I've been able to be more open with her than I have with anyone in my life. I've never loved anyone in a romantic way, and if I'm being totally frank with you, the idea of loving her is killing me because it puts her in danger, but I do. I knew it from the moment she first came into my home and I realised that I didn't want her to leave." The words coming out of his mouth may have been about me but until now they've been aimed at Crow, but now he looks at me. His eyes shine beneath the dim living room lighting, "I don't care if I have to share you, I don't give a damn about you loving him as long as I get to love you too. As long as I get to love you, I have everything."

The revelation stuns me because although I had thought it through so many times and I knew I didn't want to lose one of them, I didn't ever contemplate having them both. I didn't let myself think that it was ever a possibility.

"I can't do that. I can't choose, but I don't want

you, either of you to feel like you're not my first choice. I want both of you to be with someone that can give you everything, and I just don't know that I can do that, not only because of everything that is going on right now but also because I don't know for sure that I'll ever be able to choose and I don't want you to wait and miss out on someone else, on finding someone that can choose just you while you're waiting for me."

Crow and Victor don't look at me. They're looking at each other, their gazes intense, though they don't look hurt or angry, they look as though they're somehow communicating something without my knowledge. If I ever believed in telepathy, it would be at this moment. It seemed like they were having a conversation between themselves without any words being spoken.

"What if we don't want that? What if we both want you? Together? Do we get a choice in this?" Victor turns to look at me, slowly, ever so slowly as he speaks, his eyes trained on mine as my head spins between his and Crow's unrelenting gazes.

"Together?" I ask anyone that will answer, somewhat dumbfounded at the mere idea of them both taking me, having me.

"Why don't we show you?" Crow suggests as he lifts himself up from the armchair to kneel in front of me.

With Crow on his knees beneath me and Victor to my side, I feel undeniably nervous. Not the bad kind of nervous, but the kind of nervous that makes me want to nod my head and tell them yes. Yes to whatever you want, anything you'll offer, always yes. Victor edges closer, his thigh tight against mine as he looks at Crow and nods, before gently moving a few strands of my hair away from my neck, behind my shoulder. Everything seems to be going in slow motion as he gives me time to say no, to stop whatever is about to happen. I can't fathom what is about to happen and yet not a single part of me wants to stop it.

Crow's rough hands run along the top of my thighs, making me thankful that I wore shorts, allowing him to touch every part of me that he wishes too. I find myself watching him intently as his hands begin pulling my legs apart, running his hands along the inside of my thighs, higher and higher, until he's so close. So close to my core, doing so little and yet doing so much at the same time, making me feel like every atom, every inch of me is ablaze with want and need.

Victor chooses that exact moment to begin coating kisses along my neck, and despite my need to not seem so desperate for them, my body takes control over my mind, my senses. My body arches, my core towards Crow and my neck perfectly placed for Victor in a desperate attempt to beg them, to plead with them - hoping that they never stop.

"That's it, pretty girl, let us in," Victor whispers in my ear, only magnifying the tension I feel, knowing that this is real, knowing that they're

201

both here, giving me more than I ever anticipated wanting, let alone having. I try to catch my breath as they devour me, even knowing that being anything but breathless around them is impossible.

Crow's fingers move tantalisingly slowly as he grazes along the material of my shorts, pushing them aside, as well as the underwear beneath them, leaving his fingers stroking me gently. I like to think that I'm not completely inexperienced and innocent but at this moment, I feel like I've never been touched before and wonder why I've never initiated this very touch sooner. Victor's hands begin kneading at my breasts as he continues to place his lips along my collarbone. He places kisses along my jaw and then my chest until he uses his teeth to pull down my vest, revealing my bare breasts. At any other moment, any other time in my life, I would be disgustingly embarrassed and shy being laid bare so freely before these men and yet in this moment, I feel so much desire for them that I can hardly stop myself from asking them, begging them to do more, to give me everything.

Before I have time to think about what is happening, Crow is pulling my shorts and underwear from beneath me, lifting me so easily to do so. He discards the useless material before lowering his head to my clit, leaving open mouthed kisses along my most sensitive area. Without thought, my hand finds his head, holding him in place, refusing to let go of this euphoric feeling.

"Fucking perfect, so tight," Crow mumbles as he licks and fills me, entering me for the first time with his fingers, forcing my body to arch further, push his head down even more. I've never needed someone, let alone two someones, so much in my life.

Victor sucks and bites lightly at my nipples, leaving me achingly close to the release I know they'll bring me. The touch from them both feels like it's reaching every soluble part of my body. I've never felt more alight and needy than what I do now.

"Please don't stop." I gasp, unwillingly letting out a moan of pleasure I had attempted to keep in from the moment they began touching me.

"Which one of us don't you want to stop, pretty girl?" Victor whispers with a sexy chuckle before putting his mouth back on one nipple, while kneading the other breast with his free hand.

"Both," I practically cry out, feeling my body pound back into them both as we seem to move as one. "Both of you", I moan, "don't stop, please." I beg, incapable of saying anymore as my head rears back and my body tenses, knowing how close I am to finishing all over Crow's hand.

Crow's tongue joins his fingers at my entrance, using his other hand to rub his finger against my clit while Victor continues biting and sucking at my nipples, using his free hand to reach for the back of my head, pulling at my hair from the roots. The tingling pain only accentuates the pleasure coursing through me from their joined attentive touch.

"You gonna cum for us, baby girl? I wanna taste every fucking bit of how much you need us," Crow breathes out before returning his attention, his lips, his tongue and face back to penetrate every wall I had ever put up.

"Don't be greedy, I want to taste her pussy too," Victor says with a glance up at me as he gets on his knees beside Crow.

The mere sight of them both on their knees before me has me as close to orgasm as their touch. These men, so mighty and deadly in their appearance, give me everything, all of them just as I open myself up to them completely.

"Open wide for us pretty girl, let us in," Victor encourages as they nudge my thighs even further apart. The slight burn my body emits from being in a position I haven't before is diminished by the immense pleasure that takes its place as they simultaneously suck and lick, nibble and finger my entrance and my clit. Their hands alternate so that one of them continuously has their hands on my breasts, roaming along my nearly bare stomach, having only my vest left scrunched around my waist, leaving me completely bare beside it.

"You're close aren't you, baby? I can feel it." Crow practically roars out at the very moment that an unrecognisable sound comes from my lips. I don't even know whose hand, whose fingers it is, but the penetrative pleasure and the constant attention on my clit has my whole body seizing up as I reach orgasm and feel them licking every morsel from my core.

It's now as I come down from the high, watching them raising their heads from the one part of my body that has never been touched by anyone beside myself that I feel so unbelievably cold and shy, unable and unwilling to look either of them in the eyes.

"Don't go shy on me now, baby girl, you were lapping it up just a minute ago." Crow laughs huskily as he rises from his knees before reaching his arms around me and lifting me up in a cradle of sorts.

"No, seriously, put me down," I tell him assertively as I attempt to wiggle away from him.

"Take her into the bathroom," Victor tells Crow as he follows behind us, ignoring my pleas.

Crow doesn't say a word but does as Victor ordered, leading me to the bathroom. Victor puts a towel on the toilet seat and encourages Crow to sit me down which he does. I want to scream and run away. I know what's about to happen and no matter how much I am reeling from what just happened, having them see me so bare now that the moment has passed leaves me feeling more vulnerable than ever; and yet I know arguing to get away is pointless because they won't let me and the same part of me that enjoyed them devouring doesn't want them to let me go.

Victor turns on the water in the shower and puts soap and shower gel in the holder before coming to kneel before me once more.

His eyes penetrate mine, his gaze intense. He doesn't say a word as he lifts my vest top off me and discards it to one side. I subconsciously wrap my arms around my stomach, feeling more exposed than I ever thought possible in the harsh luminescent shining down on me. On every wobbly, nowhere near perfect part of me.

"We want you and until the moment you push us away and tell us no, we're going to have you. Do you understand me?" he asks. Though the words sound demanding and somewhat bossy, they fill my heart to pure explosion as I nod solemnly at him.

"Now that that's cleared up, let's get you in the shower," Crow says as he lifts me up once more and places me gently into an upright position so that I'm standing in the shower.

"This is awkward, I can definitely do this part alone," I whisper uneasily as Victor and Crow pick up a sponge each and begin leisurely covering my body in a soapy massage.

"Yeah, maybe you can, but it doesn't mean that you're going to," Crow tells me simply as he and Victor continue their assault on my senses.

I can feel the heat beneath my skin warming once more at their touch.

The confidence I had only moments ago comes back, the questions and worry in the back of my mind disappearing, waiting to resurface another time.

I want them, both of them and seeing their clothes become drenched, their bodies wet and obviously apparent through their clothes only makes me want them more.

I reach my hands forwards, one on each of their chests, their heads rising simultaneously as they wonder where my touch may lead.

"What are you doing, pretty girl?" Victor asks huskily, his voice unsteady and unsure.

"Treating you the same way you treated me," I tell them quietly as I step out of the shower, turn it off, and lead them both into the bedroom, feeling the cold hit my every nerve, only inciting the excitement and confidence in me once more.

"You don't have to do this, babe, we didn't do it so that we'd get something back," Crow tells me.

I take my time, taking off both of their tops and trousers, leaving them only in their boxers.

I push them both gently onto the bed so that they're lay down next to one another, face up, eyes intent, watching me and my every move. Their eyes are both so dark and filled with desire and a hungry passion that I can't wait to set free.

"I know, but I want to. I want both of you," I tell Crow as I crawl onto the bed between them both. "I want you both so badly," I whisper into his ear, watching as his Adam's apple sways.

I haven't done anything like this before and yet when knelt above them, I feel like the most in control, surreal goddess. I feel like I could do or say anything and they'd let me.

I begin to drizzle soft kisses along their chests, taking it in turns, to be sure I give them both my complete attention, or as much of it as I can between them.

I take a deep breath, reeling in the courage I know I need for the next part of my not very well thought out plan.

I pull down Victor's shorts, taking his cock in my hand before using my other hand to pull down Crow's boxers and placing my lips over his cock.

Crow sucks in a shocked gasp while Victor lets out a soft moan. This makes me feel like a god. And I love it.

I bring my tongue around Crow's manhood, bobbing my head up and down while doing the same with my hand to Victor's hard shaft. Crow's hand reaches my hair, his fingers tangling within it, pulling and pushing my head exactly where he wants it. I take in as much of him as I can before gagging.

"Shit, I'm so-"

I look up at Crow, his eyes filled with worry.

"Don't stop, I like it," I tell him, feeling the streaks rolling down my cheeks. His eyes fill with dark curiosity as he looks at me knowingly and pushes my head back down onto his dick.

"Fuck, I need some of that before I cum," Victor ushers out, his eyes dazed and filled with craze as he watches me take Crow in my mouth. My hand doesn't stop moving on his cock, the continuous rocking motion becoming more natural to me.

I take my mouth from Crow's cock, taking it in turns between them both. My head bobs from one of their cocks to the other, a motion, accompanied by their hands on my body that makes me want to scream with the tension and passion filling me.

"I want you. I really, really need you to fill me. Please," I beg, feeling my body arch without my telling it too. My pussy is wet, drenched at the sight of them both being so turned on.

Crow lifts himself up from the bed, pulling his boxers off completely before settling behind my bent over body.

"Keep sucking his dick for me, baby. Don't stop," he tells me. I nod and continue, hearing Victor's moans and grunts of pleasure as he grips my hair and forces my head down over and over again. My core is desperate, my body shaking.

Crow's fingers take place inside of me, the need to be filled finally coming close to being granted.

"Can I take you, baby?" Crow asks as his cock grazes my entrance in place of his fingers.

"As long as Victor will after. I want you both," I tell him, my mouth coming back down to Victor's cock, moaning and arching my body in an attempt to rectify the fire filling me.

"Tell me if it hurts too much," Crow pants out as his cock begins gently filling me. My body takes a moment to accommodate to his size. It feels like my insides are vibrating to adjust to fit him inside of me. The fire felt like it was being quenched by pain for mere seconds before it comes roaring back.

"Fuck, I can't do this for long. You're so fucking tight, baby. I'm gonna cum any second," Crow all but growls at me before steadily pumping his thick shaft into me, causing my head to move and bob even further on Victor's drenched dick.

"You're fucking beautiful, look at you," Victor whispers out as he watches me. My speed picks up, my tongue rallying around the end of his cock each time I come up for air. Each time I gag when he pushes my head so far into him, my eyes tear up and the pain and submission I feel so willing and desperate to give them turns me on as much as the actions taking place.

Crow's body and cock pounding into me send me into a frenzied woman, my hands roaming over Victor's body, desperate for more.

Victor lifts me so that Crow is holding me up by my legs, not taking a single second to do anything but pushing his cock unto me harder and faster while Victor takes the opportunity to rub his cock along my clit, making me cry out with pleasure, unable to contain myself with the onslaught of touch being handed to me.

"Please, please," I cry, tears streaming down my face.

"Please what, baby girl?" Crow grinds out, his voice taking on a dangerously dark tone.

"Please don't stop," I beg, matching his every

move with my own as my pussy desperately seeks out every inch of his cock.

Victor's teeth are latched onto my neck, bringing the painful passion back to light. The pain fires up and ignites my need for them. My mouth lets out the most sensual cries of pleasure I've ever heard before I feel one final pulse from Crows cock as he roars into my ear before he pulls it out and spins me around, telling Victor to finish me off.

Victor wastes no time, filling me once more with his giant manhood. I cry out as he does, craving more of his lips as he places them along my neck while Crow does the same on the other side, my head resting back against Victor.

Crow plays with my clit while Victor grunts and fills me repeatedly in a motion that pushes my nipples into Crow's chest. Victor pulls my hair so that my head is next to his before snatching my lips in a criminally chaotic kiss.

"I'm about to cum in you, pretty girl," Victor tells me.

"OK." I squeal out, reaching my own orgasm just as I feel the final pumps from his cock as he empties his load into me, mixing with Crow's.

"You're ours, well and fucking truly ours now," Crow whispers as they carry my drained and limp body to the bed. They take a side each, our heavy breathing mixed together as I cuddle into them both, feeling their orgasms leak out of me.

"Our girl, you got that, beautiful?" Victor asks. I nod my head, my eyes already closed as I mumble a yes and feel myself drifting off to sleep.

Chapter 21

I don't tell Victor and Crow that Liam has texted me. It is two am when I wake up to get a glass of water, nestled between the two of them, that I manage to sneak out into the kitchen without waking them and it is at that moment when I check my phone and find the message that confounds me.

Liam - *Call me and I'll tell you everything.*

He's been calling me since I got here the other evening, and I have yet to answer any of his calls or texts. I don't need proof to believe what Gray and Crow had told me. I believe them both wholeheartedly, but this text has my mind reeling.

I make sure I am far enough away from the closed bedroom door before calling him. I don't want Crow or Victor to overhear. They'll likely snatch my phone off me and insist I don't contact him again. Understandably so, given the situation and the recent revelations about him.

He answers on the first ring.

"How's my little girl doing?" I'm not sure what has happened in the last few days, but his voice sounds even more creepy now than it ever has before. Maybe it is just because I have been made aware of what he is really like.

"Don't call me that. What is it you need to tell

me?"

"Oh, tut tut, don't you want to talk pleasantries first?" he asks. I can practically hear the snide smile on his face.

"Just tell me whatever it is. I haven't got time for this," I tell him nervously.

"Where was Crow when he left you?" he asks mischievously.

"Have you been watching us?" If I didn't believe Crow and Gray before, I certainly do now.

"I have eyes and ears everywhere. Where was he?" he asks again.

"With Dad. So, we're not even pretending you're the good guy now?" I ask hesitantly. He doesn't seem to be attempting to cover the evil emitting from himself.

"You didn't answer my calls or texts. It's not hard to figure out why. Someone told you."

"So it's true? You were in on it?" I ask, knowing that he knows what I mean. The kidnapping.

"Yes, and I'd do it again in an instant. Now back to Crow, what was he doing with your dad?"

"Why? What's the point of this?" I ask curtly, not wanting to waste any more time than needed on his line of questioning.

"He may have done some research into me, at least I'm assuming it's him that figured it out, but I've got my own information about him. He's an O'Banian. I suspect he's one of the sons." I recognise the name but have no idea why or

214

where from.

"What's an O'Banian?" I ask, hating that I don't already know.

"I thought you'd be all caught up on this. The O'Banians are the Irish Mafia. They dabble within the police and the FBI. They're more tainted and potent than the rest of us put together. They send informants, undercovers to whoever they're interested in taking over or merging with. I have proof that he's one of them." I don't know what to say. He can't be right. That is ridiculous. Crow has told me about his family, his brothers. He wouldn't hide something like that from me. I am sure of it, and yet the niggling suspicion in the back of my mind doubts my own certainty.

"You're lying," I quip.

"Pay attention, little girl. He is an O'Banian. Plain and simple. Take of that what you will, but don't assume I'm the only liar around here."

"Are you the one that put the mark on me?" I ask, changing the subject. I'm not sure about Crow being an O'Banian, but I do know he is keeping things from me, that much is for sure.

I trust him endlessly. I trust him with my life, but that doesn't mean that I trust him not to lie or keep things from me. I know there is more to him, something he is hiding. That's when the reminder of the number on my phone and code words entered my mind. They aren't the Cobras, whoever he is talking to, but who is it? I need to find out.

Liam sighs, seemingly unsure of how to

answer my question.

"I didn't, but I suspect I know who did. Be careful, girl. I might be a bad guy, but there are worse than me in the world. I would have looked after you well if I'd had you as a girl." The pleasure I can hear in his voice makes me want to be sick. He would have looked after me? I dread to think what that even means.

"Goodbye, Liam." I hang up, reeling from the conversation.

I immediately find the contact that Crow had added and informed me to ring if I needed them. My finger hovers over the name, wondering what would happen if I did call them.

Kenny. Down Viper Spring. I remind myself.

I press the call button and wait.

Two rings before it's answered by a man's breathy low tone.

"Tell me the code and what the problem is," he tells me. My stomach flips anxiously.

"Down Viper Spring. It's Charlie," I tell the stranger.

"I know who it is. What's wrong?" he asks.

"Who are you?" I ask lamely, knowing that this isn't how it works.

There's silence at the end of the line.

"You're only to call if it's an emergency."

"Please, I need to know," I beg.

"My name is Kenny. Ask Crow. Only call if it's an emergency, Charlie, this is a busy line. Oh and I won't tell anyone just yet about your little chat with Liam, or this one." The man chuckles.

216

Signed with Love duet
J R Dust

The line disconnects at the same moment I throw my phone down and look around the room, wondering if there are hidden cameras. That can't be right though. This is Victor's home. Despite the fact that he hadn't ever told me so, I had no doubt that it was protected both physically and through any forms of hijacked technology. It has to be. All members, specifically those in the inner circle, are protected ferociously.

I pick my phone up again before realising that it must be the phone that's been hacked. It has to be. Whoever Kenny is, why is he willing to cover for me? It makes no sense.

The last ten minutes has left me with more questions than answers. I rub a hand over my eyes, the exhaustion of the last few weeks finally hitting me. My whole body feels completely drained. I take a seat on the sofa, knowing that one way or another, I need to find some answers to the various questions I have. Who put the mark on me and how the hell do I make it go away? What is Liam's endgame in all of this? What is Crow lying about? Where is Gray? And finally, what on earth am I supposed to do with the two of them? Can I really be with them both? Is it possible or will it end with all of us heartbroken?

I take to Google on my phone, uncaring any longer about whether or not my phone has been hacked. If Kenny can cover for the phone calls, he can cover for this too. Or not. I don't care anymore.

I search up the O'Banians. There are so

many news articles but every single one I click on seems to have so little information on. And then the articles start disappearing. I mean, literally disappearing. I click on each article and then my phone turns off. I turn it back on, search it up again, and the article will be gone. I do the same thing four times before realising that it is him. It has to be. That's how he knew about the phone call with Liam and it's how he's doing this. It has to be. Does that mean Crow really does have something to do with the O'Banians, or is there another reason why Kenny or whoever else is attempting to stop me finding out more? Is there another reason? Maybe these O'Banian dudes are just really bad news, but that didn't seem like enough of a reason. Or is he just toying with me?

I press the call button again, this time ready to give this Kenny guy a mouthful rather than a nervous few questions.

"I told you to call if there was an emergency. I'm not an agony aunt, Charlie," the mystery voice says down the phone. I can hear the amusement in his voice.

"Why are you playing with me? Who are the O'Banians? And what gives you the right to decide what I do and don't get to see on my phone?" I whisper-scream at him, feeling my heart rate rise with frustration.

"Women are so dramatic. Maybe I'm doing it for your own good. Go and wake Crow up and ask him. I'm a gossip, but I'm not allowed to be right now, so sadly I can't tell you anything. Nighty night, nosy."

"You're a dick," I seethe before hanging up again, hearing his cackle-like laugh before I do.

Maybe I shouldn't have called him a dick. I might actually need him at some point. Well, shit.

Chapter 22

"If it's happening, I'm going," I insist as I rummage around Victor's bookshelf looking for the book I was reading last night. I swear he's hidden it from me. Well, probably not, but I have no other solution as to where it's gone so I'm blaming him.

"You can't. Do you have any fucking idea how dangerous it is for you, Char?" Crow remarks, throwing his hands up in the air in frustration.

"He's right. It's not safe. I'm sure we can think up a way for you to have fun here," Victor tells me, flirting between the line of being serious and sexy as he takes a step towards me and places his hands on my hips.

I dip away from him, knowing that if I let either one of them touch me that I'll cave.

"No. You'll both be there! How much more protected can I be?" I ask them, knowing it's a low blow but also well aware that they'll take it as a hit to their ego if they have to say they can't protect me.

"Charlie, if me and Mr Kiss My Girl agree, you know I have to be right." It's back to Crow. They're tag teaming me. Against me.

"Mr Kiss Our Girl," Victor corrects him.

The simple correction gives me flutters, sending me into a girly dizzy spell that fills me with the same love and adoration that they've both centred around me since the declaration of care. Well.

Signed with Love duet
J R Dust

"Will you stop and listen to us for a minute, Charlie?" Victor says as he stops me in my tracks and backs me up against Crow. I'm in a sandwich. I'm the filling. My mind takes even that thought into a dirty frenzy, but I stop myself before I start something I know will end with me vulnerable and agreeable.

"You can touch me up all you like but I'm still going," I tell them.

No one thought the party would still be going on tonight but since it is, I want to go. I get that it could be dangerous, though with the heightened security, I imagine everything will be fine. After last week's attack, I hardly imagine they'll be scrimping by on protecting the Club.

"I just want one night to be a teenager. Everything is so chaotic right now, I just need one night. That's it. I've never even been to a real party. Please," I turn as I finish, hating that I'm begging them. I know they're worried, and I get why they are, but that doesn't change my motivation to go.

They eye one another steadily before Victor relents and nods at Crow.

"Fine, but you do not leave our side, do you understand?" Crow asks. I hardly let him finish before I'm nodding enthusiastically at them both and running off to find my book again. I need to read. Then I can get ready.

"Not once, I swear." I smile as they simultaneously shake their heads in defeat.

The book is under the cushion. That's weird.

I pick it up before skipping into Victor's bedroom to pick something to wear. I had asked Crow to go and get my clothes earlier this morning. It wasn't hard to tell that he didn't know what to bring so literally grabbed a few handfuls out of each of my drawers and hoped for the best.

It's now that I'm away from them that I wonder why I haven't mentioned the phone call with Liam.

I was going to. Before falling asleep again last night, I had told myself that I would ask them both about it. Even though the conversation with Liam centred around Crow, I am sure Victor knows more than he is telling me too.

I'm not sure what stopped me. Or rather, I perhaps didn't want to admit that I was worried about how they would react, worried that they would cover up my concerns or be frustrated with me for not telling them sooner.

———

Dad still insisted I go to the doctor this morning, which I had completely forgotten about until he rang me twenty minutes before I was supposed to be there, reminding me of it. I'm not sure why he is so insistent on the checkups when nothing is wrong. It is long, boring, and to add to matters, I am met with a grumpy doctor that is not our normal doctor. He isn't rude, he is just very reserved and seems unwilling to interact, which is always fun.

Signed with Love duet
J R Dust

I'm not sure that he does it on purpose, chances are he is just busy and sick of people. I can't say I blame him if that is the case. I would be bored stiff of seeing people day in and day out too if I were in that situation. Dad used to get everyone check-ups with the Club Doctor every few months but he hasn't done it in a few years. I wonder what made him change his mind so suddenly.

I have spent the afternoon jazzing myself up in Victor's bedroom, insisting that he and Crow leave me alone to have some girl time. I have spent the time pampering every inch of skin I have. Shaving, waxing, moisturising, creaming, and preening. My body feels completely brand new. Sleek, slim, and when I look in the mirror before leaving, I am more impressed than I ever thought I would be when I was planning out my clothes this morning. It isn't often I look at myself and think I look nice, but I know that what I am wearing will blow Victor and Crow away. And as much as I hate the idea of dressing up for a man, or two men in this case, imagining their faces seeing me in this only makes me want to wear it even more.

Just the thought of the acts that had taken place in the recent days with them sends shivers down my spine, a fire filling the frenzied and constant need I seem to have when around or thinking about them.

I had crimped my hair, loving the volume it gives it as well as the slim shape it gives my face.

Signed with Love duet
J R Dust

I put on some blood red lipstick, black mascara, and some smoky eyeshadow.

I didn't bother with foundation, blusher, or contour. I never usually wear makeup, so having on what I already do makes my face feel full as it is. Plus I'm not great at doing it in the first place, so I am sticking with the safe, easy options.

I love makeup on other girls. They always make it look incredible and flawless, but applying makeup is not a skill I have and most of the times I've tried it, I look orange. Not the look I'm ever after and yet the only one I seem to be able to get right, so it's easier to just avoid it all together.

I had decided on red strappy heels, a black skin tight dress that showed just enough cleavage, accentuated my curves, and is short enough to make my legs look longer than they really are.

I had chucked a leather jacket on top, mainly just because it is cold and I need some sort of cover or I'll never make it to the club, let alone inside to enjoy myself, but also because it is my favourite one that I wear with just about everything.

Dad picks me up and drops me off outside the club, the boys saying they'd meet me there. They didn't mind me being away from them since I was with my dad.

The music at the club is monstrously loud. I am only at the gates and can hear it already. I am surprised it is still going on but as Crow had said, we can't live our lives avoiding the very things that we want for the fear of something bad happening. He is right.

There are at least a hundred people standing outside, smoking and drinking, swaying from side to side, probably so intoxicated that they are completely unaware of what is going on around them.

I have never been drunk like that, and I never want to be either. I hate the idea of being in a state, physically and mentally, where I'm not fully in control of what I am doing or saying. I mean, I got that it could be fun, that it was a release that everyone needs at some point. I just never want to be in a position where I have no control. That's my worst nightmare come to life.

My goal is to find Crow, Victor, and Alice (and maybe even Eggy) and just be a teenager for a little while. A few drinks won't hurt.

"Yo, Char!" I'm nearly at the door and turn towards the voice that I instantly recognise as Crow's. He is walking straight towards me, having spotted me before I saw him.

He pulls me inside of the club, and I find myself immediately surrounded. It's packed in here. How anyone is dancing is beyond me. There's hardly space to move or breathe, let alone actively dance to whatever the hell is echoing over the speakers.

Crow hands me a drink. I take a sip and recoil in shock.

"Fucking hell, Crow!" I exclaim. "What are you trying to do to me?" I ask with a laugh.

Signed with Love duet
J R Dust

Vodka, and vodka alone, is filling the red plastic cup he has handed me. It burns my throat and starts a fire in my chest from breathing through the cold air outside.

A cup later and a chat with a still working, but ignoring any customer that isn't me Alice, and I can feel the alcohol taking effect on me.

I don't recognise most of the people here. A few say hello, bump into me by accident, and apologise, or try to flirt, but I push most away or simply ignore them.

I'm sitting on a bar stool talking to Alice about a man in the corner that looks like he's about to be sick. His friends are around him trying to get him in the taxi outside to get him home, and Alice is informing me that this far too drunk man is a regular that does this every time a drop of anything alcoholic passes his lips.

Crow went to the bathroom about twenty minutes ago and hasn't yet come back. I wonder what he's doing. I wonder where Victor is too, I've not seen him anywhere.

I tell Alice I'll be back soon, down another cup of vodka that I know I'll soon regret, and unsteadily clamber off the bar stool in search of Crow and Victor.

So much for not letting me leave their sides. I can't even find them, let alone stay with them.

Through the main hall, I enter the corridors, leading me to the quietest part of the club. The people in the party were only allowed in the main hall or to the toilets to the left of the main hall.

226

Crow wouldn't have used them though. A lot of the men have designated rooms here, and chances are he would have gone to his, so that's where I start.

Before I get very far though, in one of the guest rooms, I hear roars of laughter, male laughter, and decide to check inside to see if Crow has found some of his friends that he's got distracted with.

I can feel my body moving from side to side without my consent. My head seems to be swimming in thoughts that I can't straighten or comprehend.

I crash into the wall through my drunken stupor, but quickly lift myself from it in the fear of someone realising how drunk I am.

I'm still in control. My body is just a little out of sync with my mind. That's all.

I push open the door, apparently forgetting formalities and knocking in my drunken state and find two guys that I vaguely recognise.

I can't pinpoint their names. Sober me would probably know, but vodka drinking Charlie has absolutely no idea.

I think the one on my right, the one dancing on the bed, might be Matt. Or is it Max? It might even be Marty. It starts with an M, that much I'm sure of. I think. He's got ice blonde hair and the darkest eyes. He's always covered in cuts and bruises from fighting. My dad doesn't like him but has never had enough evidence of bad behaviour to get rid of him.

Signed with Love duet
J R Dust

The one on the left looks similar with light hair. This one has darker streaks through his though, a disgusting smirk stuck on his face, and clothes that reek of weed.

Stoner and maybe Matt. Wait no, we'll call him Marty.

I notice probably a moment too late that there's coke laid out on the dressing table in the middle. This must be one of their rooms. There are pictures and posters all over the place, men's clothing and odd shoes hanging here, there and everywhere.

"Sorry, wrong room." I salute to them for whatever stupid reason as I go to leave but I am pulled back by hands on my waist.

How did they get that close to me without me realising?

"Get off me!" I scream, but watch as I struggle in the ones embrace, the other shuts and locks the door.

Oh fuck.

Why did I drink?

I can feel it. My arms, my legs, my whole body. It's not as capable. Not as strong or decisive as what I am in a fight when sober.

He lets me go but I don't move.

It's Matt/Marty that locked the door. He's blocking the door. Stoner is watching me with a smug expression plastered on his face.

"You think you're so high and mighty being his daughter, don't you?" Matt asks me as he inches closer.

228

Signed with Love duet
J R Dust

"Oh, shut up and let me out." I don't let my fear show or at least I don't think I do.

I'm not stupid. I know what stupid guys like these think they can get but they're not getting it from me.

Before I have a chance to turn to see Stoner laughing, I feel the heaviest sensation against the side of my head and collapse to the floor from it, my eyes becoming dark, the room dim as I feel nothing but heavy darkness.

I wake in a new room, my eyes adjusting just enough to see that I'm not in any place that I recognise. How did they get me out of the Club and somewhere new without me waking? I must be in the club. My mind must just be playing tricks on me.

Is this about the mark that had been placed on me? Or is it purely bad luck?

My eyesight is blurry, my head drumming. I can see their lips moving, but I can't hear them. I can see five, no six of them even though I know there's only two. The same two.

I try to move, to get up but Matt, or was it Marty? No, Matt is on me in an instant, pinning my arms down from behind me, above my head.

My body is shaking, and I can feel my cheeks are wet. I'm not sure if it's me crying, or blood from whatever Stoner guy hit me with. I can't tell.

I feel like my head's been flushed down the toilet ten times. Nothing I can see is making sense. I can't hear him but I can see Matt laughing. My legs are flailing, kicking. I'm screaming.

I can't understand what's happening.

I need to get them off me, but no matter how much I kick or try to move my arms and fling my body from side to side, nothing's happening.

Am I even moving?

Stoner guy says something to Matt and they both laugh.

Stoner guy punches me. It happens so quickly that I don't even have time to move my head away to stop him. He hits me again, and all I can feel is the swelling and my head hitting the floor as he lifts it up with one hand and hits me with the other.

I can see the blood. I don't know how I can see it, but my eyes are red.

Everything looks red and bleary. He hits over and over and over again for what feels like hours.

I can hardly see now. My eyes must be swollen or blocked with blood.

He stamps on my stomach with his boots and my automatic reaction is to curl up to protect myself but with my arms being held down, all that happens is my legs moving, but I'm just giving him more of a chance to get his leg in just the right place to do it again.

I can hear myself screaming, I'm just not sure if it's really happening, if I'm physically screaming or if it's just in my head that I'm rejecting this moment, in denial that this is happening.

No one in the club is supposed to hurt anyone, let alone women. It's not because I'm special but because I'm supposed to be able to look after myself.

They know that the music is too loud for anyone to hear me. They know no one is allowed into that part of the club unless they are a club member.

I don't know if they were going to do it anyway or if it was just a matter of wrong time, wrong place. They're at least smart enough to know that they won't get caught right now and that's what scares me the most. There's no one here to come and save me, and I seem incapable of saving myself.

They're talking, probably shouting, but I still can't hear.

They're laughing at me.

Matt is slapping my face. I can't feel it. It doesn't hurt. The only reason I know is because of my head lolling to each side as I watch the actions take place.

My head hitting the floor when they hit me and being thrown to either side when they slap me.

My whole body feels like I've been run over by an artic lorry. I don't think my body's ever felt so weak.

So scared.

I'm sure I'd normally be filled with rage in this situation, but all I want to do is cry, sob, scream and ask for someone, anyone to come and save me. To help me.

Stoner guy gets down between my legs. He lifts my tattered dress up, rips my underwear off me, and tosses it aside.

I use every last ounce of energy and strength I have to try and twist and turn every part of my body out of their grasp, but all that I get in turn is Matt hitting my face more. Stoner guy is brushing my lower half, and more screaming fills my mind.

Matt has worked out the obvious. That even without him holding onto me that I can't move. He's knelt on my arms now, just in case and pulls down the top of my black strapless dress.

His face goes down towards my breasts just as Stoner pulls apart my incapable stupid legs.

Matt is biting me. Biting me. And I can hardly feel it because all I can think about is what's about to happen and what the monster in front of him is going to do next.

Matt sits back, weight killing my arms, probably turning them in all kinds of directions they're not supposed to be in.

He's pulling my hair, sneering in my face.

Forcing me to look at Stoner.

I do.

He's already got his trousers pulled down and his cock out.

It's disgusting.

I think I'm going to be sick.

I'm gagging, coughing, spluttering and retching.

I'm screaming, fighting, in pain, not capable of saving myself.

He's holding my legs apart no matter how much I try to fight it. My body is at the end of its tether.

He pushes himself inside of me and it hurts.

It hurts so much that I feel the screaming off my lips change from a scream to an outright cry. I sound like a little child desperate for her mother.

But I don't have anyone to come and save me.

He's pumping his body in and out of me as Matt slaps me some more.

It feels like a fire is going off inside of me. Stretching, scratching, and a burning fire is killing me. I feel like I'm being torn apart.

It hurts so badly I feel like I'm going to pass out.

Matt has a knife in his hand and I can hardly move to watch what he's doing.

My whole body is moving on the floor from the movements happening within me.

I'm crying. I'm begging. I'm asking a God I've never believed in, I'm asking anyone to stop this. To save me. To give me something to hold onto.

I feel a scratch on my neck, though when I look I know it must be so much more than that. There's a knife on my neck.

I feel no pain when he drags it up onto my face, across my cheek.

He stabs my arm and I feel a searing pain both inside of me from the monster inside of me but also from the knife that is being repeatedly stabbed into my body.

He puts it into my stomach.

Passes it to Stoner who takes a break and

shoves it into my leg. Again. And again.

My stomach. Again.

They're going to kill me.

I'm going to die today.

My body isn't my own anymore. I feel like I'm watching it from above. From a whole different place.

And then the door opens.

My sight is blurry, my mind a puddle of despair and horror as I attempt to call for help from whoever the new entry into the room may be. I look up, my sight clearing slightly and I see two faces, both of which make my throat feel like it's being strangled. The air leaves my lungs, the room becomes smaller, my mind confused as I look upon the face I always assumed would forever be my saving grace.

It's Gray, but my brother hasn't come to save me. And neither has the man stood next to him.

Diary Entry #1

I will never sign my story again, for my body has been signed in ways that kill me, and I never wish to instil that horror onto anyone or anything, not even these sheets of paper beneath my hand, but for this one time, for once, for the only time there will ever be - I'm signing my story for you.

CK

Charlie Keller

Part 2

Signed for Him

Chapter 1

Gray - 3 weeks earlier.

"Have you checked on Charlie tonight? She's going to that party at the Clubhouse, isn't she?" I ask as he walks ahead of me. I hate that I could only watch her from a distance. At least he gets to see her, even if he does have to keep his distance. Not as though it seems he is doing a very good job at it.

This whole thing is the most fucked up situation I've ever found myself in, and I've been in some very fucking precarious situations before now, so that is seriously saying something.

"Yeah, she's got Crow and the shithead with her," he tells me.

He doesn't like Victor. I'm not exactly too keen on him myself. We knew Crow was an O'Banian. Hell, I was the one that had helped him get into the Cobras to start the investigation into the club for his family so the whole merging shit could move on a bit quicker. Not as though anyone besides me and the fucker next to me knows that. Well, Crow, too, of course.

But Victor - he is a whole other issue. I don't know enough about him and I don't like that. I don't like that someone is around my sister that I haven't had the chance to fuck around with a bit to see his true colours first. I mean, I am not exactly thrilled about anyone being with my baby sister, but at least I trust Crow. I know he would do anything to protect her. It had started as an assignment, but even I saw the way they looked at each other before I left. It was the only reason I could leave and trust that she would be ok. I sigh at the thought.

Yeah, and look how that turned out, you idiot. Look at where you are now.

"What room did he say they'd be in?" I ask as we continue walking through the hallway towards the main rooms.

"197. They got a new girl in tonight. I dread to fucking think what they're doing to her. Apparently this one's into pain though, so they'll probably be ripping her up," he mutters as his face distorts in disgust.

Matt and his wannabe Danny class themselves as 'Doms'. From what I am aware of, that includes respect, consent, rules, and a safe word. None of those things are included in Matt and Danny's sex life. It is rape. Simple as that. No matter how willing girls are to come back with them, they are no longer interested when they realise they'll likely end up in hospital or - like too many of the girls I've seen carted out of here - dead. They meet girls on dating sites, claiming to be things they aren't, and then drug and drag them back to this slice of hell to ruin and rape them.

"Has Dad figured out that they're crossing him yet? Shit, even just their attitude should get them kicked out, shouldn't it?" I wonder aloud. My dad gives people too many chances. Like way too many chances.

He is a man so loyal to some stupid MC code that he doesn't even see what is right in front of him.

He had this vision of me taking over the MC after Liam is done, but I can't think of anything worse. I don't know exactly what I want to do or where I want to be in life, but running the Club and the Cobras is not it. I know that much. But then again, maybe now that I have seen this darkness I would have a better chance of taking charge and knowing a fucked up person when I meet them. There are definitely plenty of them here.

Matt and Danny had been planted into the Cobras before I left. At different times so as not to gain too much interest or query. I had no idea they were anything but your typical Class A fucking bastards until I got trapped here and he started telling me more than he should have.

Matt and Danny are lunatics. Legitimate psychopaths with no care or consideration for the women they break. They seem to think that because they don't have STIs and wear condoms most of the time that it is fine. It isn't.

And if I say anything? Charlie. Charlie is always the threat. Every single person here knows they only have to mention her name and I'll do anything they ask, and I fucking hate it.

I don't think I'd ever wished to be an only

child. Even when Charlie was pissing me off as a kid or wanting to hang out with my friends when I didn't want her to, I never wished she wasn't there. But for the sake of my sanity and both of our freedoms, I wish I was an only child now, even if only so that they couldn't threaten me with her safety.

I have complete faith in Crow's ability to take care of her but then again, if you've got a bunch of twats planning and attempting to get to someone, there's only so much that one man can do.

I look to my right and find he's slowed down to match my pace. He isn't any more keen on this than I am.

It isn't exactly a friendship me and this fucker have, but while we're both stuck in a scenario we don't want to be in, we definitely trust each other more than anyone else in this shithole.

"Nope. No one likes them, but you know what your dad's like. He thinks he has to have evidence of bad behaviour to kick them out. He won't just do it because they're twats." He huffs out as we round the corner.

My head shakes of its own accord, mad at my dad for being too trusting. Mad at myself for landing myself here. Mad at Charlie for being vulnerable and someone I care so highly for. Worst bit is, I knew my mum was in with some bad people. I knew there was a chance they'd get to me before I got to them, but what I didn't expect was to be carted off by a whole other fucking band of bastards while I was busy worrying about my mother's men.

"I swear to god, if I have to act happy when I walk in and see them carving up some poor girl again, I'm gonna lose my mind." The minute I show even an ounce of disgust at what the animals in this place do to women is the same moment they use Charlie's freedom against me. They know she is my weakness and I can't fucking stand it, but if being a prisoner here means that she is safe then I'll survive it for as long as I have to.

"Just smile and wave. They'll be going to see the boss and then we can get the girl to the doctor. Problem solved." He says it like it's so simple. I've been taught my whole life to protect women, to love and care for them.

He's so used to seeing screwed up and messed up shit that I don't think it phases him anymore. Well, no, that's a lie. It does. I know it does. I can see it in the twitch of his eye that he tries to hide every time we walk in on something gruesome or every time he's tortured and hurt as punishment for caring for Charlie, but he handles it a lot better than I do. Maybe if I'd grown up the way he had then I would too.

I'd asked him once how he managed to see the women be treated so badly and do nothing about it. He told me that you can respect women all you like but that doesn't mean that everyone else will too.

I might be gay and so the whole holding the

woman and loving her thing doesn't apply, but that doesn't change the fact that I still respect fuck out of the women around me - whether I know them or not. I hate the fucked up things the men here did to the girls they take, but I can't do a thing about it without more threats to Charlie's life.

You go out on a mission to find your mother and you end up held hostage and threatened. I know how to land myself in the furnace of fuck ups, that's for sure.

"Here we go, this one," he says as he taps my back, gives me a fake smile and encourages me to do the same before opening the door and motions for me to enter first.

The smile plastered on my face doesn't falter while I greet them until I see the carnage they've created.

Fuck.

There is blood everywhere. All over them and the poor girl underneath them. Her body is red with very little sign of life. I can hardly even see her face. But that's the way they like it.

"Oh shit," Danny says as his body stops pumping into the poor fucking state of a woman underneath him. My horrified eyes drift up to Matt kneeling on the girl's arms as he slaps her again before looking up at me with fear filling his eyes.

Why does he look afraid? They're usually cocky as fuck when someone finds them in this sort of situation, happily showing off their conquests and the pain they've caused.

And that's when I look at the woman's face for the first time since they've leaned away from her and feel the instant horror and rage coat my vision.

Charlie.

My mind seems to enter a desolate state, my body unmoving as I stand wide eyed and nearly delirious with anger and shock.

Before I can convince my body to register the shock and move, the fucker beside me is on them as he lets out a monstrous roar. His hands grab the knife I hadn't noticed that was in Danny's grip. I watch on as he crouches down between them, over Charlie, and swipes his hand back and forth, stabbing them both repeatedly until they're still and nearly lifeless beside her.

"Get the fucking doctor. Now," he roars out as he picks her up gently, with utter fury in his eyes.

I thought I was saving her by doing as they said but now they have us both.

Fuck. How did this happen?

Chapter 2

Charlie - present day

My whole body feels heavy. My eyelids refuse to open, despite the many attempts I make to move them. It feels like my eyelashes are fluttering from the small tickle on my face and yet nothing happens. I can feel my eyes moving, but all I see is darkness. I try to make my hand move and feel only the smallest twitch of my fingers. And that's when the pain hits. The excruciating pain that courses through my body and is unrelenting in its desire to make me wish for death. It's a burning, throbbing, stabbing pain that seems to attack every part of me.

"She's awake," I hear a shallow feminine voice say, a voice lacking any emotion or care. A voice I don't recognise, I realise.

Footsteps follow the words spoken. Three sets of footsteps. One is light, leading away from me while the two others are heavier, louder footfalls that get closer and closer to my side.

"It's time to wake up now, Chars." It's Gray. Gray's here. Why is Gray here? Where is here? Am I at home?

No. This doesn't feel like home.

What happened? Why am I in pain in a place that I don't recognise the feelings and smells of? What do I last remember? My mind draws a blank

243

as I think of the morning I spent getting ready for the party at the Club after being to the doctor. After the time I'd spent with Victor and Crow. I recall going to the club, having vodka—

And then I remember.

The men. Waking up in a place I didn't know. The brutal assault they laid on my body. I instantly want to rip at my skin, feeling the disgust and turmoil within me wanting to claw its way out.

I feel disgusting and helpless knowing what happened to me as I wonder how I'm still alive. I am alive, aren't I? I must be, I heard Gray.

Am I in the hospital? But no, I realise, I can't be. There would be doctors and nurses that would be surrounding me in a hospital.

I think back to Gray. Gray is here. The same Gray that I haven't seen for a lifetime. They greeted Gray like a friend, not an enemy, I suddenly remember. Where are we?

I subconsciously twitch the moment Gray's warm hands connect with mine, my eyes shooting open at the contact - my eyes connecting with his.

I can feel the fear he must see in my face. I don't want to be here. Wherever here is. I want to be at home. I want to cry and scream and ask the world why I deserved this, but before I even open my mouth, my body hits me with the most excruciating pain I've ever felt. Except it's not in one place. There's not a single hit of pain. It's everywhere. Every wire and line within my body feels like it's on fire.

Signed with Love duet
J R Dust

"It hurts," I cry out quietly to Gray, my voice barely more than a whisper as tears escape and run down my cheeks.

His eyes fill with sorrow as he looks down at me with his eyebrows crammed together.

"I'm so fucking sorry, Chars. I'm so fucking sorry," he tells me as he places his head in my hand.

I watch in utter confusion, the pain ebbing to the background as I look around and try to work out my surroundings and why I'm here. Why I'm not home in my bed.

I just want to go home. The anxiety in my stomach rolls and shifts, waves of nausea hitting me at the uncomfort. Not just the physical discomfort but the idea that I have no idea what is going on or why I'm not where I'm meant to be.

It is a hospital room, though I don't feel that I'm in a hospital. I'm not sure why, but I'm certain I'm not safe. I don't feel like I'll ever feel safe again.

As my head slowly turns, looking around the room, my eyes connect with a monster. Not a new one but one that does make the fear that lingers rise to the surface.

I spent so many years looking up to him, thinking that he would be my saviour, my family forever and yet the last time I spoke to him, I knew. I knew there was a deeper and darker part to his soul than I had ever realised or wished to see.

"I'm not going to hurt you," he says as he

takes a few tentative steps closer to me. His presence is as overpowering and outrageous now as it ever had been and when I'm feeling most vulnerable, it terrifies me.

"What's happening? Where am I? Why are you here? Where's Dad? And Crow? And Victor?" I ask, my throat dry and my voice hoarse. I feel the tears rising to the surface, though I do my best to blink and blink, to make them go away.

Make them go away.

"Please take me home." I turn to Gray, unsure that I can trust him but knowing that I hold more trust in my brother than in the monster on my other side.

Gray dabs at his eyes as he lifts his face, his eyes still filled with a mixture of guilt and remorse as he shakes his head at me.

"I can't leave, let alone take you home," he tells me sadly.

I fight through the pain consuming my body, shifting so that I'm sat up in the bed, pulling the blanket with me to cover the hospital nightgown underneath.

Who changed me out of the clothes I was in? Who saw the damage that I knew was done to my body? I didn't need to see myself; I could feel the bruising and stiffness in my very bones to know that I was inexplicably and fatally changed.

"Why can't you leave?" I ask him, my eyes alternating between him and the monster beside me, unwilling to turn my back on him for the fear of what he may do.

"They promised that if I stayed, they wouldn't hurt you. They wouldn't take you but now that they have you, if I try to leave or help you leave, they'll hurt you even more," he wrenches out, his face looking like he's about to sob in my lap at any given moment.

I think through what he's said. They? Who are they? The same they from the letter he left me? Just sitting up in the stiff bed has my body and muscles aching, I'm certain I don't have the energy to escape, let alone ask the questions I want to right now.

"Can you take me home?" I ask quietly as I turn to Liam. The monster. No doubt the devil behind all of this.

He watches me, his eyes filled with nothing but darkness.

"I can't. I can demand that you're mine though. No one else will hurt you then."

A laugh gurgles through my dry throat, a sound that resembles a choked sigh more than the sarcastic laugh that was intended.

"Right. Then only you could hurt me," I say.

I'm trapped. One way or another, whichever way I go, I'm trapped. I can't move. I can't leave. I can't get off this bed. There are monsters everywhere. I want to curl up in a ball, close my eyes, and not open them again until I'm in the arms of safety. Until this is all over and someone wakes me from this nightmare, telling me that none of it was real, that everything will be OK, but

I'm not sure that anything will ever be ok again.

I want Crow. Despite my care for Victor, it's not him I crave. I want Crow's warmth, his laughter, his reassuring smile. I want his arms around me and his voice whispering in my ear, telling me that everything will be OK. I want him to hug me and hold me and carry me home.

"I'll take care of you. I may be the villain in your story but I promise you, I won't hurt you."

I inwardly cringe at the statement, the irony of his insistence on keeping me uninjured when I'm sitting in a hospital bed feeling more physically and mentally drained than I ever have in my life.

I had been hurt in every way before from different things, whether that be illness or heartbreak; from those I love dying or leaving; and yet the pain I'm in now doesn't even come close to comparing. It's a situation I never envisioned being in and one that everyone warned me of. You never think it will happen to you until it does, that's the saying, right? I can't count how many times I was told that when I was younger when Nina, my best friend, and I wanted to go out alone.

Liam looks at me with a hint of what looks to be shame or remorse in his eyes, but I dismiss the notion that he could possibly feel bad for this situation or for me when I have no doubt he was at least a part of the reason I'm here.

"How long have I been asleep?" I ask Gray, not wanting to spend any more time than necessary looking at Liam's face or thinking about the implications of what I assume he's done.

"The doctor put you into an induced coma to let your body heal. You've been out for just over three weeks," he tells me, his voice gentle and hushed.

Three weeks.

My God, three weeks.

"Why haven't they found me?" I rasp out. I want to cry. I can feel my chest filling with emotion. If I've been gone for three weeks and they haven't found me, who's to say that they ever will? They have so many resources at their disposal and if they haven't found me yet, I dread the idea that they won't at all.

As I shift further up the bed, pulling the thin, crisp sheet along with me, Gray and Liam look at one another, a silent conversation passing between them. Gray's face looks even more grim now than it did moments ago.

"What happened? Oh god, please tell me they're ok," I demand, knowing for certain that I couldn't handle the idea of anything bad happening to any of those that I care for. I would rather they didn't find me at all than get hurt in the process of trying to get to me.

"This place is well covered. Hidden. It's unlikely that they will find you. The boss has spent years making sure that this place is impossible to find. They're fine. No one is hurt outside of you," Liam says as he moves to sit on the chair next to the bed on my left.

249

My mind doesn't seem to know how to comprehend what I'm being told. Nothing and nowhere is impossible to find. They will find me. I just have to wait. I just have to wait for a little while and they'll find me, I tell myself. The comfort I attempt to bring to my mind is pointless though. I know that the first twenty-four hours after a disappearance are the most important - the most likely time for a victim of kidnapping to be found and if after three weeks I haven't been found, it's unlikely that I will be.

Not impossible though. Not impossible. Even if I have to find a way to get out of here myself, I will. I just need to be patient. There is always a weakness, I just need to find it.

"I want to get up. I need to go to the bathroom. I want to shower." The truth is that I want a moment alone to cry my heart out and repair it before I have to face Liam again, but I'm not going to say that.

"I'll give you a hand, come here," Gray says as he helps me up from the bed and holds onto my arm as I walk on unsteady and jelly-like legs to a door on the opposite side of the room.

He walks me inside and shows me where everything is, telling me that he'll be just outside if I need him. There isn't a window or an accessible vent. No way out aside from the door that will lead back to Gray and Liam. I can't face leaving without Gray anyway, and I'm not sure my body has the resources to do much escaping right now as it is.

Signed with Love duet
J R Dust

I turn on the shower and step inside, hating the new scars surrounding my body from the assault but lapping up the warm water on my skin like heaven and hell. My skin feels so sensitive to the pellets of water being thrown its way, but the warmth engulfs me. My mind races at the conundrum I find myself in, but I cut off the thoughts abruptly, knowing that if I start crying alone, I'll probably never stop. I throw my head back under the cascade of liquid and wash myself quickly before stepping out and drying myself off.

"I've got some clothes here for you. Open the door a little and I'll hand them to you," Gray says. I do as he says and grab hold of the clothes.

Once dressed, I find the mirror above the sink and stare horrified at the face in front of me. Tears brim to the surface as I look on at the woman staring back at me. That's not me. It can't be. But it is. My hands lift and the woman in the mirror copies, tracing my fingers over the monstrous scar still healing over my face. I remember them cutting me. Hurting me. I thought I was going to die, but it isn't until this moment when I look in the mirror that I realise how truly broken I look. There are dark circles under my eyes, nearly healed bruises over the top of my body that are visible even with the clothes on.

I always thought that scars weren't a big issue but now that I have one running down my face, I want to break and cry and scream at the prospect of never looking the same again because having physical scars means that it isn't just my body that will never feel the same, but my mind too, and while stuck in this furnace of hell, I have no idea how I'm supposed to recoup. I have no idea who to trust or how much.

Chapter 3

Charlie

My backside throbs and burns as he pulls the whip back again, my body convulsing over the table, shivers running through me as I await the continued physical assault that lashes through my senses.

My fingernails dig into the side of the table, the pain tremendous as splinters from the wood embed themselves into my skin, but it's serving as the only distraction I can find. I hear the sound of the whip flying through the air towards my backside once more with a guttural roar filling the room as the cold material smacks against my uncovered skin, causing another twitch of my body, another sob. I do everything I can to hold it in as my head shakes of its own accord, the tears spilling onto my cheeks and the table below me as I try to stop myself from wailing out in pain.

"What number is that?" Liam rasps out, his breaths as harsh as mine are as he pants and takes a moment's respite.

"Twelve." My voice is barely above a whisper as he rounds the table and crouches down to meet my eyes, lifting my head by my hair in his hand as he does.

"How many? I couldn't hear you," he asks again, his voice steady as I watch his chest through my blurry vision, my eyes filled with tears.

"Twelve," I mutter quietly, acid and bile filling my mouth as I speak.

I don't want to be here. I want to go home. It's the only thought that occupies my mind - the only thought that I allow to keep me company. The thought of Crow pulls me through the depressive daze I find myself nearly submitting to daily.

Liam places my head back down on the table, my cheek on the cold wood beneath it. He strokes my hair as he takes a deep breath, "Do you need more or is that enough?"

"That's enough." I give in.

There's no point fighting it. I've been fighting it since I first entered this apartment. Fighting him, fighting the inevitable that I knew would end up happening if I wasn't found soon enough. I just hoped I would be found before I lost the strength I needed to keep fighting. But it's too late. I can't keep going - not mentally nor physically.

"I'm not doing this because I want to hurt you, I'm doing this because I don't want you hurt," he emphasises as he rounds the table, reaching the back of me as his hands begin roaming along the back of my bare thighs.

He made me strip, so that I was in nothing but my bra before he punished me. It wasn't unusual but that didn't mean that it was any less cruel. It is humiliating being covered in scars. I hate it, but to have to bare them to someone unwillingly makes it so much worse.

Signed with Love duet
J R Dust

The punishment doesn't usually go on this long, but I think he sensed how close I was to breaking, how little fight I had left in me. He knew that he just had to go that little bit further before I surrendered.

His hands are wet, likely covered in my blood and sweat as they draw closer and closer to my entrance. The feeling of anyone, let alone him, being that close to the intimate parts of me makes me want to be sick, but I know that will cause me more pain so I hold back the urge and wait, unmoving as he does as he pleases with the body that is barely mine anymore.

He can do what he wants to the shell of me. He insists that he is doing it to protect me, but the notion seems as laughable as it is improbable.

"It's me or them and despite what you may think, I'm the better choice. They would take it in turns with you, pass you around their friends, take you without any preparation, do whatever they wanted with you. At least here, at least now, it's just you and me." And it was that thought that makes me shiver, that makes my body shake uncontrollably rather than the hands and fingers that are caressing my folds.

Though I'm sure he takes pleasure in feeling my body shake, assuming that he is the cause through pleasure rather than sickness at the idea of it being just me and him.

I understand but that doesn't mean that I believe him entirely. Gray had told me that what he was saying was true - that the other men here

255

had declared that if he didn't use me then they would, and from the stories Gray had told me of what transpired outside of this apartment, I have no doubt that I don't want to be a part of that. I know that in his own mind, Liam feels he is the better option, but that doesn't change the fact that I am certain he is happy about it and that was why I fought it.

Despite the fact that I hate it, it isn't because he is unattractive, it isn't because I can't let him do it, nor is it because I hadn't ever thought about it because I had. It is because I feel like every time he touches me, I am cheating on Crow. I have no idea why Crow over Victor is the deciding factor. I adore Victor, but the more time I spend away from him, the more I realise that I only miss him in the way that I miss Nina or Alice, not in the way that I miss Crow. When I sob into my pillow next to a sleeping Liam at night, it is Crow's touch I crave, his words, his hushed whispers. Him.

Liam's heavy breathing stops my thoughts where they are, erasing any thoughts of those on the outside from my mind.

I knew what the options were and I didn't want either one. He'd repeatedly told me that he was being threatened, that he didn't have a choice. I knew that, but that didn't change the fact that I still didn't want it. I wanted to be saved. I wanted the torture and punishment to go on for as long as it could before I had to finally give in so that I could be saved before that time occurred, but I

Signed with Love duet
J R Dust

can't take anymore.

The thing I hate, probably more than him touching me, is the fact that him touching me makes my insides warm and my core wet. I hate that my body seemed so willing and pliant as he touched me for the first time. The last time I was touched there, it was taken from me so violently that I never wanted to be touched again and yet through his touch, my body seemed intent on not only surviving that but on enjoying it orgasming again.

The hand not on my core's entrance flicks and rubs at my clit, my body responding tenfold despite my attempts to stay as still as possible. The friction he is creating has me arching my body and biting down on my palm to cover the cries that threaten to spill free.

"You're so wet, my baby girl, you're so responsive to my touch." His voice is molten, like lava as his words do nothing but set alight my body once more. I hate this. Mentally, I hate it. I want his hands off me, I want to go home, I want to cry and wash his touch away and never be near him again but he is right, my body seems to adore his touch. My abdomen feels more and more full as his finger gently slips inside of me, his other hand rubbing against me between my folds, the pressure building higher and higher until I feel the one thing I dread. I dread it because he knows. He knows that my body isn't against him as much as my mind is, and that brings the sobs forward the moment I feel the tightened orgasm release all over his hand as his fist pumps slow down before he finally takes his finger out of me and pulls his hand away, the cold air suddenly making my body shiver again.

His hands reach around my waist and lifts me to my feet, my legs wobbling, my backside still throbbing from the pain that, although not nearly as bad, is certainly not diminished. My core throbs as violently as my backside does, coming down from the most horrendous and yet mind-blowing orgasm.

His breath falls down on my hair, his head above mine as he turns me towards him, my eyes downcast, unwilling and not wanting to look at the man and monster in front of me.

He leads me to the bathroom, my body aching and burning with the aftermath of both the pleasure and pain that he forced upon me.

"Stand there. Don't move." I don't acknowledge that he's spoken, nor do I disobey. My body feels numb and tingly outside of the pain, wondering why it was so easy for him to get me to a place of lust filling my gaze even through the pain.

I feel like I've cheated on Crow, despite logically knowing that he would want me to do whatever I could to stay alive and well, and yet I don't feel either of those things. I'm surviving, sure, but it feels endless, this cycle with him, and the longer we spend together, the more I can feel the brick hard barrier I had put up crumbling at his feet. He knows it as well as I do, and that kills

258

me.

I care for him in ways I hate admitting. After spending so many years with him as part of my family, I know there's good within him, even if I feel like I haven't seen any of it for aeons. I wonder if he faked it but realise that he surely couldn't have. He used to care for me, genuinely, with a ferocity that I admired as a child and a teenager and yet, as I stand here now, I question what changed and how it occurred. Was he always this way and I just didn't see it because I was looking at him through the eyes of an adoring child?

Liam interrupts my fraying thoughts with a flannel in his hands, him on his knees in front of me as he gently rubs the cloth across my thighs and my outer legs; over and over again he puts the flannel under the warm water and returns it to me, to my skin, cleaning the blood, sweat and remnants of the orgasm away as I stand unmoving.

There's something sensual about his movements, about this vulnerability and the silence with no words spoken. Something strange. He washes me delicately, as if I'm a vase that could break at any moment. Maybe if he had been this gentle with me from the start it would have been easier for me to give in. Not that I should, but maybe I could have. I could have even wanted to.

When he's finished and uses the towel to dry my naked and marred skin, he pulls his fluffy robe around me, taking me to the bedroom and laying me on my stomach on top of the mattress. My hands find themselves attached underneath the pillow as I lay my head upon it. I'm not sure what he's expecting from me, and a small part of me dreads that he'll come onto me again, but as he kneels by the side of my head and looks into my eyes, I see only hurt and despair. This is the man I knew as a child. The one that was caring and thoughtful, the one that didn't want me injured. Ever. Unless it was by his hands apparently.

"You're going to rest," he tells me as he pushes a strand of my hair from in front of my eyes backward. I don't respond, watching silently as he eyes me curiously.

He leans down, his lips finding my forehead as he plants a kiss upon my skin.

"Sleep, my beautiful girl. I'll read." I fight the urge to do just that, but I feel my eyes closing of their own accord as his voice reads the words that lull me to sleep and his fingers comb through my hair.

Chapter 4

Charlie

"Do you think I could see Gray again soon?" I ask, adjusting my voice to sound as sweet as I can possibly make it without Liam noticing how fake I'm being.

Five hours and all hell is going to break loose. Five hours and I'm going to be saved.

I hope.

Liam was right when he made that promise to me while I was in the hospital bed, wishing for death to take me home if no one else could. Well, right to an extent. He could protect me from everyone else. He hasn't let anyone near me besides himself and Gray since I've been here but that also means, exactly as I had suspected, that it is him I found myself subjected to instead--and the strangest part about that? Liam is a completely different man to the one I thought he was. I mean, no surprise there, and I do not mean that in a positive way.

I had known from my conversations with Crow and from Gray's letter that he wasn't as he seemed, but even then I don't think I knew or even suspected how mentally unhinged he was. I'm not sure if he acted sane or at least partially so because he knew he needed to or if something had happened that had changed him,

261

because this man in front of me is a completely different character to the one I knew as a child.

His eyes lift, meeting mine from across the table. The very same table he bent me over while he whipped me and made me cum. God, even thinking about it makes my stomach twist and my mind revolt. I hate how easily he can sway my body.

He watches me as he chews his food. The food I made, like the perfectly capable housewife he wants me to be. So I do, I act amazingly. I'd never been interested in drama or the theatre classes in school, but my gosh, have I put on the largest and most deceitful act of my life since being in his presence. If being what he wants me to be allows me to be hurt only by him then I can cope with that. I would prefer to be hurt by only him, even over and over again, than to be tortured and tormented by the animals I have caught glances and whispers of in the hallways.

Gray has told me of the barbaric things that go on outside of the confines of Liam's apartment, and as much as I hate being a prisoner and hurt by him, it is preferable than being treated even worse by those outside the door that holds me here.

"I'm not sure you seeing him so regularly is a good thing. He acts out after he's seen you, and you give me more attitude too. I'm not sure I like it," he tells me, his lips lifting into a smirk that he knows will goad me. He does this on purpose - tries to antagonise me so that I say something he doesn't like or act aggressively and then enjoys punishing me for it.

Five hours and he won't be in charge of me anymore. I just need to make sure he doesn't know that.

Despite my initial reservations about giving in to him, I knew I had to. It was the only way to live here. I spent my first few days out of the hospital in this apartment with him, with the occasional visit from Gray when he was allowed to see me. I also spent the first few days telling Liam exactly what I thought in between my crying fits and outbursts of anger - until he snapped. I had since decided that I would be smart. Wise. Use the brain that my father had raised me with and be exactly what Liam wanted until I found a way to get myself and Gray away from here.

The strong, independent and stubborn part of me hated it but it was the safest way to live.

I had just about given up on the hope of being rescued. I had no doubt in my mind that my father, Crow, Victor, and both clubs would have been looking for me, but wherever I am must be far enough away and so far off the radar that they can't find me, or else I wouldn't still be in this hellhole. Assuming that Gray's plan works though, I can be out of here tonight.

"What if I promise to be good? And I'll make sure that Gray doesn't act out anymore either. You know how hard I've been trying," I insist as I look at him once more, masking the frustration and anger I wish I could unleash without consequence.

Liam hums for a moment, twisting his fork over and over in his hand before placing it down on his plate and looking at me with a triumphant grin.

"I tell you what, how about we go to the bedroom and if you're a good girl, I'll let Gray come and see you later when I go to work." I can feel the bile rising up my throat, but I fight to hold it down.

I thought the pain would be the worst form of torture he would put me through while being in this cage, but I was wrong. So wrong. Within hours of returning from the hospital room after his first beating of me, he insisted that I kiss him. To show him how sorry I was. Within a week, he insisted that I hug him, to show my care and gratitude. A few days later, he whipped me, making me promise to always call him Daddy or Master when he forced himself inside of or on top of me. As if my body hadn't been through enough. As if my mind could handle anymore forms of torture. I didn't always give in to begin with. I fought. Hard - and ended up once again covered in bruises and cuts. So now I do give in.

I'm not someone that enjoys pain, or someone that is good with pain. I remember hearing stories from the Cobras wives about how well they had handled the pain in childbirth, how high their pain threshold was. Mine is not. I am terrible with pain and I can't claim otherwise. Between the mental and physical torture of being here, the forced orgasms are the better option.

Liam stands from his chair, the scraping of the wooden chair on the tiled floor sending shivers through me as he tucks it back in and begins his walk to me, his hand out, waiting for mine to be placed over top of his.

Five hours and this won't be my life anymore.

I lift my unsteady body up and place my hand in his calloused one, feeling revolted at even our hands touching - in part because I'm not at all revolted. His warmth and his soft touches do things to my body that I despise.

I always used to think holding hands was such a romantic gesture and now the only thing romantic about my life is the overwhelming sadness when I wake from a dream filled with Crow.

I close my eyes, willing away any thoughts of him or anyone else outside of this place, knowing it will only make this next part harder as he pulls me along to the bedroom.

So much of why I hate it is because I don't. I don't hate it at all and that guts me more than anything else. The first few times I pleasured him, I ran to the bathroom to be sick as soon as he left, but the longer it goes on, the more I've learned how to push the right buttons with him, how to get my way without him knowing that I'm doing it.

I've learnt a lot - one of the newest things I've learnt is that Liam is very capable sexually. Although I would much prefer I didn't have to do it, to give in to him, the fact that he insists on making me have an orgasm daily kills me because every single time, it makes me feel like I am losing my sanity. Losing my sanity because my body adores his touch while my mind will do anything to get rid of it. And the longer I'm away from Victor and Crow, the more I start to wonder if it might be easier to let the submissive, vulnerable, darker side of me learn to care for Liam. But now Gray has a plan.

Five hours.

I feel like my whole mindset is altering every day, every time he touches me or becomes tender with me.

"Strip for me, baby girl. Let me see what's mine," he whispers in my ear as we enter his bedroom.

I waste no time, immediately taking off the dress covering my body and placing it on the nightstand on my side of the bed. I'm left with a slight chill, wearing only my bra and underwear. Ones that Liam picked out, of course. I keep my eyes downcast, gazing at the cream carpet - just how he likes it.

"Now get on your knees, baby. Show your master how good you can be," he demands, the lust already filling his voice, thickening it if possible.

I take a step closer to him and fall to my knees, waiting while he strips himself of the clothes he's wearing.

It's so strange to be in such a fucked up

266

routine. To know what I'm meant to do and yet somehow, knowing gives me comfort. I know what I can and can't do now. I know what makes him angry. I know what pleases him and until the moment I'm out of this place, pleasing him keeps me from being hurt. Pleasing him pleases me in the most screwed up way. The sounds he makes when I turn him on fuels me to do it even more.

His length bobs in front of me, already fully erect as his hands grasp my hair, forcing my head forward until his length takes residence inside of my mouth.

I move my head rhythmically back and forth, sucking and licking at the muscle in my mouth as Liam rocks his hips into me further. His moans fill the air around me. My eyes water incessantly as he pushes his cock to the back of my throat, choking me on it.

"You're such a good girl, aren't you?" he asks as he juts forward once more before pulling his cock from my mouth, signalling for me to move to the bed.

I lay on my back on the bed, exactly as he likes, as he stands at the base and watches me with a smile on his face.

"Take your bra and panties off for me. Daddy wants to treat his little girl," he tells me, unmoving, watching me as I hastily do as I'm told.

I can handle the whole 'master' thing. I hate admitting it, but it turns me on as much as it seems to turn him on, but it's when he refers to himself as Daddy that I cringe.

"Now open your legs for me."

The cold air brushes along my core as I do, my eyes not moving from him, taking my cues on what to do from his every move.

"So fucking perfect," he mutters as he pulls me by my ankles to the bottom of the bed so that my core is mere centimetres from his face.

He lifts my legs over his shoulders before spreading my lips with his fingers, his tongue lapping up the space over my bead with haste and greed. The sensation and friction from his tongue and stubble has my body arching from the bed, my legs tightening around him. He has me melting and moaning in seconds.

His hands move to my waist, holding me in place as he laps up the inside of me, his tongue darting in and out of my body while his fingers squeeze my sides. The mixture of pleasure and pain has an involuntary groan leaving my lips, much to Liam's pleasure, his dark chuckle surrounding me.

My hips move of their own accord, desperate for more, to be closer to the tongue and face between my legs. My insides cramp and pulse as he crams his tongue into me and over my bud continually, lifting me higher, closer and closer to release.

He's done it so many times now that he knows exactly how to get me there. How to make my body writhe for him and his touch.

His hands climb down from my hips to my thighs, pushing my legs apart until it's painful, his tongue not once halting in its assault of my core.

His face lifts, his eyes finding mine, his smirk and my pleasure coating his face, making it glisten.

"You're going to cum on my tongue like a good girl now, Charlie. Do you understand?"

I nod. Yes.

"Tell me. Say the words." My body moves closer, desperate for the friction.

"Yes," I whimper out, the words tasting bitter in my mouth as I do.

"Yes what?"

"Yes, Master." I close my eyes as I speak, hating the way it affects me.

He smiles once more at me as I open my eyes again before bolting back down to take what's his, his tongue flicking desperately along my clit while his fingers enter me, thrusting in and out continually as I grow closer to the release he wants.

A whimper and a groan escape me as my hands find their way to his hair, pushing his head closer, torturously closer, the friction and need of him overwhelming as I claw at him, my legs tightening around him as my pussy pulses and releases the orgasm it was dying for.

My breathing calms, my body sated as he lifts his naked body on top of my own.

"You're such a good girl for me. Well done. Now it's time to ruin you and fill you up," he tells me, his voice thick with need and lust as his length slips over my entrance, teasing my body

269

as my hips lift to him, taking the tip without permission.

His constant want to impregnate me terrifies every part of my soul - for more reasons than I can even begin to count. I was on the contraceptive injection, which lasts three months. I know I've been here for over a month, but I lost track of the days eventually, meaning that I now have no idea if the one thing inside of my body meant to protect me still will.

He chuckles heartily with his hands beside my head, his lips on my arched neck.

"So desperate for this cock, aren't you, my greedy girl." His lips catch mine in a dangerously rare kiss, the taste of myself on his tongue filling my mouth.

It's at that moment that his length fills me, a gasp leaving my lips, straight into his as his thick dick penetrates me and every part of my body that counts.

His jagged breath beats over my mouth as he thrusts in and out of me in quick succession, my hips meeting his every thrust, my body being unaware of how bad this man truly is. My body adores him and his touch, even when my mind knows it shouldn't. But in moments like these, moments when he takes me, it's easier to let him, to allow it and to force the logical side of me that wants to fight my want and need for him to be quiet. Any time I've fought this it only ended up in more pain. A pain that I won't ever feel again if I can get past tonight.

His hands come to my throat, squeezing and ebbing away at it as my vision darkens and my lungs begin to struggle. Not long now. When he grabs my neck, I know it's not long. The pleasure filling my body intensifies, seemingly in awe of the pain and pressure he puts on me, a second orgasm only a few thrusts away as he consumes my body.

His juts become rabid, his groans immeasurable and his hands tighter around my neck as his seed fills me, my pussy clinging to his cock in bursts as my own orgasm wraps around him.

My body relaxes at the same time that his does, his head nestling between my shoulder and neck, his chest and stomach landing directly above mine as he puts his weight on top of me.

"You're such a good girl for me," he whispers in my ear as my eyes begin to flutter closed, the daylight from the window ebbing away as the sun hides for the evening.

"Come here," he tells me as he lifts his sticky, sweat-covered body from mine and lies beside me, his arm out above my head. An invitation to curl up beside him. I check the clock as I do, my heart hammering in my chest so hard I'm terrified that he'll feel it. Four hours. Four hours until I can go home.

My body fits next to his disgustingly well, the touch of his body moulded to my own bringing me more comfort than I would ever dare admit.

271

Signed with Love duet
J R Dust

His hand twists and turns the lockets of my hair as the other holds me close.

"I wasn't always like this. I'm sorry you only got to meet this version of me." His voice is soft, possibly softer than I've ever heard it as his words fill the empty void around us.

I don't say a word, worried that anything I do say may trigger his anger.

"I'll go in willingly with them, I won't fight it. Just let me hold you one more time before it's your time to go." His words send a cold shock through my body - startles me in the worst possible way. He can't possibly know. He wouldn't allow it. He can't.

"I know this is goodbye. I'm not going to stop them. I just want you for a little while longer before our time is over," he tells me as he places a kiss on my forehead, bringing me closer once more, leaving no space between our bodies as his breathing evens out while his hands caress my skin.

He knows. He knows, and he's letting me go.

Chapter 5

Charlie

Gray is pacing. Tapping his fingers against his outer thigh and pacing as if the action will gain us our freedom or calm his erratic thoughts. If only.

We had a plan. Well, Gray had a plan that was supposed to be our escape. I waited and waited and when the sun came up, I realised that something had gone terribly wrong. So here we are with plan B. Presumably. This is what he was doing the last time he had a plan. Pacing and panicking.

"What is it?" I ask aloud, unable to cope with the built-up tension he's brought into the room from the moment he entered.

I don't think he has even heard me. He doesn't make a single notion that signifies he did. He's still pacing. Back and forth, from one end of the living area to the other, over and over again.

"Gray," I say gently as I walk over to him, placing myself in his line of sight. I don't want to startle him.

Despite how much he's attempted to hide it, it's clear to me that he's been as much of a mess as I have since the moment I woke up. He's had to be here and endure it even longer than I have.

He stops abruptly in front of me, looking at me, into my eyes, as if he's searching for the answers to so many unheard questions.

"I don't know if it'll work. I hope it does, but if it doesn't, it'll get worse," he says before taking a step around me as he continues pacing.

It will get worse? The only thing worse than what I'm currently living through is being out there, and even including Liam's many, many flaws, I know for certain that he would do anything to be sure that I didn't end up out there. But that doesn't mean that he can't hurt me. He knows, as well as everyone else being aware, that to get to me or Gray all you have to do is threaten the other. We're each other's downfalls in this wretched place.

"Do you mean a way out?" I wonder, the hope I meant to keep tucked away now firing through every nerve ending in my body.

I hope like hell that's what he's talking about. What else could it be? I can handle things getting worse so long as we know that we've tried, but then the more I think about it, the more I realise that it's not just me that has to be willing. It's Gray too. Am I willing to put him in danger to attempt an escape? I don't think I am, and that thought terrifies me because that's probably exactly how he feels about me.

Gray continues his obsessive walking, thinking over whatever it is that has him so desperately consumed.

"The less you know, the better, but I managed to contact Dad. He can get us out but they need more people, they'll get butchered otherwise.

Signed with Love duet
J R Dust

They'll be here in five days," he pants out as he stills and hovers in place, his fingers tapping his thigh again as his head flits left and right, paranoid of anyone overhearing us.

We can get out. As much as I want to know every detail, I couldn't care less about the nitty gritty of it so long as it means that we can leave. I can go home, and that thought fills me with as much dread as it does excitement. Now that the prospect is genuinely a possibility, the option of going home, the thought of being anywhere but here, makes me realise how much I've undoubtedly changed in such a short space of time.

I know they'll want to know everything, and I know that even if I refuse to tell them that they'll have a pretty good guess going off the sight of me now in comparison to the last time they saw me dressed up ready for what now seems like the most silly night. All of this because I wanted a night out. A night to go out with my friends. I could have stayed at home or at Victor's and none of this would have happened. Or, at least if it had, then I would have had so much more protection around me in an attempt to stop it from occurring.

I hate that I question whether they blame me. I had to convince both Crow and Victor to let me go that night, and look at what happened. Look what happens when I get what I want. I'm completely transformed. I left my father childless and alone all because of my selfish wants and needs. It was bad enough that Gray had already disappeared, but to have both of us gone must have been heartbreaking.

"Do you think they blame me?"

Gray stops, his brows creasing together as he looks at me.

"Blame you for what?" he asks, the confusion evident in his tone.

"For this," I say as I wave my hands around the space we're in. "I'm only here because I wanted a night out." I laugh bitterly.

"Char, no. No, fucking hell, no. I hate to admit it but one way or another, these people, these fucking animals," he snarls, "would have got you. Christ, I've been here for months, and I've never even met the top dog and even the mention of them has me fucking shaking. He's a stubborn fuck by the sounds of it. I can tell you that nothing you did or didn't do would have made a difference. It might not have been that day, or even that week or month, but you would have ended up in their grasp no matter what. But now is our time to get out, Charlie. Now is our time to move on from this. You're with me, right?" I nod feverishly at his words, my head bobbing of its own accord as my chest fills with emotion, with love for my brother that's been as tortured as I have, if nothing else by simply knowing what I've been through while here.

"Midnight. Midnight in five days' time, and they'll be here. Just act normal until then and the rest is sorted, OK? Just be who you need to be to survive until then. Can you do that?" I nod again, not trusting my words to come out with as much strength or conviction as I would like.

"OK, right, now sit down and play a game with me, you know what Liam's like if he thinks we've been scheming," he mutters as he takes to the table and pulls out the board game. I follow him over, taking a seat opposite him, watching and imagining the reunion I've wanted for so long as he puts the board out between us.

He's right. Liam hates when we're just sitting chatting when he walks in. He always asks what we're planning, what we've been talking about when in actuality up until today, we've very genuinely just been talking to each other. He's a paranoid man - admittedly with good reason because he knows as well as I do that I would love nothing more than to leave, but I'm certainly not going to be the person to give in to his paranoid state.

Five days and I leave. I hope. The last plan was the furthest thing from successful. Gray had a plan, told me the day and time, a day and time that Liam somehow also knew about and then it came and went. Nothing happened. It turns out the guards had changed rotation which put the whole idea in jeopardy.

This one might work, and then I'll really say goodbye to Liam. And then what happens to him? I hate that any single part of me even wonders, let alone cares. I'm going to need some serious fucking therapy when I get home.

277

My mind wanders back to the thoughts of Gray and the potential consequences of his plan going wrong. Come to think of it, aside from being aware of him having his own apartment in here, I've never asked what he does, what's taken from him.

"Gray, where do you go when you leave here? What do you do?" I ask.

I watch as his eyes lifts slowly to meet mine.

"I usually go and stay in my apartment. They ask me to do menial jobs - cleaning up, doing the accounts, crap that no one wants to do. I don't have the same problem you do," he tells me.

We haven't spoken about it. He's not asked, and I've not divulged the information, but I have no doubt that he knows and by the look of wrath filling his eyes, I know that he doesn't like it any more than I did to begin with.

"He's not all bad. He's better than what you've told me happens out there. Much better. He does care about me in his own fucked up way. I know how to get around him, how to get what I want sometimes," I tell him honestly.

He nods his head at me, likely unsure of what else he can say or do. We're both stuck here with no one to save us. Yet.

"I know he's not what I thought he was, but that doesn't change the fact that I don't like what I suspect happens when I leave." He rolls the dice, effectively stopping the conversation there as he makes his next move on the board.

Chapter 6

Charlie

"I'll be out in a second," I call back to Liam through the bathroom door. He doesn't like leaving me in here for too long. He's probably afraid that I'll find a way out or possibly drown myself in the bath. I couldn't pretend that I hadn't at least thought about trying both of the above. I have never been so uncertain of myself, my mind and my mental strength or the lack of it, since being held as a prisoner.

They don't happen often - panic attacks - and when they do, Liam is usually at work so I am alone or Gray has been here once, but I can't cope with this while he is around.

"What are you doing?" Liam questions as he taps on the door again.

The tears brim to the surface and don't leave as I feel my breathing speed up. A sudden and overwhelming sense of anxiety and helplessness overcoming every part of me.

I can't do it. I can't be here. I can't be in this room or this place or in my mind. My mind is shutting down, my body not far behind it.

I can feel my body shaking, and violently so as I quiver in a seated position underneath the spray of the shower. The water is the only thing keeping me from losing it entirely. It's freeing

279

knowing that it comes from the outside world. The only thing from the outside world that is coming for me.

My chest feels like there's a stampede of beasts stomping on top of me, my heart beating so quickly from the never-ending pressure on me that I can hardly breathe. The breaths coming out of me are short and sporadic in nature, leaving me feeling even more panicked than before.

"Open the door or I'm coming in." Liam.

But I can't move. I can't speak or think or do anything aside from ride the wave of the all-consuming panic and pain filling me.

My chest pumps as the sobs shake my body under the water, my eyes closed, unable to distinguish and explain or cope with the situation I'm in.

Breathe. I just need to breathe.

Fucking breathe.

"Charlie." His voice sounds so close but with my eyes closed, I can't figure out if he managed to get in. I locked the door. Did he unlock it? Is he in the bathroom?

Open your eyes.

But I can't. My eyes won't open, unwilling and unwanting to see what's in front of me.

"Charlie. Look at me." His voice sounds panicked, afraid almost as I feel his hands find my shoulders. He shakes me. He's inside.

I force my eyes open, seeing Liam crouched down in the bathtub beneath the shower opposite me fully clothed, now soaking wet too.

Signed with Love duet
J R Dust

"You're having a panic attack. That's what this is, right?" I nod, not trusting my voice as the tears continue to roll down my cheeks, falling into the tub alongside the shower water still spurting out.

"Charlie, I need you to breathe for me. Breathe in, copy me," he instructs as he takes a deep breath and encourages me to do the same.

I try to follow his instructions but all I can feel is the pain and fire in my lungs.

"I can't," I sob, my words coming out practically unintelligible as he shakes his head, lifting his shirt over his head and throwing it aside before reaching over and pulling me onto his lap.

"Feel me. Feel my hands on you, feel my heart beating, Charlie. You can hear my voice and no one else's," he tells me firmly as I fall into his chest, my legs pulled up beneath me.

His hands stroke my hair, my back, my shoulders.

"Touch me, baby girl. Don't think about anything else. Touch me and know that while you're here, while you're in my arms, that I will never let another soul near you," he whispers, his hand pulling mine up to his chest, my palm above his steadily beating heart.

"Match me, baby girl. You used to try and make our hearts and breathing match when you were little. You used to copy my breathing pattern. Do it now. Feel me, trust me, and copy me." I listen to his words, let them consume me as I take nothing else in.

281

He's right. I remember him cuddling me as a child and trying to make myself breathe at the same time as him. His breaths always seemed too slow, meaning that I'd end up out of breath quickly, but I ignore that and do it again. I imitate his breathing, feel his hands as they slide over my shivering body, and feel his heart beating beneath my hand, his chest rising and falling at the same time as my own.

"I will never let anyone get to you, Charlie. I might be the bad guy, but I know you know I'm being truthful when I say that you can trust me at this moment. I would skin any man or woman alive that dared to even think about harming you." His words are harsh, though what's even more brutal is the truth in them. He's right and despite the way he's treated me, even if just for his pride or his fucked up way of caring for me, I do know that he wouldn't ever let anyone else hurt me.

"Breathe with me, baby girl, keep breathing." I don't say anything as I take his continued commands in and do as he instructs.

The world seems a little clearer, not as hazy or blinding and within minutes that feel like hours my breathing has regulated to match Liam's.

"No one will ever get to you again. The only devil that you need to worry about in your life is me."

"Is that supposed to help?" I strangle out, my voice croaky from the tears.

"You might not realise it but you have limits,

282

and I'd never push you past them. I know what you can handle from me and what you can't. You might feel like I've pushed you out of your comfort zones, but I have never and won't ever tip you over the edge."

I think his words over, my mind reeling back to the torture he had inflicted upon me until I had given in. He truly didn't think he had pushed me too far. Had he? Despite these panic attacks that are more based on my lack of control than Liam, I have always known, even in the worst events with him, that I could stop it or at the very least make him stop even if the actions that happen afterwards don't stop. I think.

I knew that he didn't want to hurt me permanently, maybe I did know subconsciously that I could get through it and he did too. Or maybe he's just saying what he thinks will help. I'm not sure any part of me will ever truly know.

His hands comb through my wet hair as he carefully detangles it with his fingers. The slight tugging as he undoes the mess brings my breathing down, using the unusual comfort to help tame my wildly beating heart.

"Come on, you're going to bed. You need to rest," he tells me with a huff as he lifts my body, still clinging to his as he stands and steps outside of the bathtub and begins the walk towards his bedroom.

"Why are you so nice to me sometimes and so willing to hurt me at others?" I ask, braving the question even though I know it could end badly if it makes his temper flare.

He doesn't stop, doesn't answer me either. He places me on top of the duvet on his bed, pulling the covers from the other side to wrap me up so I'm practically cocooned in the embrace of the warm and familiar material.

I watch as he walks away and returns only moments later with a glass of water and what looks to be two paracetamols.

He sighs, eyeing me with a curious smile before sitting beside me. The bed dips with his presence and weight and for the first time in a long time, not a single part of me feels afraid with him so near.

His jaw tics and tightens as his eyes roam over my face.

"What started this? What are you worrying about?" he asks, the question catching me off guard as I look up at him with my brows creased.

"Are you joking?"

"Obviously not, Charlie," he tells me sternly, his hand circling in front of him as if encouraging me to speak.

"Liam, I've been kidnapped, taken away from my family, raped, beaten and forced into sex with no idea of how or even if I'll get home." My voice is surprisingly strong and loud. I almost expected to break down saying all of that out loud, but Liam's face doesn't alter, his face a mask as I watch his Adams apple bolt up and down as he takes in my words.

"You miss them. Crow and Victor. Your dad

and that Alice girl. Is that what this is?"

My bravery seems to have no bounds as my eyes roll of their own accord.

"Of course, that's part of it, but it's not just missing them, Liam. I don't want to be here. I don't want to be made or coerced into doing things I don't want to do. I don't want to feel like I'm cheating on anyone. I don't want to have to avoid thinking about them because the moment I do, I feel so guilty and dirty and filled with shame." My eyes become glassy as I continue, determined to be honest with him since I imagine it's the only chance he'll give me to do so.

"I feel like I'm in a never-ending cycle of torture and pleasure and even the pleasure I hate because I know it's just my body reacting and not what I really want. I hate that I find comfort in you even though you're so awful to me. I hate that I'm not reacting to this the way I should. I should be crying every day and trying to find a way out and yet I just act like your 1960s housewife, making you food and cleaning up and waiting for you to demand sex or a blow job and more than any of it, I hate the times when I don't hate it at all because no matter what you do or say to me, there will always be a part of me that treasures and cares for you. I despise the fact that I enjoy you pleasuring me. I hate that I have no idea what I'm thinking from one minute to the next. I don't even know how I feel about being raped because I've not had time to acknowledge it because I feel like I'm constantly in danger. I feel like if I hadn't gone to that stupid party that I wouldn't be here. I want to go home, and yet I dread it too, because I know that I'm going to have to face my dad and Victor and Crow, and I have no idea how I'm going to feel or what I'm going to say because I can't even understand how I feel or what I think, let alone have any idea how to explain it to them." I take a deep breath, feeling as though I hardly let my lungs inhale a good dose of oxygen as I spoke.

I watch Liam process my thoughts as his eyes scan my face, as if in search of something more.

I feel surprisingly better for letting it out. Gray and I have spoken briefly about everything going on but with the fear of being caught talking about something someone doesn't like, we hardly ever get to truly talk about how we're feeling or what we're thinking. I've just admitted more to Liam than I've even admitted to myself since being here.

Liam runs his hand through his hair as he sighs, his hand rubbing against the back of his neck as he looks down, seemingly speechless as I watch and wait patiently. He must have something to say.

"I can't make this better for you, not how I want to. You know that if I don't have you, they will and I won't allow that. But what I can tell you is that none of this is your fault and when you go home, because you will go home, you don't have to tell anyone anything or explain anything to anyone if you don't want to. If they can't accept you while you heal then they don't deserve you at all." His words surprise me. He says them with so much brash honesty and conviction that it very genuinely shocks me.

His hands reach out, hesitating before touching me. He reaches for my jaw, stroking his thumb against my skin as his eyes dart between my eyes and my lips.

"Get to sleep. I'll read," he says, though I'm certain he wants to say more, his face filled with concern and something else that I can't quite place before he stands from his place, tucks me into the covers again, and leaves the room without turning back.

Chapter 7

Charlie

Cottage pie. It's been one of my favourite meals since I was a child and as I portion the meal onto two plates for myself and Liam, I let the familiar smell take me back to a time when Liam and Dad used to argue about who made it best, when there was nothing more complicated or dreadful in my life than my mother not being a part of it. Gray always voted that Dad made it best. I always took Liam's side. Even though his tasted like roadkill.

I take the plates into the living room, placing them on the table where I've already put the cutlery and our drinks, knowing Liam will be back at any moment. He always returns by 7pm. It feels so wrong to be so easily domesticated for a monster and yet the more time I spend with him, the more he opens up to me and shows me kindness, the more I wonder if maybe I've seen everything that's happened in a light filled with negativity for reasons that aren't all that logical. At every turn, he's tried to protect me, even if his ways haven't been the best.

He's been violent, something I've hated at times and yet craved at others. His domineering presence and demands don't give me time or the emotional and mental time to think or rather

288

overthink as my mind seems to do, and I hate that I like that. I hate that I need his demanding nature to truly allow my mind to be free while submitting to him. I asked Gray if he thought I was submitting to Stockholm syndrome more than I was submitting to Liam, and he simply told me that Liam and the situation we're in was no more a choice for Liam than it was for us. I wasn't sure what he meant since he refused to explain further, but it made me wonder if perhaps there was more to the whole thing than I had realised.

As I fold two napkins for each of us, the front door bangs open, the handle hitting the wall behind it as Gray enters, holding up an injured Liam at his side.

My eyes protrude from their resting place as I take in the scene in front of me.

There's blood covering Liam. His head, his neck, his chest. I can't tell where it's coming from or how bad the injuries are beyond the darkening and deep red that is seemingly everywhere.

"What the hell happened?" I ask as I rush towards them, taking Liam's other side, his body slumped.

"I'm fine," Liam grunts, his eyes bruising and beginning to discolour as he looks up at me.

"You are the furthest thing from fine, Liam." I tell him as I help Gray bring him towards the sofa.

Liam sits down in a rush, his body pounding down, his blood staining the material beneath him as he puts his head in his hands and his legs spread apart to hold his elbows in place.

I find the first aid kit and ask Gray to get warm water and a flannel from the bathroom as I take out some bandages, not knowing the extent of the damage done to him yet.

"Why did they do this?" I ask, not needing to have it confirmed that it was them. Those in charge of this operation.

Liam says nothing but shakes his head, refusing to answer me as I use the wet flannel to rub away the blood from around his face. The largest of the wounds seems to be a deep cut beneath his eye. I dab at it gently, not wanting to cause him any more pain than what he's already endured.

Gray stands at my side, his menacing silence filing the room.

"Are you going to tell me what happened?" I ask him pointedly as I continue to clean the blood from a stoic still Liam.

"He wouldn't give you up," Gray says, his voice conveying the same mixed emotions he has towards Liam as I do.

And then his words sink in.

"What do you mean he wouldn't give me up?" I ask, the anger that's been building within me brimming to the surface.

There are so many parts of me that hate this man in front of me but I know, without a doubt, that in his own fucked up way he cares for me beyond measure, and whatever happened to cause this, this pain that he's in, just shows the lengths he's willing to go to protect me.

"She doesn't need to know the rest," Liam tells him, his voice sounding as broken and exhausted as I was when I first came into this apartment.

"For once in your life, Liam, give up the pretence and tell me what the hell happened. Please," I ask, needing to understand.

I was under the impression that he was one of the perpetrators in this scenario, but if they're willing and able to hurt him this badly because of me then that surely isn't the case. Maybe Gray wasn't as far off the truth as I thought he was when he suggested that Liam had as little choice in being here as we did.

"It was me or you. Either I gave you up for them to have you or I gave myself up. That's it. Nothing more, nothing less. I just need to go lay down for a bit and then I'll be fine," he tells me as he rises to his feet, his stance unsteady as he does.

"That wasn't fucking it, and you know it," Gray says.

Liam's eyes become deadly as his head rises to find Gray's eyes, the argument passing between them needing no words.

"I said that was it so that was fucking it. Say another word about it and I'll fucking end you here, Gray. I might not be in charge, but I've got more fucking power than you do," he tells him, his eyes lethal and filled with promise.

"I'll get him to the bedroom. Stay here." Gray huffs out as he takes Liam's arm over his shoulder and leads him away from me, cussing and muttering something to him that I'm not close enough to hear.

From behind I see even more damage. His clothes are completely covered in dirt and blood, the jeans he's wearing showing none of the denim blue that was there just this morning.

I take the bowl of water and the unused first aid kit to the kitchen as I run over the situation in my mind. There's not a single part of me that can look at Liam when he's like that, when he so willingly goes through so much torment and pain for me and want anything but better for him. I have no idea how he got here or why, but I do know that he doesn't deserve it.

I realise now that until I'd come here and spent time with Liam and Gray in a hostile environment that I looked at Liam and his wrongdoings as so black and white and yet when I look at him now, I know for a fact that he didn't get here, to this place mentally or physically because of his evil but rather for reasons he won't share with us.

"He's in the shower. I put the chair in there which will probably be ruined in minutes but he wanted to get in there and couldn't exactly stand, so yeah," Gray tells me as he walks out, his eyes casting glances in each direction as he walks towards me as if checking the room for possible danger.

"I'm going to go, but call me off Liam's phone if either of you need me, yeah?"

"Yeah, of course. Thank you for helping me with him. Can you come back tomorrow?" I ask, wondering if Liam will finally allow the pretence he's used for so long down now that we seem to be on the same side or as close to it as anyone can be in such extreme circumstances.

"I don't think Liam has the energy to care if I come by or not anymore. He wants out as badly as we do," he tells me.

I nod and take him into a hug at the door before he leaves, hating that he's alone.

"They did to him what they did to you when we found you. It's not the first time. He's a monster, but he's a monster that is somehow in love with you and willing to go through anything so you don't." He holds my head close in his embrace as he whispers the words to me before looking into my eyes, nodding when I'm sure mine are wide as saucers in realisation of what he's admitting to me.

"They raped him?" I ask, my words barely there as tears spring to my eyes, unable to comprehend the pain he's repeatedly allowed himself to go through to keep me here. Safe.

Gray nods, his eyes dark, angry I realise. I doubt anyone will ever understand it, but I know as well as he does that we both care for Liam far more than either of us would care to admit. It's fucked, like completely and utterly deranged of us to care, but the longer I'm here, the more I see and get to know the Liam that is truly him rather the one I thought I had known my whole life, the more I realise that he's an entirely different man under the armour.

"He spent his childhood being abused in the same way. Dad told me about it years ago and now here… he went through it over and over again before you got here. They kept telling him if he did then they wouldn't take you and when they did, he knew it wouldn't end. Now you're here, they use you as his weakness. They know they can do anything to him because he'll allow it to protect you from the same fate. They've just not gone this far before by beating him too." His words stun me as I take in the reality of what they mean. My stomach drops, feeling empty and hollow yet so sickly at the same time as I think of what he's repeatedly been through, not just throughout his childhood but since being here, for me.

"How have I never noticed?" I ask aloud, unsure if I truly want the answer or not.

"He's used to putting up a front. It's something he's done for years, Char. I don't have a fucking clue who he really is, but I have a feeling it's not someone that's as bad as we think, or at least not someone that's just bad, you know?"

"Yeah, yeah I understand." He gives me another hug, waves goodbye, and walks away as I shut the door and find myself on the floor with my back to it, my knees curled up to my chest as I contemplate the information I've just been given.

I hear a door shut in the apartment and as my

294

head lifts, my eyes connect with Liam's, his body now clean of blood as he stands in the doorway to the living room with nothing but boxers covering him, the bruises and damage from the torture he's endured clear on his skin.

"Don't you fucking dare, Charlie." His voice is ice cold and filled with venom as he stares at me, his words making no sense in my mind.

"I'm not doing anything." It's as I speak the words that I realise I'm crying, the tears causing my voice to crack.

"He told you. I fucking told him not to say anything, the stupid fucking bastard." he mutters as he walks towards me, his steps still a little unsteady but far better than when he walked in.

"Stop looking at me like that. Stop feeling sorry for me, I don't need it and I don't fucking deserve it. Stop it," he orders as he crouches down in front of me with a hiss, the movement obviously causing him pain which only fills me with more sorrow and sadness.

"You don't get to decide what you deserve. If I want to feel sorry for you then I damn well will," I tell him, bravery and anger that I've not felt for a long time brimming and bubbling as I answer him back. Something I wouldn't have dared do mere hours ago. But I realise now, I know with complete certainty that he's been so hard on me because he knows nothing else, because he's been so determined to be sure I don't land upon the same torture that he has at the monsters' hands.

"Why are you so stubborn?" he asks with a small smile as he sits opposite me on the floor with his knees bent in front of him.

"Why are you so secretive?" I answer back with my own question, one I genuinely wish he would give me an answer for.

He huffs out a grunt as he watches me, his head shaking. "Why the hell do you have so much empathy for me?"

I sit silent for a moment, pondering his question.

"Either because I legitimately have Stockholm syndrome or because you're genuinely not as bad as I thought," I tell him honestly, curious about how he'll take my words.

His lips lift up in a boyish grin and then his body shakes as his head falls back, a laugh finding its way out of him.

"You think you have Stockholm syndrome? You've thought this through?" he asks as he wheezes, his laugh filling the air and lifting my sadness along with it as I smile at him.

I remember seeing him smile and laugh before he went to prison, but I'm not sure I've seen it or perhaps just paid attention since he's been out and yet as I watch him laugh now, see the happiness in his face, my stomach fills with unwelcome butterflies as I realise that I wish I could do this constantly. Make him smile. Make him happy.

"I don't know why you're laughing. I mean,

296

I've been kidnapped, it's a legit option here, Liam," I tell him, though seeing how free and open he looks as he laughs at me and my thought process has me denying the possibility.

"No, you're right, it's just funny that you've actually thought this through. I thought I'd broken you, and maybe I have in some way, but I don't think you're as broken as I thought you were. And since when do you answer me back? What's happened the last two days?" he asks, his voice light and happy.

"I'm pretty sure I'm broken beyond repair at this stage, but I still have a mind. I answer you back in my head mainly but I feel like I've seen you, like really seen you and you can't go back to being a dick now," I tell him honestly.

His smile drops as he watches me. He nods his head before letting it fall back again, his eyes looking heavenward before finding me again.

"I really didn't want to hurt you." He stops himself then, a small grin overtaking his face, transforming him completely, showing me how handsome he truly is when he's joyful and carefree. "OK, that's a lie. I'm a sadist in the sack but I mean, I didn't want to hurt you like I have. I didn't want to hurt you permanently, just for pleasure. I just didn't know how else to make you give in," he tells me, his honesty shocking me.

"A sadist in the sack," I repeat. He looks at me with a sly grin as he gets up, grabs my hands and lifts me to my feet, bringing us chest to chest. Or rather, bringing my head to his chest as I look up at his much taller frame.

"That's right. I don't know if you noticed, but I did say other words too. I like how it's just those words that you pick up on though," he tells me as he puts his hands in my hair and plays with the strands he finds.

"I'm well aware you said other words, I just got stuck on those. Does this all mean you'll stop being a dick and work with me now?" I ask.

His eyes lift above my head, searching the empty space beyond us as his teeth catch his bottom lip.

"Can I hug you now?" he asks, his eyes penetrating my own, this being the first time I recall him asking if he can touch me in any way. I take his question as an answer. It's the first time since I've been here that he's given me a choice rather than taking, manipulating, or forcing my touch.

I give him my answer without words as my arms reach around his back, meeting behind him as my face falls to his warm chest, his skin warm to the touch. He sighs into my hair before placing his arms around me, his body quivering and his breath catching as I land a small kiss on his chest.

"I'm feeling like I need to be a bit more frank with you considering we've just had a breakthrough, so ask me anything. Whatever you want, and I'll be honest. I'll tell you whatever you want to know. I can't be fucked with this anymore. Anything."

My mind whirls with possible questions, knowing that I have more than we could possibly have the time to ask.

"Is Crow really an O'Banian?" I ask, remembering the phone call with him from before I was taken.

Liam pushes me away, looks into my eyes, and nods at me with hesitance.

"Yeah, he's the son. Well, one of the sons." He nods.

Even with the hatred running through my veins for him before any of this happened, I believed him and I still do.

"How did this happen? Any of this?"

His hand reaches for my neck. He slides his fingers to my nape, running them along the back of my neck and my lower scalp before he speaks.

"Come and sit down. It's not exactly a short story."

Chapter 8

Charlie

Liam passes me a mug full of hot chocolate before taking a seat beside me on the sofa. I turn my body so that I'm facing him, my stomach filling with dread as I wait for the answer I've wanted to know for what feels like an eternity.

"I'm going to start right at the beginning. If you need me to stop or explain anything then you can ask, but it might take a while. It's… complicated," he finishes with a jerk of his head as he finds the word most suited to the story I'm patiently waiting to be told.

"I was abused as a kid. Gray probably told you that, but he nor your dad knew the extent of it. It wasn't just beatings and rape. I was groomed from the first moment I can remember to be what my father and his men wanted me to be. He was powerful. A business man that had more money than sense. More fucking insanity and hatred and want for more money than he ever really needed. So he used me. His friends had the most fucked up fantasies - all involving children. Me. So he charged them. They'd get time with me to do whatever they wanted, and he'd get a hefty cheque at the end of it. I never went to school. He hired a tutor and for the longest time, I would cry myself to sleep wondering how other kids

300

coped with this, because I assumed it was normal. I didn't know any different." He takes a breath, watching my reaction or purposeful lack of a reaction on my behalf. The sorrow I felt filling me made me want to cry for him, but I knew he wouldn't appreciate that and probably wouldn't continue if he saw me react that way, so I schooled my expressions.

Dad had hinted at Liam having had a bad upbringing, but I thought he meant divorced parents or an alcoholic father or a dead parent. Not for one moment did I assume it was ever this bad. I want nothing more than to comfort him, but I also don't want him to stop talking. He looks as though he needs to get it out as much as I want to hear it. I need to know what makes him tick, what makes him him, and what brought me to the situation I'm in now. I know that if I attempt to comfort him, he will take it as a sign of me not being able to cope, or he'll hate the sympathy and stop telling me anything, which is not what I want.

"So, this went on for years, until I met your dad. My father had asked me to go out and run some errands. I'd already tried to run away and was left nearly dead for it so I didn't ever try again. Your dad was there. We hit it off immediately, even though I had no fucking clue how to act around anyone aside from my dad, his friends, and the very few people I'd met outside of that circle of people. Your dad lived right by the depot my dad sent me to do errands and every time he saw me, he'd come out, take me inside, and feed me more food than I knew what to do with. I went there one day after a particularly bad beating. I was used the night before more brutally than I'd ever been and the moment your dad saw me, he told me he'd get me away from there. And he did. I never saw my dad or his men after that. I lived my life with you and your dad. Your mum, too, until she left and I thought I was healing. Until I was walking home with you from the shop one day and saw my dad stood right outside your front door. I shoved you inside of one of the men's houses closest to yours, told them to protect you with their life, and walked up to my father as if I wasn't more terrified than I ever had been in my life."

He takes a moment, his brows creasing together as his eyes look skyward, his gaze completely dazed as if recalling the events of that day as they happened exactly, unwilling to miss any small detail out now that he's started.

"What did he want?" I ask, though I have a creeping feeling that I know.

He looks at me after I speak, his eyes withdrawn somehow even though his gaze feels intense.

"He wanted me to work for him. In prison. If I refused, he would take you. He'd obviously been watching me for long enough to know that no matter who I was close with - your dad, Gray, the men at the club… he knew you were my one true weakness. He insisted that he had men that

302

could get you with a moment's notice, that he'd let me go when I had done what he wanted and that if I didn't do what was needed then he'd make sure his reach got you too and I had no doubt it would." His words shatter me completely. He'd lied - sort of at least when he'd told me the reasoning for his jail sentence when he first got out. But now that he is here, as his story is unfolding, I am beginning to understand and my heart breaks at the thought that I'd ever questioned him.

He had sacrificed himself for me in more ways than I ever truly realised, and I'd done nothing but question him and be unwilling to believe or understand his side of the story. I remember my dad telling me as a child that there were always two sides to every story and I realised now that I had never given him the chance to truly, openly give me his.

"That's why you were going to take me? So Gray and Crow were right, they just didn't understand why they were right." Liam nods as I put the pieces together - pieces that in all fairness, no one could have guessed or assumed without the knowledge that Liam is giving me.

"I planned on taking you away, but I got caught by two of my dad's men and they tried to take you instead. I killed them both and didn't fight or run when I was arrested. I worked for my father inside of prison and did everything I could to creep you out and push you away when I came out despite how much I wanted to do the opposite so that when he saw my life, he didn't see you actively in it. He knew I'd be living with you and your dad, but I needed you to despise me. I needed you to hate me or think badly of me. I didn't want him to know that you mattered, but he'd set a price on your head before I even got out of prison."

"A price on my head?" I question, reminding myself of how I ended up here or at least why I suspected I did. The money. The black market. The various people after me because of the price on my head. I had assumed it was something to do with the club, a rival or competitor, but it had nothing to do with me all along.

"We're in my father's domain, baby girl. That's the reason I can't get out."

I take in what he's said, trying to process why I'm where I am, and realise that it's because of his father wanting to hurt him. It's not my fault. Hell, it's not really got anything to do with me. I had assumed that it was a personal attack on my dad or the club, but I couldn't be more wrong.

It's not my fault.

It's not his either, but this time when I tell myself that it isn't my fault, I believe it. It was some fucked up attempt at Liam's father wanting to get to him. I could have been anyone Liam cared about, and although I can see why Liam has that grimace on his face as he sits there and undoubtedly blames himself, I know that it isn't his fault either and that he's protected me from the worst - giving me the lesser of two evils.

Signed with Love duet
J R Dust

Always. He has been taking my place to ensure that I'm kept safe or as safe as he can keep me.

My heart soars as I watch him, his face in his hands with his elbows on his knees. He looks completely shattered. Broken. Beyond repair, and so much of me wants to fix that.

"Why didn't you tell my dad? How did Gray end up here?" I ask, realising that there must be more he needs to tell me.

Liam doesn't move from his crouched over position but does begin to speak.

"When I saw my father all those years ago and even up until you got here, he insisted that if I told anyone, if I did anything to jeopardise him, he would make sure you all went through a worse fate than death. I had no idea who I could trust. He made me a paranoid mess, thinking that everyone was out to get me. I had no idea what to do. I know I could have done things better but in the moment, I had no idea how. This isn't some excuse; I know I've done things to you that are unforgivable. I know that, but I'd prefer to be the one to hurt you than them. I can't bear the thought of any of them having their hands on you. I'd prefer to be the villain in your story than them." His voice is barely above a whisper, his admission halting my thoughts.

He has been the villain in my story for so long and I've let him be. He's let himself be. When I spoke to him on the phone, he didn't try to redeem himself or make excuses, he let me think the worst.

"What about Gray? He said he was looking for our mum."

He sits up now, running his hand through his hair before looking at me and letting out a low, humourless chuckle.

"He did. He found her. She's with my dad. I have no idea if it was a coincidence or if my dad planned it that way, but he found her with my dad. They're together," he says with a wince.

My brain seems to be having a momentary lapse in sanity. A manic and crazed laugh leaves my lips as I watch Liam for any signs of a lie, but there are none. He's deadly serious.

"You're wrong."

Liam watches me carefully, obviously realising how utterly confused I am as I attempt (and fail) to process what he's told me. She can't be here. In the very same building that I am.

"Why hasn't Gray told me?"

"He didn't want to hurt you. He didn't want you to know that the person that birthed you, the one that was supposed to love you, was in all of this fucked up shit." He sighs.

"She knows about everything?" I ask.

I knew that she must have been heartless to leave two children behind, but to help or even just know about her two said children being taken, held against their will and her daughter being raped and doing nothing about it is a whole new level of bad. I've not had a child. I'm not a mother but surely, surely that can't be right. I know it's not.

306

Signed with Love duet
J R Dust

"Everything," Liam says with a small nod of his head.

My eyes flit back and forth, unable to still themselves as I think over the situation I've found myself in.

I need comfort and at this moment, Liam is the one I want that comfort from. I shift across the sofa and plant myself on his lap. He seems momentarily stunned before he wraps his arms around me and buries his head in my hair.

"I know it's not the fairytale kind of love that you probably wish for but I do love you, Charlie. I'll never let anyone harm you ever again, I hope you know that." His promise and truth mean more to me now than anything ever has before - mainly because I believe him. Without saying a word, I curl up on his lap and snuggle up to his chest, listening to his heart beat for me.

Chapter 9

Charlie

Assuming everything went to plan, we would be leaving tonight. I am going home. I did everything I could not to get my hopes up too high. It didn't go to plan last time, and there is nothing to say that it will now.

I wasn't sure if Gray had told Liam about the plan to leave. I hadn't, but I hope that he knows. I want him to come with us - to leave this hell hole and live a life away from the father that had controlled his every waking moment. I know he is on my side but that doesn't strictly mean that he is OK with me leaving, so I have stayed silent.

"I'm going to fucking kill them all one day," Liam roars as he slams the door open and walks into the apartment.

His hoodie is, as usual, stained with blood - whose I don't know. His body is recovering, and I can't see any obvious or new wounds on him, so I assume it's not his blood.

"What happened?" I ask as I pause the television to give him my full attention.

"They get off on beating the initiates. They killed one tonight," he tells me, his arms flailing around, signalling towards the door.

My heart sinks at the idea of someone being killed. Even if they weren't a good person by society's standards, that doesn't mean they deserve death. If the initiates here are anything like the ones that often join the Cobras, they're likely younger people trying to get away from a life they dread going home to.

I highly doubt it's the first time it's happened, but it is the first time he's come back and told me anything about his day. It seems our breakthrough really did mean honesty from here on out.

"Is there no way you can leave? Get out of this and get away from it all? If me and Gray found a way out, would you leave with us?"

"It's not as simple as that. If I left, he'd only find me again." He sighs as he takes a seat at the dining room table, his hands clasped together in front of him on the table as his eyes drift off in thought.

Unsure of how best to alleviate his stress, I do the one thing that I know I shamefully crave and he always wants. Touch.

I stand behind him and let my hands travel over his neck, his shoulders, and to his front. My hands wander over his chest as I press light kisses along his neck, feeling his muscles tense before relaxing under my touch.

"What are you doing?" he asks, his voice strained and thick with desire.

"I'm giving myself to you," I whisper into his ear.

"Willingly." I'm not sure if he's asking or stating a fact as he says the word, so I show him.

Signed with Love duet
J R Dust

I move his hands from the table to his sides and straddle his lap, my hands on the back of his neck.

His eyes are dark - hungry as he looks into my eyes, as if looking for any sign of hesitation on my behalf. There is none. Some deep part of me feels endlessly guilty, as if I'm cheating on Victor and Crow, consensually giving myself to Liam without force, coercion, or physical violence forcing my hand, but the part of me that's at the forefront of my mind now wants him.

I want him.

I want to please him. I want to give him the part of me that he's not yet willingly had. I need to be his as much as I need to breathe.

I can feel his hardening length beneath me, his breaths harsh and uncertain as he watches my every move.

I run my hands through his thick hair as I trace my lips along his jaw and his neck, sucking on the delicate skin ever so slightly. My lips find his. He doesn't move or engage for a moment - and then the world ends and begins with us as he ravages my mouth, his tongue finding mine in a fiery battle of wills for dominance. His hands cling to my hips, the pain from his rough grasp on me setting my core alight above the hard length of his cock jutting towards me, jolting me skyward. His mouth doesn't leave mine, though he does end the hungry kiss, our breaths mingling and violent as he fists a hand in my hair and pulls my head from his.

310

Signed with Love duet
J R Dust

His eyes sear into mine, his gaze alluring and confounding.

"If you don't really want this, you have to tell me now because once I start, I'm not going to stop, Charlie. You can tell me no a million times, but it's not going to happen unless you say no right now." His words are somehow the sweetest he's ever said, which has got to make me the most fucked up person to think so but for the first time since I got here, he's letting me out. He's letting me say no. He's giving me a choice even if he's not giving me one after that word comes out of my mouth.

"I want you, Liam. I want you inside of me," I tell him shyly, my adrenaline-filled bravery from only moments ago having evaporated and leaving me meek and small once more.

He lets out a sound not dissimilar to a roar as he picks me up, his lips finding mine again as he devours me while carrying me towards what I have to assume is the bedroom.

My body is thrown down onto the bed, the whole bed shaking under the weight of me being thrown its way. I lay there startled but brimming with excitement as I watch Liam undress in front of me, his thick and powerful muscles rippling as he moves and throws his clothes to the ground beneath him.

When he's done and stands stark naked in front of me, my eyes automatically draw down to the erect cock wishing for attention.

"Strip for me, baby girl."

I stand and strip slowly, accentuating every movement I make in the hopes of turning him on even more. When I finally see his face, I realise that it worked. His eyes look practically soullessly dark as he appreciates the sight of me, his eyes appraising every bare part of me.

"You're so fucking beautiful." His words and the low hum of his voice have the desired effect, shooting straight to my core.

"Lay on the bed for me." His command is simple, and yet my mind wanders and jumps as I do as he says.

"Spread your legs for me."

I do just that, waiting with eager anticipation as I bare myself to him. He takes a moment to look, his eyes filled with adoration and lust as he does before his face fills the gap between my legs, his tongue gliding from my clit and back down, the feverish actions of a starved man.

His teeth nip at my bud, my hands grasping his hair as he squeezes the skin on my inner thighs while working me closer and closer to the brink with his tongue and his fingers beginning to fill me.

A sound unlike any I've made before leaves my lips, my desperation leading my hands to claw and pull at his hair, pulling him closer to me as if he could possibly be any nearer.

When my orgasm rears to life, I hear myself as if unpretentious calling his name, my thighs closing in around his head as he rides and laps up the wave of the lust-filled sin that escapes my body.

He rises from his position, holding my legs apart as he settles between them, his cock sliding along my entrance with ease, my wet embrace urging him on as he looks at me with love filling his eyes before entering me in one swift and harsh motion. A low gasp escapes me at the shock of his abrupt entry. He waits a moment for me to adjust before he begins pounding into me, my legs clinging around his waist as I thrust my hips up to match his quickening pace.

His hands take hold of my waist and hips as he rocks our bodies together as one, the actions along with the friction from his body on mine causing a yielding heat to pool between my legs. The slapping sound of his body beating against mine does nothing but make the frenzied look in his eyes more hungry and desperate as he roars to life and flippantly rolls into me repeatedly.

The orgasm within me begs for release, my body pathetically desperate for more as he utters curses, his hand in my hair as he ruggedly releases his load within me, his cock twitching and sending me just far enough for my own orgasm to follow his.

His body falls limply on top of my own, the warmth and security of his body on mine bringing me peace as I close my eyes and smile while he plants light kisses along my face. My eyelids, my cheeks, my lips, my jaw, and my neck.

"Come here," Liam grunts out as he flips us

over so that he's on his back and I'm lying on top of him while he's still nestled inside of me.

"I need to go to the bathroom and clean up," I insist with a smile, watching as he shakes his head and looks at me with mocking disapproval.

"No, you don't. You're staying here. I'm staying inside of you and not a single bit of my cum is leaving your body. You're mine, baby girl, and anyone that tries to tear you away from my body right now will be fucking sliced and fed to the pigs."

I can't help the sudden laugh that leaves my lips as he speaks, the seriousness of his crinkled brows and the wonder in his eyes as he watches me laugh.

"Why are you laughing at me? I'm being fucking serious," he says. "Unless you need to piss, then you can go. I'm not into piss play. But if you go to pee then I'm filling you back up when you come back," he tells me sternly.

"I'm laughing because you sound crazy and I don't hate it," I tell him honestly. He opens one eye to look at me again, his arms wrapping around my body before sighing and closing his eyes again.

"Wait, do you need to pee?" I shake my head with a blinding smile and fall asleep nestled into his chest with his arms cocooned around me.

Chapter 10

Charlie

The soft shaking of my body jolts me awake. I had tried to make sure I didn't fall asleep but my eyes closed and surrendered to sleep before I knew what was happening.

My body moves, suddenly aware of what's happening anytime now. *What time is it?*

"You need to get dressed. They'll be here soon." Liam.

I'm stunned into silence as I listen to his words, confirming his knowledge of us going and yet he's doing nothing to stop it. Why? Why is he letting me go? Is he coming with us? Despite the many terrible things he's done, I can't bear the idea of leaving him here. Or leaving him at all. After the truth and heartbreak of his life, I realise that no matter what he's done, I want him, his life entwined with my own somehow.

He gets out of bed and begins dressing himself in his usual clothes and then pulling out his riding leathers. Why is he putting his leathers on? My mind is racing with possibilities as I sit, stunned, unable to move as I attempt to process what's happening in front of me. I shift my eyes to the clock. 11.45p.m. Fifteen minutes.

"Baby girl, listen to me. As much as I'd love to stay here with you all night, they'll be here any minute and even though I have no doubt you'll tell them everything, them walking in on you naked in my bed isn't high on my priority list, and I somehow doubt it's what you want either. You need to get dressed," he tells me hurriedly, his hands on either side of my face as his eyes beat into mine before he begins rummaging through his drawers and pulls out some of my clothes.

I take action and get dressed as quickly as I can, part of me questioning if this is some kind of trap, but I'm so uncertain that I have very little idea what to say. No. He wants out as much as I do. Where's Gray?

"Put these on," he says as he hands his leathers to me. So, they're not for him.

"Why?" My voice is more timid than it's been in months, the confusion I'm feeling coming front and centre.

"They're not much but they'll protect you more than your clothes will if shots are fired," he says as he pulls the jacket around me and zips up the front.

"Why are you letting this happen?" I ask, realising too late that it sounds like I'm sad at the prospect of leaving when in reality all I should be feeling is joyous at the idea, yet his apprehension and willingness to let me go confounds me.

Liam stops, turns, looking at me with nothing but sincerity as he steps closer. The heat from his body is felt all over mine even though he's not touching me.

He sighs, his eyes low before he looks into my eyes again.

316

"I've already taken up too much of your time and inflicted more hurt on you than I wanted to. It's time for you to go home, baby girl. It's time for you to heal and live your life." My mind is blank as I take in his words, unsure of why or how he's come to this conclusion, but thankful all the same.

"Thank you." My words are a whisper, barely spoken, but I know he heard me, his eyes filling with sorrow as he wraps his arms around me and pulls me into his chest. I hug him, my arms around him as I nestle my head into him further, holding back the unshed tears that threaten to spill over.

It's not a moment later that I hear what can only be described as pure chaos in the building surrounding us as the front door to the apartment bursts open.

Gray rounds the corner, a gun in his hand, his eyes scanning the scene in front of him with confusion and a sad understanding - myself pulling away from Liam's embrace.

"Charlie! Is she in here? Charlie!" a voice I would recognise anywhere shouts from the lounge and before I know what I'm doing, my legs are leading the way to him. The moment he comes into view, the tears I previously held captive lose the battle, the tears and emotion pouring out of me at the sight of him as he takes me into a bear crushing hug, the tears that I attempted to hold in falling freely down my dad's shoulder as he hangs onto me for dear life.

"Oh, Charlie," he whispers, his voice sounding hoarse in my ear as he holds my head in place at his nape.

His hands move from my back, placing me down as his eyes turn to black slits of anger when he looks up to see Liam mere feet away from him.

Liam looks at me and nods his head with a weak smile before laying his eyes back upon my father's, his guard down, his eyes forgiving of what he knows will come. And it's him giving up that stops me because no matter who he is or what he's done, the stupid, stupid part of me that could feel empathy for anyone doesn't want this.

"He stopped them from hurting me," I practically yell as my dad's hand halts mid-air with the gun faced directly at Liam's head. I don't dare look at Liam or Gray, knowing that they'll both be as surprised as I am, understanding more of the why than my dad ever will.

My dad's eyes find mine, his arm not moving.

"What happened?" he asks, his words coming out harsher than I've probably ever heard.

"I have no idea, I just know that he protected me and took more beatings to protect me than I ever had to take," I tell him honestly. "And he knows things, it might not be much but it's more than me and Gray know. He knows a lot more than we could tell you. He can help." I feel like I'm manipulating him. My words aren't a lie, not in the slightest but I, as well as Liam and Gray, know that I'm stalling. I'm stalling the end of Liam's life. For some unknown reason that even I can't fathom. Except I do know, my clambering and shattering heart knows damn well why I can't and won't let him die.

"Did he do that to you?" he asks, not moving, though I know exactly what he means. The scar - the one that tears across my cheek. It's the first time he's truly seen it, having only seen me run up to him in a flurry moments ago, not giving him the chance to see the physical change in me.

"No. I don't have a single scar on my body from him."

"Fuck." My dad drops his arm and brings the gun to his side at the exact moment that I hear footsteps to my right.

"Is he on our side or theirs?" my dad asks me, his gaze not leaving Liam.

"Ours. I promise you; he's been forced into this as much as Gray and I have been." I watch my dad as he nods his head, his body posture relaxing as he goes up to Liam and takes him into a hug, patting him on the back. Liam looks as stunned as I feel.

"Charlie?" The voice is low, filled with pain and anguish, a quiet wonder as I turn and lay my sights upon one of the two men that have filled my dreams and nightmares since the first moment I found myself trapped in this hellhole.

The room stills, time slowing as I take in the outgrown and messy beard covering his lower face, the black under his eyes, the ruthless muscles soaring from his clothes and the heavy breathing of Crow. My Crow.

He takes a step towards me, his eyes assessing and curious as he looks me over, his gaze roaming over my body, presumably checking me for injuries.

His eyes seem to land on the scar on my face. It's strange, seeing him now mere feet away from me when it's the very thing I've hoped for and dreamt of since I first arrived here.

I feel my chest heaving, my face shaking, my eyes stinging with unshed tears that come to life for what feels like the millionth time tonight as Crow puts his hands on each side of my face, his eyes not leaving mine.

"Come here, princess." Crow's voice sends shivers down my spine as I recall the comfort he brings me just being in his presence. He wraps me in his arms and I feel my body sinking, floating, revelling in his strength as he holds onto me for dear life.

God, I've missed him.

"You're never fucking leaving my side again. Not to fucking shit or piss or fucking breathe. Nothing. Never again," Crow tells me as he pulls me into his arms, the warmth of his body surrounding me as he strokes his hand through my hair.

———

"This really wasn't necessary. I promise I'm fine,"

320

I tell my dad as Gray shakes his head at me from behind him.

I knit my brows together, wondering what he's trying to get across to me with his stern expression and the shake of his head.

"Yeah, well, I'm sorry if I want my recently kidnapped daughter checked over," he tells me sarcastically as he grips my hand tighter.

He's not let go of my hand since we left a few hours ago. I was stuck in what I found out was a hotel Liam's dad owns and uses as their base as we left. I hadn't been allowed to leave Liam's apartment so aside from seeing trees and parked cars outside of the windows, I had no idea where I'd been. Crow and my dad's best friend, Tin, escorted Liam back to the Clubhouse while Dad drove me and Gray to the private hospital The Cobras and a few other MCs uses. It is paid for solely through the cash of multiple Clubs, meaning that only they have access.

I wonder for the first time where Victor is. Considering the way we left things, I found myself surprised that he wasn't with them. I know from the way my thoughts have ventured that I need to talk to him, to be as honest as I could be. I'm not sure that I care for him in the way I do for Crow.

The bright lights in the private room the doctor had taken me to makes my head ache. I am exhausted. I need sleep.

The doctor has examined me, taken bloods, checked all of the freshest injuries to my body, and is due to come back any moment with results. Although my physical injuries are less than pleasant, I know there is nothing permanently wrong with me. I hope. The only shameful thing I am concerned about is contracting an STD. I have no idea where Liam or the others have been and dread the idea that I have been given something potentially permanent that could alter the rest of my life but with my dad and Gray by my side, my mind was thinking positively, even with the niggle of negativity being thrown in every few minutes. I push it back and force my concentration on my dad.

"We're going to have to talk to you properly when we're back. We need to know everything that's happened. Everything you've seen and everything that's happened to you," my dad tells me gently. He must have an idea of what's gone on, even if he doesn't want to admit it to himself.

I keep forgetting about the scar across my face, having lived with it for long enough and having seen it so many times in the mirror as I stare back at myself, but I forget that he isn't used to it. Every time he looks at me, his eyebrows draw together, his cheeks pinch, and his mouth twitches. I can tell he's doing his best not to stare, but I also know how I used to be if I saw someone with a scar. I think back to the way I used to look at Edgar - one of the rival mc president's sons. Admittedly he had a bad enough reputation to want to keep me away anyway but with the reputation he held alongside the burns covering so much of him, it scared me and I often found myself staring in wonder without even realising it. Only Gray and Liam had seen me since the first night aside from the doctor that was there so I hadn't had to witness the stares, but I have no doubt I will now that it is time for me to go home.

Thinking about Edgar gives me the reminder of Alice who I have avoided thinking about at all costs. I still don't know if the Clubhouse had been attacked the night I was taken or if it was just me that had been attacked. If it was the club, I have no idea if Alice is alive or not and, until now, I hadn't had anyone to ask that would know or give me the answer.

"The night I was taken, what happened?" I ask my dad as I rub my fingers along his hands, my attempt at comforting him as I ask him to think back on what must have been a horrendous night for him.

I had spent so long thinking about it in the earlier days of being away from my life that although it stung to think about the events that took place that night, it doesn't hurt now the same way it once did.

"Crow was ambushed. That's how they got to you. A fight broke out in the rest of the club, but only five men were found. They were killed on sight. No one was lethally harmed from our side if that's what you're wondering." He always has a knack for knowing where my thoughts are, and at this moment I am grateful for that.

323

"Is Alice OK? Is she still with the Cobras?"

My dad looks at me in question as if it's such a stupid thing to ask then shakes his head, wiping whatever thought it is entering his mind away.

"You could say that. There's been… a truce of sorts since she and Edgar got closer. She hasn't seen him in months though. She said she couldn't bear to since you were gone and she had no idea if he was a part of it or not. He helped us get to you though. All of his men did," he says begrudgingly. Accepting the help and being thankful for the help offered to you are two very different things, and despite how grateful I am to be more free than I have been for what feels like an eternity, I can understand his hesitation at using the support of others to get here. The Cobras will now owe them, and knowing my father and his love for us, he would have offered anything.

"What was the deal?" I ask, concern filling my voice as I watch him for any giveaways or signs of admission.

"There wasn't one, that's the problem. I didn't even ask. They offered their help willingly with no stipulations, but you know what this is like. They'll ask for something. Eventually." The unknown is worse. That's why he is so on guard. He has no idea when the request for a favour returned will come in, nor does he know what it will be, but as a man of loyalty and worth, he will pay it - whatever the cost.

I watch as my dad pulls his hands away from

324

me and begins twitching with them in his lap. I'm not sure if he's just nervous and anxious, considering how tense this must have been for him, or if it's something more.

"Are you OK?" I ask him. His cheeks puff out as he sighs and takes a deep breath before speaking.

"I need to apologise to you, Charlie."

"What for?" Gray told me that Dad would feel guilty for not getting to us sooner, but I didn't once anticipate him being right. I have no doubt that he did everything he possibly could to find us the moment he knew I was gone, as well as Gray.

"For Victor. The marriage. The deal and the merge of the Clubs. I knew you weren't ready, that you didn't want it, and I made you feel like you didn't have a choice despite knowing that. Having you disappear made me realise how much I've done wrong as a father and I'm sorry. I'm sorry to both of you for not being better than I have been," he finishes as he looks between myself and Gray before looking down to his twiddling hands again.

Gray and I share a look, Gray's full of sadness that I understand.

"Dad, it's fine. This is your life. It's hard for you to separate them and us, we get that, but I'm pretty sure I can talk for both of us when I say that things won't be the same anymore, and I don't think we want them to be. We all need change and that includes you, old man," Gray says as he pats my dad's shoulder and throws a

Signed with Love duet
J R Dust

small, hesitant smile my way.

Chapter 11

Charlie

I thought I would be thrilled to be home and though a part of me is, the most prominent part of my brain feels lost being in a bedroom that I know is mine. But it seems nothing like mine anymore.

I purposefully stayed downstairs with Dad and Gray for as long as I could, putting off the inevitable return to a space that was once mine but no longer feels that way. Dad asked if we - Gray and I - wanted to go to bed. It's just past 6am and neither of us have slept since we woke yesterday morning, but my mind is wide awake, no sleepiness in sight as I attempt to adjust my mind to the freedom we now have.

We could go anywhere and yet I don't want to venture anywhere at all. When I stopped on the stairs and wondered where I'd rather be, knowing that I didn't want to be here, nowhere felt like home. Not my childhood home I was now standing in, nor the Clubhouse, or the houses of the Cobras men surrounding us. Not my best friend, Alice's home or Victor's. Nowhere.

I've aged only a few months and yet it feels like I've been gone for decades when I look around the room filled with innocence and evidence of my youth and naivety.

Everything is exactly as it was. My bedsheets

have been changed but my diary is still out, the books I was reading are still misplaced on the floor and my makeup is still open on my desk counter.

"Are you OK?" Gray asks.

I spin around to find him searching the room similarly to myself. Remembering the years we spent having sleepovers in here and found joy in the simplest things. Only, it's not just me that left and came back a different person. He did too.

"Are you?" I wonder as I watch his eyes spin around the space surrounding us.

His eyes find mine, no doubt mirroring my own with the sadness and guilt.

"I honestly have no fucking idea, Chars. It's going to take some time for both of us. I don't know where we fit in anymore or where we go from here, but we'll work it out, alright? Together," he says solemnly and with promise as he takes a step towards me and engulfs me in his arms.

"Together," I repeat, knowing that he and only he understands what my mind is doing because his is surely doing just the same.

Gray pulls away as I hear the familiar sound of our dad's heavy footfalls on the stairs. Gray gives me a sad smile, knowing unlike anyone else how I'm feeling.

It's at times like these that I can't even begin to imagine how it must be for those that don't have siblings. It makes me all the more grateful to have Gray by my side throughout life.

Signed with Love duet
J R Dust

"Knock, knock, you decent, Charlie?" my dad asks, accompanied by a couple of thumps on the door.

"Yeah, come in." I plaster on a smile as the door swings open and reveals my dad stood there accompanied by Tin. Dad said he was there during the rescue, but I hadn't seen him with all of the chaos.

"Oh, look at you both, my little spy and the troublemaker," Tin says as he pulls me and Gray into his embrace and squeezes me enough that I have to tap his back and let him know to loosen his grip a little.

As someone that's been in my life for as long as I can remember, he's like the unofficial uncle I never really had or knew I needed.

I notice as he pulls away and gazes down at us both that his smile is genuine. He doesn't seem to worry about his every move or word, unlike everyone else I've come across so far since being home - not as though that's very many people in all fairness.

"They might not be comfortable with that, Tin," my dad echoes under his breath in the background. He looks uncomfortable as he watches the three of us, seemingly unsure of how to proceed but obviously wanting to protect us and our sanity, even from Tin.

"It's fine, honestly, Dad. The more people faff to me and make me feel like I've been through something, the more it makes me feel like I have. The closer to normality I can get, the better." I feel uncomfortable saying the words despite them being the truth.

I'm usually open and comfortable with my feelings but having to repeat anything to do with the experiences of the last few months makes my stomach churn.

"Agreed," Gray chimes in as he wraps an arm around Dad's shoulders and knocks his head against the side of Dad's.

"See, it's fine, you old whinge bag. Now go make me a cuppa, will ya?" Tin pushes my dad out the door before giving both Gray and I a wink and a smile as he turns his head and leaves behind Dad.

"It's going to be like this for ages, until we've seen everyone again, isn't it?" Gray asks me as he falls back on my bed and pats the space beside him, signalling for me to join him.

I do just that, enjoying the soft material and familiar comfort of my bed.

"Yep, I have a feeling it is. The more I sit here and wallow in my self-pity, the closer I'm going to get to losing my mind. I don't want to be stuck in here. I want to live my life," I tell him quietly as I stare up at the blank ceiling above us.

"What do you want to do?"

"I want to be a writer. I'm going to make it happen. I'm so sick of bad, just bad everything, I'm going to make my life good," I tell him with a determined smile.

I have no idea where I'll start or what I'll do to get where I want to be, but I do know that I want to try. I don't want to hold back or wait for anything anymore. If I want something, I'm going to be a stubborn sod and bloody well make it happen.

"What about you? What do you want to do?" I ask him as I flip onto my stomach and watch him as he bites the inside of his cheek and pinches his brows together.

"I honestly have no idea. I've never known. I just know I want more than this now. I don't know what more is though."

"You'll figure it out, I'll help. We need to move on, make our own lives." Gray nods his head at me, agreeing before closing his eyes.

"I'm just going to rest for a bit and then we can make new lives, OK?" he says, sleeping as he rolls over on the bed and pulls a pillow under his head.

I lay my head down but know that sleep won't be coming for me anytime soon. I can very rarely switch off and fall asleep quickly, no matter how exhausted I am.

I think back to what it is I want to do. I want to write. I have more ideas than I know what to do with, but I have no idea if that's really something I could pursue.

When I think about my life in the years ahead, I can imagine myself with children one day. I can see myself living peacefully in the countryside not far from where we are now and despite how much I've always envisioned a future without the Cobras in it, I can't seem to shake the feeling that they'll always be a part of my life and so much of me is grateful for that. The Cobras have been a family to me for the longest time as I've grown up, adapted to the world, and tried to figure out who I am.

_____

Dad squeezed me fresh orange juice that tastes heavenly to go with my breakfast - well, it's mid-afternoon but I've just woken up and Gray is still sleeping and since I haven't eaten since last night, I feel practically starved.

I eat the food from the plate in front of me, devour it more like. I feel as though I have a never ending and never full stomach to contend with right now. Being away from constant danger will likely have that effect on you, though, I imagine. I mean, I ate well before but I feel insatiable today.

Through my breakfast, I notice, but make a point not to be obvious that I've noticed, Dad staring at me. I'm not sure he even realises that he's doing it but every time I glance in his direction, he's watching me. Sometimes with a small smile and other times with a gaze filled with worry and wonder. I can't imagine how awful the last few months must have been for him, but I also don't know how to comfort him. I'm not sure that giving him a hug will help. In all honesty, I don't think anything will help aside from him knowing I'll never leave his side again.

Signed with Love duet
J R Dust

"Who gave you that scar, Charlie?" My body freezes at his words, his question.

I'm not sure I want to answer but I also can't not. If I tell him who gave me it, he'll ask how I got it and even though I've had the all clear from the hospital and they have my full reports and want to start counselling to help me talk through things at which point I'm sure I will be honest, I'm not sure how I can be right now with him - and yet I don't want to lie either.

"One of the men that took me," I tell him, figuring it's the truth and hopefully enough.

"Did they…" He pauses, scratching the side of his face along the scruffy beard that's grown. "Did they hurt you in, you know, in other ways, Charlie?" He grimaces as the words come out, his intention with the question clear.

I find myself hesitant to answer. I don't want to answer - not just because I don't want to have this conversation but because I know it'll break his heart. But I also don't want to start lying to him. My mind whizzes with possible answers that I could give him without lying but without telling the truth and yet they all seem ludicrous or unbelievable, even in my own head.

"Just once. I never saw them again," I tell him, sticking to the truth. I didn't ever see them again and I didn't ask what had happened, where they were, or if they were in the same building that I was living in because I didn't want to know.

His face contorts in agony, his eyes closing as he takes a deep and ragged breath before opening his glassy eyes and looking at me again.

"Liam didn't let me out of his apartment there – he said it was too dangerous. I only saw him, Gray, and the doctor the whole time I was there. No one else was allowed in, and I didn't go out. Even if he had let me, it's not as though I would have wanted to." My dad nods at me, his face clearing as he takes in my words.

"They looked after you?" he asks, his voice sketchy and unsure.

"Yeah, they helped me a lot. I wouldn't have got through it without them." It's the first time I've said it or even thought about it and truly meant it. I hadn't thought about it before, but it is true. If Liam hadn't done what he had for me, I have no idea what would have happened to me or how I would have survived. If I had survived at all.

"Charlie, darlin, I need to talk to you about a few things..." My dad sounds so unsure of himself, and I dread to think what comes next as I wait for him to continue.

In a moment that I thought was about to be either heartfelt and comforting or downright dreadful, the front door springs open, hitting the wall behind it with a thunderous roar as scuffling sounds from behind me. I twist in my chair to look down the hallway only to freeze in place as I take in the scene in front of me.

What the hell is going on?

Crow and Liam are scrapping, if you can even call it that, as they are both attempting to get into the house. My dad must have got up without me

334

realising because between the unintelligible shouting, my dad is trying to split the two up, his own voice shouting and joining in with theirs.

It isn't until Gray comes down the stairs, his hair dishevelled and his eyes still half closed, that I lift myself from the chair and make a move towards the three men currently having a very tightly contained shouting match in the hallway. At least they'd got inside the house now. Most of our neighbours are members of the Cobras, but for the ones that aren't, they would not be happy about this chaos on our very literal doorstep.

Gray's eyes travel from the scene in front of us to me, back again and then land on the ceiling as he sighs, rubs his eyes, and comes down towards me.

"What's happening?" he asks, his voice still hoarse and filled with sleep.

"I have got absolutely no idea," I tell him as I continue watching as my dad pushes Crow and Liam apart, one hand on either of their chests.

"Will one of you please tell me what the fuck is going on here?" My dad's voice reverberates off the walls. His back is to me, but I have no doubt he's glaring at them as his head swivels between the two men.

Silence. Gray stood at my side, obviously just as curious about what and why they woke him as I am.

"Well? Someone. Fucking. Speak." Dad exaggerates and articulates his every word, honing the message home that he's not putting up with this shit right now.

"He hasn't been interviewed yet and when I got to the door, he just fucking shows up when he's supposed to be at the Club being guarded since we don't have a fucking clue who's side he's on, and now he's staking some fucked up, old man shitty fucking claim on Char," Crow says as he takes a breath and steps away from my dad. And then I replay his words in my head. Oh shit.

"I swear to fucking God, I'm gonna lose my mind," my dad says as he pinches the top of his nose and looks heavenward. "Liam, what the fuck Is going on? Why aren't you at the club?" my dad asks, his head swinging to Liam as he does, his hands flying up in the air in exasperation.

Liam looks at me, his eyes tender and sincere before he looks stone cold as his gaze returns to my dad.

"I am not staying away from Charlie for another second, I don't give a shit what you think or want. They're still fucking out there and until someone annihilates the lot of them, I'm not leaving her side. You can interrogate me with her there, she knows everything anyway." Liam's words practically gut punch me.

I had spent so long since being home just becoming accustomed to being away from that place that I hadn't considered the possibility of being taken again. Without Gray and Liam there, I have no doubt so much worse than what did would happen to me. Things that I wouldn't recover from.

"It's an interview, not an interrogation." My dad sighs as he shakes his head in defeat, letting both Crow and Liam pass.

Crow reaches me first, taking me in his arms and filling me with warmth. It feels unbelievably nice to be in his arms again.

After being with someone nearly 24/7 daily for months to being without them for so long, I probably missed his presence the most.

"You alright, man?" Crow asks Gray as he pulls back from me and gives him a bro hug and pats him on the back.

I watch as Liam stands unmoving in the hallway, my dad telling him that it's not an interrogation. Liam doesn't seem to be listening or caring for my dad's words though.

It's hard to imagine how close they've been for so many years when I see Liam so detached now. It's as though the front he's always put on has been wiped away and he's been left a very nearly empty shell of the man I remember as a child.

And then for the first time since any of this happened, I think of my dad. Really think of my dad. And Liam. And the fact that I've had sex with Liam. Willingly. Encouraged it even.

Oh fuck.

How on earth I hadn't thought of or considered this before is beyond me. I knew he was my dad's best friend. I knew it shouldn't have happened and yet even through the force, I let it.

337

I allowed it and even wanted and begged for it.

I've not spoke with anyone about how things unfolded with Liam. I have no doubt that the people closest to me at least will ask for more details soon enough and though part of me wants to hide the undeniable connection that Liam and I have, I hate to see him in a place surrounded by people and yet looking so isolated and lonely.

I take a step closer to him, my eyes not leaving his as he gives me a small, lopsided smile, unsure of himself and undoubtedly unsure of how I want this to go. It's one thing to be open and vulnerable and true with him when it's just him and me, but it's a whole other matter when those I care for most are around me. And yet, like Gray said - things aren't going to be the same and I'm determined to live the life I want to, doing whatever it is I want to rather than holding back for the sake of anyone else so I do the one thing that I know we both need and rush into his arms, relief filling me when I feel his head come down onto mine and his arms wrap around my smaller frame.

"Where's the shithead?" Liam asks as he pulls back from the short embrace and looks around.

"Who's shithead, exactly?" my dad asks as his brows bunch together.

"Victor," Gray answers for him. I find myself looking towards him while he speaks and see Crow watching me with a curious gaze, his eyes flitting to Liam occasionally before he nods his head as if in answer to his own question and throwing a mischievous grin my way.

"Victor wants a word with you," Crow tells me, his eyes portraying nothing as he watches me, and yet I watch as the look on his face changes when my dad turns to him and gives him a small shake of his head.

"What's going on?" I ask. It seems they both know something they aren't willing to share with me. Why am I not surprised?

"You'd think after being kidnapped and held hostage for so long, you guys would reflect and realise that I need to know stuff at this stage," I tell them both, understanding that it isn't necessarily Crow that isn't willing to tell me but rather my dad, and Crow is simply going along with my dad's orders.

"I'll go get him. The sooner you know, the sooner you can make your own decision about where to go from here," Crow says, his hooded and wary eyes catching mine as he eyes Liam once more before kissing my forehead and leaving through the front door.

Chapter 12

Charlie

Victor looks nervous. Very, very nervous. His eyes keep shifting around the room towards my dad and Crow, who won't stop glaring at him.

"What happened? Why are you staring at him like you want to murder him?" I ask, hoping it'll lighten the mood and one of them will tell me that they don't actually want to murder him, but they don't speak.

I look towards Victor again, realising now that I don't feel the same way for him as I initially thought I did. I'd realised while away that I didn't feel as strongly for him as I did for Crow and Liam, but seeing him in person only cements that feeling.

"Go on. Tell her then," My dad encourages impatiently, his hands sliding in the air between Victor and I.

"It's my fault you were taken," he says, his hands fidgeting on the table in front of us.

My brows crease, not understanding how it could possibly be his fault.

I look at the men around me. My dad. Crow. Liam. Gray. Victor. They're all sat at the table and it seems myself, Gray, and Liam are the only ones in the dark here. Their faces are as confused as I expect mine is.

But then I look at Crow and my dad again.

They know something.

"How was it your fault?" I am tempted to tell him it wasn't, but I have a feeling I'm missing some rather significant pieces of information here considering how tense and awkward everything currently feels. The air around us is filled with a nervous energy that seems to be emitting from myself and Victor in waves.

"My dad wasn't really interested in a merge with the Cobras, but I had a meeting with an unknown source which wasn't unusual. This person explained that he needed a way to get close to you and he needed my potential connections to do it. I, of course, refused initially. I didn't know you and I had no interest in getting involved in whatever this was, but he threatened my father's life and despite how little we get along, I do love him and couldn't see his life being taken because of me, so I agreed." He winces as he looks up at me before returning his gaze back to his hands. "Except then I really did care for you but I still had this in the back of my mind. Crow didn't want to," he looks around awkwardly, "share you, but I did everything I could to convince him. I needed you both to trust me, so when the source explained that I needed to get you to the club alone that night, I told you I was going but never showed. I didn't ask what their plan for you was, but I knew it had to be bad. I just thought that you'd be safe in the club with Crow," he finishes.

I take a moment of doing nothing but staring

at him before I speak.

It was him. It wasn't his fault. I don't for a second feel that it was. I am angry with him, sure, but I know that in his situation, I'd do just about anything I could to protect the people I care about as well.

He wasn't the one that set it all up. He wasn't the one that raped me or held me hostage, but he did trick me. Lied to me. Made me vulnerable.

"Who was the source?" Liam asks, his tone lethal as he eyes Victor.

"I don't know. I never got a name. Just some bloke with a skull tattoo over his face. Creepy as fuck if you ask me," Victor says with a shiver.

"Jonesy," Gray says with a nod from Liam.

I have no idea who this Jonesy bloke is, and I have absolutely no interest in finding out. If he is a part of the reason that happened to me then he can stay as far away from me as humanly possible.

"Right. So, what happened to you?" I ask Crow. "Dad says you were ambushed."

"Yeah, this fucker told me at the very last minute what was going down, so as I was freshly out of the shower, I put my boxers on and ran the fuck to my bike. Basically naked, might I add. Got on, got all of a mile down the road, and got fucking ran off the damn road. Wake up in hospital and here we are," he says with a huff, his eyes never leaving Victor.

"What? That's not right. You gave me vodka at the club," I tell him. I remember it. Clear as day.

342

I remember going in and him giving me a drink of vodka.

Crows head spins to me so quickly I'm surprised he's not got whiplash.

"What are you talking about? You can check the CCTV, Char, I wasn't there. Not at all that night. Not once."

"Alice saw you. She was at the bar, she saw you," I tell him, not understanding what's happening.

I know he wouldn't lie to me. Not about this. Dad would have said something if Crow was wrong. He would know if this had or hadn't happened, and he doesn't speak up to tell me otherwise, so I have to assume that Crow at least thinks he's telling the truth - but he's not. He can't be because I remember him being there.

"You gave me a cup of vodka and then went to the bathroom and didn't come back. I went looking for you but because I was drunk, I accidently stumbled into the wrong room. That's where they were," I say, not needing to go into any more detail than absolutely needed into what happened after I entered the room.

"Do you really think I'd leave you? I take you to the fucking bathroom with me in your house half the time, baby, let alone in a Club packed full of people," he says, his hands reaching mine over the table and rubbing my palm softly.

He's right. Shit, he's right, but I saw him. It was him.

"Do you have the CCTV?" I ask my dad,

who's already got his laptop out without me realising.

"Fuck. Who were you around that day, Charlie? That isn't Crow. I don't know what happened or what you saw but that was not Crow," my dad says, his voice weary and scared as he looks at the screen on the laptop.

He spins the laptop around to me and I watch in horror as I take the drink, the vodka from Matt's hand before he walks away. To the bathroom.

"That's not possible. I'm telling you, I saw Crow," I say as I back away and begin shaking my head.

I don't understand. I thought the vodka was spiked. I mean, it probably was but how was it possible that I saw Crow?

"Hallucinogenics can make you see things. He wouldn't have known that you would have seen Crow but that probably just worked to his advantage. He couldn't have guaranteed you'd see anything in particular, he probably just thought it would help. We didn't find out until afterwards but the plan was for them to come and find you when the fighting broke out, it was just bad luck that you found them first. Fuck, that makes so much more sense. When you told me that Crow left you, I didn't understand it, but he didn't leave you. He didn't even manage to get to you," Gray says as he watches the screen with me, terror filling his eyes, mirroring my own.

"How would they have got it in me before then though?" I wonder as I think through the events

344

of the day.

I'd been to the doctors and then been here all day getting ready. The only people that I had been around were Crow and Victor.

And then I see a wincing Victor and I know.

"You did it?" I ask him, horrified. I understood all of it. I understood why he did what he did. I'd do anything I could to protect the people I cared for, but this was just too much.

"You've got to be fucking kidding me," Crow hisses as he jumps from his chair and rounds to Victor, grabbing the top of his typically immaculate white shirt and holding him mere inches from the floor, the chair he was sat on tipped over beneath him.

"No, wait! I want to hear it!" I yell at him as I get up from my seat and lean across the table towards Crow.

"Oh, you'll fucking hear him scream in a damn minute," Crow says as he unsheathes a gun from the holster beneath his jacket and places the muzzle of the gun at Victor's forehead.

"Crow, no!" I shout as I move towards him, knocking the chair over in the process and moving to grab his arm before he truly lets loose.

"No, Crow. I mean it. Don't you fucking dare," I tell him as he looks at me. He stares back down at Victor for a moment before nodding at me.

"Fine. I won't shoot him," he says with a glint in his eye as his arm rears back before crunching his fist into Victor's face. I watch with my mouth splayed open as Victor's head falls back and hits

345

the hard floor beneath us, his face wincing in pain as he hisses out a string of curses.

"Oh, for fuck's sake, Crow. I love you but you're like an out of control, testosterone filled teenager," I inform him as I move him out of the way and crouch down to a hunched over Victor.

"I love you too, baby," Crow says sweetly as he kneels beside me and places a soft kiss at my temple.

I roll my eyes at that being the only thing he got out of what I said. Of course, that's all he heard.

"Are you alright?" I ask Victor. I nudge Crow away and put my hand out for Victor to take.

I might not be all that keen on his actions right now, but I'm also not a complete animal. Most of the time at least.

"I don't know why you care. I'm sorry, Char. Honest to God, I'm genuinely sorry," he tells me as the men around me mutter and shake their heads.

"I know. Don't stress, it's done now. Nothing can take it back. You've just got to move on," I tell him with a strained smile as he takes my hand and stands from the ground. I'm trying to be a better person, OK?

If nothing else, this whole situation has taught me that I can do whatever the hell I like and right now, forgiving Victor for doing something he felt he had to is what I want to do.

"Do you still wanna know?" he asks as he stands to his full height while rubbing his hands through his hair and over his rumpled clothes.

"Yeah, I do. How did you do it?"

"Well, I didn't. I knew they were going to but I didn't. It was the doctor. Well, not him but his assistant. I don't know how they got to her or knew you were going to be there - I hadn't told them that part but they knew and when they were taking blood, they injected something too," he tells me solemnly.

"But I felt fine all day, right up until I had that drink," I say as I turn to the men behind me for guidance.

"I'm not exactly a drugs expert, but I'm guessing the alcohol didn't help and some take hours to kick in I've heard." I nod at Gray's words. I'm not convinced Victor's right, even if he thinks he is. I surely would have known if I'd been drugged in the morning.

"This better not be you forgiving him and getting back to where we were because I am not doing that," Crow says as he eyes up Victor again, his eyes vicious as he looks him over with a disgusted curl of his lips.

"I forgive him just fine, but I did realise that I don't think I care for him in that way. I would love to have you as a friend though, assuming there's no more lying and setting me up to be kidnapped involved," I tell Victor with a rueful smile.

He winces at my words.

"Too soon?" I ask with a laugh.

"Way too fucking soon, Char," Crow answers behind me.

"Right, is there anything else anyone needs to tell me before we move on?" I ask, my eyes swinging between the men around me. My attempt at being confident seems to be waning when I catch Crow smirking at me.

"Don't even start, we're talking later," I tell him as I roll my eyes at his lack of seriousness in a situation I am attempting to be very serious in.

Gray, Liam, and Dad all shake their heads.

"Well, there is one more thing. More for your dad and Liam to know than anyone else but..." Victor cuts himself off as he backs up when both Liam and Dad begin walking menacingly towards him.

"You realise he's about to tell you whatever this is anyway, you don't need to act all hulk on him," I tell them. I hear Crow snicker in the background before pretending to zip his lips closed when I glare in his direction.

"What is it, boy?" my dad asks him.

"Well, the thing is, my dad wasn't interested in a merge but now he sort of is-"

"I might forgive you, but I am not marrying you if that's where this is going," I rush out, watching as Victor smiles and shakes his head at me.

"No, no, I know. It's honestly probably worse. Since you two stepped down-" I don't let him get anything else out before I put my hand up to stop him.

"What is he talking about stepped down?" I step in between Victor, my dad, and Liam as I look up at them both with the most incredulous

348

look on my face.

"You know, when I asked 'does anyone have anything else to tell me?' This is what I meant. This is the type of thing you're supposed to tell me. Why the hell have you both stepped down?" I hiss out, my eyes closing and my breath hitching with frustration as I take in the absolute fuck fest (in the worst way) that is the situation I'm currently stuck in.

I genuinely spend more time wondering what the actual fuck is wrong with the male specimens surrounding me than I do thinking about real, logical, normal things these days - which is pretty bloody concerning.

"Char, I'm not exactly in a position to lead right now if you hadn't noticed," Liam tells me with a pointed look.

OK, fair. I'm not telling him so but he has a valid point. I don't even need him to explain. I get it.

"Dad?" I ask, though before he even speaks, I know what's going to come out.

"I was only watching over the Club until Liam got out, it was never supposed to be permanent. I never wanted it to be. I need to move on with my life, with you and Gray," my dad says, the harsh lines and dark circles under his eyes becoming apparent. He may only be in his thirties, but you can see how tired he is - from the mayhem of club life and the consequences of it.

"So, who does that leave in charge?" I wonder aloud.

"By our laws, people fight - both physically and through the votes of our men as to who the new MC President is. It usually goes down the line of succession if everyone is happy with that but Gray doesn't want it, he never has and I'm not going to force that on him," Dad says with a glance in Gray's direction.

Gray has always trained hard. He's a much better fighter than I am, but I'm not sure that he's suited to the role even if he wanted to be.

"That's where the problem kind of lies," Victor interrupts. "Theo, my dad's righthand man, wants to try and become the Cobras new Pres to merge the clubs."

"Would that be bad?" I ask, though from the ashen look on Victor's face, I assume it indeed would be.

"He's a sadistic fuck that gets off on power and hurting people, so yes, it would be bad," Liam says while scratching the stubble along his jaw.

"And what are the chances of him getting in over anyone else that tries?" I have no idea if anyone has put their name forward, but I imagine the Cobras would want one of their own ruling them.

"None of the Cobras want the responsibility so right now, assuming he has the most support and can gain the most allies, we wouldn't have much choice but to accept him," my dad says.

So it needs to be someone that the Cobras trust, someone that can gain support, and

350

someone that can help form allies. Crow's eyes catch mine as I find a sly smile creeping on my face. I have the best idea.

Chapter 13

Charlie

"This feels weird," Crow says as we walk together towards the lake and the forest we used to visit regularly.

"I know. It feels like nothing and everything has changed all at once," I agree as I take in the scenery surrounding us.

Spring is now in full swing, a fact that is blatantly obvious when looking at the vibrant and newly growing leaves, trees and flowers beginning to bloom once more.

"I'm surprised Liam let us come out alone. He's a stubborn fucker." Crow sighs as he takes my hand in his.

His calloused hand overwhelms my smaller one. I've always thought of myself as someone that's strong, independent, and a fierce feminist, but I'm realising more and more that the safety of a man I care for, a man's larger presence being near me, and offering me their security sends flutters through me.

He's right. I think the only reason he didn't very genuinely superglue himself to my side was only because Dad insisted that if he didn't at least start the interview process that they wouldn't let him near me. That got him moving. And glaring. There was a lot of glaring involved too. He's good at that.

You know that annoyingly attractive and brooding frown that men do? That one.

Crow's hands are rough and yet they are inviting and comforting too. I peek down to see the way our hands connect.

"Yeah, he's a little protective," I agree.

"Are you scared?" Crow asks me as we pass the street of houses.

"Of what?" I wonder as I look around us and wonder what there is to be scared of.

"Everything."

I think for a moment before responding, trying to think of a way to effectively communicate the way I feel.

"I feel fidgety and paranoid - a little bit wary of touch but overall, no. I mean, it might be a weird realisation to come to but I feel like there's nothing I can do to stop bad things from happening. I could train or carry a gun, or have you or Liam with me twenty-four seven, but if someone really wanted to get to me, I have no doubt that they would eventually. Just like they did before. And even though I'm petrified of that happening again without Gray and Liam to protect me like they did, I don't want to let the fear of that stop me from doing what I want," I tell him honestly as I take a deep breath and attempt to force myself into enjoying the fresh air that I've missed. Being stuck inside for so long drove me crazy or at least it felt that way.

"Are you scared of my touch? You know I

won't ever push you, don't you?" he asks as he watches me delicately.

I turn to look up at him as we walk and see the concern written all over his face.

"I know," I tell him with a small smile. There's not a single part of me that questions Crow and his motives.

"Can I ask you something else?" he asks as we near the clearing and the entrance to the woods.

"Yeah, of course." I take my hand from his and run it down my side. His hands are hot. Sweaty even, or is it mine? I can't tell.

"Did anything happen between you and Liam? He looks at you like I imagine I do."

His question stops me immediately, my hands freezing for a moment. I'm not going to lie to him, but I also feel like I've put him through so much already that I don't want to put him through more.

"Yes. We slept together. I care about him," I tell him honestly, worry coating my voice as I shift uncomfortably and walk towards the peak and our den, not wanting to see the horror and disgust on his face. I'm being a coward. I did this and I have to live with the consequences. I turn to him again just as he speaks.

"And you trust him?" he asks, his hand ruffling his already ruffled and short hair.

"Yeah, I trust him just as much as I trust you."

"I hate to tell you, Char, but your judge of character ain't great considering the whole Victor fiasco, so maybe we should take it slow with him. I mean, he's admittedly better looking than Victor so I wouldn't mind seeing him fuck you while you suck my dick but even so, we'll take it slow, yeah?" I nearly drop the travel mug I'm holding, my eyes going wide as I turn to see a sly grin covering his lips.

What did he just say?

I don't know where to start processing his words.

I splutter out some sounds, unsure of what I'm even trying to say as he smirks and wags his eyebrows at me.

"If I'm a bad judge of character, you realise that it includes my judgement of you, right?2 I ask with a crooked brow as I fold my arms.

"I'm amazing, thank you very much," he says with a laugh as he takes the mug I'd put on the floor and begins filling it with tea.

"Also an O'Banian though," I say. Not a question - a fact. I don't think he'd lie to me at this stage, but I still don't pose my words as a question, not wanting to give him the chance to lie.

I guess this is as good a time as any to bring it up. I watch as his face contorts and he shakes his head with his eyes closed briefly, the twitch of his lips my only sign that he's not annoyed by my accusation.

"Yeah, Crow O'Banian at your service, ma'am." He salutes me with a smirk on his face. The words, along with the action and his stature, is appallingly attractive when it so shouldn't be. I know he's trying to keep things light by joking but shit, he is really handsome.

Shut up, Charlie.

"Does everyone else know now?" I wonder as I watch him watch me.

His eyes are so intense. It feels like he's trying to read between the lines, read my mind, and figure me out all at once, and although the intrusion would usually bother me, with him, I find that maybe I don't mind. Crow has seen so much of me, I don't think he'd run no matter what he saw or found in my mind's depths.

"Yeah, everyone knows. My lot were the ones that helped us get in contact with Liam. It's the only reason I haven't bloody shot him down myself because he helped. I don't trust him, but I dunno, maybe he's not that bad."

I follow suit when Crow sits on the floor with my bag between us.

"Are they the mafia?" I ask, realising after speaking that I categorised a them vs us mentality without meaning too. I also note that I didn't ask if Crow was, but rather they as if he wasn't a part of them but rather a part of us when I suppose he isn't at all.

It makes sense, far more sense than I'd like for it to. Crow's laughter and banterful side makes him seem so at ease but when he's angry, frustrated or even in his own bubble with his thoughts, I've seen how deadly and meticulous he can be.

"Yeah. It's not as bad as it sounds though. I mean, it is," he starts, "but probably not like what you think. My family is normal, they're just like the Cobras, it's just a different brand of Club and bad I guess."

"What do they do? What does it mean to be in the mafia?" I ask, unsure of how any of it works aside from what I've read in books or seen on TV, which I have no doubt is incredibly inaccurate.

He laughs, a hearty laugh as he lets his head fall back, his skin lighting up from the sun's streaming through the cloud and trees.

"It doesn't feel any different being an O'Banian in the mafia than it does being a part of the Cobras to be honest, Char. We protect what's ours, do what we need to do, and keep going. That's it." Like it's that simple. I doubt it is as simple as he's making it seem but then again, if he's grown up his entire life living inside of that, then it probably doesn't seem all that strange to him.

"So, what were you doing here?" I'm pretty sure I know the answer. I remember spying, or attempting to spy on my dad's meeting a while ago and hearing that the O'Banians usually place a spy in the ranks of any base they planned to merge with.

"My family sent me to see what the Cobras were like, where their values and morals lie, what they could offer us in return for what we could offer them." He offers me the truth, which I appreciate now more than ever.

357

"So now what? What did you report back?" I ask curiously as I turn to watch him.

"I told them that we're merging," he says with a laugh, as if it's the funniest thing in the world.

"You told them? You have that much power over what happens?" I'm not sure why it seems so shocking that he does. If he's the son of some mafia god then he's bound to have sway.

I attempt to look at Crow as I did the first time I saw him. I remember thinking about how intimidating he was, how large his personality and presence was. I remember noticing so many people cowering under his stare. His personality as I got to know him has allowed me to see him as the teddy bear he really is, but I'm certain he could be just as deadly as any other when needed.

"I didn't really give them a choice to be honest, babe. I've grown to love the Cobras nearly as much as I do you," he says softly as he takes my hand in his and uses his free hand to run his fingers across my palm.

"OK."

"OK? You don't have any more questions?"

"Well, I mean, I'm sure I will at some point but right now I'm just going with the flow, so OK." I nod at him, enjoying his hands in mine.

He gifts me with a small smile that sends my stomach somersaulting.

"I got you something. It's nothing exciting, but I saw it and it made me think of you. Do you want it now?" he asks as he pulls his hands away from mine and goes in his pocket, pulling out a small black box.

"If that's a proposal coming, the answer is no. I'm still pissed at you, at least wait until after you've made me hash browns." I laugh.

"I think you've had plenty of marriage arrangements for a while. I'm not in a rush." He chuckles, holding his hand out for me to take the box.

I take it hesitantly, watching as his eyes show me the nervousness that he's emitting.

"Is it going to make me cry? Because I've cried enough for a while too," I tell him as I feel the smooth box in my hand.

"I hope not, I never know what to do when girls cry. Just open it," he tells me eagerly as he shifts closer to me, moving the bag between us out of the way.

I open the box up slowly, not wanting to rattle or accidentally break whatever is inside. There's a small section of black paper that I move to reveal a necklace. On a black chain with a silver pendant is a necklace with paper inside. Paper covered in words - a segment out of my favourite book that only Crow would know about.

A bright smile takes over as I touch the pendant delicately, lapping up the thoughts of how caring and sweet Crow can be. I've never seen anything like this before, but of course Crow of all people would somehow find something so small and yet meaningful to gift me.

"Do you like it?" he asks nervously as he

peers in my direction, his neck craning down to see my face.

"I love it. Thank you," I tell him as I close the lid of the box and smile up at him.

"Is it your dad that runs the O'Banians?" I ask suddenly, my earlier idea coming back to me in the silence.

"Yeah, he's the one in charge of our patch, why?" Crow asks, his gaze infiltrating my own suspiciously.

"What's he like?"

"He's pretty chill. I mean, he can be a scary bastard when he wants to be, but he's not that bad really." He laughs lightly, his eyes still watching me as if I'm about to pounce.

"Would you be able to arrange for me to meet him by any chance?"

"I'd love for you to meet my dad knowing that you're mine, but I have a feeling this isn't one of those 'meet the family because we're together' type of dinners, is it?"

"I have an idea I'd like to run by him," I tell him.

"Are you going to tell me this idea of yours?" he asks as he places a hand on my leg and begins caressing it steadily.

"Arrange a meeting with your dad and you can be there to find out."

Chapter 14

Charlie

I said that I would go to the club today and up until about five minutes ago, I was feeling completely at ease with that thought. Now that I'm standing outside the Club doors, however, I am suddenly feeling like I'm either about to very literally shit myself, cry, or have a complete breakdown. Or maybe all three. Hopefully not at the same time.

Aside from when they've had no choice, Liam nor Crow have left my side once and they're both here now, insisting that everything will be absolutely fine. Liam needs to be interviewed. Again. And I need to get over the built-up fear of being inside of the Club.

"Come on, why don't we spend the afternoon together? After we've done everything we need to here?" Crow asks as he pulls his leather jacket on.

"The three of us?" I ask, confused.

Although neither have left my side, both Crow and Liam have also somehow managed to avoid being with each other all that much. If I'm upstairs, one of them has been with me while the other is downstairs. Usually, Liam is the one downstairs. We've hardly had any chance to talk since being home.

Signed with Love duet
J R Dust

We've not managed to speak about anything that happened, what's going to happen now, or if what did happen was just a case of us both being in a rather sticky situation where we used each other as an outlet for that. I don't think that's the case but until I have the opportunity to ask him what the hell is going on in his mind, I also have absolutely no idea either. He's hardly touched me since being home and though even a few weeks ago, that would have pleased me, I find myself now missing his touch and the comfort I'd become used to from him.

"Yeah, Liam will too, won't you?" Crow asks him, giving him a look that says 'say yes or else' but I don't stop him. If these two could get on, it would make everything so much easier.

"Yeah, course," Liam says as he opens the door in front of us and waves his arm in front of me, signalling for me to go in front.

I stand there transfixed, listening to the music coming from inside for a moment, doubting my ability to overcome this so quickly. But if I don't go in now, will I ever? I have Liam and Crow right by my side. They weren't here last time, and that's why I managed to get taken. They wouldn't let anything happen to me. They won't. I'm safe. I'm ok. Everything will be fine.

I walk inside with Liam and Crow at my side, heading straight towards Ben at the bar. He's the first familiar face that comes into my line of sight. I take hold of that and aim for him. He hasn't noticed me yet, but when I take a seat on one of

362

the bar stools, his head rises and a line of confusion crosses his eyes before a smile lights up his face as he sees me.

"Char! Oh, bloody hell, girl, I haven't seen you in forever," he says as he opens the flap of the bar, walks through, and comes to give me a hug.

Ben is one of Gray's usual hookups. Not as though he's told me that, but I've noticed the way that Ben looks at him and very conveniently gets to finish work and follow Gray to one of the rooms here and then comes back dishevelled and messy. Gray thinks I don't notice these things, but I most definitely do. Ben is only a few inches taller than me, maybe 5'10 at a guess, has a slim build and no hair on his face. He has dark, nearly black eyes and hair to match that goes in every which direction.

"Oh, you're looking good, babe! You want a drink?" he asks as he lets me go, looking at me once more with a smile before going back behind the bar and waiting eagerly for my order.

"Yeah, I'll just have an orange juice please. Way too early for the harder stuff," I joke as he laughs and takes Liam's and Crow's orders before collecting our drinks.

"So, what are you doing here? Alice isn't around today, but she'll be back in tomorrow if you were looking for her," He tells me as he slides my drink over the counter and waves away the notes that Liam offers him.

"No, Liam and Crow have got a meeting and are busy this afternoon, so I thought I'd stop by with them instead of waiting at home on my own. Is Dad around?" I ask as I glance around and see many other familiar faces but not my dad's. He said he was going to work early this morning but that didn't necessarily mean that he was here.

"Yeah, he's in one of the meeting rooms. Probably waiting for you lot. Are you late?" he wonders with a wag of his eyebrows.

"I don't actually know," I tell him with a small laugh as I look towards Liam. "Are we?"

He looks at the clock above Ben's head before turning to me with a smirk. "Yep. Half an hour late, as it happens."

"Why the hell didn't you tell me? Dad's gonna go bloody crazy. Come on," I tell him as I grab his arm and yank him towards the doors to the meeting rooms.

"I'll see you later, Ben!" I shout back at him as I walk off while dragging Liam.

"There's no rush. You wanted to do your hair," he tells me as he swipes my hand away, straightens himself, and then grabs my hand again.

"I could have just put it in a bobble if I knew we were on a time crunch," I hiss out.

"Nah, he's right, your dad won't care," Crow tells me as he catches up with us and takes my other side.

"Do you even know my dad?" I ask, exasperated. "He will most definitely care." I huff out as I continue plodding along towards the meeting rooms.

Signed with Love duet
J R Dust

I pull to a stop outside the door I can hear conversation coming from while I wait for a very slow Liam and Crow. They seriously could not take any longer if they tried. They both have such confident walks, I realise as I watch them with agitation filling my face. If nothing else, speeding ahead gives me a moment to take in the absolute god given beauty of them. Now that I'm looking at them standing side by side, I realise how similar they are. I've never thought about it or noticed it before but they both have buzz cuts - well, they did, Crows has grown out a bit since but Liam's is still short. Their hair is only a few shades apart from one another and their builds are also eerily similar aside from Liam being maybe three inches or so taller than Crow.

"You look like you're eye fucking us, princess," Crow tells me as he staggers towards me with a smirk on his face.

"I was most definitely not doing that," I tell him with a terrible hair flick as I turn around, mortified because I absolutely was doing exactly that.

"You look like one of those popular girls when you flick your hair like that." Crow laughs as he loops his arm around my shoulders and kisses the side of my head.

"I do not, at all. I look cool and dignified when I flick my hair," I tell him even though I know for a fact that I am lying through my teeth.

"You really do. You know that blonde one in Mean Girls that you used to make me watch? Her." Liam joins in with a smirk on his face.

365

"Yeah, man, that's the one!" Crow laughs, his head falling back as he does.

I whack Crow in the stomach lightly in an attempt to either hurt him or shut him up.

"Are you done picking on me now? Are we going in or not?"

"We're still ten minutes early, there's no need to rush," Liam tells me as he checks the time on his phone and shows it to me.

"It's three o'clock. I thought you said we were half an hour late?" I ask, confused.

"I did. I lied. No one's supposed to be meeting us until ten past. I just knew you hate being late and I know your dad likes it even less, so I thought if I distracted you then you wouldn't worry as much about being here and walking down the hall," he tells me simply, with the most 'duh' expression ever, as if I should have known something so seemingly obvious.

I look at him, completely dumbfounded at the thought that went into him doing something so simple that helped so much. He is right. I hadn't thought about my clammy hands, my erratically beating heart, or the harsh breaths that were coming out of me even once since he mentioned us being late.

"Did you know about this?" I ask Crow.

"Well, no, but I figured it out when he told you we were late when I knew damn well that we were not and then he kept smirking at you so I put two and two together and made eleven point seven, so yeah, I knew before you," he tells me with a nod of his head as if everyone should understand his maths.

A smile creeps up on my face as I glance between them both.

"Are you lot coming in or just standing in the hall all damn day?" I hear Tins gruff voice shout from inside the room. The door is open slightly, his voice loud enough to echo and be heard down the hall.

"We're coming now, chill ya beans, jeez," Crow says as he saunters inside and takes a seat at the table, totally unbothered by Tin's huffing and puffing. One thing about Tin is that he hates waiting. He likes to be busy all of the time, so if he's got something to do, he likes to get it over and done with so that he can move onto his next task.

I'm sat between Liam and Crow with my dad, Tin, and Mal sat opposite us. Mal is very introverted and prefers to spend his time away from others, but in these situations, he's the only one that's had any genuine history in his life with questioning, interviews, and psychology. He was a police officer with a psychology degree so although this isn't anything official, he knows how to conduct himself a lot better than anyone else my dad could have asked in the Cobras.

"Right, everyone here? Let's move on. Liam. Mal, let's go," Tin says pointedly as he nods in Liam's direction.

"We've gone over everything we need to. I just have a few questions for you, and then we'll

367

talk among the three of us and get back to you with an official decision."

Liam nods, looking completely unphased. I'm not sure that Liam wants this life anymore. I know that he adores the Cobras and the men within, but that doesn't change the fact that after everything he's endured, I'm sure he'd prefer a peaceful life away from the chaos of club life or at least a lesser part in the Cobras that doesn't demand as much of him.

"Are you happy for me to proceed with Crow and Charlie here? Some of the questions are of a rather intimate nature," Mal says delicately.

Liam avoids my eyes but looks past me at Crow, who gives him a tentative smile. Crow may be the joker but he has a bigger heart than most people I know. He's one of the least judgmental people ever, but I'd also understand if Liam doesn't want me or Crow to be here to listen to whatever it is that needs to be spoken about.

"It's fine. Go on," Liam instructs Mal, who opens up the stack of papers in front of him.

"The first question was in relation to your father. You said that he has a vendetta against you and with the evidence you've given, we have reason to believe you. What I want to know is if you feel he has the ability to take down the Cobras with the assets he has. Our main concern here is the Club and those within it. This isn't a question so much about your character but rather what your father is capable of."

"He's got intel coming from most areas of law

enforcement and is friends with more people that can help him than I care to know about. Between his connections and his men, I have no doubt that if he came while the Cobras were unprepared, he could annihilate us all." Liam says it with so much nonchalance that it terrifies me. I know that he's not a particularly dramatic person. If he genuinely thinks that his father and his men could take down the Cobras, I'm certain he's right.

My dad's jaw tics as Tin huffs, but none of them make a move to speak. Mal continues.

"You said that your main weakness, the one way he'd be able to get to you, would be through Charlie. Is that correct?"

"Yes."

"Why is it that she is your weakness over anyone else in your life?"

"Because I love her." My eyes practically bug out of my skull at hearing him say the words so relaxed, as if he's saying 'duh - obviously' without saying it at all.

"And in what way do you love her?" my dad asks as he leans forward over the table and towards us.

I don't meet his eyes when he speaks, though even if I wanted to I couldn't, his eyes are glued on Liam's.

"In a very different way to the way you lot love her." He chuckles deeply, so calm and confident in his declaration.

My dad's jaw clenched and releases as he continues, "Make it clear for me here, mate, so that I'm not stuck making assumptions. In what way do you love my daughter?" Oh Jesus, this is not going well. The frustration is brimming in my father's eyes.

"In exactly the way you don't want me to. I love her so much that I want to spend every single fucking second with her, so much that I'd happily live my life with her, so much that I'm willing to put up with him for her too." He rushes out with a smirk as he points his head in Crow's direction.

"Oh thanks, make it sound like I'm a fucking side piece, why don't you? I'm the OG, you're the bloody late comer," Crow huffs out with a roll of his eyes.

"You're telling me that you want to be with my daughter?" my dad asks, surprisingly calm in his demeanour. I mean, he looks understandably tense but overall he doesn't look like he's about to hurt Liam too badly. He doesn't look like he wants to maim him, you know? That's good.

"What if we don't trust you? What do you plan to do then? Go back to your father?" Tin asks, completely ignoring Liam and my dad's dispute.

"Why are we moving on? I'm not done!" my dad exclaims, his hands in the air as he looks at Tin in shock.

"Does no one else care that my best friend wants to be with my fucking daughter?"

"Not really. He's a dickhead, but he ain't a bad man and you know it. Moving on," Tin says, ever the one to not want unnecessary chatter, unless

370

it's from me or Gray, who seem to get away with it of course. The positives of being like one of his own children to him.

"We're talking about this later. Don't be thinking you're staying in her room anymore," my dad says, his eyes not leaving Liam.

"What, so you'll let him stay with her but not me? You've known me for years," Liam argues.

"He's earned my trust unlike some," my dad hisses out, though I can tell his anger is waning.

"He's a fucking undercover O'Banian!"

"Well, that's fucking rude," Crow butts in.

"OK, how about we move on like Tin said? I don't think we're going to achieve anything positive by carrying on this conversation right now," I interrupt, knowing that despite my father slowly calming that the more we talk about it, the more his wrath will grow again.

My dad and Liam nod their heads, not looking at each other as Tin and Mal continue firing questions at Liam.

Once the initial disagreements are over with, so too are the questions rather quickly.

It doesn't take long before we're out of the Club house and left alone again. Since both Liam and Crow aren't in the best of moods after the meeting, my wonderful idea is to let them pick what we do for the afternoon.

Crow chooses go-karting or paintballing while Liam picks the cinema or hiking. Complete opposite choices of course. They're crazily similar sight wise and yet their personalities can't

371

be more different.

I end up deciding on something completely different. We go to the wildlife park. I am your typical young woman that adores animals, coos at every newborn baby I see, no matter what form it is in - human or animal. Plus, my decision means that they can't argue over who gets to pick what we do.

Chapter 15

Charlie

After spending the afternoon with Crow and Liam, I feel like a weight has been lifted from me. Joking and messing around with them makes me realise just how much I'd missed being myself without the chaos. Crow and I were usually together 24/7 so to be away from each other for weeks felt like years, at least in my mind.

"You alright, darlin'? I got chippy!" my dad shouts as he comes through the front door.

"You know I love you, don't you?" I ask with a laugh as I get up to retrieve some cutlery and drinks for us.

"We eating in the lounge, Charlie?" he asks, though I have no idea why since he's already settled himself on the sofa and opened up his food.

"I want to have a chat," he tells me.

I lower myself to sit next to him. Crow and Liam said they had business to take care of at the Club, but that they'll be here soon.

"Just wait a second, you knew I was getting knives and forks, you idiot. You're worse than a child." I scoff, handing him a napkin from beside me as well as his cutlery.

"And you're like a bloody mother hen, my girl," he says laughing.

I smirk at his comment, knowing full well that it's true. These men would never survive if it weren't for me.

I dig into the chips, sausage and gravy he'd got me - my absolute favourite takeaway meal.

We eat in silence for a while, with just the tv as background noise. I soon finish up and chuck the plastic container in the bin and place the cutlery into the sink.

"So, what is it you want to talk about?" I ask as I walk back in to sit down again.

The doorbell goes before Dad has a chance to say anything. I roll my eyes at our uninvited visitor's terrible timing.

"I'll grab it." Dad jumps up from next to me and catapults to the door.

"Alright, old man?" Liam.

I can hear them muttering something to one another, but not their words.

Dad follows Liam and Crow into the lounge. Liam takes the seat next to me, Crow sitting on the arm of the chair, whilst Dad takes his seat in the corner.

Liam gives me a pointed look, but I have no idea what it's supposed to mean so I don't respond with my voice or my actions, turning to face Dad.

"They're gonna stay for this conversation, Charl," Dad says. He seems tense, which makes me nervous. He is sat upright, which makes a change for him since he's usually laid back in the comfiest chair we own. His hands are knitted together too, fiddling with the cutlery still in his hand.

I look towards Liam and Crow for any indication of what's going on, but neither of them are looking at me. Liam shakes his head slightly as if in answer to me though. No? Don't ask. Is that what he's trying to say?

"So, what is it that's got you all twisted up?" I ask, concerned more than curious seeing the state of the three men.

"You know you had that doctor's appointment a while back?"

"Yeah, is something wrong?" I wonder.

"No, not physically. No one's ill." Well, that's a start. He's staring at the ground as he speaks though. Something is wrong.

I nod at him to let him know I heard. Waiting for him to continue.

"I don't really know where to start to be honest with you, darlin'," he explains. He looks up at me this time with a weak smile that I return, encouraging him to continue.

"You know all about your mum, about what she was like when we were together." My mind reels, wondering why on earth she had anything to do with this. I do know though. I've been told by so many people how awful she was to him.

I don't remember much about her, but I hear enough and remember her golden hair and her hard, green eyes refusing to ever play with me or cuddle me. She didn't want me, but Dad did. He took over when she disappeared. I've had a

375

better life with him and without a mum than I would have had if she had stuck around. Considering what she'd recently let her only two children witness and go through, I have no doubt about the horrendous stories I've been told of her over the years.

"She cheated on me a lot throughout the years." I already knew this, but say nothing, waiting for him to continue. "I had a tip off a few months ago, a random letter in the post telling me that you weren't mine."

A letter in the post? Who the hell would come up with something like that? There are always rumours about everyone in life. Rumours and speculations are what create half the things the world talks about, but to tell a man their daughter isn't theirs eighteen years after said daughter is born, it just baffles me.

"But I am though. We're exactly the same," I say with a light laugh. If this is what is worrying him then he is just being silly. Our personalities are exactly the same.

"We like our tea the same way, we both love hash browns, we can both shoot better than this dead shot over here," I say, jerking my thumb towards Liam. "We practically have identical personalities, Dad," I say with a chuckle.

"You're right. We're very similar, but do you realise what you just said, darlin'?" I think back to the words I used but don't understand what he's referring to.

"They're all learned habits, Charlie. All things

that anyone would grow up being if they were brought up by me. You've always been a daddy's girl, followed me, copied me. You wanted to be just like me, and you are." I realise then what he meant.

I always thought we looked alike too, but now that I'm looking at him, I understood it.

Our hair and eye colours are different. Our face shapes are complete opposites, as well as our individual features. I don't have any of his physical features. His pitch-black hair in comparison to my mousy brown doesn't match. My nose is annoyingly small in comparison to his prominent one. My lips are full and plump whereas his are thin and small. Small differences but differences all the same.

"I could have just taken after Mum instead of you though," I say hesitantly.

It's true. We don't have pictures of her around, not because my dad doesn't want to or wouldn't, but because I've never been that interested in her. I've been told so much about her that's negative, and the small memories I do have of her are never anything good either, so neither of us really see the point. So many people look like one parent and not the other. Crow showed me pictures of his parents and he looks identical to his dad, but nothing like his mum.

"I contacted a man I knew your mum was sleeping with at the time we were together, around the time you were conceived. I explained the situation and he was willing to give me a DNA sample so that we could compare it in case it came to it." I shake my head, standing.

A man? What man? A DNA sample. My mind works at a mile a minute, repeating Dads words back to myself. The doctor. He took a swab from inside my mouth. I knew that was a bit strange at the time but didn't think much of it. Why didn't he tell me? Why did no one mention it when this letter arrived?

I answer my own question before I even get a chance to ask. My dad does everything within his power to avoid me having any stress in my life, any worries or problems. He wouldn't want to worry me. That's why he wouldn't have told me.

"The doctor did the test," I state, feeling like my mind is spinning in circles but realising when Crow's arms stop me that it's not my mind but me slowly spinning in circles.

I stop abruptly and look up to Liam's fallen face.

Neither he nor Crow would look so distraught if I was my dad's daughter. My dad wouldn't look so devastated if I was his.

They'd be overjoyed. Happy. Truth was, they probably wouldn't even mention it or, if they did, they wouldn't look as concerned as they did now. My dad's face is not that of a happy man.

"This man you got the samples from, do they-" I can't say it.

"They match yours. He's your biological father. I'm not." My dad's face falls even more, and I can feel my eyebrows knitting together.

Signed with Love duet
J R Dust

No. No. No, this is not happening. Absolutely not. I feel my head shaking again, wishing more than anything that I could shake this whole conversation away. Dad isn't my dad? But he is. He is. My mind can't process the mess that's happening right in front of me, and I find myself looking at my dad, checking his face for a smile, a smirk to tell me that this is some sick joke. But he's not smiling, his lips aren't lifted. He's crying.

I'm still as a statue. Unable to move. My mind seems to freeze in place, incapable of understanding what I'm being told.

Why is Dad crying? Am I crying? I lift a hand to my face to feel my cheeks, but there's no water. No tears. I'm not crying. Dad's crying.

I move away from Liam's arms and kneel in front of my dad, gently tearing his hands away from his tear-stained face.

"I'm so fucking sorry, Charlie," he cries.

"Why are you sorry? Just because we don't have the same DNA, it doesn't mean you're not my dad, you bloody idiot," I say with a laugh.

I might cry later, but I can't handle dad being upset, being torn apart. I need to help him now. He's my dad. He read me stories as a child, and rocked me to sleep. He hand-fed me food when I was being a lazy toddler, and he taught me the truth about life. He taught me how to live, how to take care of myself. My dad lifted me and kissed me when I fell and grazed my knee so many times whilst learning to ride a bike. He's my dad, and now my dad is upset. My poor dad is in tears, and I have no idea what I need to do to make him feel better, the way he's made me feel better so many times throughout my life. He needs me. He needs reassurance.

"Come here, you big baby," I say as I stand up and pull him into a hug. This is how it was at the start after what happened. Me trying to take his sorrow and sadness away. He's strong but sometimes he needs help, and that's ok. I need to help him now and think later.

"You're such a good woman. I'm supposed to be the one consoling you, and here you are comforting me. You're too good, I should have known sooner," he says with a disgruntled sigh as he pulls away from my embrace.

"Well, I mean I am pretty amazing," I tell him, "but like you said, that's learned, so it's gotta be from you." I shove his arm lightly before tucking myself back into his arms.

He needs me to be his baby girl right now. He needs to know I'm his, so I let myself get lost in my dad's arms.

"I love you so much, you know that, don't you, darlin'?" he mutters into my hair.

"I know. I love you too, you fool," I say with a chuckle.

He pulls back and lets me go, looking at me like he always has. Like I'm still a tiny little baby he still needs to look after.

"His name is David Bancroft. He didn't know about you until I explained. He got the results at the same time as me. He's desperate to meet

380

you, but I asked for a few days so that you can decide. I hate to say it, but he does seem like a good guy, darlin'." He rubs the back of his neck in an awkward gesture of uncertainty.

"I'll meet him, but I'm doing it here. I hope you didn't think you could get rid of me that easily," I say with a smile.

"Wait, what about Gray? He really does look just like you," I say as I think of the physical similarities between the two of them.

Gray's been absent more than he's been here since we got back. I've not wanted to push him, so I've done my best to let him experience life again in whatever way he sees fit.

"Yeah, he's mine, and he knows about this. He didn't want you to feel overwhelmed so he went to work," my dad says with a sad smile.

We spend the rest of the night talking things through, my dad explaining and me comforting him whilst Liam and Crow comfort me.

I don't want to imagine anyone else being my dad. I can't imagine anyone else doing a better job than what my dad's done. I'm not always a grateful daughter, but I do my best to always be a loving one. I think I sometimes forget or perhaps just don't realise how hard it's been for my dad, bringing up a daughter on his own alongside trying to work, run a club, and earn money. He's given up so much for me, and now to find out that it was all for a daughter that isn't biologically his – I'm not surprised he's so upset.

The logical part of me knows my next

thoughts aren't true, but I can't help but wonder if perhaps he feels differently about me now that he knows our DNA isn't shared, if maybe that's why he's so devastated because knowing I'm not biologically his has made the love he's always showered me with diminish some.

Liam hardly says a word, not wanting to interrupt I assume, but he keeps his arms on me throughout the night, whether that be by placing his hand on my back, locking our hands together, or having his arm around my shoulder. He is making it known that he is there when I am ready, and I appreciate that.

Crow, unlike the brooding Liam, jumps in with jokes and banter to ease any tension that arises when certain topics are brought up. His naturally charming and humorous nature serves to be something I'm beyond grateful for.

They're the perfect mixture of everything I need, I realise.

Chapter 16

Charlie

"He's not your dad? Holy shit!" Alice huffs out as she sits back, eyes wide, and takes a sip of the wine in her hand.

"Yup, tell me about it. I thought my head was full on going to explode," I say with a forced laugh. If I don't laugh, I'll cry, right?

"Wait, is your real dad hot? Matt's hot," Kira butts in as she watches me eagerly.

"He is definitely not hot. He's old enough to be your dad." Liam laughs as he shakes his head at Kira.

"So are you, but you're still hot." Kira is thirteen. Thirteen.

"Kira, no! You can't say stuff like that to grown-ass men," Alice chastises her as she rubs a hand over her forehead and eyes.

"Well, I just did, so boo-hoo, baby," she says as she glares mockingly at Alice.

She has more sass than anyone I know. More confidence. More arrogance and more insanity, but she's also the coolest thirteen-year-old you'll ever meet too.

"What about me? Why am I being left out? My mum always told me I was handsome," Crow says as he fakes a pout and flutters his lashes at us all, causing a laugh to break out between me,

Alice, and Kira.

"Why are you all laughing? I'm bloody gorgeous," he informs us as he looks around at us all with a crooked brow and confusion marring his beautiful face.

"You're hot, too, don't worry," I tell him as a giggle escapes while I pat his leg.

"It's the older men. The girls dig it," Liam tells him, his face as confused as Crow's.

"First of all, no one says dig it anymore, which just shows exactly how old you are. Secondly, you're not that old. Third, how the fuck old are you?" Kira asks Liam as she leans in closer.

"Will you stop swearing? You've literally just become a teenager, you do not need to be saying that kind of stuff," Alice says as she takes another large gulp of her wine.

I have no idea how she does this alone. No parents or family, and although the Cobras and a few neighbours help her with Kira, I genuinely can't understand how someone so young can cope with the responsibility alone. I need to make sure to come around and help more often. Not as though I do much to help, but just being there is more than their own family offers.

"I'm thirty-two. Not that old, but far too old for you to even be joking about, kid. Stop giving your sister a damn heart attack, will you? It'll upset Char and then I'll have to take your Haribo off you," Liam threatens as Kira looks mortified and hugs her packet of sweets closer to her chest.

"Jeez, that's harsh! I'll be good, ugh. Men,"

she mutters as she slides another sweet into her mouth while glaring at Liam.

"How did things go with you and Edgar? Dad said you haven't seen him for a while."

I'm not sure how willing she is to talk about him but considering she was practically gushing over him the last time I'd spoke to her before I was taken, I'll bet that she isn't over him as much as she probably wants everyone to think.

"She's being difficult. He has flowers, a note, and different snacks delivered here every single day. She won't even open any of them," Kira tells us, rolling her eyes at her sister - the consequence of which is a whack on her arm from Alice.

"It's not that simple," Alice tells me, shaking her head.

I wait, sensing there's more she wants to say.

"At the start, I was worried that he had something to do with your disappearance and then I realised when he helped so much that he can't have, but I don't think it's really that at all. I think I'm just terrified of him leaving. Kira and I both got so attached to him after just a few days, imagine a month or a year and then him leaving us," she says quietly. Kira's face falls as well, as if thinking about that and how much it would hurt.

Considering the way they've been abandoned before, I can see why, but Alice particularly has worries.

"I know that logically you must know this, but I'm going to say it anyway. If you don't let anyone in enough to let them hurt you, you'll miss out on some of the best opportunities in the world. Not just in a romantic sense but in so many other ways too. Sometimes you have to risk being hurt and just hope for the best instead," I tell her, watching as she nods at me softly.

Alice is one of the brightest people I know, with a personality to match, but since I've been back, I've noticed that the flame burning inside of her seems to have diminished. I thought that maybe Edgar had hurt her in some way and she was trying to get over him, but it seems she's the one that broke it off despite not wanting to get over him. I can't say I'm particularly keen on the man, considering my past and the stories I've been told about him, but if someone as lively and lovely as Alice got to know and appreciate him for who he is then who am I to judge? Especially considering my current predicament with the two men sitting beside me. Someone even more traumatised and hurt than I am and another man that lied from the first day I met him.

"If it's any consolation, I did a lot of research on everyone, including him before joining the Cobras, and I can safely say without giving his whole life away that he doesn't attach himself to anyone unless they mean a lot to him. He's not close to many people but the people he is close with get the fiercest form of protection and love from him. He doesn't leave anyone," Crow says, his usually bashful and humorous tone now gone, giving way for the sensible and caring side of him that I adore just as much.

I think I knew; I must have known that Crow did his research before joining us, but what I didn't think about was him potentially knowing a lot more about all of us than we perhaps realised. He'd never, so far as I know, used information about anyone against them and yet I have a feeling that he knows enough that he could if he ever needs to.

"I told you he won't just leave," Kira murmurs to Alice.

I watch as the two sisters smile at one another, Alice's eyes looking lighter and filled with promise as she takes Kira's hand in hers.

Chapter 17

Crow

She's nervous. I can't figure out if she's nervous because she's meeting my family, nervous because she's meeting the head of the Irish Mafia, or nervous because she's about to ask for something that I really hope I've guessed wrong. I take her hand, relishing in the way she automatically brings her body closer to mine for comfort. I press my body into hers, bringing her head to my chest as I breathe in the fresh ocean scent of her. Her body taught against mine does unexplainable things to me, setting the very rarely placed dick in my pants into overdrive.

Her arms wrap around me, her head beneath my chin, fitting perfectly in the space between my neck and chest. She folds her body into mine further, my cock over the soft curves of her stomach. Fuck, she feels nice. I could happily live the rest of my days with her body against mine.

Shut the fuck up, Crow.

You do not need a boner right now.

I let her hold on for another moment before gently pulling away from her, watching as Liam walks up from behind her towards us.

He gives me a nod, a knowing grin, and juts his head towards the door behind me. My family are in a hotel suite, the door of which is currently

388

behind me.

"Whatever this is, Char, it can wait, we don't have to do this now," I tell her, hoping that she understands, that she knows what I'm trying to say when I'm not even sure myself half the time.

"Just stay close, both of you," she tells us as Liam puts his hand on her lower back and guides her towards the door.

I've spent so long worrying about her that I hadn't even considered that this would be the first time I'd seen my family since I began the infiltration of the Cobras. I spoke to them constantly; Charlie had heard me on the phone to them a lot. Despite what everyone seems to think, we are way more average than you'd assume. You know, give or take a few deaths, murders and wars here and there obviously.

"You ready?" I ask her as I take her face in my hands and place a kiss on her forehead. God, she's fucking beautiful. She makes me want to pray to a deity I've never believed in just to keep her by my side for eternity. I'll happily fucking burn in hell for as long as needed so long as I get to her at the end of it.

She nods, throws a smile that I know damn well is filled with fake confidence my way, and then proceeds to push me towards the door.

Right. OK. It'll be fine.

There's not a single part of me that is worried about my family not liking her or her not liking them, even though I'm sure that's got to have been something that has crossed her mind.

Signed with Love duet
J R Dust

Despite the way she often sees herself, she's one of the most self-aware and selfless people I've ever met. I mean, how often do you meet someone that can forgive the guy that set her up? Even thinking about Victor makes me want to fucking pummel him. I shake thoughts of the stupid fucker away and pull myself towards the door.

I knock on the door once, not even getting a second rap on the wood in before it's sprung open, revealing my mum.

"Oh, my baby boy!" She squeals as she pulls me into her embrace and holds my head down to her level while squeezing me with all of her might.

I might be a grown ass man, but I'm not going to lie and say that my mum's hugs aren't the best. The best familial hugs at least. Char gets top spot for all other types of hugs.

"Let him up, Mary, no one else will get a look in if you don't." My dad huffs from behind her.

"He's my son, and I'll damn well hug him as much as I want, thank you very much!" she sasses back as she squeezes me some more.

My mum's a little shorter than Charlie and small in build, but her sass and attitude definitely make up for it. She lets me go, her eyes finding Charlie, and I watch in awe as her face lights up.

"Oh, look at you! You are just beautiful, sweet pea!" my mum gushes as she rushes over to Charlie and takes her in her arms.

Char looks momentarily panicked before relaxing a little and awkwardly hugging my mum

390

back. Liam seems about as astounded as Char is, and I can't help but laugh at that. Talk about a fish out of water and you've got Liam - a man who looks pretty uncomfortable right now. Can't say I blame him. He's in uncharted territory.

My dad gives me a hug, patting me on the back and ruffling my hair a little before shaking Liam's hand and introducing himself to Charlie.

"So, I hear you wanted a chat with me, Charlie girl. Shall we get to it?" he asks gruffly.

"Yes, please. I really appreciate you coming all this way," she tells him, her voice taking on that of a professional as she talks to my dad.

She may not have been involved with the Cobras dealings, but she definitely gets the confidence, even if it is a show, from her dad. I've watched him in the most intense and intimidating situations act cool and collected, and that's exactly how Char appears despite the hidden terror and nerves I know she's feeling. I have a feeling I know what's coming and even though a part of me is dreading it, I also can't be more proud of what she's willing and able to overcome to ask for something so outrageously out there.

"Well, I needed to see this lad you've got hooked on you, it's not a completely selfless trip," my dad says with a smile as my mum takes his arm and leads him to the two sofas facing one another. There's a glass coffee table between them that my dad collects his drink from before taking a seat and encouraging Char to take a seat on the sofa opposite him.

I grab a chair from the table and sit next to her, letting Liam take her other side on the sofa.

"I'm not sure I'd say he's hooked." Char laughs while looking at me with a smile that makes her eyes look even brighter. Fuck, her smile kills me every time. I need to take more pictures of her smiling. Not right now, though, shut up, Crow.

"Oh, he definitely is. Did you know that he talks about you every single time we speak?" Zak, my youngest brother, says as he walks in from an adjoining room. He gives a quick fist bump before taking a chair and sits by us.

Zak took after our mum more than Coran, my oldest brother, or I did. Zak is taller than me by maybe an inch or two but more slender too. He has more of a swimmer or a runner's body, with his light hair matching my mums. Coran and I both look much more like our dad with darker hair, more natural muscle as well as our father's obsession with tattoos. Zak always says he wants a tattoo or two, but I don't think he'll ever get one. He's smart, like stupidly smart, and says he doesn't understand the enjoyment from causing yourself pain.

"You alright, man? Where's Coran?" I ask, knowing that my parents wouldn't have come for too long without him. He and my dad are the ones in charge of the business side of things and are constantly in meetings together online, over the phone or in person, always consulting one another.

Signed with Love duet
J R Dust

"We've left him at home to take care of things while we're here. He'll be taking over when I retire so it's about time he has the chance to prove himself without my help," my dad says, his hands gripping onto the glass of what I've got to assume is whiskey in his hand.

So, this is a business meeting, I realise. My dad rarely drinks but anytime he's in a business meeting, he has whiskey.

"He'll do just fine, I don't know why you insist on acting like he won't," my mum scolds him with a light whack to his shoulder as she sits next to him.

"I didn't say he wouldn't do just fine," he objects, rolling his eyes in exasperation at her.

My mum glares at him a little more before turning her gaze back on Charlie.

"So, what can we do for you, dear?" she asks as she leans forward in anticipation.

I watch Char for any clues or worry emitting from her, but she's the picture of confidence and grace as she smiles kindly at my mum.

"Well, as it happens, I'm after your official support," she starts, and I'm thinking nothing other than fuck no as she continues, "I'd like to run for President of the Cobras."

There's absolute silence as my father's lip twitches into a smile he tries to hide and my mother's eyes light up as if it's the best thing she's ever heard. Zak doesn't look surprised in the least and, as I look at Liam, he's doing nothing other than glaring daggers at Charlie's head. OK, great. Going well. No problems here.

Hey, God. If you're up there, I'd appreciate it if you could come down and just re-wire Char's brain for a super teeny tiny second so that she changes her mind. Cheers, mate.

I don't want to make her feel like I'm disrespecting her, but I also want to rip her off the sofa, drag her home, and not let her out ever again. How Tamlin of me. She told me about him, one of her redeemable book boyfriends. I genuinely think she prefers the men in books to me half the time but then again, they're made by women for women most of the time so who can blame her?

Back to the present, please, Crow.

Right.

"Why do you want to do that?" my dad asks her, his face clearing of emotion though from the small twitch of his brow, I know he's already made his decision. Fuck.

"It's either me or one other contender. A man from The Laidens that, from what I've been told, will run it to the ground. The Cobras are my family and I want to protect them in the same way that they've always tried to protect me. I want things to be as legal as possible, for them to be a part of society rather than be estranged from it. I want them to be a part of the local community that people feel they can come to if they need help, and I want future generations to have what I've had from them," she says as she lets out a breath, sits a little taller, and straightens her shoulders as she waits for my dad to say something.

Well, shit. I thought she was going to suggest that I take over the Cobras and I was worried that I'd have to ever so kindly refuse, but if this is the way she wants it to go, that includes a lot of change. But if anyone's capable of enforcing it, it's her. She's so much stronger than she realises. Her stubborn streak is made of iron, her mind made of tougher stuff than I've got in me, and her will and wit capable of anything. But she will need help. A lot of it. And there's no one else I'd trust to help her aside from myself.

Well, fuck. Here we go.

"I'd like to rescind my title and offer myself as a second for Charlie in the Cobras. I want to make the transition permanent and official," I tell my dad. I watch as my mother's face lights up even more, my dad smirks, and Zak rolls his eyes at me.

"You have that much trust in her or are you blinded by love?" my dad asks me after another moment of silence.

"It's got nothing to do with love. I believe in everything Charlie wants to do, and I want to help her achieve it, which I can't officially do unless my title is taken from me." It's the way it works in the Irish Mafia. You can't be an O'Banian and a Cobra.

My dad looks between us, his gaze indecisive and curious.

"You'd be willing to give up your future for

this?" my dad asks me.

I nod my head, not needing to expand on it. Charlie's eyes find mine as she gives me a gentle and tentative smile.

"Very well then. You both have my full support. When you become the Cobras President, I expect a merge as well, and so long as you're OK with that happening then Crow needn't give up his title."

"Can we have dinner now? I need a proper catch up with you all, and I want to get to know this handsome little so and so a bit better," my mum says as she wiggles her eyebrows at Liam. Ew. What the fuck is wrong with her? I take everything good back that I've ever said about my mum. Even worse is Liam lapping up the attention and Charlie finding it hilarious. Brilliant. Fucking brilliant.

———————

"Was anyone going to tell me about this plan before you set it in motion?" Liam asks, frustrated as we walk back down the hall towards the entrance of the hotel.

"Not really, no," Charlie says dismissively as she does something on her phone. An abrupt laugh leaves me at her tone. She sounds like she's in charge already, though I suppose between the three of us, she is in charge. She knows well that both of us will do anything she says.

"Excuse me, I'm technically still the Cobras President, and what about your dad?" he asks, exasperated as he stares at her in horror.

"I'm texting him right now, and not for long you're not," she tells him with a sly grin and a condescending pat to his shoulder before she continues walking onward.

"Have you heard this?" Liam asks me as if I'm not finding the situation the most hilarious thing I've ever witnessed.

"Come on, we're going to see the Devils Dealers now. I don't want to be late." Char whistles through to us and clicks her fingers at us impatiently.

"We're going where?" I ask, confused. She cannot surely mean we're asking them for support as well. They hate us.

"Edgar said he'll help us if I put a good word in for him with Alice. I've already told her, I'm not lying to her about it but I also do think he's actually good for her," she says simply. Right. Right, sure.

"And what are we? Just your bodyguards?" Liam asks.

"Pretty much. Come on, my pretty little bodyguards, let's go. Stop being drama queens and move your butts, please. We're on a tight schedule."

Chapter 18

Charlie

"You need to be quicker at dipping out from under me. You're tiny in comparison to him and if he catches you, you're pretty much done for, Char. The only way you're going to win this is if you can avoid him, wear him out, and then throw a sucker punch his way when he's not expecting it," Crow tells me as he helps me up from the floor again and begins circling me once more.

We've been at it for hours, with Liam watching and instructing from the sidelines, and although as we've already determined I can throw a decent punch, if I'm caught, I'm dead. Well, as good as.

The meeting with the Devils Dealers went as well as expected. With Alice, and therefore Edgar's support, we could potentially have their help. Maybe.

"I need to take a break, I'm dying over here," I tell them as I use the towel on the bench to wipe over my sweat-covered face. I have no doubt that my face is currently as red as a tomato but with how exhausted my limbs feel, I couldn't care less.

"You don't have time for a break. We have very little time to get you ready, and I'm not watching you get beat up so you need to figure out your shit and do it," Liam tells me harshly

398

from the sidelines. I know he's just worried, and I know that I probably need the tough love he's currently throwing my way, but shit, a breather would be nice.

"Fine. Once more and then I'm done for the day," I tell them both as I attempt to shake the exhaustion from my body and stand upright again in front of Crow.

He watches me, his eyes penetrating my every move as we circle each other.

In a split second that I very nearly miss, he comes running towards me. I skirt under his arms as they reach out towards me and grab his ankle, lifting it from behind him and spin around as he lands on the floor beneath me. I jump on his back, bring his hands behind his back and smile triumphantly up at Liam.

"That's once. Do it again. Good job though, baby," he says sweetly. Butterflies flit through my stomach at the praise.

"Wanna let me up now, princess, or am I flipping you over?" Crow asks from below.

I get off his back and run my hands down my now crumpled clothes as they practically stick to me.

"I seriously need a shower. This is gross," I tell no one in particular as I peel off Liam's shirt so that it's just my sports bra underneath on display.

"Who are they from?" Crow asks as he juts his head towards my stomach. It's only now that I am realising that he hasn't seen the rest of my body since I've been home. He hasn't seen the scars littering my skin.

"Matt and Danny," I answer simply, not wanting to get into a conversation about it. The anger and fury in his eyes shock me, but he says no more as his jaw tics and his teeth grind one another.

"Stop, I'm fine," I tell him, my hands on his jaw as I lay a light kiss on his chin.

"Did you kill them?" Crow asks Liam.

"No, Gray stopped me. Said Char might want to get her own revenge one day. The rest of them have probably scattered by now, but those two are at the club in one of the interrogation rooms." This is news to me as much as it seems to be to Crow.

"They are?" I ask, wondering for the first time if revenge would help. I feel OK most of the time. Like genuinely ok, but then there are other times when I look at the scars littering my body and all I want to do is sob and sit in a bath of bleach to rid my body of the invisible dirt and grime that only I can see.

Liam nods next to me but doesn't say anything else.

It doesn't take me long to imagine a scenario in which I could harm them. I know I'm not the first person they've nearly killed. They've killed and damaged many women before me from what Gray told me, but does that mean they deserve what my imagination could conjure? Yeah, actually, they do deserve it.

Signed with Love duet
J R Dust

"If I wanted that, you'd help me?" I ask them both.

"I'd love to fucking kill them myself, but if seeing you do it is my only option, then I'll bring the damn popcorn," Crow says as his hand grazes mine.

"I nearly killed them once already, I'm not opposed to helping you finish the job," Liam confirms.

Knowing that they're both so willing to lay down themselves to help me makes me feel more powerful than I should. I remember wondering if part of the reason that Liam is attracted to me is because of the power role he had over me - being older, more experienced, and having lived and experienced more, but I realise now that the truth with both of them is that I'm the one in charge. I'm the one with the power, and I like that thought more than I assumed I would.

I decide to be brave, if that's even the right word, as I ask them, "Would you kneel for me?"

Crow and Liam both have near identical confusion flitting across their faces before they both nod as they look me up and down.

"Then kneel."

I watch as hunger begins to fill their gazes, their minds obviously realising how this could end up. I want to test it. I want to see how it feels. I've always submitted, even when fighting, I've always been the one to submit and for the first time in my life, I want to be the one in charge. Of everything.

One by one, Liam slightly more hesitant than Crow, they kneel on the floor in front of me. I know no one's going to walk in. Crow locked the door behind us when we came into the gym earlier, not wanting anyone to interrupt me while training.

I inch closer to them, their heads directly opposite my upper stomach. I'm only around a foot away from them now, and I find my insides pooling with a heat I didn't expect. The sight of them submissively knelt beneath me has me feeling more in control and powerful than I ever have. I feel like a queen sitting on a throne with someone worshipping me. Only in my case, I get two someones.

"Lay down," I instruct them. They do exactly as I say within seconds, their speed almost comical as I watch them.

"Closer. I want your sides touching." They don't say a word but shift closer together. Crow has a smirk on his face while Liam looks more tentative and confused.

I walk towards them and take a seat on Liam's hips, feeling his cock lengthen beneath my core instantly as I smile down at him, my face no doubt coating with desire as I grind my body along him. He lets out a low moan as his eyes roll back and his hands grapple to find my waist.

I look to Crow and find him still smiling deviously, his head lifting and finding mine, our lips connecting as I continue the movement over Liam.

The moment Crows lips find mine, Liam begins thrusting up into me. Even with our clothes in the way, the warmth filling me is undeniable. The multi-layered pleasure has me bucking and reaching for Crow's dick with my hand, allowing Liam's hands on my waist and Crow's hand wrapped around my head to hold me up.

"I could fucking eat you, princess. Fuck, I've missed you," Crow grunts out as he pulls my head towards his, his tongue fighting with mine for dominance as Liam's hand pulls my head back by my hair. My eyes catch his. The pleasure and hunger in his eyes as he watches Crow and I ignites the burning desire within me even further.

"Open the fucking door! We got a problem!" I hadn't heard anything before that, but the abrupt voice pulls me out of my daze as I pull away from Liam and Crow. I stand immediately with the worry of someone barging in through the locked door.

"Fuck me, he had to come now?" Crow groans as he stands and adjusts himself, followed by Liam who does the same before going to the door and opening it to find my dad there. He's glaring at Liam until his eyes find mine. I have no doubt that my skin is as blushed as I feel and my hair as messy as my heart as he rolls his eyes at me and instructs us to follow him.

403

Chapter 19

Charlie

The problem was not in fact a problem but rather us being too obvious. Oops.

We've been going at this fighting malarkey for days, which I understand isn't really much, but it feels like years and in that time, the only thing I've mastered is hiding, avoiding being punched, and tiring someone out--which was exactly the goal so that sounds great but today, Crow said he was going to put in real effort. I thought I was ready, more than ready. I was not ready. It took me three attempts before I managed to avoid getting hit. He wasn't hitting me hard at all, just little jabs, but he was using his full speed and skill as my opponent will and I failed epically. The problem with this is that I don't have long left and whereas Crow was taking it lightly on me, I know that Theo will not give me the courtesy of trying again or going easy on me.

"As long as you can wear him out and avoid him grabbing or hitting you, you'll be fine. Wait until he's tired and then put your all into it. Get him on the floor. You want to go for his head, try and twist or break some bones if you can. If he's weak, he'll give in easier or the ref will call it," Liam tells me. I've heard this so many times and yet the closer we get to the match, the more

404

terrified I become of getting into a ring with someone that is nearly twice my size. Someone that is going to put everything he has into beating me up.

"Why did I sign up for this again?" I ask with a defeated laugh as I slump down on the kitchen chair.

"Because you're a badass bitch with the Irish Mafia, The Cobras, and The Devils Dealers supporting you. Maybe," Crow tells me with a smirk and a light knock to the shoulder as I wince.

"Don't touch me. Everything hurts." I moan as I close my eyes and lay my head down on the table in front of me.

"What are you thinking about tomorrow?" Liam asks as he retrieves the ice from the freezer and fills up a glass of juice for me.

Tomorrow. Oh, shit, I had practically forgotten all about tomorrow. My dad had arranged for David, my biological father (that sounds too weird), to come and meet me. He is coming here, to my dad's house, which helps the anxiety but that doesn't make me any less nervous to meet some random man.

"I'm thinking that I have way too much going on in my life right now already, but I know that if I put off meeting him then it'll just make it harder," I tell them honestly.

I've been so busy during the previous days that I hadn't had time to think about tomorrow and how I expected or wished it would go, but that doesn't change the fact that now that I am

405

thinking about it my stomach is tensing and my mind is racing in the worst possible way.

"Do you know him?" I ask Liam. He was around when my mum was, so maybe he does. Maybe he can tell me something to calm my nerves.

"Not personally. Your dad said I met him years ago, but I don't remember it. We've done plenty of looking him up so that we know he's a decent guy but honestly, that's about it. I'm sorry, baby," he says as he runs his hand through my hair.

"It's alright. It's life. It'll be fine. Everything is always fine eventually," I tell him with a weak smile.

I'm not nervous. Yet. Although I'm sure I will be come morning.

"You two will stay here, won't you?"

"We'll always stay, I told you I'm never leaving you again and I damn well meant it," Crow tells me with conviction as Liam nods in agreement.

"Who damn well meant what?" Gray asks as he waltzes into the kitchen.

"You look a mess, Chars, what the hell did you do?" he asks as he looks me up and down, horror written all over his face, before he goes to the fridge and gets his overnight oats out. He's obsessed. Has them every morning without fail.

"I damn well meant that I ain't leaving her," Crow repeats.

"Oh yeah, he won't even come to the bloody Club with me. He's besotted," Gray comments

406

casually as he sits beside me and begins eating.

"You would be, too, if you let yourself open up to a certain someone," Crow tells him with a look that says *'mhmm, I know'*.

"You need to stop gossiping with the Cobras like a bunch of old fucking ladies is what you need to do. You're meant to be my best friend," Gray says with a mouthful of food as he points at Crow and then to himself as he speaks.

"I am, but since you won't listen, I'm just reiterating my point that you're a fucking idiot that'll end up alone unless you let someone in."

"Someone isn't who I want, I don't know who I want otherwise I would," Gray utters.

"Are you not even gonna stick up for me here? We went through legitimate trauma together and you're letting him rip into me?" Gray asks Liam, his face an image of shock.

"If I didn't agree with him, I'd totally take his side but as it happens, he's right for once," Liam says as he continues roaming his hands through my hair, totally unbothered by anyone around us.

"You guys are shit today, I am so not keen on you two right now. So much for being my fucking bestie beans. What time's your maker coming tomorrow?" Gray asks me as he changes the subject.

Crow covers his mouth as he attempts to hide a laugh - failing epically too, might I add. I give him a short glare before turning my attention back to Gray.

"He is not my maker," I hiss out, "and I don't

407

know, I'm pretty sure Dad told me but I've forgotten. Are you sticking around tomorrow too?" I wonder.

"Are you kidding me? I love you, but hell no. It's weird enough knowing our mother's a hoe that kept half your DNA hidden, but I do not need to meet that half. What if I find him really attractive and end up screwing your daddy? Oh, that would be a good story. You should write that. Take notes." He hands me my phone and waves his hand around in a writing motion as if to tell me to get on with it.

"You are so disturbed," I huff out with a laugh that follows as I take my phone from him.

"For being gay or for potentially being into your daddy?" he asks, his eyebrows wagging my way with a smirk.

Even though I've suspected as much many times, this is the first time Gray has ever openly told me that he's gay, and the fact that he's doing it in such a relaxed way makes me beyond happy. I worried for such a long time that he felt the pressure of making an announcement when I don't think it should ever be that way. It should be as simple as saying, 'hey, I love this person'.

"Definitely the second option." I laugh, enjoying the glee on Gray's face.

"What type of guy would you go for? I mean, if I ever potentially found someone that I thought would be a good fit for you?" I wonder.

"Are you kidding me? Isn't it obvious?" Crow asks, his head falling back with a laugh as he pats a glaring Gray on the shoulder.

"What? No, why would it be obvious?"

"He's a little baby bottom, aren't you, bro?" Crow says as he ruffles Gray's hair.

"I honestly don't know why we're friends at this point," Gray mutters grumpily.

"I thought you were fucking Ben?" Liam asks, his eyes wide as if trying to figure out how that worked since Ben gave off major bottom energy.

I'd been curious about their flirtatious nature for a while but didn't want to intrude by asking.

"Haven't found anyone worth being a bottom for." He shrugs.

"Wait, so are you and Ben actually a thing?" I ask.

Liam nods his head at me and gets a glare from Gray.

"No, we are not a thing. We just mess around sometimes. He's too... nice," he says with a grimace just as Dad walks in behind him.

"Who's too nice?"

All of our eyes divert to my dad, Gray's wide eyes included.

"Liam," I say, completely unsure of why, but it was the first name that came into my head.

My dad's brows crease. "Liam's too nice?" he asks, his voice totally unbelieving. "For what? A fucking mass murderer? That's about the only thing he won't do." He huffs and rolls his eyes and pulls his phone out of his pocket.

"How's the fighting going? Victor said Theo's in impeccable shape," he tells us, showing us a clip on his phone of Theo sparring with someone.

"Victor sent you that? He's a fucking shithead, I don't care how much sucking up he does," Crow says, shaking his head and leaning back from the phone screen so that I can see.

"Yep, he's been keeping me in the loop," my dad tells us.

I watch the video, my face practically glued to the screen as I witness the brutal punches and lethal force that leaves Theo as he trains with a man I don't know or recognise. The strength and power behind his punches terrifies me. The idea of him coming towards me with that force sends shivers down my spine, makes my hands shake, and my heart race far more quickly than should be possible.

"I'm not trying to put you down here, darlin', but I'd prefer the club go to him by you forfeiting than see you get hurt in the process of trying to win it." I understand why he's worried. I'm worried and I'd be surprised if he wasn't. He's seen Gray and I go through so much pain that I can understand why he doesn't want to witness anymore of it, but despite how much Theo terrifies me, I know that I can't give up now. I know that I have to at least try.

"I'm not giving up to that," I say, my head nodding to the screen still held out towards us in his hand.

"I'm not letting the likes of him run the Cobras into the ground after years of them having us. They have us or they have nothing. He's not winning anything other than a trip to hospital," I tell them all with far more confidence than I actually have.

I remember my dad telling us that confidence is all you need. He said you could scare people with confidence. So long as they thought you could beat them, then you could. I've never put that theory to the test but now is as good a time as any, right?

Chapter 20

Charlie

"Will you stop fidgeting, darlin', it'll be fine," my dad says as he gets his rucksack together for work. I untangle my hands and place them on my lap.

I'm meeting David today. He's driven two hours to meet me for the first time, and it's only because I don't want to be rude and disrespectful to the effort that he's gone through that I don't bolt out the back door right now.

"I know."

"What is it about meeting him that makes you so nervous?" he asks.

I ponder his question, not completely sure of the answer. In less than five minutes, David will be here. I can't decipher what I'm thinking, let alone put it into words. I don't really know why I'm nervous, other than knowing that this meeting could go wrong, feel weird, or be a lot more tense than I'd like.

I've had different scenarios running through my head all night and every moment of the day since I woke up. This could go terribly. He might see me, see the scar on my face that I've done my very best to forget about, and wonder what happened, as any normal human being would. I don't want to lie to the man the very first time I

412

meet him, but there's also no chance of me telling him the truth. He might meet me, begin talking to me, and decide that I'm a terrible person that he doesn't want to get to know, and it's not as though I particularly want to impress him or anything, but it would be nice for him to meet me and think that I'm not a bad person. I don't ever try to be. I try to be the opposite, although I admittedly don't always succeed in that.

"I don't know. It's just a weird situation. I'm just stressing," I state.

"That it is," he says with a chuckle.

The doorbell goes, and I'm sure I'm about to pee my pants as Dad gives me a warm smile before heading to open it. I follow behind him. He's acting so chilled out, though I'm willing to bet at least some of that is for my sake because he can see that I'm nervous.

He opens the door and I'm presented with a man that if I wasn't sure before that he was my biological father, then I am now.

I instantly see it, the resemblance between us. He has the same shade of grassy green eyes as I do, the same freckles under his slightly wrinkled skin. He's older than Dad is, that much is obvious, though not by more than ten years I'd say.

I smile weakly at him and see an identical one trained back onto me. We have the same smile. It's like looking into a mirror if I take away the fact that he's however many years older than me and a man.

413

Ok, maybe not a very good mirror, maybe a blurry mirror or the strange ones you get at amusement parks for kids.

He's wearing dark jeans and a white long-sleeved shirt. He looks smart, posh almost. He has no stubble, no beard or moustache, and has hair the same dull brown colour as mine cut neatly atop his head.

"Come on in. You can sit in the kitchen with Charl, I was just heading out," Dad says as he leads us back through to the kitchen.

I take a seat in the same spot I was before, easing myself into the comfortable worn wooden chair as David does the same in the seat opposite me after Dad gives him the nod of encouragement to sit.

"I can see the resemblance between us already, you look just like my daughter," David states as he smiles warmly at me.

"You've got a daughter?" The question I was about to blurt out comes out of Dad's mouth instead. I like that he is just as curious as I am.

"Yes. Yes." He smiles. "She's just a few years older than you. I have a son as well."

"Will you tell me about them?" I ask enthusiastically.

"You know what, I'm gonna head off to work, I'll leave you two be. Liam and Crow are in the living room if you need them," he reassures me with a small smile.

He walks over to me and gives me a kiss on the top of my head before saying a swift "love you" and running off.

"You can see that you two love each other a lot," David says with what looks to be a genuine smile.

"I don't mean to offend you when I say this but he's my dad. It would probably be stranger if we didn't love each other."

He smiles knowingly at me.

"No, I completely understand. I do want you to know, though, that I do love you as well. Since the moment your dad rang me and told me everything, I've loved you and it's only grown more and more every day." I feel so cruel not being able to return the kind sentiment, but I'm hoping he understands that for me it's just too soon, something that isn't yet there or formed. I'd only be lying if I repeated his words back to him.

"So, you were going to tell me about your kids?" I encourage.

"Ah, yes!" he exclaims.

He leans down to the bag I didn't notice before and pulls out what looks to be a scrapbook.

"I know it's a little childish, but we've all been creating little notes and pictures for you since we found out." He hands me the book and nods at me to open it.

I open the first page and find a picture of David, with who I assume to be his son, daughter, and wife.

His wife has beautiful fiery, short red hair, warm grey eyes, and a large smile. She looks like the mums you see in movies, the ones that want to constantly make sure you're fed, hydrated, and hugged just enough.

The girl in the picture does look surprisingly similar to me. She has her dad's dark hair that falls just above her shoulders. She has a button nose like I do, with grey eyes like her mother. Our face shapes are very similar, but her skin is lighter than mine.

The young man in the picture had the same warm smile as his mum; stood next to his sister with his arm around her shoulders. He's looking directly at the camera. He has auburn hair, a mixture of both his mother and father's, though he has the same green eyes as I do. The shape of his eyes is similar to mine as well. His smile is infectious, even through the picture.

I look down at the names below the picture. David. His wife Amanda, Robin, and Dustin.

I turn the page quickly and find a handwritten letter attached to the page alongside a bookmark.

I'm not really sure how I'm supposed to start this letter, but I wanted to write something to you, so I'm going to start again.

Dear Charlie, (that seems a little too formal, doesn't it?)

To my new sister (that seems too cringey)

Signed with Love duet
J R Dust

Hey! (I'm giving up with the greeting now, so stopping here)"

I find myself laughing at the letter before carrying on.

Considering I'm a writer for a living, I'm really not doing very well here.

Dad's told me a bit about you, but I don't think he knows loads yet, so I'm still a little clueless.

He says you like books, so I've given you one of my bookmarks. I love to read too, I'm actually a professional writer so if you ever fancy turning reading or writing into a career then hit me up!

I already have one little sister but because of how old we are I didn't think I'd ever get another. Mum and Dad definitely aren't going to be starting all over again with a baby anytime soon. So, when he told us about you, I've got to admit that I nearly had a legitimate heart attack. I mean, not exactly but I full on thought I was going to. He came into the lounge calling a family meeting one night and came out with that! He says you only just found out, too, and I'm sorry for that. We're all excited to meet you, but I get that for you it's probably more stressful than exciting.

I really can't wait to see you.

I'm not really sure what I'm supposed to be

saying in this letter. I'm just rambling at the moment, as I'm sure you can tell. But I just wanted you to know that I'm happy that you're going to be a part of our family, I'm happy that I've got another little sister. With any luck you won't be as annoying as my other one. But overall, I can't wait to meet you.

From the best big brother that you'll ever have (yes, I hear you have a brother but I'm competitive. I'll win.)
Dustin
P.S Can we meet you soon?"

I find myself laughing again at his all over the place letter, but I do appreciate it all the same.

"Dustin seems keen to meet me," I say with a laugh.

"I had to fight him off coming with me today, he's persistent alright," David tells me with a smile.

"What's he like?" I ask.

He takes a moment, searching off in space as he conducts his words.

"He's thoughtful, caring beyond measure, and a complete nuisance too, though he'd disagree with me about that." His soft smile looks so honest that I can't help but trust the words he's telling me.

"I take it he didn't convince you to let him come then?"

David physically cringes at my words, and I

watch as he pulls his eyebrows together. What's that about?

"I didn't want to tell you in case you felt pressured, but I don't want to lie to you since you've asked. He's in the car. He said he wanted to come even if he just got to see your face from the door," he tells me hesitantly.

I find myself laughing again.

"Can I go get him?" I ask, curious to meet the grown man that is sitting in the car alone just to get a five-second sighting of me. I suddenly feel like a statue in a museum. It makes me feel like a celebrity with paparazzi on my tail. I smile at the thought.

"You really don't have to if you don't want to. He knew there was a chance he wouldn't meet you. You don't have to meet him just because he came here," he rushes out. I like more than I'll admit how diligent David is in making me feel comfortable.

"It's ok, it would be nice to meet him," I admit.

David looks up at me warily, obviously unsure of my words.

"Plus, he's probably less likely to annoy you for two hours with questions on the way home if I meet him," I say with what I hope to be a convincing smile.

"As long as you're sure," he tells me with a weak smile.

I nod and enter the hallway towards the door, walking past the mirror and stopping abruptly. Because I'm so used to it now, I forget the scar

419

is there, but I realise that David hasn't looked at it once, nor asked about it and although I'm surprised by that, it pleases me to no end. I wonder if his son will have the same reaction, or lack of, as his dad or if he'll be curious enough to ask.

I walk out the front door and find the man from the picture leaning against what I assume to be David's car, looking down at a book in his hands. He's not noticed me yet.

"Dustin?" I ask.

He looks up instantly and a wary smile fills his face.

"Are you Charlie?" he asks hesitantly. He closes his book and takes a step towards me.

"Shit, you look just like Robin, you must be you." I laugh at his logic.

"Are you coming inside?"

"Seriously? You don't mind?" I don't ask, but by his appearance I'd say he's probably early twenties, but the way his voice lifts with excitement, he seems like a little kid.

"Yeah, come on." I usher him inside behind me and lead him into the kitchen. He takes a seat next to David.

"Do either of you want a cuppa? I forgot to ask when you came in, sorry, David," I say as I begin boiling the kettle.

"Tea would be fantastic, please, Charlie. We both take one sugar," David tells me.

I make the tea quickly and hand it to them before taking a seat back at the table.

"You're really pretty." I blush at Dustin's abrupt compliment, not used to being told that by anyone other than Liam, Crow, and my dad occasionally.

"Thank you," I tell him with an awkward laugh.

"It seems weird hearing you call Dad David. I know you've got your own dad, but it still seems strange," he says with a chuckle.

"Yeah, I suppose I'd think it was weird too if I was in your situation," I say with a smile.

"My sister's going to hate how pretty you are," he says with a boisterous laugh.

My eyes go wide as I look at David.

"Have you not seen the scar on my face? She's got nothing to worry about." I laugh.

The idea of her hating me instils a panic inside of me that I didn't expect. I don't plan on becoming besties with them all, but I didn't want her to hate me.

"How'd you get it?" Dustin asks causally as he takes a sip of his tea.

"Dustin, stop it. You're making her feel awkward," David admonishes. Although he's right, I don't like the idea that Dustin feels bad for trying to get to know me.

"No, it's ok. Everyone's naturally curious about things like that, I get it. I would be too if one of you walked in with a scar covering half your face," I say with a tender smile.

"I was attacked not so long ago, the same day as I had the swabs for the DNA sample actually, not as though my dad told me this is what they

421

were for. I ended up in hospital and am now covered in all these wonderful scars that I should totally make up stories about to make me sound like a badass," I say with a laugh.

David and Dustin look at each other briefly before turning back to me.

"Did your dad sort the people out that attacked you?" David asks warily.

I realise that he didn't ask if the police had. That makes me curious. Does he know about the Club? Liam said he knew David when he was around years ago, so I suppose he would, but would I jeopardise them by saying yes, they did? I don't actually know the answer.

"I don't know, I haven't asked to be honest with you. Do you... do you know what Dad does?" I wonder.

David smiles at me. "Yes. I'm well aware of what your father does for a living. I have no issue at all with your father or the lifestyle he lives," he says to me reassuringly.

"That's great and all, but are either of you going to tell me?" Dustin asks, and I can't help but smile at his impatience at being left out.

"Charlie's father owns a Club. A Club that's," he pauses for a moment, "that's not completely legal in all of their actions," he tells Dustin.

I smile at his evaluation of it. He's not wrong by any means, but he's put it so delicately that it almost makes it sound ok, when I know that the majority of society don't think it is.

"And you haven't intercepted yet?" My ears

perk at this. Intercepted? My narrow eyes find their way towards David.

"Why would you intercept the Club? How?" I ask, my tone making my thoughts clear.

David shuffles uncomfortably before he puts his hand in the breast pocket of his jacket and brings out the one thing every one of us dread.

Detective.

"Get out." I stand as I say the words, pulling the gun from its hidden spot under the table as I do, thankful that I remember years after my dad told me about hidden guns around the house. Pointing it directly at David's head, I wait patiently for them to leave. I've been through far too much shit to even contemplate letting a man like this worm his way in. He's probably just using me to get to the Club.

"Get out or I will kill you right now," I say when David doesn't make a move to go.

He's using his connection to me to get in. He's using it to arrest and hurt the Club and the family I've always loved. I will not allow him to hurt them. I couldn't care less about who he is.

Dustin's eyes bug so far out that if I wasn't so pissed I'd probably have laughed at his cartoon-like face.

"Woah, woah, it's ok." He has his hands up in front of him as he stands, towering above me.

"Get out. Now." I try to keep my voice as low and steady as I can.

Liam and Crow barge in, their eyes flicking to me for only a second before they get their own guns out and point them at David.

Crow turns to me, asking, "Sorry to break the tension here, but why are we holding him at gunpoint, princess?"

"He's a detective," I tell him coolly.

"That's why you have a gun pointed at him?" Liam asks as he brings his arm down and places the gun back into the behind of his jeans. Why is he putting it away, the bloody idiot?

"I'm not here to take anything down. I've known about the Club for years. I have no issue with your father running it, none at all," he says.

"What the actual fuck is happening?" Dustin asks more to himself, I think, than anyone else as he watches the shitshow commence. I pay him no mind.

"He's not going to do anything to put anyone away or put the Club at jeopardy, Char, do you really think your dad and I would have let him in if we thought he was?" Liam asks.

"You knew he was a detective?" I ask incredulously, pointing my narrowed eyes at Liam this time.

"Well yeah, but he's not bad, baby," he tells me.

I realise he's right. Dad and Liam would have done every possible check they needed to before letting him in, especially with all the crap going on at the moment.

I bring my arm down, the gun alongside it, and watch as Crow does the same, following my lead.

"Fine. I don't give a shit who you are though, you hurt my family and I will kill you and make sure no one ever finds you." I know I shouldn't threaten people, especially this guy. My biological father. Especially a detective that I don't actually have a way of getting rid of or plan on shooting. My plan is just to scare him which apparently now makes me look like an idiot.

"I don't doubt that one bit," he tells me steadily.

"Sit down and drink your damn tea," I tell him with a sigh and a roll of my eyes at my own ridiculous jump from A to Z.

"I'm sorry for threatening to shoot you. Probably not the best first impression," I say as I smile and shift uncomfortably.

He chuckles as he looks at me. "One of the best first impressions I've ever experienced actually."

"You're a fucking badass bitch!" Dustin exclaims excitedly. I roll my eyes again and laugh at his absurdity.

"That is definitely not something I've ever been called before," I lie as my eyes meet Crow's, holding back the laughter that threatens to spill.

"That was insanely cool!" he says to me, before turning to his father. "Why didn't you teach us to do shit like that?" he asks.

I laugh at him and take my previous seat.

"You may as well stay now that you're here," I tell Crow and Liam.

425

"Dustin, David, this is Liam," I say, nodding to Liam. "And Crow," I say, smiling up at Crow.

They all nod at each other in greeting.

"You literally live in a film. That was so cool. You've just given me the best idea for a new book," David says as he shakes his head in astonishment.

Chapter 21

Charlie

"I feel like I'm literally going to shit myself," I announce to Liam and Crow as they start putting the weights back on the shelves in front of me. We have the gym to ourselves again. My last training session is over, and now the fight that could change everything is mere hours away.

An abrupt laugh leaves both Crow and Liam.

"OK, don't do that, not only would it be extremely unattractive-" Crow starts.

"I don't aim to be attractive," I interrupt.

"And that's not where I was going with this if you'd let me finish my sentence, little miss stress head. I was going to say, not only would that be extremely unattractive but it would also put you in a bad mood for tonight which is not what you want. You want to be in a good mood," he finishes as he comes closer to me and lifts my lips into a smile with his fingers.

"No, a bad mood would mean she was more lethal. Do it. Shit yourself," Liam says from across the room as a laugh escapes me at his stern expression and simple order of encouragement.

"I vote no," Crow says with a look of confusion in Liam's direction.

"Do you think it'll help if I puke? Maybe I just

need to be sick," I think out loud, nodding my head as if answering my own question.

"I vote no for that too. But I'm sure Liam would love to disagree with me and suggest that you simultaneously shit yourself and puke. Shall we add piss in, too, Liam? You into that?" Crow asks before turning to me again, "Go for it. Shit, piss, and puke on yourself, it'll help," he says mockingly in a tone that I assume is meant to be Liam's.

Liam knocks his shoulder, "I do not sound like that and no, I'm not suggesting she let every bodily fluid suddenly hammer out of her. I'm just saying that her being in a happy go lucky mood isn't going to help her win a fight," Liam says, pinching the bridge of his nose as he looks between me and Crow.

"OK, you two are ridiculous and not helping at all." I laugh, watching as the two men smirk at one another.

Fuck, my body sees them and within seconds just wants to pounce.

So not the time, Charlie.

"What do we do now? I feel like I need to stay busy or I'll get nervous, and I don't want to be nervous." My goal is to appear as confident as possible even if that's not actually how I feel.

"I can think of plenty of things to keep you busy," Crow says with a dramatic wag of his brows and a wink in my direction.

"Even when being ridiculous, you are ridiculously handsome. Flop it on out and I'm all for it," I joke with a shrug.

"No, that is not going to help. Not right now at least," Liam intercedes, rolling his eyes once more.

"I mean, it might help me relieve some pressure."

"Then let us relieve your pressure, not the other way around," Liam says as he stalks towards me and takes my face in his hands, his lips crashing into mine in a show of dominance and passion that I am all for.

He arches my head backwards, so that my face is directly below his as he devours my mouth with his own, his tongue darting between our lips as I feel Crow's presence behind me, his lips on my neck and his hands between my legs.

"Knock, knock, I'm coming in!" a voice shouts from outside the door.

Oh, for fuck's sake, not again.

Crow groans behind me as he steps away, Liam simultaneously pulling his lips from mine as he lets out a sigh of frustration, his pants tenting without care as Gray walks in.

"I feel like I just interrupted something," Gray says as he takes in our positions. Crow is mere inches from me at my back while Liam still has his hand around the back of my head.

"You did. You can go now and come back later," Liam says as he walks towards Gray and begins ushering him out.

"Uhrm, no actually, I can't. I need advice. Like, now," he says as he skirts around Liam and comes barrelling towards me in a rush, as if worried that Liam will catch him and physically toss him out.

"What's up?" I ask as I take a seat on the gym benches and gesture for Gray to do the same on the ones in front of me.

"I think Ben likes me," he blurts out, cringing as if it's the worst thing in the world.

"Why do you think he likes you?" I'm not even sure why I'm asking this question considering the way that Ben looks at him. Every time they're in the same room, Gray is completely unphased and Ben acts like a man starved for the sight of my brother.

"Because he told me he likes me."

"So, you know that he likes you?" I ask.

"Well, he could have just been saying it."

"Why would he do that?"

I'm sure my face conveys the confusion I'm feeling because he quickly starts talking again.

"I mean, I know he's attracted to me, we've been fucking on and off for ages, but he said he likes me," he emphasises as if this makes more sense than his previous statement.

"Is that a bad thing?" I wonder, unsure of why this is such a problem.

"Well, yeah, that's why I'm seeking advice, Chars. Duh." He rolls his eyes, watching me as if I've completely lost my mind, which I may very well have considering I don't understand what the issue is.

"Oh, I get it, you don't like him, you just want

430

to fuck him," Crow says with a nod of understanding.

"Exactly."

"So, what is it you need advice on? How to make him not like you? Just be yourself. I don't like you," Liam states - a complete lie if I've ever heard one.

"You only don't like me because I interrupted your weird time with my sister and Crow, which might I add for a second time is weird," Gray acknowledges.

"You told me when I was like ten that you would never judge me. This feels pretty judgey," I argue.

"No, no, no, I'm judging him," he says with a look in Liam's begruntled direction, "and him," he says as he nods towards Crow, "but I'm not judging you." he clarifies.

Despite his reassurance, I somehow don't think the words coming out of his mouth are making the situation any better.

"That's judging, mate," Crow tells him.

"OK, well fine, I'm judging. Now back to the problem at hand please. What do I do?"

"Be honest with him. Tell him that you don't see him that way and that you're not going to carry on having sex because you don't want to lead him on," I tell him, not understanding how this is even a question he needs to ask.

Is it not common sense to do the above? I mean, obviously not if Gray seems to be having so much difficulty coming to the same conclusion that I have.

"Yeah, but I get stressed if I don't have sex for too long."

"Have sex with someone else then, it's not hard, mate."

"It is when there's fuck all gay people around. I don't mess with baby bi's, and I literally don't know any other gay person," he concludes.

"Aren't there apps for shit like that?" Liam asks as he grabs Crow's phone from out of his hand and begins looking up gay hookup apps and showing Gray.

"Yes, but I'm a depresso espresso that doesn't want to just meet random people for sex. Who knows what they'll do to me? I don't want to be kidnapped and raped, thank you very much. Not my kink," he says as he lifts his hands in the air and shakes his head.

His eyes catch mine at the exact moment he realises what he's said.

"OK, that was bad. I should not have said that. I'm sorry, I didn't think. Too soon, always gonna be too soon," he hashes out in a panicked rush as he waits for a reaction from me.

"It's fine." I smile, knowing he meant no harm and that he just doesn't have a filter between his brain and his mouth. "I get what you mean and from experience, I can vouch that you do not want that. Been there, done that, got the t-shirt," I say as I pull the shirt I'm wearing in front of me as if to show him.

"You realise how weird you two are, right?"

Crow asks as he looks between Gray and I with confusion marring his brows.

"Yeah, we're odd, get over it. You love us both; now hush while my sister gives me some solid advice," Gray tells him with a pat on his shoulder and a hand on his mouth to silence him.

"Ew, don't lick me, you freak! Jesus, keep your animals under control, Charlie," Gray says as he pulls his hand back from Crow, wipes his palm on his trousers, and watches him in disgust as an obnoxious laugh leaves me, Crow, and Liam at Gray's reaction.

"OK, OK, my advice is to find someone else to hook up with, be honest with Ben, and be chill. Meet in public places, tell people where you're going, and do that thing where you check peoples' criminal records."

"Ugh, you just don't understand." He groans as he gets up to leave, "Oh, and Dad wants to see you." He checks the time on his phone and holds it up for us to see. "Like twenty minutes ago."

———

"Are you ready?"

No.

"Yep," I lie, watching as my dad paces nervously around the room.

I'm nervous, I'm anxious and I'm scared, but the nervous energy emitting from my father is absolutely killing me and making me so much worse.

"Stop pacing, she can't stop watching you," Liam tells my dad, his eyes not leaving mine as he speaks. He's been doing this all day. Watching me as if waiting for me to break down. I mean, I very well might so it's not a bad idea for him to keep an eye on me.

"Hey, princess!" Crow shouts from across the room as he jogs over to me.

"What?" I ask, not wanting to let too many words come out for the worry that I may very well just tell them all that I'm giving up and not doing this anymore.

"The crowd's filling out, Theo's looking like a bitch boy in his spandex, and you're about to become the president of the mother fucking Dark Cobras. You ready for this shit? My princess is about to get queen status people, it's time to move your butts!" he yells at the people milling around us as the few people in here smile, nod, or shout a cheer in our direction.

We're currently in the gym - again with Tin, my dad (Matt), Alice, David, Gray (who said he did indeed find David attractive - great), Liam, and Crow.

"I'm not doing nothing, I'm just waiting," my dad responds to Liam.

"You're about to boss the fuck out of this shit and if for any reason you want to give up, just give me or Liam a shout and we'll come save your ass, k?"

So not ok.

"OK." I nod. I attempt to drown out the chatter and noise from around me with my music but every time I put the headphones in, someone comes up to me to say something and I zone out again.

"It's time to go, baby girl," Liam whispers to me, his face so close that I can feel his breath on my lips.

"OK."

Be cool. Be calm. Be confident.

Chapter 22

Victor

Even though it's one of my father's men fighting, I'm not sure how welcome I'll be to attend considering the way things panned out between me and Charlie.

I hold no ill will towards her, despite what I can understand those that care about her believe and by some miracle, she doesn't seem to have any hatred for me.

She saunters in, the complete image of someone cool and collected, gives me a hug, asks me to secretly spike Theo, tells me she is joking, laughs, and off she goes. So simple. Elegant. Confident. I highly doubt she is truly feeling that way, but the air of it is the perfect persona for this evening's events.

I've already drugged him, unbeknownst to her. I'm not going to tell her that - or anyone for that matter. I needed to do something in an attempt to gain the forgiveness she has already granted me, after all. I had no illusions of what I was doing. I know I need to do much, much more to truly attempt to gain her trust, but this is a start even if she will never be made aware of it.

I watch from the bar as the area fills with people. I know most of them or, if I don't know them personally, I recognise or have heard of them at least. It's how it often works in this world. You may not know someone, but you always know of them. Usually because of some story that has been told with dramatic changes to enhance the truth of the situation.

"Can I get you another, sweetie?" the bartender, Ben I believe his name was, asks.

I shake my head, but notice that his eyes aren't on me as he speaks, they are across the room. Out of curiosity, I allow my eyes to follow his line of sight. Gray. Ben is looking at him with an intensity and hunger I recognise. I wonder to myself if it is a one-sided crush or if Gray swings that way. I don't recall Charlie ever mentioning it, but perhaps she doesn't know. Or perhaps I've got it all wrong. Or perhaps it is simply not an advertised fact.

My mind takes me to unimaginable places as I witness made up images of Gray bending Ben over and pounding into him. The thought of it has me feeling more uncomfortable and hotter than I'd like. I haven't ever envisioned a man in a sexual way before, but the images keep coming and coming. I attempt to distract myself by looking around the room and taking in my surroundings but nothing does the trick, the images won't leave me. They are all I can see.

Gray on his knees.

Gray on his stomach, arse up.

Gray begging, pleading, screaming.

Fuck, I can imagine absolutely ruining him. I can imagine his hair soaked with sweat and cum as he looks up at me.

Shake out of it, for fuck's sake.

I have no idea where or why the pictures of him naked for me are appearing, but they won't stop. I have absolutely no problem with anyone's sexuality but mine has always been very simply straight - until I noticed Ben watching him with desire, that is.

I'd only met him the once at Charlie's father's home when I explained myself to her. I wince just thinking about that day - not because of the physical pain caused - I'd had much worse but rather because of the devastation it had caused Charlie and the trust that we had grown that had been so irrevocably shattered.

It wasn't as simple as I'd made it out to be, but without jeopardising the person I care for most in the world, I couldn't very well go and explain that to anyone, could I? No, I need to protect them from anyone that could know of their existence and if that means taking the consequences of actions I wish I didn't have to take in the first place, then so be it. I am surprised that they believed that I'd taken action based off of threats towards my father considering how little love there was between us, but they did believe it and that's all that matters. I don't need questions asked that I don't wish to answer.

I realise that through the process of my thoughts wandering astray that I must still have been looking at Gray, who was now looking at me with eyes filled with hatred. Great. One more person to add to the list.

I can't help but notice how attractive he is. He has a rather boyish look about him that seems to appeal to me. I'm sure Charlie mentioned that he was a few years older than her, possibly around twenty-one, but he looks like the type of man that could be fifty and look half his age. He has an innocent look about him that I know holds no fact. He is far from an innocent person. Not a bad one that I am aware of, but certainly not innocent either.

His attire replicates that of a teenager in college with his grey tracksuit bottoms that get tighter towards his ankles and a dark hoodie that looks to be far too big on him. He has a slender body. He is built with muscle from what I saw the other day, but more of a swimmer's fitness level than that of a fighter with hordes of muscle. Sandy blonde hair covers his head and sweeps lightly across his forehead. I'd noticed him moving his fringe out of the way the day at their father's but hadn't taken much notice of anything else about him. He's a few inches shorter than me, though given how tall I am, that's not a surprise.

Stop staring, Victor.

Right, right. I'm here for Charlie.

I turn my attention back to the self-made ring in the centre of the room and watch as Crow, Liam, Tin, and Matt gear Charlie up. She looks surprisingly level headed considering the jibes and curses coming her way from Theo across the

439

ring. He's doing his very best to antagonise her, I can see it in his eyes. He's wearing an evil smirk that I've seen many times before. He's a big man. Maybe six feet two with a lot of muscle. A beer belly stands up front but if nothing else, the muscle on his arm and his weight alone could easily flatten Charlie. She's small, petite, and not made for this. I hope like hell they've trained her well enough. I doubt any of us want to see her pummelled. Although, I doubt it would ever get that far. I can't imagine Liam or Crow would allow a single punch to be thrown her way before they intercede. But then again, hopefully with what I've given Theo, any punch he throws shouldn't be too deadly or dangerous. He should be on his knees with just one punch once it kicks in.

The fight begins with Theo and Charlie inside the ring, circling one another. Theo is throwing a string of words her way that I frustratingly can't hear while Charlie looks completely unphased and remains silent as she eyes up her opponent.

Good, very good.

The tension building in the room is magnified by the silence that ensues. The room is eerily still as everyone waits for the first punch or kick to be thrown. There are bets made by everyone - on who will hit the other first, who will go down first, who will get back up, how long it will last, and if others will end up intervening. I didn't take part, but that doesn't mean that I'm not aware of them.

My phone vibrates in my pocket but I ignore it, knowing that it will be one of my few very annoying friends wondering where I am. I had insisted that I wouldn't be coming tonight. Not only did I not want to see Charlie get inevitably hurt, but I also didn't want to cause a drama that wasn't needed, but I realised too late that I needed to be here for those exact reasons. I don't want to see her get hurt, but I can't stand to be away and hear about it without seeing it. I don't want to cause a drama and yet I am the first one to cause one by drugging Theo.

It isn't that I care about Charlie in the way I perhaps thought I did originally, but I do still care. A lot. She is one of the only people in my life that allows me to so freely be myself and I think I clung to that with everything I had when I first met her. She surprised me - astounded me even.

Theo throws his arms out with a fist towards Charlie that she narrowly avoids. The moment he throws the first punch, the noise in the room resumes. There's shouting, booing, screaming, and screeches coming from every direction. There are people cheering and throwing their hands up. Others are clapping while some are stood as stock still as I am while watching the fight unfold.

For too long, Theo throws punches and kicks that Charlie avoids as she practically and tactically chases him around the ring. It looks as though she's trying to exhaust him before she starts using her body against him, which is good. That's exactly what she should be doing.

What I don't anticipate is Theo catching

441

Charlie, and yet he does. He manages to grab her ponytail, holds her still for just a millisecond as he throws a punch with all of his might straight into her face.

He lets her go and I watch with horror as she falls, crashing down, her head hitting the floor too quickly, and that's when absolute carnage ensues.

Crow's and Liam's eyes are filled with death wishes as they scramble to get inside, but what they don't see that I have the absolute glee of noticing is Charlie as she opens her eyes and looks up at Theo with a lethal danger and predatory fury unlike anything I've ever seen before. Theo isn't looking at her. His arms are in the air, rejoicing with what he assumes is his win.

The people surrounding the ring are too occupied to notice, but I do. I notice the smirk that lands on Charlie's face as a presence seems to consume her entirely. It's like watching a woman possessed as she lets her leg go out and trips Theo up. The shock on his face is beyond pleasurable to see as her men pause their attempts to get to her. Once they realise that she may indeed have the upper hand; a better chance than they originally assumed.

Theo falls heavily to the ground beside her, his eyes filled with confusion, but in less than a second, she's on top of him, throwing one punch after the other at his face, in motions so quick I can hardly keep track of her arms moving. She looks heaven made, God like, lethal as she

442

descends her fists upon him. She looks like the most incredible monster I've ever seen, her eyes lighting up with the pain she's inflicting. Blood spurts out from Theo's face and covers her, but she doesn't stop. Doesn't hesitate. Doesn't slow. She pummels her fists into him until he's stopped moving completely, and then the smirk that covered her face returns as she slowly gets off him.

Crow and Liam, as well as everyone else around us, are deathly silent as they watch on. She stands above him, spits on his face, and walks around the ring, looking into the very soul of every person her eyes encounter.

"Now you fucking bow to me," she says, her voice travelling, loud and clear. I watch in awe as the people around us take her order very literally and begin getting down on their knees, smiles and roars once again filling the room as they cheer her on. Awe fills me as I replicate the actions of those around me and bow with a laugh nearly bursting out of me at the ludicrousness of the situation, watching as her eyes catch mine. Her lips twitch into a half smile as she nods my way, before Liam and her dad walk into the ring, holding one of her arms up each and announce her as the new President of The Dark Cobras.

The damn queen.

I glance once more at her brother that I know will haunt my thoughts before leaving the queen and her attentive bees to their business.

Chapter 23

Charlie

The last time I was alone looking for Crow in this Clubhouse, I felt weak, afraid, and had a nightmare in store that I could never have anticipated but this time, as I look around for Crow, I have people nodding their heads, acknowledging me, I'm the President of the Dark Cobras.

"They're in Crow's room waiting for you," Gray whispers in my ear, his presence unexpected by my side as I look over at him.

"Why are they in there?" I ask.

Crow hasn't stayed in his room here at the club once since I've been home, and neither has Liam. Other than to pick up clothes or any other essentials, they've hardly left my side; I can't imagine why they'd be in there now.

"They've asked me to keep everyone away, to keep Dad distracted especially, so I'm going to guess that I don't want to know why they're in there waiting for you." He laughs lightly as he pushes me towards the hallway door.

The last time I walked down this hallway, I was out of my senses and alone. This time, I feel more powerful and majestic than I ever have in my life. I feel confident and like I could take on the world, and yet the niggling in the back of my mind won't leave me.

It doesn't take long to get to Crow's door. I stand, unsure of myself and what's waiting for me as my hand reaches for the handle. Anticipation runs through me as I open the door and find the absolute last thing I expected to see.

My heart soars, my body reacting immediately as I feel my core warm and my body shiver at the prospect of what's to come.

Liam and Crow on their knees, in only their boxers, their heads down. Waiting for me.

Their tattooed torsos and muscle-ridden biceps and chests while they kneel before me are inexplicably hot.

"Whatever you want, baby. We're all yours," Liam says as he looks up towards me, his eyes connecting with mine, his face filled with earnest caring and adoration as he waits for me to make my move.

Despite how powerful I feel in this moment, I want nothing more than for them to take me. To use me, to screw me and to make me feel nothing but them.

"Whatever I want?" I ask, curiously.

"Anything," Liam says as Crow looks up and nods at me.

"I want you both to ruin me. Make me yours, mark me, taunt me, please me. Do anything, I just need to be yours completely for tonight. I want you to take control."

Liam smirks while Crow's eyes go wide, always the more cautious of the two.

"Your wish is our command, baby girl," Liam says as he rises to his feet and strides towards me.

Crow's more hesitant but soon takes the hint and follows Liam's path to me. He stands back and watches for a moment as Liam undresses me. I'm suddenly glad that I took that shower after the fight. The last thing I needed right now was to be covered in blood and sweat.

Once I'm completely bare before them, Liam takes my hand and pulls me towards the bed, bending me over it. He falls to his knees again, the thud clear as the silence consumes me.

"Do you want pain?" Liam asks, his voice low and seductive as he speaks, his breath echoing along the insides of my thighs.

"Yes," I whisper, needing everything they can give me.

"Then stay still and count." It dawns on me instantly the memory of the last time he ordered me to count but unlike then, I am now completely in control despite our positions. I know that I can tell him to stop and he will. I can tell him to kneel or beg or jump from a damn plane and I know that he will.

"Make sure you're loud enough for me to hear." It's Crow this time that speaks, his low timber of a voice that penetrates me and makes me wet without a single touch.

I nod my head, words unable to form as I wait anxiously for his hands to land on me.

Only, what I expect doesn't come. What I find

446

instead are lips on my inner thighs as he bites, over and over again, just hard enough for it to cause a bolt of pain and pleasure to run through me as Liam spanks my behind with his palm.

Crow's lips on me send shivers throughout my body, goosebumps all over me, my pussy wet and pleading for his touch. His lips hover over my clit and the lips of my core, just close enough for me to feel his breath on me, but he never dares to go further while Liam continues spanking me as I count loudly enough for them to hear me clearly.

"Are you ready for something special, baby?" Liam asks as Crow's mouth disappears from my body. I turn to find him standing again, his eyes not leaving the space between my open legs, his eyes filled with hunger and desire.

"I'm ready." I nod.

"Then get on your knees, baby girl. Let's see how much we can pack in your mouth."

I turn and get on my knees in front of them, realising that they both must have taken off their boxers without me noticing. They both stand completely naked in front of me, their cocks hard and pulsing in front of my face as I lick my lips.

"Just seeing you down there makes me want to fucking ruin you, princess," Crow says as he strokes his thick cock and presses the tip to my lips. I open for him immediately, taking him in completely, my eyes bugging and my throat tightening as he pushes himself all the way down my throat.

I suck and lick, the head of his cock hitting the back of my throat repeatedly as his head rears back, his hand in my hair while he controls our movements. My eyes flit between his and Liam's as I continue the repeated motion. Seeing him so turned on because of me makes me feel mighty and horny beyond belief.

"You ready to add another into the mix?" Liam rasps out as he takes his hand from his dick, his eyes hooked to mine. I nod, my mouth still full of Crow's pulsing cock.

Liam enters me alongside Crow, my jaw aching, my lips hurting and yet my core wetter now than it's ever been. My hand finds my clit, needing the tension and friction to help me. I find myself writhing and panting around their dicks as I do my best to take them in as far as I can. Their movements are identical as they pull on my hair, my scalp stinging from the motion.

The moans and noises escaping them send me into a fever as they fill my mouth, wanting nothing more than for them to fill me elsewhere.

"Is that your hand on what's ours, princess?" Crow asks, his eyes watching my hand.

I nod my head, just slightly.

"How about we do something about that?" he asks.

I nod again, my jaw and mouth sagging and panting as they take their cock away from me.

"Open her up, get her ready for us both," Liam commands, his order clearly intended for Crow who doesn't hesitate for a moment, his hands

448

pushing me onto the bed, his face taking residence between my legs while his tongue and fingers immediately start ravishing me, stretching me and driving me wild. My hips lift and shake, my mind completely obsessed with the hands that are on me.

Crow's fingers slide in and out of both holes in a rhythm so quick that I can hardly comprehend it. My body moves and jolts with each movement, my eyes closing as I take in the overwhelming pleasure consuming me.

Hot lips, a wet tongue and rough hands encase my breasts and nipples, toying and taunting them tantalisingly slowly in comparison to Crow's speedy thrusts of his hands within me.

"You're so fucking wet, princess. You're such a fucking good girl," Crow utters before he very literally dives his head back between my legs, his tongue doing torturous things to me.

"I need you in me. Please," I beg, tears leaving my eyes at the all-consuming and unknown frustration and angst filling my body.

"Well, since you asked so nicely," Liam teases as he bites my nipple and makes a squeak escape me.

Liam and Crow seem to have an unspoken conversation, Liam nodding at Crow without any words spoken.

"Get up, baby girl. I want you on top of me."

I move to allow Liam to climb onto the bed beneath me, his cock protruding and filling my entrance. The immediate relief at having him fill me makes my body sag backward onto Crow just as he pushes me forward and coats my arse with lube.

"Fill her," Liam tells him. Crow takes the command and rolls with it, his hands pulling on my hair as he thrusts into me in one fluid and painful motion that halts my breath and fills me with a fire that I'm unsure will ever truly die down.

Within moments, I'm being moved and bounced on their cocks, feeling like I'm about to explode or be completely ripped apart and yet not wishing a second of it away as they use and ruin me just like I wanted.

"Fuck, your tits look fucking delicious like that," Liam utters as he holds my waist and moves me up and down, my breasts bouncing simultaneously with my body. He lifts himself up and grapples with my moving breasts, sucking a nipple into his mouth and holding on with his teeth as I move and thrust between them.

"You ready to cum, princess? Because I'm about to fucking break you," Crow whispers in my ear, his movements pausing, my arse so full of him that it feels impossible to think of anything else.

"Do it, please," I beg, needing everything and anything they'll give me.

"Don't say I didn't warn you." He chuckles lowly as he grabs hold of my throat, pulling me back towards him so that our bodies are flush up against one another. Crow behind me and Liam attached to my breasts, pounding into me from

450

beneath.

And then he does exactly as he promised. He absolutely breaks me in two. He pounds into me in a quick, harsh, thorough succession while Liam holds me in place and moves me up and down his shaft.

I'm moaning and pleading in words that make no sense and mean nothing while they assault my every sense.

"Now cum, baby girl," Liam instructs as they both pound into me fluently and at identical moments, sending my mind and body to a place I've never dreamed of being, in some high up lost world only known for the strength of the orgasm that rips through me.

I feel both of their cocks pulse and release within me as I collapse onto Liam's chest, feeling completely and utterly ruined in the most earth-shattering way.

Crow rolls off me and lays next to Liam, pulling me between them. I curl into Crow's side, my head nestled on his chest while Liam spoons me from behind.

"Ruined enough for you?" Crow asks with a weak laugh as Liam brushes the hair from my face.

"Mhmm," I mumble and nod, feeling my eyes close.

———

"I've decided that I want revenge," I tell Crow and

Liam. I mean, they're still sleeping but I'm practising telling them in Crow's bathroom mirror. Like any young woman does the night after becoming the President of a Motorcycle Club and having sex with two men. Right, so apparently I've not magically matured and gained a shit load of confidence overnight. Good to know.

I think back to the fight and the confidence and fury that felt like it was possessing me. I've never felt confidence or power like I did in that moment. I have no idea what made me say or do the things I did. Dad told me afterwards how much I'd shocked him and yet in all honesty, I think I had shocked myself as much as anyone else around me watching on as the power rushed to my head.

It was at that moment that I realised what I needed, what I craved. I craved very bloody vengeance. I enjoyed hurting Theo far more than I'd like to admit but I realised that it wasn't him I wanted to hurt as badly as I did, it was them.

I woke up about an hour ago and have been sitting on the floor of the bathroom for eighty percent of that time, thinking. Definitely over thinking, but thinking all the same. I feel like everything is finally starting to come together thanks to last night's victory. My dad, David, Crow and Liam, The Cobras. It all seems to be falling into place slowly. The only thing really holding me back from healing is my nerves, and the nerves only originate because I'm scared of Matt and Danny coming after me again, which means that I need to get my revenge. I need to see them bleed, and I need to make sure that they can never hurt me again.

That sounds logical, right? No, probably not, but I feel like it would make me feel better knowing that they're not in the world anymore. I know from what Gray and Liam told me that I'm far from the first person they've hurt, so I know that I'm doing what's right by the whole female population. I just feel like Crow and Liam might look at me differently if I tell them that I want to exact revenge on them. I have no idea why, I imagine they'd probably support me in it, but there's still a part of me that wonders if they think I'm going too far.

"What you doing in here? We snoring?" Crow asks me sleepily as he rubs his eyes and comes to sit next to me on the floor. He's got boxers on, but nothing else, and even that doesn't manage to distract me from my thoughts.

"Nah, just thinking," I utter.

"Penny for your thoughts."

"I'm not cheap. I want a pound," I tell him with a smile, watching as he gets up, goes back into the bedroom, and returns with a pound coin.

"One hundred pennies for your thoughts then," he tells me as he hands me the coin.

"I think I want revenge. I think that's the final thing I need to do before I can move on."

"Then let's go get ready to get your vengeance, princess," he says with ease as he

453

stands and reaches for my hands, pulling me up
with him and embracing me in his warm arms.

Chapter 24

Charlie

"They're in there?" I ask Liam as I stare blankly at the door ahead. It's ordinary. Wooden. Nothing special. And yet inside of that door are the two men that set the whirling chaos in my mind in motion.

They are the ones that hurt me, scarred me, and rearranged my brain.

"They are." His words are heavy, his voice low, quiet.

The two guards outside of the door stare straight ahead, not looking at me even though I'm only mere feet away from them.

"You don't have to do this. We can take care of this for you, Char," Crow tells me as he brings his hand to the back of my neck and begins rubbing his hand back and forth.

I know I don't have to but I really, really fucking want to. They hurt me, and now it's my turn to hurt them. I'm feeling surprisingly strong but maybe that's because I haven't had to look at their faces yet.

"Are they healed from what you did?" I ask.

"Healed and tied up. They can't move," Liam tells me.

I nod. Good. That's good.

I walk forward with Crow and Liam to my rear

455

and open the door, the guards not leaving their posts as I do.

They're each sat in a chair with a hospital gown, the only thing covering their bodies. They're facing me, the chairs around two or three feet apart from one another.

"Shut the door and tell the guards to come back later."

I'm not sure if it's Liam or Crow that listens to my command, but I hear hushed voices speak and the door close as I stand watching the fear filled faces of the imbeciles in front of me.

They're nothing. Ragged men probably not much older than I am, and yet they thought they had the right to touch me. To hurt me. To take what they wanted. But now it's my turn to take what I want.

Their manhood.

I twist the knife in my hand by its handle, my hands desperate to take action, but I remind myself of how I want this to happen. Slowly. I want them to feel the worry and terror that I did. I want them to see the blood and red and soaked skin that I did.

I walk towards Matt first and watch as he attempts to move away from me. His body can't do anything aside from sweat with the chains around his ankles, arms, and neck. The chair moves a little as he shoves his weight from one way to the other.

"Hold him." Crow and Liam take one side each, going to his back and holding him still.

Signed with Love duet
J R Dust

The tape covering his mouth stops him from speaking but doesn't stop the noises that leave him as he attempts to speak or scream.

I've always thought of myself as a very empathetic individual but in this moment, I feel truly heartless. Psychotic. Uncaring.

I fall to my knees directly in front of Matt and lift the hospital gown up his legs until it reaches his waist. His penis hangs loosely between his legs as he attempts to shake his head, his eyes wide and terrified as tears begin to fall.

"That's right. Cry. Roar. Scream," I whisper to him as I look up into his eyes while a monstrous grin covers my face.

I take his flaccid penis in my left hand and begin severing it with the knife in my other hand. His movements and muffled screams do nothing but urge me on as I attempt to cut through the surprisingly tough skin and muscle. Blood squirts out and covers my face. I wipe the blood away from my eyes with my arm before continuing my pursuit, watching with keen curiosity as his eyes begin closing. His head lolls to the side as I finish the job I set out to do. The pouring blood doesn't stop as I finally slash the final piece of thin skin and take the severed skin and muscle in my hand.

It's tiny. Maybe an inch long. I'm not sure if it'll work for what I have planned. One can only try.

I stand and face who I now know is not Stoner but instead a man named Danny.

"Get me some more tape," I tell Crow as I look

into his worried eyes.

In every other moment of my time with Crow and Liam, I've cared. Truly cared, but in this moment that I know will never leave my mind, I know that all I care for is getting revenge as I see fit.

This is my time. My decision. My right.

Liam leaves Matt passed out in his chair and follows me to Danny.

I rip the tape from his lips and spend a few seconds taking in his pleads.

"I'll do anything, anything you want. I'll do it myself; I'll chop it off myself. I'll never touch anyone ever again. I fucking swear, I swear." His begs and pleads continue until Crow reaches me with the tape I requested.

"Just cut enough off to cover his mouth again, please, and then wait." My voice sounds hollow and monstrous and yet I don't care.

"Stop talking or I'll make it worse for you," I tell the man in the chair. He immediately stops speaking, his eyes full of hope.

"You were inside of me. And now, he shall be inside of you. Open your mouth." I tell him as I feel an evil smile spread across my lips.

His eyes are as wide as saucers as he does the exact opposite of my order and closes his lips, jamming them shut.

A laugh bursts out of my lips as I watch his eyes soar between the three of us. No one is going to save him.

Crow and Liam may think of my tactics as

wrong, sick, extreme, or fucked up and not one bit of me cares. This is my way.

"Hold his nose closed. He has to open his mouth to breathe at some point," I tell Liam, knowing that between him and Crow, he's the most accustomed and able to perform acts of violence.

Liam does as I say. I wait nearby with the bloody and useless muscle of penis in my hand.

It doesn't take long before Danny opens his mouth with a gasp. I don't miss my opportunity and shove the penis in his mouth before holding his jaw shut and telling Crow to tape his lips shut with the tape. He does.

And then I get back to work. I do the same to Danny as I did to Matt. Sever his manhood even though he's long since choked and passed out since then.

I take a step back and admire the work I've completed.

Only one more thing to do and then I can turn on the sane side of my brain and return home.

I look down at myself, seeing that the black leggings, black vest top, and navy zip hoodie are covered in blood.

"Are you done?" Crow asks.

"Nearly," I tell him as I smile, my sweet smile, the sane smile and take a step towards him.

I watch as Crow visibly gulps. He knows me well enough that I have no doubt he knows exactly what my plan entails from here. In order to remove and heal from memories, you have to replace them. And there's no one else I'd rather replace those sordid memories with than Crow and Liam.

"Our baby girl needs us. You can do that, can't you, man?" Liam asks with a sly grin thrown in Crow's direction.

I would never force him to do this if he didn't feel utterly comfortable doing so. So I watch Crow's face, searching for any signs that he's going to say yes and mean no.

He looks from me to Liam and then back to the now quiet men in the chairs beside us.

"Go and sit on his lap. Face me," Crow tells me, his words a command. An order. His face and eyes are filled with hunger and determination as he watches me sit on Matt's lap.

"Uh uh," Liam says with a shake of his head and a mock shake of his finger.

Crow and Liam look at one another before returning their gazes to me.

"Naked," Crow fills in for them both. They seem to have a connection whereby they can communicate without words - and I love it. I love that the men I love and need have as much of a connection with each other as I do with them. Admittedly in a very different way but even so.

I stand and take off my hoodie first, throwing it to the ground beside me, not phased in the slightest if it ends up dirty or covered in more blood. I then remove my vest, my bra, my leggings and underwear so that I'm completely bare before them.

460

Signed with Love duet
J R Dust

"Now what?" I ask sweetly as I watch them stand beside one another and adoring the carnal attraction I have to them.

They're so different from one another and yet as I stand patiently waiting for my orders, I realise that I definitely have a type. Tall, tattooed, and deadly seems to sum it up.

"Go and sit on his lap again," Crow tells me.

I do as he says, feeling the still-spilling blood cover my bare behind as I sit on his lap.

He begins twitching as I do, the weight of me obviously waking him from his painful slumber. I pay no mind to him, his body beneath mine making me want to fidget and get out of the room, but determined to do what I set out to.

Liam is the first to come over to me. He falls to his knees and pulls my left breast into his mouth, sucking and laying light bites along the sensitive flesh.

Crow watches, his eyes alight as he takes in the scene in front of him.

"Aren't you joining us?" I wonder aloud breathlessly, the pleasure from Liam's lips, teeth, and tongue filling my every ending.

Crow's nefarious smile lights a furnace within me as he crouches down beside me, his hands immediately drifting to my entrance. I watch as his fingers use the blood covering me as lube while he enters me harshly with two fingers.

Liam's lips find my own just as a gasp escapes my lips and fills his.

Crow's fingers don't stop their insanely

pleasurable assault on me, his thumb coursing along my clit as I hear the muffled moans enter my ears from the man beneath me. I pay no mind to him, giving Liam my all as his tongue darts out and fights with mine for dominance.

I realise too late that I'm grinding down on not only Crow's hand but the stub I left of the man beneath me. I don't want him feeling my pleasure, I decide.

I pull my lips from Liam's reluctantly. "I don't want to sit on him anymore," I tell them both and watch in awe as they say nothing but immediately take action. Crow takes his hands away from me, my insides feeling empty as soon as he does. He instead puts his face in place of his hand and then lifts me with his hands underneath my legs and reaching behind to my back to keep me upright. I look up to find that I'm very nearly touching the ceiling but feel incapable of concentrating on anything but Crow's head between my legs as he carries me so effortlessly above him while walking towards Danny.

"I don't want their bodies on mine," I whisper out, unsure of what Crow's plan is.

He adjusts his hands and my body, pulling me down so that I'm standing in front of them both.

"You aren't touching them. We are," Liam tells me huskily as he takes a seat on Danny's lap and pulls out his already hard cock, his hand sliding up and down the length.

I'm not touching them. They are, I repeat in my mind.

462

Signed with Love duet
J R Dust

I go over to Liam and take his hand away, instead covering his length with my lips as I swiftly roll my tongue over the head of his cock and revel in the moan that leaves his lips.

I can feel Crow's presence behind me as he places his own dick at my entrance and impales me harshly, with so much force that it pushes me down further onto Liam's cock, the head of which now feels like its bulging out of my throat and yet as I look up with teary eyes from the sudden assault, the pleasure that fills me from Crow's continuous, rough thrusts and Liam's moans of pleasure taking over every sense I have. My hands on Liam's thighs help steady my body as I take and push back for more of Crow to fill me.

"Fuck, I need in her before I cum," Liam grunts out to Crow as he grips his hands through my hair and lifts my head off his stiff and leaking dick.

Crow leaves my body, much to my annoyance, leaving me cold and empty from the air around us taking his place.

Liam spins me around and pulls me towards his lap. I hear him spit in his hand before his fingers reach for my rear entrance as Crow's hands lift my legs so that they're held above his elbows. Liam lifts me in one swift motion and slowly puts me down onto his cock. The overwhelming sense of being so full halts my breathing for a moment as my arse adjusts to having his size and length filling me.

When I've had a moment to adjust and nod at

Crow, he brings himself closer and pushes his cock inside me once more. The immense elation taking over me ends abruptly when they both begin pumping in and out of me, seemingly perfectly in time with one another as I let go and allow my body to be moved and jolted by their movements, immersing myself in the euphoria soaring throughout me.

Crow's hand reaches for my neck, squeezing it to the point of pain at the same moment that Liam's hands begin playing with my nipples.

"Oh fuck," I breathe out, unable to keep quiet any longer as they continue to beat into my body in the best way imaginable.

"Cum for us, princess," Crow tells me as his eyes glaze over with hunger while he watches my breasts bounce up and down from their pumping actions within me.

"Be our good girl and scream. Let them hear you roar for us," Liam whispers in my ear as his hands grip my waist and pinch. The pain of his harsh grasp and Crow's hand on my throat has me doing just that and screaming out as an orgasm rips its way from my body.

Chapter 25

Charlie

"Has he been acting weird to you?" I ask Crow as we leave the Clubhouse after my first official meeting as the President and head home.

"I don't think so. I mean, he's been a bit quieter than usual, but there's been a lot going on so I can't really blame him. It's a lot to process along with his own shit."

"Yeah, I suppose you're right." Liam has been off and when I say off, I can't exactly place what it is that's been off about him, but he just doesn't seem to be himself, which is worrying me.

He's had more trauma to work through than any of us. I'm on a waiting list to see a counsellor, and I tried to convince Liam to do the same, but he wouldn't. I'm not sure what it is, but there's something going on in his head that he won't tell me about and I hate it. If I don't know what's going on, how can I help him?

He'll be home soon; I can talk to him about it then. Dad has been at the Club more and more lately, to the point now that he's hardly ever at home. I think he's doing exactly what I advised to Gray by keeping himself and his mind busy and therefore not allowing the negativity to have time to fester.

It doesn't take us long before we're pulling up

outside the house. I go straight up to my bedroom to get dressed in something more comfortable and have a shower. My whole body is aching and although the shower helped, I can't help but feel so exhausted - mentally and physically, completely drained. I've been sleeping like the dead at night, and yet I'm still ready to have a mid-morning nap daily. It must be the chaos of everything going on.

As I leave the ensuite bathroom and walk into my room, I'm surprised to find Liam sitting on my bed, facing me with something silver and shiny in his hands. I can only see the end of whatever it is. It's small, and the way he's fidgeting with it in his hands makes me think he's nervous.

"Are you alright?" I wonder aloud as I begin drying myself off and getting dressed. His eyes don't leave the item in his hands once which considering I'm wearing nothing is rather surprising.

I pull leggings and a baggy top of Crow's on to cover myself before sitting next to him on the bed. Our thighs touch as I do, even through the clothes I feel his warmth.

I wait in silence for a moment, wanting him to know that he can talk and I'll listen. I watch him as his brows crease and he bites his lips uncomfortably.

"I've got something for you, but I want to say something first," he tells me, his eyes still downcast, not meeting my gaze.

"OK," I say, not wanting to spook or panic him

466

by saying or asking too much when he's so clearly feeling anxious.

"I've been trying to be everything you need, but I know deep down that I'm too broken to be the man you deserve. I see so much of myself in Crow, and I realise that if I'd had the right kind of childhood then maybe I'd be able to be the sort of man that he is for you. I've done things to you that can never be forgiven, things that I can never tell you how sorry I am for. I feel like I can't live in a world like this when all that happens in my head is you. You and then the bad again. You're the only good in the dark, and yet even you aren't enough to make the darkness go away. I will never, ever be able to make things right between us, but I want you to always have a part of me, no matter what, so I thought I could get you something like Crow did. I found you the matching set so that no matter what happens in life, no matter where I go or where my mind takes me, you'll always have this because I know that no matter how complete you make me feel that I've been through too much to ever be whole for you."

He holds out his hand, a small silver key inside of it with the end containing parts of a story, just like Crow's necklace that currently hangs around my neck and yet, no matter the beauty and sincerity of his gesture, it's his words that cause the tears to leave my eyes and my arms to wrap around him as I nestle myself into his chest.

"You are more than enough, Liam. We're both a little broken and that's OK. We've got time to heal, time to get better. We can heal together," I insist as he sighs and wraps his arms around me.

He doesn't utter a sound for such a long time as he holds me. Feeling him breathe against me, his arms, his warmth, makes me feel both more alive and more fortunate than I have in a long time. Knowing how much he struggles and yet how much he fights that every single day to remain here with me is more than enough, more than I could ever express to him or make him truly believe.

He pulls back, his hands on my cheeks as he looks into my eyes with a vulnerable innocence that portrays his feelings in a way that no words ever could.

"You're so fucking perfect, you're practically blinding. I'll make it all better one day, I promise." His lips catch mine before I can respond, taking me off guard as he takes control, pulling my face towards his as his tongue skirts gently into my mouth. The dominance and soft touches are complete opposites, and yet utter perfection until he pulls away too quickly, leaving my lips feeling plump and pink from the sudden onslaught.

"You make everything better already." I smile up at him, knowing that he needs what I'm offering, even if it seems so slight to anyone else. To Liam, the smallest things mean the absolute world.

"Come on, we need to get going. Your dad's

468

going to be back soon," he says as his usual smile reappears. He takes my hand and leads me to the stairs.

"Why do we have to go downstairs just because he'll be home soon?" I ask, unsure of the relationship between the two things.

"He's got your new leathers, girl. First woman to enter the Cobras and somehow ends up the boss at the same time. That's not bad going, baby," he says as he winks and drags me down the steps.

I hadn't even considered getting my own leathers, nor had I thought about how much that would mean. I'm not sure that I ever thought I'd want a set of my own but now that the prospect is being presented to me, I feel myself welling up at the truth of the responsibility and family that I've taken on.

"You alright there, baby?"

"Yeah, I'm fine, I just didn't expect to feel so emotional at getting my own leathers." I laugh lightly, feeling dizzy with excitement that I never anticipated that I'd experience.

I never thought I would even be a Cobra because of the rules surrounding women, or rather the lack of women on the Dark Cobras and yet, just like Liam said, here I am taking on the ultimate responsibility by not only being the first woman to join the Cobras but by being the President of them as well.

It's definitely time to make some changes.

Alice is my first call I note in my mind as I feel

469

over the possibilities. She more than anyone deserves the title held with being a member of the Dark Cobras - if she wants it, that is. She's been there for everyone, through everything, despite her own tremendous battles and problems.

Liam watches me, his eyes inquisitive as I think over my potential plans for the future.

"You realise that you're doing that thing where you just freeze and think. You know you can sit down and think as well," Liam jokes while pulling me along towards the lounge.

"Yes, I know, I just didn't want to forget so I had to stand still to remember." I laugh as he sits next to me and pulls my legs over his, stroking his fingers along my thighs as he does.

"OK, well that sounds strange and like you have some memory problems. Is it time to see the doctor again?" he asks with a wink in my direction.

"Why's she seeing the doctor?" Crow has a mouthful of food as he speaks - ever the attractive gentleman, which means that his words come out more like a grumble of vowels and random syllables than an understandable set of words mashed together to make a sentence. I understand him all the same, but I still send him a roll of my eyes and a confused look.

"Are you ill?" he asks, stalling down the food and rushing over to me, feeling my head with the back of his hand and looking into my eyes.

"No, she's not ill, she just has a terrible

memory," Liam tells him as he whacks his arm away from my head.

Crow throws a glare his way.

"You said doctor. I panicked. No one explained. What do you expect me to do?" He looks at Liam as though he's stupid and has completely lost his mind which just earns him a second set of eye rolls directed his way.

"Pretty sure that's your dad's bike out front," Crow says, completely unaware of what my dad's presence means as he nods his head in the direction of the window for me to see.

Chapter 26

Charlie

"He hasn't replied to me at all," I tell Crow as he ushers me along towards Alice's door.

"He will. He's probably just having a mini breakdown and then he'll be back," he says nonchalantly.

I look at him incredulously. "That's not ok," I emphasise, wide eyed.

Crow does nothing but roll his eyes at me.

"He'll be fine. This is a lot for him. You know it is. There's no way he can just go from being his dad's slave to this and it not affect him, Char. You need to give him time. You know he'll come back to you, he fucking adores you," he says as we reach the door.

I take in his words, realising that he's right. Liam has never had anyone truly care for him aside from my dad and some of the Cobras and even then, he felt he had no choice but to sneak behind their backs to protect me. Of course, it would be a big deal. He needed time. I can do that. I just need to give him time. It will be fine.

I nod at him and knock on the door to Alice's flat, attempting to wipe my mind of any thoughts of Liam so that I could give my full attention to one of the only friends I have.

"They're here, they're here, they're here!" Kira

squeals as she comes to the door and opens it with a wide smile on her face.

"Hey, Mini," Crow greets her as he ruffles her hair and steps inside.

"Alice is peeing but she said she'll be out soon," she tells me brightly as she closes the door behind us and tells us to sit down.

"I did not tell you to tell them I'm peeing, I said I was going to brush my teeth," Alice utters at her sister as she walks through from the bathroom.

"Where's Liam? He's my favourite," Kira says grumpily as she mock pouts and looks outside of the door again.

"Firstly, that's rude, little mini, I thought I was your favourite and secondly, he's having a magic moment where he disappears and then reappears, but he'll be back soon, little Haribo lady," Crow jokes as he takes a seat on the sofa, his legs spread wide as he invites me to sit between them. I shake my head, not wanting to be too physical in front of Alice and Kira, especially with what Alice is currently going through with Edgar.

"Fine, come here then," Crow says as he grabs my arms and yanks me down so that I fall right beside him, tucked into his arm as I do.

"People in love are so weird. Why do you touch each other so much? Makes me wanna hurl," Kira tells us, throwing her fingers down her throat and gagging as if to reinforce her point.

"You'll be in love one day too and then you'll eat your damn words, girl," Alice tells her as she walks into the kitchen and returns moments later with a tray of drinks.

"Can I tell you your future?" Kira asks excitedly, her eyes filled with wonder as she pulls out a tiny bottle of crystals and rocks from her pocket.

"Sure. What do you need me to do?" I ask with a laugh as I watch Alice shake her head and roll her eyes at her little sister's antics.

"Just put your hand out and keep it still," Kira says seriously as she shakes the bottle of rock in her hand and then tips them out onto my palm.

Her head dips, her eyes squinting as if to check the stones a little more and then looks at me, her eyes wide and curious.

"People are going to die."

My heart stops for a moment. Even though I know the likelihood of a thirteen-year-old girl telling me my fortune isn't going to be the thing to make her predictions come true, the crass mention of death has me feeling sinister and concerned.

"Jesus, Kira, what did I say about telling people fake and horrible fortunes?" Alice exclaims from her place in the kitchen.

"What? It's true, that's what it says!" Kira spurs back at her sister, picking up the rocks and crystals from my hand, pouring them back into the small container.

Signed with Love duet
J R Dust

"I think you've come on your period, princess," Crow says as he shakes me awake softly.

My eyes feel tired and groggy as I look around the bed, my mind not comprehending what it is he's saying.

"Come on, Char, let's get you in the bath."

I allow him to pull me up off the bed while still half asleep as I follow him into the bathroom. The bath is full with bubbles and my iPad on a tray, Netflix already on there, ready to play.

"You didn't just wake up?" My words sound slurred and sleepy as I speak.

"Nah, but I didn't want to wake you until I had a bath run," he says as he lifts his shirt over my head before he takes my underwear off and instructs me to try and go to the toilet while he turns around and then lifts me into the bath.

"I'm gonna go change the sheets and then I'll be back, alright? There's some water and chocolate behind your iPad too," he tells me with a sweet smile before kissing my forehead and leaving the room.

I nod and close my eyes as I feel the water cover me.

I take in the silence as I lay back and appreciate how lucky I am to have the likes of Crow in my life. I realise how often before I admitted my feelings for him that I wished for a partner similar to the men I read about in romance novels and yet Crow, with his ability to make me feel content, is more than anything I could have ever wished for.

475

His laughter, his energy, his kindness and thought is beyond anything I dreamed of when wishing for someone to love me because he does so much more than that. He doesn't just love me in the way that I do him, but he treasures and reassures me through simple acts rather than meaningless words without any need or want for reciprocation.

"Char." His voice sounds panicked and far away even though I see him right next to me as I open my eyes.

"You need to get out. Now." I look around, wondering what the problem is and come across it immediately. I can't have been in the water for more than a few minutes and yet the bubbles are nearly all gone and in their place is water that's turned red.

I've had plenty of baths while on my period before, but I have never experienced this.

"Crow, this isn't normal," I whisper as he gets a towel and carries me bridal style out of the bath, his clothes now soaked as I look up to see his worried face.

I get dressed and fill my underwear with more padding and sanitary equipment than is probably needed as Crow empties the bath.

The pain hits so suddenly that I find myself leaning over the bed in an attempt to ease it.

"Princess, you're leaking already."

"Matt! Matt, Gray! Fucking wake up, now!" Crow roars as he slams open my door and bangs on my dad's and Gray's doors before returning to me.

"I'm taking you to the hospital, baby. You're ok, everything's going to be ok." Only I suspect that both he and I know that nothing is ok because I think we both know what's happening.

My bedroom doesn't feel familiar. Not the curtains or the bedding that Crow replaced only hours ago or the soft carpet beneath my bed. Not the ensuite or the wardrobe or the clothes inside of it. Nothing does. Not even Crow. Not my dad or the people that flock around me, whispering things to one another that they think I can't hear. I practically laugh at myself internally. I'm hilarious. I feel hollow and empty. They all seem to think I'm scared or upset or ashamed, but I'm none of those things. I'm nothing. I just am.

A knock echoes around the space surrounding me, leading my eyes to drift towards the door that slowly opens as Crow's head peeks around the side of it. My mind aches at the sight of him.

I see it in his eyes - the wishing for me to be me again. He doesn't say it or show it, but I know he must want me to just shake out of it. To go back to being me. He must. I do, so how can he not? I feel like the moment the bleeding started, the moment the doctor confirmed something so dreadful, was the same moment that I truly began to mourn - not just for the life leaving me but for it all.

"Can I come in?" he asks, his voice low and husky, still filled with sleep. He must be exhausted. He's been with me the whole time. Point blank refusing to leave. I haven't asked him to go but my dad has. Numerous times. Not because he doesn't want him here, I don't think it's him personally that he wants gone. I think he just believes that if things go back to normal or as normal as they once were that I will too. He keeps looking at me as if he doesn't know me. He looks as lost as I feel. I hate seeing him feeling anything other than himself.

I nod my head at Crow, letting him know that it's OK.

I smile weakly at him, and find myself staring at the wall above his head again as he kneels at the end of my bed.

"Do you want anything to drink or eat?"

"No, I'm OK, thanks," I tell him as I huddle into myself further, cringing as I feel myself bleeding again.

I can feel it leaking out of me. The blood. The life. Mine and its. The thing that was inside of me. The life that I didn't want but didn't have a choice in keeping or losing. The doctor said my body couldn't cope with the physical strain I was under and that was what they suspect caused the miscarriage. My body lost a baby. I'm losing a baby. A part of me.

They did a scan that made me sob the moment I looked at it. It was black and white and mine. And Liam's. I remembered that and sobbed even more. I thought for a moment that the universe was giving me something - something unwanted but still something of my own that would get me through the rest of my life, and then I remembered that he wasn't here, that I had no idea where he was, and that the blood meant that the universe was taking away the very thing it had gifted me. I hate that I don't have the choice to decide what I want to do. I hate that my body is taking that decision away from me. It feels like every choice I'm supposed to have in life is being and has always been taken away from me, and I'm not sure what choices I have left.

I'm not sure what I'm supposed to do now when I feel so little and so much all at once.

"Do you want to talk about it?" Crow asks gently, his voice barely above a whisper as he peers up at me huddled on top of my blanket.

"Talk about what? I don't know what to think, let alone know what to say," I tell him honestly, the exhaustion from my mind's exertion tiring my brain and body.

"Will you let me hold your hand? I just want to help you, comfort you," he insists as his eyes widen and offer me more comfort than any physical touch could.

"Will you cuddle with me until I fall asleep, please?" I plead as my eyes fill with tears, blurring the vision of him in front of me.

"Oh Char." He sighs as he manoeuvres us so

that I'm in his arms under the cover. "I'd cuddle you every damn moment of the day if you'd let me."

His arms immediately offer me comfort as I turn and sob in his arms, appreciating more than ever the soft touch he allows me.

His hands roam between my tangled hair and my back, rubbing gently along the clothes covering my skin.

He holds me until the sobs subside and sleep takes over, all while whispering the sweetest things in my ear.

"Did you know that a baby stays with you, is a part of you even after you've lost it? Alice told me that," he tells me softly.

"Did you know that you're the bravest person I know?" he whispers.

"I'll always be here, princess. I'll always be by your side," he promises.

"You'll never lose me, you'll never lose Liam, and you'll never truly lose this part of you," he assures me.

"You'll never lose the baby because it will always be yours," he reassures as he strokes my hair.

"You'll always remember and so will I and so long as we remember then it's never truly lost," he tells me as I cry harder and harder in his arms.

"We'll plant a seed, let a tree grow, and watch as it blooms just like you and your baby would have," he says kindly as he wipes my tears away.

"We can bake a cake, throw a party, and

decorate the tree as it grows every year," he decides.

"Just because you hadn't decided if you wanted it or not, that doesn't mean that it's any less yours or any less loved. You would have loved it and so would Liam and so would I. Any part of you would be adored and cherished."

"Thank you." My sobs subside while I cling to his chest, listening to his voice and appreciating his calming melody and his presence more than ever.

Chapter 27

Charlie

Crow's red Ferrari is waiting outside the house, but as I look inside for him, I notice that he's not there.

I pull my phone from my pocket with the aim of texting him, but at the very same instant, I feel arms lifting me from behind. I have a moment of panic before recognising the smell... Crow.

I spin in his arms, a smile appearing despite my mellow mood. It feels like one of those reunions you see online. The tear-soaked eyes, hugs that are never ending, and the light inside the eyes of the people reuniting. That's exactly how I feel. Like everything wrong is being lifted for just a moment as I wrap myself around Crow and squeeze him with every single bit of might I have inside of me. His arms are around my back, mine around his neck. He's lifted me so high that my head is above his and as he looks up at me as he slowly releases me down, I remember every single reason why he's both my best friend and everything more - because he makes me feel like this when it's the last way I think I deserve to feel.

I follow him to his car and find myself smiling again when he gives me a blanket to put over my lap and a hot water bottle for the pains that are

482

slowly lessening.

Crow kept me smiling through times when I wasn't sure I wanted to even be alive. He protected me from my demons, made sacrifice after sacrifice to make me happy, and did everything imaginable to keep me going.

"How about we get some bad food for lunch?" he asks, looking at me with a nervous smile.

"You love bad food," he says as he continues driving onto the back alleys.

"Where are we going?" I ask, wondering why he's not going towards the main street where the usual restaurants and takeaway bars were located.

"Wherever you want, tell me what you want to eat, and we'll get it."

"No, I mean where are you heading right now?" I ask, confusion coating my question.

"Oh, I was gonna take you back to mine, but we'll get food first," he says as if it was that obvious.

Crow's hand reaches for my jaw with his eyes still on the road, and he squeezes.

"I can hear your teeth from here, woman. Stop it." I always do it when I am nervous or stressed or frustrated. My teeth start grinding, my jaw clenching, and he always knows whether he is looking or not, and he always holds my jaw tight as if it will solve the problem. It doesn't solve the bigger problem that is plaguing me, but it does immediately stop my teeth from chattering.

"You're an idiot," I say with a tight laugh.

"Yeah well, you'll be ugly and old with no teeth if you carry on that way, and we can't have that, can we?"

"You cheeky bastard!" I say, feeling a full belly laugh emptying its way from my mouth.

The guilt I feel for experiencing happiness as life escapes me haunts my mind. Crow and I spoke for hours upon hours last night and although logically, I know that I'm allowed to feel happiness, I also know that it will be a while before the happiness isn't plagued by guilt and sorrow.

"I'm trying to help you out here, Charl." He chuckles. "Do you want to be old, ugly, and lonely?"

"Oh, so I'll be lonely now too?" I ask. "And where might you be whilst I'm busy being a toothless old granny?"

His face lights up as he tells me, "I'll be out doing your shopping because you'll be too embarrassed to go anywhere in case you laugh too hard and your falsies fall out."

This is why Crow is and will always will be my best friend, no matter what else he is to me too.

"Oh, shut it. You're a prick," I tell him as I shove his arm just enough.

"Don't touch the jewels, love, don't touch the jewels," he says as he pulls away in mock pain.

"I'll be shovelling your damn jewels up your bleedin' arse if you carry on this way," I tell him with a glare. Not as though he sees it as he's too busy driving.

Signed with Love duet
J R Dust

He pulls up outside of one of the most beautiful houses I've ever seen in what feels like seconds.

It's small and quaint, a cottage really, not a house. The walls are made of stone, different shapes and colours ranging the outside of the house, with vines and flowers flowing from the ground right to the tip of the tiles and slightly off kilter roof.

The garden is brimming with life and as I open the door to get out and look around, I notice a swing identical to the one I have at home painted in the most striking sunset orange that I've ever seen. It's my favourite colour, and I have a feeling Crow is well aware of that.

I turn to face him and find that he's watching me, waiting for my reaction.

"Is this place yours?" I ask in wonder.

"Something like that. I wanted to be in the city for such a long time, but I realised not so long ago that this was so much more beautiful," he tells me sombrely.

"It's incredible, Crow."

"You were the inspiration. You went on and on about your dream home often enough that you made your dream mine, and this is the result of that, so really, I've got you to thank."

I smile up at him, and rush over to the swing before plopping my bottom onto the cold surface.

Crow chuckles as he wanders over and takes a seat beside me.

"This is a home for all of us. I mean, I

originally got it for you and me, but I've even added a shooting range for Liam." Hearing his words, his uncertainty about whether that will now happen crushes me.

I snuggle up to him, placing my arms around his back and his chest as he places his head on mine and whispers the words that he knows I love most in the world.

"Do you want some hash browns for dinner?" he asks.

"I'm not sure hash browns work for dinner. I'll put something together. Lead the way," I tell him as I elongate my arms in front of me.

I follow him up the cobble path as he leads me into the most beautiful entryway. It's like something from a film. The walls and decoration are all autumn shades. Yellows, oranges, purples, reds, and browns surround me.

As Crow shows me around, I'm taken aback by the natural beauty of the place. The inside is furnished with oak and it's breath-taking to say the least. It's a small, quaint place but it's so utterly beautiful that the size is just an added part of its charm.

"How did you have time to do this?" I ask in astonishment.

I turn to look at Crow and find him smiling mischievously at me.

"I started a few months ago when I bought the place. I knew you wanted to get away. Not far away, I know, but enough so that you had independence and a home you loved, so I've

486

been working on it for us. When I wasn't looking for you, I was doing this," he says with a small, tense smile.

I swing my arms up and around him, squeezing him in ways that would surely suffocate anyone else, but has him only chuckling into my hair.

———————

"I take it this is the mighty Charlie Keller then?" a voice asks from behind me. I twist on the bar stool I'm sitting on in front of the breakfast bar to find a man I've never seen before.

He's tall with ice white hair sweeping across the top of his head and ridiculously bright, practically translucent green eyes.

"Oh, you alright, man? Yeah, this is Char. Char, meet Kenny. He's come to set up the security for the place."

Kenny. Kenny. Kenny.

"You called me a dick last time we spoke," Kenny tells me with a mischievous smile as he puts his hand out for me to shake.

"You were being a dick that night. Super unhelpful," I say pointedly as I shake his much larger hand. Firm, but not intimidatingly so handshake though. My dad would be impressed. He always used to tell me that I needed to improve my handshaking skills - as if that is even a thing.

"We're just heading off but you've got a key,

haven't you?" Crow asks him as he rounds the table and helps me off the stool.

"Yeah, I'll be fine. I'll message you when I'm done. Nice meeting you, Miss Keller. A mini O'Banian in the making, this one," he tells Crow with a nod in my direction.

"What do you mean?" he asks.

"She hasn't stopped glaring at me since I walked in." He laughs.

I have not been glaring at him, at least not on purpose. I'm pretty sure that's just my face. Oops.

"Sorry, I didn't mean to. It's nice to meet you too." I smile as Crow takes my hand, utters a few more words Kenny's way before he's taking me to his car out front.

"Do you think Liam will come back now? He's had long enough to think, right?" I ask as Crow begins driving off.

"Yeah, he'll be back, I'm sure o-fuck!" he exclaims as I feel the seat belt tighten around my chest and neck as the car jolts forward and stops abruptly.

"What the hell was that?" I mutter out, looking towards Crow as I notice a man pulling Crow's door open and grabbing him, pulling him out of the car.

By the time I take my seat belt off, there's a presence behind me and I know I'm done for. Again.

Chapter 28

Charlie

There's bad luck and then there's me it seems. Who manages to get taken twice in a short amount of time? Yep, that would be me, it seems, so as I sit up groggily on the surprisingly comfortable bed and look around the bare room, I wonder why the fuck I was taken this time.

My thoughts immediately run to Liam's father. Maybe Theo or Victor's father on behalf of Theo, though Victor had said that the two of them weren't particularly close. His father seemed more interested in the wellbeing of his club as a whole than the actions of an individual within it.

My body feels fine, other than half asleep. The pain in my stomach is still there though dulled by the magnitude of the situation that I am trying to play down in my mind in an attempt not to have a full-blown panic attack without anyone around and no idea where I am.

The bleeding is now lighter than it has been, which upsets me at just the thought that the loss is nearly over. I don't want the loss to last forever but knowing that I still have even just a small part of my baby inside of me fills with a strange sense of joy, but the bleeding stopping often means that it is coming to an end and that the baby, the foetus, the whatever you want to call it has left

489

and I am alone again. Despite the fact that I wasn't aware I was pregnant, the thought of now being truly alone having lost the smallest thing that means the most absolute courses me. The door creaks open at that exact moment, and I realise that I don't have time to mourn. I only have time to do what needs to be done and, in this situation, that's working out who's taken me and form a plan to escape.

And yet as the man walks in, completely relaxed and calm, I realise that I am completely fucked because I don't need him to tell me who he is. I know exactly who he is because he looks identical to his son.

Liam's dad doesn't say a word as he enters the chamber and just watches me in silence for what feels like a lifetime.

"What do you want from me?" I ask, finally giving in after an eternity of his hard glare facing my direction.

"I took Liam and now he's here. I took you and now you're here. Your goal is to kill Liam and then I'll let you go. Simple." His voice is rough, low and commanding as he speaks.

"I'm not doing that," I insist with a voice that is nowhere near as confident as I hope it sounds.

"I thought you'd say that." He chuckles darkly.

"See, the thing is - if you don't do it, then my men, who thoroughly enjoy violence and men's weak spots will do it, and I can assure you that you doing it is a lot less painful and humiliating than them doing it."

Signed with Love duet
J R Dust

—————

The walls are soundproof. No one will hear anything that I say. No one will know what I do. And now that he's sat in front of me on a metal chair with his hands tied behind his back and blindfolded, I find myself completely unaware of what to do or say. I can't do this. I can't let them hurt him but I can't not do this either. Seeing him like this takes me back to the events that unfolded that night with Matt and Danny.

I was sure that someone along the way would insist that I was demented, evil, and wrong for what I encouraged and did but in my mind, they deserved it. But this - Liam does not deserve this.

"I know it's you. I can feel you." His words stun me. He doesn't move, not as though I imagine he could move very much even if he wanted too.

I rush towards him and undo the blindfold from around his eyes, hating that his own flesh and blood could do this to him. The torture he'd been through his whole life was horrendous. The things he'd done and that had been done to him in the name of protecting others was unimaginable and even still, his life was a never-ending array of demonic torture and evil events - through no fault if his own. And now we are stuck. If I don't kill him, they will while making me watch, and I highly suspect that that won't just kill him. I have no doubt that they will drag it out. Hurt him. Maim him. Rape him. To hurt him as well as me.

"Are you here to kill me? I don't mind. I'd

prefer my life be ended by your hand than theirs." He sounds confident somehow, even though his voice is hoarse and broken when he speaks. His words are emitting a confidence I'm sure he can't truly be feeling.

I don't speak. I don't respond, largely because I just don't know what to say or how to respond. I suddenly don't even know why I agreed. Except I do. Of course, I do.

"Let me hold you. Please. One last time," he begs, his eyes pleading with me. As if I could possibly say no.

My mind is still reeling and attempting to figure out an escape plan, but as I look around the nameless and empty room, there's nothing. No window, no vent, no way out.

I move to his back and use the knife they gave me to kill him to undo the ties holding him down. He waits patiently as I cut through the thick rope tying his hands together before rounding to his front letting my knees hit the concrete floor beneath him as I bend to cut the same rope from around his feet so that he's free.

My eyes stay downcast for what feels like an eternity, my heart racing as I attempt to compose myself and stop the incessant nagging in my brain. I realise now that I'm so close to him that he somehow still smells like him. Not like the alcohol that so often overpowered the senses like when I was a child but him. The man that I've grown to love in an entirely different way to what I thought I should. The same man that I know

492

would conquer any army thrown his way to protect me.

I don't move as his hand drifts down to my chin and ever so gently places two fingers below it and lifts my tear-filled gaze to meet his.

"It's OK. I'm ready. I know what needs to be done. There's no way out of this, Charlie." I hate how accepting he is. I've never seen him give up or even give in to anything besides me. I don't want to see him give up now. I hate that he's accepted this lethal fate as if it means nothing. Maybe it doesn't. Not to him, but it does to me.

"Please don't cry, you know I hate it when you cry." His words are soft, low, quiet, barely spoken as I look into the forgiving eyes of the man before me.

His body looks stiff from being in such an awkward position for so long, but I soon realise that he must have saved strength somehow - somewhere, as he crouches down beside me, leaning back against the wall and pulls me onto his lap with what looks to take so little effort from him, my head against his chest while his chin rests on the top of my hair. I can feel his heart beating against my body, the steady thud thud thud that keeps mine from going into overdrive as I listen to his breathing and match mine to it.

"You're matching me again," he says with a sad laugh and a smile I can feel forming above me, one I have no doubt would wreck me if I saw.

"Will you say something please? I don't mind going, especially by your hand, but I just want something good before I go. Tell me anything," he insists, an order more than a question - one I'm willing to oblige as my heart shatters that tiny bit more every time he speaks.

I shift just enough to face him, seeing that his eyes are as glossed over as my own feel as he looks at me with his own screwed up version of love. No one else can see or understand it but I know it's the truth - that he does love me in the only way he knows how. It's the exact type of love I need though. No matter how misunderstood or strange it seems to others, it's his warped, overwhelming and all-consuming love that I've always longed for. I didn't realise until I was given the chance that I needed him. Him and Crow. My only constants. My every breath. My everything.

I swallow down the emotion clogging my throat as I decide to tell him the truth and a fact I've only now come to realise as more true than I knew it to be.

"Three things," I tell him, watching him as he intently watches me in return. "Firstly, you're not giving up. I don't understand why you're just allowing this to happen without even trying to get out but it's not... It's not happening and secondly, I need you, Liam. I thought you'd just left me," I cry out, my hands reaching for my eyes, rubbing the tears away as I continue, "I've been bleeding. Profusely. I thought it was just a heavy period, but Dad got the doctor out and it turns out that I was pregnant. I was pregnant, Liam. With what would have been your baby." I sob as I let out the words I'd been wishing to tell him since I found out.

His breath hitches at my words, his hand around my waist twisting and moving me until I'm straddling him, sitting atop his lap and looking directly at him as his eyebrows crease together and his face looks like it's about to shatter along with me.

"You had a miscarriage?" he asks, his eyes as haunted as his voice sounds while I numbly nod and grasp his hand in my own, intertwining our fingers together while he looks at me, eyes filled with more sorrow than I know what to do with.

"Did you know, that even after a loss, the babies DNA stays with you, as part of you forever?" he asks me, his free hand taking up residency in my hair as he softly runs his fingers through it.

"Alice told me that. I have no idea how or why she knew, but she did," I tell him with a nod.

"I'm so fucking sorry, baby," he cries, his eyes now streaming as he shakes his head and looks heavenward before returning his glassy eyes and tear-stained cheeks towards me. "Not just for that, but for everything. I'm so sorry that I'm so fucked in the head. I'm sorry that I've fucked you up just the same as me. I'm sorry that I took from you what wasn't mine to take. I'm sorry for everything," he tells me on a sob as his head falls and I instinctively catch it, holding his head against my chest this time, allowing him this moment to release it all on probably the only person in the world that cares and it's that thought and that thought alone that ruins me even further.

"You didn't. That's just it. You healed me, Liam. You and Crow have given me everything I never knew I needed or wanted, and that's why you can't let go now. Please, we just need to work together and we can figure this out. We always do," I insist.

Maybe I really am just so fucked in the head that I can't compute what happened and process it like a normal person would, but then I'm so grateful that I care for him the way that I do because despite what he's done and said and who he's been, I know that he deserves this. We deserve this. This moment - probably one of the only moments in his life aside from the time he's spent with Crow and I when someone has truly, with no ulterior motive, comforted and cared for him.

Liam lifts his head, his hands so gently holding my face as he searches my eyes.

"What was the third thing?" he asks, his voice that of a broken man, which serves to tear me apart even further. All he needed was the right childhood, the right people to love and care for him and this could have been so different. This moment would never have come to be.

I watch him as I speak, taking in every emotion and facial movement he makes. "I forgive you. That's what you need, isn't it? That's what you need to stop this and try for me? I've seen you torture yourself for what you've done. I always thought me being with you was enough but it's not and that's OK because I forgive you. I thank you. I want you. I'm glad that you did what you did," I tell him lightly, the words barely above a whisper. I know he's heard though; I hear his breathing stop and sigh as he places his forehead against mine.

He moves his hands so that he has one behind me, keeping me steady and the other on my hand, my wrist, the one that I forgot was still holding the knife and the moment I look back into his eyes, I know what's coming.

"No, no, not yet. I can't do it, not yet. We can get out, Liam. We can get out," I rush out, my chest filling and feeling heavy as more tears shed from my eyes and I try to escape his grip on me. I move and shift my body, trying to fight his hold on me as he does what he sees as the inevitable.

"It's time now, baby, it's time to say goodbye," he tells me as he guides my hand and in turn the knife towards his chest with enough pressure that I feel his body's weak attempt to fight it before he gives in as he slowly presses the knife further into himself. I fight it, using my body and my hand in an attempt to stop it but even as I manage to pull myself away, I realise that it's too late. He's stabbed himself in the chest. His hand is on the knife. In my struggle to get away and stop him, he took the knife from me and did the job I'd been sent here to do himself - so that I didn't have to.

The blood is covering both of our hands as I reach for him and cry in his arms, his arms never leaving me.

"The next time our souls meet, I'll be a better man, I'll be what you need but right now I'm going to go and tell our baby how much we love them," he tells me in between his gasps for breath.

His face is becoming so pale as I try to pull the knife out from his grasp and chest and yet even with the pain he must be in, he still manages to stop me, to continue the murder of himself.

"I don't want you to go. I want you to stay," I tell him, my head shaking from one side to the other as I pull my hand away from the knife and the contact his calloused hand has with it as my eyes fill over and over again with tears that I don't even attempt to hide or keep inside.

"Will you stay until I go?" he rasps out, his eyes filled with a vulnerable hope I wish I could memorise and keep.

"Always." I nod, letting him put his arms around me one last time as I put my head against his chest and hold onto him with every bit of strength I have in the naive hope that some miracle will come and save him. Save me. Save us.

"I, I, ugh." I lift my head to look into his dimming eyes as he attempts to speak, his breathing becoming haphazard and uneven as the space around us becomes wet with his blood.

"I love you. Forever mine," he tells me as I watch his eyes dim and flutter closed for longer than I'd like.

"I know. I love you too." I have no idea if this was the moment I was waiting for, if fate knew that the words were needed now. I only know that it feels right at this moment to tell him. I know that he needs to hear it, and I need to be the one who says it.

I hold his face in my hands, bringing my tear covered wet lips to his in what I wish was a greeting but is instead a goodbye. I take in his last breath as I pull my lips away, watching his eyes take me in one last time before they close and his breathing halts completely, his eyes closing as my chest feels like it's being ripped apart, pressed down on and squeezed simultaneously.

I don't move from his lap, holding his hand and clinging to his shirt as I pull his arms back around me, taking in the comfort he offers for what I know will be the last time as I sob into his still chest, missing the heartbeat that kept mine beating in sync from only moments ago.

He's not gone though. He's not gone. Not yet. No. He's not gone. Not yet.

I move his arms from around me and stand, adrenaline kicking in when I finally realise that in order to save him, I need to move. I check his breathing, thankful that although low and irregular that he is still breathing.

He's still here. He's not dead. Yet

I go to the door and bang, over and over again, shouting and screaming and willing my body to make as much noise as I can while pushing the weight of my body against the metal door frame with hopes that something may budge. Or if nothing else, that someone will get fed up and see what's going on.

What I didn't expect was to have the door open and find Crow standing there.

"Crow." My mind seems to blank at the reality of what's happening finally sinking in.

Liam is in a literal puddle of his own blood and Crow - somehow, by some miracle is here.

"I need help. He's got a knife wound. We need a doctor," I tell him as I rush back over to Liam, taking my hoodie off as I do and covering him with it.

"Get the doctor!" Crow yells out the door as he joins me and lifts Liam off the ground, cradling him like a baby.

They might have an unconventional relationship, but I know that Crow isn't wanting to save Liam just for my sake anymore. They've connected on more levels than I could have ever hoped for.

Chapter 29

Charlie

"You need to let go of his hand, princess. We need to get to your appointment. Your health is just as important as his," Crow tells me as I wish for a miracle and pray to a god I've never believed in.

Just let me be happy with them and I'll never ask for anything else again, I promise. Keep them both alive and happy and healthy. I promise not to ask for anything else. You can take me if you like, just don't take them. They deserve to live. To love. To heal.

I don't hear a voice or see a light, nor does any godly figure appear, and yet I hope that if anyone, someone or something is up there that they've heard my prayer and that I've done enough good in my life to have my prayer answered.

"Come on, Char. We need to go. We need to make sure you're ok." I let Crow guide me from the room, my hand in his as I curl up to his side, needing the closeness and comfort that him being near brings me.

I can't imagine a life without either of them. Without Liam or Crow. I know that one day I will be ok because that's what everyone says when someone dies. They say that one day, after years of healing, that you'll be ok but I don't want to be just OK. I want to be whole. I want to be the version of me that I am when I'm with them both.

———————

"That's not possible. I've been bleeding so heavily that... that just can't be right," I tell the doctor sitting opposite me at his desk. He must have got it wrong. Even doctors get things wrong.

"I checked three times, I found the heartbeat. I would assume that you were pregnant with twins and lost one of them. I'm so sorry."

My eyes jump from one place to another, not truly seeing anything as my mind attempts to take in the words he is saying to me. That's not right. I would know if I was pregnant. I would know, wouldn't I? I would know that. Of course, I would. But then, I remind myself, I didn't have a clue until I started bleeding and saw a doctor to confirm something I had absolutely no clue about so maybe I wouldn't know at all.

The doctor slides a scan image towards me, his eyes and face gentle and unassuming as he watches me for a reaction.

"Is that the baby?" I ask, my voice sky high and yet quiet as can be as I stare at the darkened image with curiosity.

"It is. You're not too far along, so there's not much to see but I saw a steady heartbeat and right now, that's the main thing we need." His voice is gentle, as if he's afraid that I'm about to break, though that assumption may not be wrong.

I pick up the image in front of me and watch as the doctor points out what the different shaded areas are. He shows me the heartbeat, the baby. My baby.

I had completely forgotten that Crow was at my side until he places his hand on my thigh and gives me a reassuring smile.

"I'll give you both a moment alone," the doctor says kindly as he exits the room and leaves me stunned and unsure of what to say.

When the very same doctor confirmed the loss, I had mourned. I had felt sorrow and sadness beyond measure. I hadn't even considered how I would have felt if I found out I was pregnant without the loss and yet here I am, my mind scattered and lost as I wonder how I'll cope. How I'll be as a mum. I'll be packing lunch boxes and school bags, getting them dressed and bathed, taking them on trips to the beach and hikes, and I have no idea what I'm supposed to do.

My whole world seems to freeze and turn on its axis, the future I had envisioned completely upturned and forgotten and yet there isn't any part of me that is saddened by that I realise as I look up to see Crow's tentative smile.

"I'll help you. I know you know that but whatever happens with Liam, I'll be there to help you both. You, him, and the baby. I'm not leaving you, Charlie, I never will," he promises me as a hand floats to my still pudgy but flat stomach. I am going to be round. Oh god.

"What are you thinking?" Crow asks me as I stare into the space between us, my eyes unfocused and as unsure as my mind is.

"I'm going to get round," I tell him simply, honestly, the first thought that enters my mind or rather the most recent one.

"I really don't think that's what you need to be worrying about." Crow chuckles as he takes the scan picture out of my hand and looks at it.

"That's your baby, princess. What if it's another princess? Shit, I'll never cope with two of you." He huffs out with mocking amazement coating his face.

"Oh, shut up, we don't even know yet. It might be a mini me and end up ruling the world."

Signed with Love duet
J R Dust

Chapter 30

Liam

My chest feels tight. As if it's wrapped in a bandage with a tonne of steel sat on me. I feel heavy and wonder why.

I force my eyes open and then it all comes back to me. My dad. Charlie. The knife.

Shit.

Well, I mean, I'm still here and that's got to count for something.

My eyes shoot down to the layers of dark hair on my lap. Charlie. Her face is turned in the other direction. I want to see her. I need to see her.

Fuck. I tried to make her kill me. I don't have much luck with women. I've never really tried to. I hadn't ever been interested in anything but a quick fuck before I saw Charlie as a woman for the first time. And then it all changed. And now I tried to make the one woman I had ever truly loved kill me.

Way to go, man. Way to fucking go.

And then I notice the hospital admittance band on her wrist and want to stab myself over again for leaving her and not finding another way out. The baby. The miscarriage.

My heart breaks more for her than myself, knowing that she's had to go through it all without me by her side.

I seriously need to see her face now. I need to know she's OK.

I lift my hand, which takes much more effort than I'd like, and place it on her head, my finger roaming through the loose and untidy curls. She stirs and pushes my hand away, which does nothing but force an abrupt and very rough sounding laugh out of me.

Charlie does not like to be woken up.

"Don't wake her yet." I didn't even notice that Crow was in here. I'd been so hyper focused on Charlie that I hadn't even thought to look around the room once she was in my view.

He looks as tired and worn out as I feel.

"Is she alright?" I ask, my voice quiet.

Crow raises a single eyebrow in my direction.

"She's fucking mad, dude and she's got every right to be. I'm pretty fucking angry at you myself as it happens," he hisses out as he leans towards me, his eyes filled with fury.

Oh, for fuck's sake. As if what I need right now is for them both to be pissed at me.

"I didn't think I had a choice," I tell him, knowing it's a lie and knowing damn well that he knows that too.

"Oh, fuck off with your bull, man. You were the one that put the fucking tracker in her. You knew that you could have halted the semi heroic, all together stupid suicide mission for a few more minutes and someone would be there."

We still hadn't told her that I'd done that. I did it the night before they'd come to get her from

506

that hotel. God, it seems like a lifetime ago and yet like only yesterday too. How is that possible?

I hate even thinking about the things I'd done to her there, the positions I'd put her in all because I cared for her and my dad knew that she was my weakness.

"It's better for her if I'm not around. There's no danger then," I tell him, refusing to look at him as I speak, instead choosing to watch Charlie's still hair on my lap.

"He's dead. Your father. I killed him myself. Most of his band of bastards are dead too. No one's coming for you. Or her. You can be with us. She doesn't give a shit about what you did, and you damn well know it, now gather your fucking balls and be there."

He's young and yet wiser than I've ever been.

"Look, I'm sorry that you're mad I hurt her-"

"That's not why I'm pissed. Well, not all of it." He huffs out as he wipes his palms along his jeans.

"I'm fucking angry because you left us both. You promised both of us that you'd be there. You promised both of us a life and you fucking left. You left and let her try to kill you with no consideration for how the fuck it would leave us. She can't be with you without me, just like she can't be with me without you. I don't love you the way she does, but you're one of the only people I don't have to bullshit around so until both of us tell you to fuck off then you fucking stay put and pull your shit together. Got it?"

Signed with Love duet
J R Dust

He's right. I know he's right and so does he. He's a cocky bastard, much like myself, and when I found that we actually got in better than I'd anticipated, I found something in him that I didn't want to let go of. Not a love like I had for Charlie but a bond, a connection, a friendship that I knew would last. I just didn't realise that he felt the same way.

"Alright, enough with this sappy shit. Can I wake her up now?" I ask as I cover the shake in my voice with a cough that just about kills my damn lungs.

Rule one after a self-inflicted stab wound to the chest - Do not cough.

"Go on then. Her mood's on you though," he tells me with a sigh as he sits back in the chair and watches on with keen interest - probably wondering how I'm going to go about waking her without getting a fist to the face.

"Charlie, you gonna wake up, baby?" I ask as I stroke her hair, willing her to wake up so I don't have to go any longer without seeing the face that keeps me sane.

She fidgets a little, a small and weak groan escaping her lips, but shows no sign of waking.

"Baby, wake up," I tell her again, this time allowing my voice to be an octave lower and louder.

And then she does wake and true to form, she whacks me right in the ribs, sending a shooting pain through me.

"Fuck," I hiss out as I lean forward in the bed

508

and grab my middle.

"Oh shit, I'm so so-" she starts but stops herself. "I'm not even sorry. What the fuck was that?" she inquires, her words striking me.

"Me waking you up?" I ask gingerly.

"No, not you waking me up. What was that? Crow told me about the tracker." I find myself eyeing Crow up. He lifts his hands in surrender as if to say what do you expect, dude? "You tried to kill yourself, you stupid fucking bastard! You're lucky you're in a hospital bed, or I'd bloody whack you again," she says as she scrunches her nose and brows together, appearing frustrated and annoyed, but I know she's not, or at least not as much as she probably wishes she was.

The tears fill her eyes within seconds before she rushes to me and falls in my arms. It takes an enormous amount of effort to shift my body and wrap my arms around her but like fuck am I doing anything besides comforting her in this moment.

"I'm sorry," I whisper, meaning the words but feeling nothing short of ecstatic - taking pleasure in having her so close. Her scent draws me in, makes me feel at home as I feel her soft body against mine. The pain it causes is practically numb, no pain being worth thinking about while having her here with me.

"Do you remember what I said? About forgiving you? Because I do. I really, really do," she quivers out, her sobs racking my chest both physically and mentally and fucking ripping me

509

apart.

"I know. I'm sorry, I just… need to do better," I tell her. I know I need to overcome some of the shit I've done and that's been done to me, but I also know that until I've done that, I'm not the man I need to be for her and since I can't imagine a time that I'll ever be able to leave her side, I guess being better is what has to be done.

She lifts her tear-stained face up to look at me, her soft eyes all-consuming and mighty in their stead.

"I don't want you to be anything other than you, Liam. We can work the rest out together. Crow's the least traumatised, well - we've probably traumatised him ourselves at this stage, but he can be the sane one, OK? Right, Crow?" she asks him with a ridiculous innocence covering her face as she looks over to him hopefully.

He rolls his eyes and laughs. "Yep, that's me. Protector of the traumatised," he says as he puts his hand over his heart and bows mockingly before saluting us both.

"See?" Charlie says, her face beaming.

I wouldn't ever admit it, but I dreamt of having someone that gave me everything as a kid. Before I knew how fucked the world was, I dreamt of having someone care for me and now that I have it, there's not a fucking chance in hell I'm letting it go.

"Yeah, yeah, I see," I tell her with a small smile.

"Oh, and one more thing," she says as she sits up on her chair nervously, her hands leaving my body.

"Don't pout," she orders me. I didn't realise I was, though considering she stopped touching me, I'm not surprised to find my automatic reaction is to act like a stroppy toddler.

"Anyway, so, I had to have a scan last night to make sure that everything was... gone," she stutters, "and well, it's not. They think it must have been twins and that I lost one because there's still one healthy baby. I'm still pregnant."

My eyes shift between her nervous smile and Crow's cocky and laughable one as I take in what she's said.

Well, fuck.

The dream fades as quickly as it came, the black scenery in front of my eyes taking over again as the vision leaves my mind.

"I'll protect her, I promise you." It's Crow's voice. I can't see him, but I can hear him. His voice is thick with emotion.

I think about his words. I don't trust him with my life, but I trust him with hers. Above anyone else, I trust him.

This is it. I could feel my body failing, my mind short circuiting as sobs fell on my ears and soft hands touch the hands I can't move. I wish I could comfort her. I wish I could be for her what she needs but instead, my eyes won't open and my body won't move.

"Tell them we love them. We'll wait for you,

OK? We'll-" The sobs start again, her voice breaking.

I'm so sorry, baby girl.

"We'll see you again. We'll come together again in another life when we're all better. I'll find you; I promise." Charlie. Charlie. Charlie. I need to find Charlie. I need to find our baby.

Charlie.

The beeping signalling my heart rate stops and turns into a continuous open ending ringing.

Charlie. NO.

———

Charlie

I've never experienced grief before. Not really, not like this. It feels like I'm experiencing grief for more than just myself. I'm grieving for the baby inside of me that will never know their father. I'm grieving for Liam, for the person he could have been with the right help. I'm grieving for my dad, who despite the obstacles they've been through, has lost a lifelong friend. I'm grieving for Crow who has to watch me in despair. I grieve for myself and everything that the three of us could have been.

But the worst part of all is that I have no idea how I'm supposed to let go of his hand that is only getting colder and stiffer. The nurses and doctors don't rush me. They don't ask me to leave or beg me to stop crying and wailing like I'm losing my own life. They don't tell me to get it together. They also don't tell me how quickly death changes a person. Liam's eyes are closed, his life having left his body. The shell of him that's left here is nothing more than a body, and yet it's the very body that deserves so much more than it was ever given.

I don't speak as Crow tells me that they're all dead. Liam's father. His father's men. The ones that took us. No one is coming for me anymore, which only makes it worse because if he'd lived, if he'd just kept breathing, if he'd just believed for a little longer that he was worthy and loved and cared for, the three of us could have lived a life together. It may not have been perfect, but it would have been ours.

I watch from the sidelines as so many people come and wish him the best in his new life, wherever that may be. I watch as they whisper what I assume are kind words or goodbyes. I watch in horror as Crow takes my hand and pulls me closer to Liam's side. I watch as he lifts Liam's hands and places it on my stomach. On our baby. I watch as his face contorts when I sob and cry and wonder why life is so cruel.

I watch as they take his body away. I experience the grief, the guilt, and the loss over and over again for what feels like a lifetime.

I spend an eternity praying to Liam, asking him to watch over our baby in Heaven while I watch over the one that will soon be on Earth. I

513

Signed with Love duet
J R Dust

promise him every night in my dreams that we'll meet again. We'll be better the next time we meet. Our souls won't know pain or depression or torture or trauma. I promise him that the three of us will live together one day with our children. One day, we'll sit together and watch our children play as the love between our souls passes through the world we reside in.

I tell him good night; I tell him that I love him and that I'll see him again one day as my heart breaks and Crow attempts to fix it in time for my baby's arrival.

———

"Do you think he can see us?" I ask, my voice betraying me. I had hoped that I could come here and not cry but it seems impossible, especially with Eli in my arms.

I look up at Crow from my spot on the floor. I feel closer to him this way. On my knees, knowing I'm above him. Just a few feet away. It sounds morbid and somewhat demented, but looking at the gravestone in front of me makes me feel like I can feel him. Hear him.

Crow rocks Eli gently in his arms, his soft snores the only noise around us aside from the whistling birds and rustling trees.

"I think he's watching you. Watching Eli. Probably watching me too," he says with a laugh as Eli snuggles further into Crow's chest.

"He'd be proud of you, Char. You know that."

He whispers so as not to wake Eli from his slumber. It seems his hushed words don't work though, for Eli's eyes start to peel open.

"Hey, baby boy," I coo as I take him gently from Crow's embrace.

"This is your daddy," I tell him with a sniffle as I edge closer to the gravestone residing in front of me.

The flowers around it need replacing. I've been coming to see him every few days since we laid him to rest but hadn't been for nearly a week since I had given birth.

It still hurts to be in the position I am - on my knees but it is the only way I feel close enough to Liam not to sob.

"He was kind and brave and-"

"And crazy," Crow interrupts with a playful smile.

"And a teeny tiny bit crazy," I add on with a small laugh as I look down into the mirror image of Liam's eyes.

"But he would have done anything to protect you both. He might not be here but I have no doubt that he'll protect you still. Come on, the weather's cooling, we need to get you both inside," Crow tells me as he ushers us up from the ground.

I take one last look at Liam's name on the stone, reminding myself to breathe as my chest tightens.

"You've got Eli and you've got me. You've got Liam watching you and one day, we'll see him again. You've got everything you need." Crow repeats the words he's said a million times since Liam passed away. I nod my head, knowing he's right.

I take Crow's hand in my free hand and continue to rock a curious-eyed Eli as we walk back to the house.

I insisted on having Liam buried in the garden of the house Crow prepared for us so that he is always close. So that we can all see him as often as we need, whenever we need. I've spent more nights out here with Crow by my side than I have inside of the house, but as time goes on, the visits become less frequent. From spending every waking moment next to him to now seeing him every few days.

I knew that one day, whether that be before or after my death, that I'll find him again. I'll have him and Crow by my side once more. The next time I have them both, I will never let them go.

But for now, Crow and I settle into a healthy pace and a lifestyle filled with bustling busy bodies keeping us occupied. We live a peaceful life with me studying from home while feeding Eli in a rocking chair with Crow watching diligently by my side.

Liam may be Eli's father but until he's returned to us, Crow vowed to help me raise Eli as his own. He adores and cherishes him more than any man I've ever seen. He is truly besotted which fuels the love I have for him even further.

Liam will look after and love our baby in

Signed with Love duet
J R Dust

Heaven while Crow and I will love the baby we have on Earth.

Chapter 31

Charlie - 5 years later

"Eli and Grace are officially with your brother and his lover. Does this mean I get my lover all to myself for a little while?" Crow asks mischievously as he wraps his arms around my swollen and pregnant belly from behind. Even after all this time, his touch sends butterflies somersaulting through my stomach. His baby also happens to be doing somersaults in there right now as well.

"Well, I was going to catch up on the washing," I tease as I continue to fold Eli's school shirt and place it on top of his pile of clothes.

We've set a list of chores for Eli now that he is a little older - one of which is taking his clean clothes up to his room, and yet I already know that it will end up being me doing it again. He has the most mischievous glint in his eyes every single time when he begins fluttering his lashes and telling me how tired he is, so of course he can't do it. I am the sucker that gives in nearly every time though.

"Have you seen yourself? All I have to do is look at you and I'm practically covering the place in cum, it won't take long," he whines mockingly as his hands begin to caress my breasts rhythmically.

518

"I suppose I can take a five-minute break," I tease with a smile as I turn and wrap my arms around the back of his neck and press light kisses along his stubbled jaw.

"Nuh uh," he says as he pulls back and wags his finger at me with a smile.

Shit, he's so beautiful. He's aged and grown more handsome over the years.

"If you start touching me, I'm not even gonna get inside of you before my load busts everywhere like some horny teenager," he says as he pulls me along to the lounge, sits on the sofa, and places me down so that I'm straddling him.

My dress rises enough that it's surrounding my waist, just under my bump.

"You're not wearing any underwear?" He hisses as his fingers find my clit and begin strumming away delicately, igniting a fever pitch of need within me. I always need him, want him, but pregnancy and a bit of a beard on him sets me in a frenzy. Even more so than usual.

"I had a feeling you might want easy access." I smile as I layer my lips along his neck and lift myself up so that he can get his thick cock out of the material currently restricting it.

The head of his cock bumps along my entrance, agonisingly slowly as he pulls the top of my dress down and begins nibbling and nipping at my breasts.

"Oh God, just put it in, Crow." I pant as he chuckles sexily.

519

"So impatient, princess. Say please," he says as his hand holds his cock just out of reach.

I look down into his hunger filled eyes and beg. Happily.

"Please. Please fuck me, Crow," I beg breathlessly and smile as he grunts and fills me in one swift motion.

He holds my hips and meets my every thrust in his direction as I lift and dip my body over his continuously, loving the feeling of being so full of him. Every time he is inside of me, it makes me feel like I am about to be ripped open. His size is otherworldly and yet I crave nothing more than to be completely and utterly ruined by him.

His roar of desire meets my moans as he ravages my neck with his mouth, my head back to give him access.

"Oh fuck, baby, you're so fucking perfect," he praises me as the pressure within me builds to unimaginable heights.

"I'm gonna fill you and then fuck you again. I can't get enough of you. You make me fucking ravenous." He groans as he grabs the back of my neck and meets me in the middle for an agonisingly slow kiss, the pressure on my neck firing cylinders within me that set my orgasm alight along with his fingers at my core, pressing and squeezing teasingly.

He empties his load in me, his warm cum squirting inside of me as I fall onto him, my head on his shoulder as he strokes my long hair gently.

Signed with Love duet
J R Dust

"I love you so fucking much, Char," he beats out breathlessly in my ear.

"I love you too," I say as the world goes dark for a moment and I feel myself begin to drift off. I love falling asleep with him still inside of me. He's convinced it's why I ended up pregnant so quickly when we finally decided to start trying to conceive.

"Come on, let's go find the kids and your brother and his lover before you fall asleep again," he tells me.

This pregnancy has taken the energy right out of me. I seem to sleep more than breathe at this stage. I'm always falling asleep in the middle of the day, finding Eli or Grace stroking my cheek and shouting for Crow once they notice I'm asleep.

Eli is the sweetest soul. He noticed that I fell asleep last night while watching a film and lay next to me, stroking my hair and pulling a blanket over us both. Grace, being so young, doesn't understand the element of silence that's needed to sleep so she often shouts for her daddy to be quiet and wakes me in the process, but I don't mind. Not in the slightest.

Being able to live and love the life that I have while still dealing with a rendered heartache is the most I could ever wish for.

I pull myself off of Crow, clean myself up in the downstairs bathroom, and rearrange my now creased dress as we leave the front door and head to the meadow where the children are bound to be with Liam's grave.

We set the kids' play equipment and toys up right next to it, which Gray told me was morbid as hell, but they both love it. Eli knows that Liam is his father. He talks to him daily, even though he calls Crow his dad too. Grace isn't that great at talking yet, but even she babbles along and brings Liam and Eli flowers while they're talking.

It might not be the most conventional dynamic, but I don't want Eli to feel like he didn't get the chance to know his dad even though that's exactly what happened. I want him to know him through us, but I want him to feel like he can talk to him himself anytime he wants to as well.

It doesn't take long to find them all. Eli is playing football with Gray and his lover, as Crow so eloquently puts it, while Grace is tiring out said lover by making him chase her around the garden. I find my smile lifting as I watch the scene in front of me with Crow's hand in my own.

Life is full of the most horrendous heartaches, and yet I'm simultaneously bombarded with the most sensational love and happiness in the simplest of things and for that, I have no doubt I have Liam and my baby in Heaven to thank for watching over us and keeping us content and happy until we can see them again one day.

But until then, I plan to spend every moment of the life I have, living for those that I have with me as well as for the ones I'm without.

"You're still a shithead!" Crow shouts at the man on the field as Gray gives him the stink eye for cursing out his boyfriend and Grace copies before giving said shithead a hug and babbling something his way.

Eli drags me towards Liam's grave and tells me that Liam wants to play a game. Crow soon joins in with Grace and with our family so close to being complete, even without all of us earthside, I thank every and anyone that's ever listened to my prayers.

Diary Entry - Last Chapter -

My dream has always been to write. To write a story that changes minds, confounds readers, and sets dreams alight. I just didn't think this would be the story I would tell.

For the second and last time, I'm signing this for you. For him. For everything we never got to be.

In another world, we'll have it all.

I'll see you again one day, but until then, I'll raise our son to be as mighty and wonderful as you were both always supposed to be.

Until we meet again.

Signed For Him. For You. For Us.

Charlie Keller (give our baby a kiss from me!)

Afterword

If you enjoyed the Signed with Love Duet, I hope you'll be pleased to know that Gray's story is next! You can pre-order it here - https://amzn.eu/d/cwk98JQ

I also have a readers group that you can join on Facebook called J.R Dusts Book Besties that we'd love to have you join!

You can also follow me on -

TikTok

Instagram

Patreon

Signed with Love duet
J R Dust

Acknowledgements

There are so many people I'd like to thank for helping me bring this story to life!

My editor (Magnolia Editing Services), my proofreader, my lovely PA Amanda Johnson as well as my cover designer and the designer that creates all of my beautiful teasers (forgetyounot.designs).

I also have the most amazing team of Beta and ARC readers that have become more than just readers but really close friends as well. They are constantly hyping me up, supporting me, and encouraging me and for that, I cannot thank them enough! It truly means the absolute world to me.

I'd also love to mention my family for always supporting me with my writing and just life in general! My mum for reading my books, my youngest sister for letting me talk about them non-stop, my partner for being the most incredible person I could have ever wished for, and my babies for being the best little humans in the world (yes, I'm biased but they totally are!) I am so grateful and thankful to have such amazing people around me.

And lastly, to those of you that have taken the time and the leap of faith with the Signed with Love Duet: I appreciate you endlessly!

Printed in Great Britain
by Amazon

26678365R00294